crying. Someone might ask her what was wrong, and she wouldn't be able to say anything. They would think the worst when she didn't say anything, of course; but the worst they could think wasn't as bad as the truth.

Something drew her in. She could have called it a feeling of hope, but she figured she'd used up her allotment of that a while back. But something called to her; not with anything so blatant as words. The something was a quickening of her pulse, a shiver in her belly, a sudden catching of her breath. Something. Something in there called her name, and she listened.

Baldwell's was new. Nestled in between Sandra's and the Everything $6, it sat bright and shiny and modern, its bright yellow interior and chrome-and-glass exterior out of place squeezed between the renovated brick buildings that made up the rest of the downtown.

A few customers looked up as she entered, then looked away. She didn't see anyone she knew; even better, however, she didn't see anyone who knew her. Her feet carried her past New Fiction, shelved to her right. She thought perhaps that was why she had come in—to find something to take her mind off disaster. But her feet kept going. Past Music. Past Science. To Travel.

Ahh. Travel. Perhaps her feet had known something her mind hadn't. She looked at the covers faced out, showing all the world that wasn't Peters, North Carolina, and her pulse raced faster. None of them are a million miles from here, she thought, but surely one of them will be far enough.

She gravitated to the neat row of gold-and-black Fodor's guides. Her hand cruised along the titles, not touching any of them. Waiting. Waiting for a sign.

Scotland.

No.

Australia. England.

No.

How about Ireland? Japan?

Not them, either.

Saudi Arabia. Norway.

No. All of those places seemed fine, but they didn't call to her. They weren't the reason she came into Baldwell's. Something was, though.

Switzerland?

No.

Argentina.

No.

Glenraven.

Yes, something inside her said, and she reached for the book.

Glenraven?

Jayjay frowned and picked up the Fodor's *Glenraven*. The cover hummed beneath her fingers, the shock of that first touch electric but wonderful. She opened the book and caressed the glossy pages; the heavy feel of the paper was sensual and compelling. And as she flipped past one of the illustrations, she fancied for a moment that she smelled wildflowers and freshly mown hay. She closed the guide again, a shivery thrill running down her spine.

"A Complete Guide to the Best Mountain Walks, Castle Tours and Feasts," the guide promised. The photo showed a delicate, airy castle built on the banks of a shimmering blue lake with craggy mountains soaring behind it. In the foreground, a smiling, black-haired, blue-eyed woman in colorful regional costume led a laden donkey along a cobbled path, and behind her the meadow that rolled down to the lake bloomed with sweeps of wildflowers in gold and scarlet and cornflower blue.

Jayjay stared at the cover. She had done some traveling. She'd seen a few castles. But she had never seen a castle that looked like that. And . . . *Glenraven*? She knew there were a lot of new countries in Europe since the Soviet Union and the Warsaw Pact fell apart. She simply couldn't remember hearing anything about that one.

She opened the guide and flipped past the Foreword, past the Highlights and the Fodor's Choice sections, and stopped at the map. Glenraven was tucked into the Alps, a tiny little pocket country squeezed into the border between France and Italy like a wormian bone in the suture of a skull, about parallel with Milan and, according to the map, no bigger than Liechtenstein.

She'd never heard of it, but she didn't care. It was far away. It was off the beaten path. It looked like a good place to run away from the world for a while. And, dammit, it made her heart beat faster, and that was worth something.

Jayjay turned two more pages to the Introduction. "For the first time in over four hundred years," it began, "Glenraven, the best-kept secret in Europe, opens its borders to a few chosen travelers from the outside world. The last outsider to see Glenraven dropped in before Christopher Columbus set out to discover a shorter route to India, and the one before him visited a hundred years earlier than that. In the centuries that have followed the complete closing of the borders, Glenraven has let wars and politics, the Industrial Revolution and the electronic age slip past without so much as edging in at its borders. It is a land hidden from time; pastoral, feudal, a tiny country where communities share their lives, where integrity and honesty and hard work are not old-fashioned values . . ."

Yes. Yes. This was what she needed. She left her thumb holding her page and stared off into nothingness. "Four hundred years."

She opened the book again, skimming the introduction. Phrases like "more working castles than in any other country in the world," and "glorious primitive festivals," and "last virgin forests in Europe" interested her; if she were going to hide, she might as well have fun. She tried to imagine the places behind the place names Tenads and Cotha Dirry and Bottelloch and Ruddy Smeachwykke. She studied the pencil sketches of neat stone walls and prim thatch-roofed houses and twisting paths through ancient forests and she got goose bumps. "Travel through Glenraven will be a once-in-a-lifetime adventure," the guide promised. "This tiny country is unique; until time travel becomes possible, untouched, unspoiled Glenraven is the last gate into Europe's mystical forgotten past."

"Mystical forgotten past," Jayjay murmured. Somewhere between Ruddy Smeachwykke and "mystical forgotten past," she decided she was going to make this happen. She was going to pack her bags, buy a ticket, and flee to this land outside of the realm of the known.

"But," she read, "your chances of touring this wondrous little country are limited. Protective of the marvels it alone preserves in this modern world, and only too aware of how progress destroys as much it creates, Glenraven will close its borders following the Solstice Festival at the end of this year. And once the borders shut, no one but the Glenraveners can say whether four years or four hundred will pass until they open again."

Not a problem. I can be on a plane inside of a week, I bet. Jayjay closed the book. She held it in her hands, feeling her heart pound, feeling her fingers tingle. She could almost imagine that the tingling came from the book. She could almost believe something larger than chance had brought her to the bookstore in the rain.

Almost.

But her practical side asserted itself. The Fodor's guide was lovely; the idea of getting away for a while felt all very well and good. However, the expenses were going to be dicey. The money for the trip could come out of her savings account, or maybe she could pitch a travel book to Bryan at Candlewick Press and do the trip as research. Her publisher was waiting for her to proof the galleys of *A Season After Pain*, the nonfiction book she'd sold on cancer survivors, but she figured she could have that in the mail within a week. Following that, she'd set aside a block of time to work on a novel—she really wanted to try her hand at fiction—but the fiction title was speculative. She didn't have a track record or a fiction publisher, and her agent kept pushing her to do a follow-up to *The Soul of the Small Town*, which had sold better than it had any business selling.

The Soul of a Tiny Country, she thought, wondering if she could pull together enough tie-ins to pick up the readers who'd bought the first one.

Of course, then I'd owe Bryan a book. And I'd have to tell him where I'm going, and why. And I don't know that I want him to know that.

The savings account held enough to get her through a year of novel writing if she didn't get extravagant or sick. Part of it could cover her for a trip. Maybe she would get something useful for the book while she was in Glenraven.

She took the Fodor's guide to the cashwrap.

The owner of the store, Amos Baldwell, leaned on the cashwrap and smiled at her. He was tall and dark-eyed and she guessed he was in his early thirties. Maybe late twenties, though she had a hard time telling. His face was young, but with his starched shirt buttoned all the way up to his throat and his greased-down hair flat against his scalp, he made himself look older. She noticed briefly that he might have been good-looking if he'd bothered to join the times. He pointed to an endcap in the nonfiction section, where *Season* covered the display. "Your last one is moving pretty well for me. A few of my customers told me it helped. That counts for something."

She smiled, hoping he wouldn't be able to tell from her eyes how much she wanted to be left alone. "I'm glad it's making a difference." She pushed the guide across the counter and changed the subject. "I found what I was looking for."

He stared down at the book, and for the briefest of instants, Jayjay could have sworn that Amos paled. Then a frown flickered across his face. He reached out as if to pick the book up, but his hand stopped before he touched it. He gave her an intense, searching look.

"This one is damaged. Why don't you let me get you another one?"

"There isn't another one."

"We have several other guides to Spain . . ."

She cut him off. "That isn't a guide to Spain. It says 'Glenraven' right there on the cover."

Then he did turn pale. He glanced from the book to her, back to the book, back to her. She would have sworn he looked bewildered, but she couldn't imagine why. He started to shake his head from side to side as if negating either the transaction or his own perceptions.

"Just ring it up for me, please."

"Why do you want it?"

She stiffened. She didn't want to offend him—he treated her well and displayed her books prominently, probably more prominently than they deserved—but who was he to ask her why she wanted a book? She didn't intend to tell him that she planned to leave town for a while. "Excuse me, Amos, but that is my business."

And mine, she thought she heard him say, though his mouth didn't move. He seemed to grow taller, and for an instant he flushed and scowled. She stared at him, suddenly confronted by a formidable stranger.

"Have you read through this guide at all? Glenraven is . . . dangerous," he said, stabbing the cover of the book with his index finger. "It's primitive. It's no place for you."

She refused to allow his bizarre behavior to intimidate her. "Ring it up for me," she said. She waited a moment, and then in a voice that made the word into a command, she added, "Please."

He looked at her so intently she could feel his stare. He raised an eyebrow and pursed his lips, and manually entered the price of the book into his register. "My apologies," he said stiffly, and held out his hand for her money. "Perhaps I was being . . . overly solicitous of your well-being. I'm sure you know what's best for you."

"I'm sure I do," she said. He put the book and her receipt into an imprinted plastic bag, then handed the bag to her. She turned to leave, then looked back at him. Keeping her voice level, forcing herself not to let her anger blast through, she said, "You're fairly new here, and I don't know what your customers were like where you came from, but I'll tell you this. Around here, you'll lose them if you try to tell them which of your books they shouldn't buy."

She stomped out of the bookstore, still angry.

The character of the rain had changed. It gusted and blew and sheeted. She found herself wishing heartily that she'd driven. She could be home, drinking a nice hot cup of tea, putting a fire in the fireplace, settling down with her galleys and a pen—

But of course Steven might be home. And Lee with him. And she was in no mood to fight again.

She leaned up against the damp brick wall of HairFantastic and wished the rain away, but without success. She closed her eyes and tried to figure out what she could do next.

Two

Sophie Cortiss watched the rain sheeting down outside her picture window. The hills fell away at her feet, the dark green of pine trees not much brightened by the stands of oaks and dogwoods and squat, broad peaches just beginning to bend beneath the weight of their fruit. The brash pink blooms of her dianthus drooped in the downpour, not cheerful at all. The two new horses waited out the storm under the shed in the far pasture, a painful symbol of everything she had lost and everything she could never have again. The cats curled on the outside sills and stared in at her, mewling piteously and making it plain they thought they ought to be indoors. The gloom outside was, she thought, more than mere storm. Day's end approached, dragging hollowness in its wake.

The rain filled the crevices of her walk and pounded down on the perennials that huddled over layered mulch. She should have gotten out and divided those day lilies last fall; they had grown far too crowded. She had let the bed slip. In the past two years, she'd let a lot of things slip.

I need to do something.

Something. Something different.

Down the hall, she heard the phone ring. Mitch is home, she thought dully. Mitch can get it.

She heard him pick up on the third ring.

"Hello? Oh . . . hi. Yeah, she's here." She wished, perversely, that he'd lied, that he had told whoever was calling that she was out grooming the horses, or that she was shopping for groceries. Maybe she could sneak out the door so that he wouldn't be able to find her.

But when he yelled down the hall, "Sophie, it's for you!" she went out of her studio to answer it.

He smiled and gave her a quick squeeze, and with one hand over the receiver said, "It's Jayjay."

Sophie frowned. The thought of Jayjay Bennington being perky and bouncy and cheerful made Sophie want to go to bed and not get up for a week. The two of them had been best friends since seventh grade, but since Karen's death they had grown apart. Like the perennials, Sophie had let their friendship slip.

She took the phone with a sigh, and leaned against the wall. "Jayjay. What's up?"

"Soph." Jay's didn't sound like herself at all. Sophie heard nothing remotely resembling cheer; in fact, Jayjay sounded as funereal as Sophie had ever heard her. "Could you do me a favor?"

Sophie glanced at Mitch; he waited, propped against the kitchen door frame, eyebrows raised. "Sure. What?"

"Can you come pick me up? I'm in front of HairFantastic—the place on McDuffie down from the courthouse. . . ."

"I know where it is," Sophie said, frowning. Why the hell would Jay need a ride anyplace? "Everything okay?" she asked, not wanting to give anything away to Mitch, in case this turned out to be something Jay wouldn't want him to know.

"I don't, um, don't really want to discuss it right now. Okay?" Sophie was certain she'd picked up a quaver in Jay's voice. Was it possible she was crying?

"I'll be right there," Sophie told her, and hung up the phone. She looked up at Mitch, puzzled, with the frown still on her face. "Something's up with Jayjay," she told him.

"You didn't talk long."

"No. I think her car broke down. She asked me to give her a lift."

He smiled. "I doubt there's much I can do for her car, but I'll come with you—" he started to say, but Sophie had already headed for the door.

"I'll be back in a bit," she told him. She made sure she kept moving, so that he wouldn't keep trying to invite himself along. She heard him call something after her, and assumed that he'd told her he loved her. She didn't answer him; instead, she made something of a show out of rattling her keys and fumbling with the lock. She didn't want to lie to him. She didn't. And if she told him she loved him right at that minute, it might turn out to be the most flagrant of lies.

Jayjay was leaning against the wall under the canvas awning when Sophie pulled up. Jay ran for the car when it came to a stop and slid inside gratefully. Her eyes were red and puffy, her nose was slightly swollen, and she kept sniffling. So Jayjay had been crying. Sophie kept quiet while she pulled back onto the street.

"Thanks for coming to get me," Jay said. She stared out the passenger window when she spoke, and kept her voice level and emotionless. Sophie couldn't imagine what had torn Jay up, she'd been fine the last time they'd talked; it had been a week ago, or maybe two. Or three. She didn't think it had been much more than three weeks.

"No problem." Sophie slowed for an elderly woman in a clear rain bonnet and prim Aigner raincoat who was getting into her Cadillac and who had her door flung open well into the traffic lane. Sophie swung around her and turned on the street that went to Jayjay's house.

"Not home," Jay said. Her usually clear voice grated, and Sophie heard . . . what? Deep emotions. Frustration and . . . anger? Yes. Anger.

"Fine. I won't drive over to your house. You want to come to mine?"

Jay met Sophie's eyes for the first time. "Is Mitch there?"

"Yep."

"Then I don't want to go to your house, either. Do you have a little time? Why don't we get some cocoa at Norris House?"

Sophie nodded, not saying anything. Jayjay didn't care for Norris House. Sophie considered this fact while she circled the block and headed down Tadweiller Street toward the restaurant Jay had mentioned. She had plenty of time to think; Jay showed no inclination to talk.

That didn't change until after the waitress had seated the two of them at a window table where they could look out onto the street and had left them with menus. Until they'd had a chance to order, Jay sat staring at the rivulets of rain that streaked down the glass, seemingly entranced. Then Jay snapped out of the gloom that held her and pasted a bright, intent, determined smile on her face. "I'm going to be out of town for a while. A couple of weeks, maybe a month. I was wondering if I could have my publisher send things to your address while I'm gone."

Sophie thought, What about Steven? What's he going to be doing? But she didn't ask; she could wait. Jay would eventually get around to telling her what had happened. "I don't think that will be a problem. What about the softball team?" Jay had been the first-string pitcher for the Peters Library Lions for the last three years. Jayjay loved softball.

"Candy McIlheny will take my place. She's been politicking for the slot for ages anyway."

"She sucks."

"So many things do." Jay didn't smile when she said that.

Sophie took her cue from her friend's response, and changed the subject. "When are you leaving?"

"I'll be out of here as soon as I can. My passport is up to date. I'll have to look into a visa—"

"A passport and a visa." Sophie's curiosity grew. "Where are you headed?" She sipped her cocoa and watched her old friend thoughtfully.

"Well . . . I wasn't really planning on telling anyone. I didn't want it to get around." Sophie arched an eyebrow, and Jayjay sighed. "Here." She reached into the huge pocket of her raincoat and pulled out a bag from Baldwell's and passed it over to Sophie.

Sophie glanced into the bag. One of those travel guides lay in it—it looked like it said Spain on the cover, but something about the light of the restaurant made her uncertain. Spain. Sophie reached into the bag for the book; when her hand touched it, a shiver ran down her spine and she almost convinced herself that the book was responsible, that she wasn't just chilled from getting wet on that rainy dreary day and then sitting in a drafty old house that had been converted into a restaurant.

She pulled out the guide and looked at it.

Glenraven.

Glenraven? She looked at the title. *Fodor's Guide to Glenraven.* The title was perfectly clear, the letters black-on-gold in a large, bold typeface. How had she ever managed to think it said Spain?

Glenraven. She'd never heard of such a place. She leafed through the guide, glanced at the map that showed Glenraven's location—a tiny country wedged into the border between Italy and France—and looked up at Jay. "There isn't a country right there," she intended to say, but the words that came out of her mouth were, "Let me go with you. I could use a vacation, and Mitch has to go up to D.C. for some lawyers' convention anyway."

She sat, shocked, staring at Jay. She hadn't said those words; well, she hadn't thought them, anyway. They had come pouring out of her mouth without any help from her. Wait a minute, she thought. I don't want to go anyplace—and I especially don't want to go on a foreign vacation with Jay Bennington . . . but she didn't take back her request.

"Go with me?" Jay looked surprised.

Of course I don't want to go. Don't be ridiculous, Sophie thought. But, "I need to do something different," she said, and with a sudden shiver, she remembered that she had been thinking that very thing when Jay had called. "I need a change." And even as the words came out of her mouth she was thinking, How can I face this? How can I possibly think I can do this? How?

Jayjay cocked her head to one side and rested her face on her fist. "You want to go? Really?" She started smiling, and even though Sophie kept thinking, No, for God's sake, I don't want to go, Jay's smile told her that now she had to. "God, Sophie, that's the first positive thing I think I've heard you say since . . ." She faltered and flushed and stared down at her cocoa.

Since Karen died. Jay didn't have to finish the sentence. Sophie knew what it was. She stared out the window, watching the rain, and she thought of walking out the back door that day two years earlier. Of finding Karen's sturdy little Morgan horse standing in the pasture, shaking and blowing, with sweat caked on his withers and his tack still on and his eyes rolling. She'd run through the field, shouting, knowing that Karen had been riding on the trails behind the pasture.

Sophie could still feel the earth beneath her feet as she ran, could still smell the cedar chips on the trail and the sweet full scent of honeysuckle from the vines that grew wild throughout the woods.

Karen hadn't been moving when Sophie found her. Hadn't been breathing. Hadn't breathed for a while. The doctor felt she had probably died instantly, her neck broken at the very top vertebra from the fall. Sophie and Mitch had gone out later, walking through the woods, trying to understand. Karen hadn't been jumping. She might have been cantering, which was a little risky in the woods, but Sophie had been careful to maintain the trails, and Karen was a superb rider. A 4-H blue-ribbon rider. Twelve years old. Their only child.

Gone.

Sophie sipped the lukewarm cocoa and kept her eyes on the sky outside. The rain kept falling. No rainbows appeared to tell her that finally the spell of her daughter's death had been broken, that finally she could get on with her life.

Life goes on, everyone said. Someday something will matter again. That was the popular wisdom, but in the past two years, Sophie had decided the popular wisdom meant nothing. Life didn't go on at all; it stopped and froze and your heart died in your chest but it didn't have the sense to quit beating.

And in spite of that, she had volunteered to go on a trip with Jay. Maybe it was what she needed.

She realized Jayjay was flipping through the book, talking and pointing out sights she hoped to see; Sophie hadn't paid any attention, but apparently she'd answered. Par for the course. She'd been walking through life without really seeing anything or hearing anything or wanting anything; but no, that wasn't true, either. She'd wanted to die for the longest time. She'd really wanted it. And then she didn't even care about that anymore. It all ceased to matter. She kept on breathing, the whole time feeling that she was a stranger in her own body, and that someday the rightful owner would come home and start running things again.

"There are no cars in the whole country?" Jayjay suddenly murmured. That comment caught Sophie's attention. She looked at the paragraphs Jay indicated, and saw that in Glenraven horses could be rented, and within towns, horse-drawn carriages were sometimes available, but that for the most part the only way to get around was to walk.

Jayjay leaned across the table and grinned. "So let's bike in."

"Bike . . . in . . ." Sophie found she was back inside herself again, able to express her doubts and objections. She rolled her paper napkin between her fingers, feeling it shred into tiny paper pills. "You're kidding, aren't you? This place is in the Italian Alps. I mean, there are roads . . . sort of . . ." She trailed to an unconvincing halt.

A whispering voice inside her head said, Don't argue, don't disagree, don't ask questions. If you do, you'll change your mind, and you mustn't change your mind. Just . . . come. And then the voice added something that she couldn't ignore and couldn't turn away from. It said, If you don't do this, you'll never know.

Know what? she wondered—but that was it. If she didn't go, she would never know.

After she dropped Jay off at her house, she realized they hadn't even discussed why Jayjay had abruptly decided to go on a vacation. Sophie guessed she and Steven were having trouble, but that wasn't necessarily the case. The fact that she'd forgotten to ask bothered her.

"Hey, sweetheart." Mitch met her at the door with an encouraging smile. "Is Jayjay okay? You were gone quite a while; I was beginning to worry."

"Jay's fine." Sophie studied her husband's face, looking at it as if it belonged to a stranger. He had found a way back from the bleak, empty world of pain she inhabited. He had found a way to go on, had found smiles and the occasional laugh. He kept trying to help her make peace with what had happened, but his own acceptance had only driven Sophie further from him. He could accept it. After all, he had not felt Karen budding inside of him, hadn't felt those first miraculous wriggles. He hadn't carried her for nine months, hadn't cradled her in his arms in the dark of the nursery, rocking and cooing with Karen at one breast, listening to the soft suckling sounds of her feeding, feeling the perfect silk skin and the tiny fingers that gripped so fiercely to life.

He'd loved Karen; Sophie knew this. She had never doubted it. But some hidden part of her wouldn't let go of the belief that he hadn't loved her as much.

"When you head up to Washington for your convention," she said, "I'm going to take a little vacation with Jay."

A shadow of unhappiness crossed his face for an instant, to be replaced by a carefully neutral expression. "I thought you were going to come with me."

"It wouldn't be any fun for me. I let you talk me into it, but you know how thrilling it is to listen to a gaggle of lawyers discuss their latest cases and their best methods for increasing billable hours."

"I didn't plan to spend all of my time at the convention. Sophie, you and I need to spend some time alone together. We don't need separate vacations, love. We need . . ."

" . . . something," she finished for him. "But I need this."

He sighed and nodded. "Maybe you do. Maybe this is what you need." He moved closer, wrapped his arms around her and pulled her against his chest. She felt his face press against her hair. "I want you back, love. You've been gone from me for far too long."

She stiffened and pulled away, not wanting to hurt him but not wanting his touch; when he touched her, she felt even more confused and vulnerable. "I know." She could almost feel his pain at her rejection, but she couldn't find it within herself to apologize or to explain. He was there for her but she didn't have what it took to be there for him.

She didn't know if she ever would again.

Three

Wraithlike, secretive from years of keeping secrets though no one now survived who could discover them, Aidris Akalan slipped through the familiar stone passageway, into the stairwell that led down and around, down and down and down into the cool silent dark hungry belly of the earth. The weight of ages rode upon her shoulders, and at the moment she felt every minute of every year. She did not hurry; she could not, though what waited below would have inspired speed from any breathing creature. Most would have hurried away, perhaps, but they would have hurried. The ache in her bones and joints and flesh had once again grown great; time announced itself again as her implacable enemy.

She pushed onward. The stairs ended in another corridor, this one rough-hewn through living rock. The sounds of the world above had fallen away; now she could hear only the shuffle of her leather-soled shoes on the stone and the coarse rasp of her breathing. The hearing didn't matter. She wouldn't hear them until they wanted her to. Wouldn't see them. Wouldn't smell them.

But she could feel them. Already. They lay ahead, waiting, not yet impatient or angry. Simply waiting, cold and incomprehensible and terrible.

My servants, she thought mockingly. My Watchers.

She had brought them to her home, had fed them, and in return they fed her. But they threatened her, too, more every day, more every hour. She did not fear their evil, though they were evil beyond measure. She did not fear the violence they could commit, for they had sufficient targets for their violence not to need her. She feared only that as they perceived the depth of her need for them, they would weary of her. She feared that they would find a way to break free from her, or that they would find another . . . sponsor. She considered that word, tasted it, decided it would serve. Yes. She was their sponsor. And she feared that she became daily more replaceable.

Their presence thickened in the air. She felt them watching, though they did not yet appear. They waited, testing or perhaps taunting her; she suspected that they hoped to make her fear them, that they hoped yet to see her subservient to them. They toyed with her. She showed no reaction. Her power was different than theirs, but she didn't fear them. They couldn't make her fear them.

A breeze started somewhere far down the corridor, the gentlest of whispers. Coming toward her. Sometimes they chose other ways of announcing themselves. This time it was to be a wind. She kept walking forward, kept her head up as much as her stooped shoulders and bent back would allow.

The wind came closer, the whispering growing as it came, and she could almost make out the sibilant threats, the taunting menace of their voices in the moving air.

Closer. Closer.

She showed no fear. She needed to hand-feed them again, to remind them of all they owed her. Her cells should be full; next time she would bring them to her, offer them treats, remind them that everything they had they owed to her.

They reached her. The cold wind snapped her skirt around her ankles, whipped her hair into tangles and shot racing spirals of brilliant white sparks past her on all sides.

The wind died abruptly and completely and the sparks of light began to coalesce around her. She watched them. They tried to seduce her with their beauty, but she was not one of their weak-minded victims. She stared straight at them, knowing how it cowed them to be less than awe-inspiring to anyone or anything.

"Watch/Watchmistress/mistress," they whispered-growled-howled, their cacophony of voices high and shrill and rich and deep as the fire in the belly of the earth all at once. "We will feed you."

"Yes, you will," she said. "When you have finished, I will permit you to hunt again."

"Thank you," they whispered in a hundred discordant voices. "Thank you." She sometimes wondered if they mocked her with their thanks. She suspected they might, but she could not prove they were even capable of mockery.

She felt them first against her skin as the simple pressure of cold air. The temperature dropped as more of them touched her, grew bitterly cold while the pressure became fierce; the cold crushed in on her and pressed down on her, fighting to force her to her knees, to topple her and break her, but she held, stood firm. They kept pressing. Pressing. She fought them, while sweat beaded on her forehead and ran in runnels down the creases in her cheeks, while her legs ached and her knees trembled and her spine felt as if it would collapse in upon itself. Then fire flashed through her veins, through her heart and lungs and bones and brain; it burned along the inside of her tightly closed eyes, burned her teeth until she felt certain they would burst from her skull, burned her flesh; and in fire and ice she stood, she held firm, she held fast and they did not crush her beat her destroy her and she became the ice and the fire, and, triumphant, she lifted herself straight and threw back her head and howled.

Yet even in her triumph over them, they mocked her. They had not fed well enough. They had not killed in sufficient numbers, or their prey had been weak or without magic. Stronger. Yes, she was stronger. But when they pulled back from her and withdrew to the dank wet earth in which they hid, she was still not young. Younger. Stronger. But not young. If anyone saw her touched by age, they would begin to think her weak. As long as she controlled her Watchers, she would never be weak.

She would summon them to her cells, and they would devour the prizes she'd captured for them. And when they had destroyed the last bit of flesh and blood and bone, they would give her what she needed.

Magic.

Four

Jay couldn't believe how quickly the last two weeks had flown past, or how easily everything had come together. Steven had been more than happy to see her leave; he'd even offered to pay for her tickets, hoping, she supposed, to bring her around to his way of thinking with his bribe. She'd refused. The travel passes for Glenraven had arrived two days after she'd written off to the address in the guidebook; Glenraven apparently had the most efficient bureaucrats in the world. She'd made all the arrangements for herself and Sophie because she was afraid Sophie would change her mind if Jay let her. And Sophie needed something to bring her back to life.

And here they were. Hard as it was to imagine, she and Sophie were biking away from Turin, where they'd spent a day resting before heading on to Glenraven.

Jay discovered that biking through northwestern Italy into the Alps could have easily been her destination instead of simply a throughpoint. She knew she wasn't the first traveler to end up breathless from looking at the scenery, nor would she be the last. But western Italy was new and wondrous and fresh to her. Better

yet, the traffic had thinned once they were outside of Turin, and she and Sophie could finally talk.

"So how is Mitch doing?" she asked.

Sophie pedaled to catch up with her; the women rode side by side on S25, heading west toward Susa and Bardonecchia in Italy's mountainous Valle d'Aosta region. Jayjay thought the Italian drivers were considerably better than Americans at noticing bicycles on the highway and not running them down, though the Italians seemed to think that speed limit signs referred to the speed below which a vehicle must never drop.

"Mitch? He's fine," Sophie said. Jay picked up a tinge of anger in her friend's voice. "He recently made senior partner and he wanted me to go to this convention in D.C. with him. He's happy and excited, and he acted like he thought if I went with him, I could be happy, too." She shook her head slowly. "He bought us horses a couple of weeks ago."

"You didn't even mention it."

"I almost can't talk about it. He said riding was something we had both loved, and that we had to get our lives back. He wants me to go riding with him." Her face clouded over with pain. "He asked me how I would feel about having a baby."

Jay winced. "Oh, God."

"As if we could replace Karen."

Jay knew Mitch. He was a nice guy, and Sophie was his sun and his air and his water, and he was doing everything he could do to bring back the person she had been before the tragedy. Jay didn't think that he'd suggested having a baby as a replacement for Karen, but she also could believe Sophie would see his suggestion that way.

"What did you tell him?"

"I told him that I'm thirty-five years old, and it's too late to think about babies. I told him we had our chance." She put her head down and pedaled harder, hard enough that Jay had to push herself to keep up. Jay could see Sophie's despair in the rounded lines of her shoulders, and she could see her anger in the stiffness of her body. Sophie said, "The way I feel right now isn't only because of the baby, or the horses, or his trip to Washington, or the fact that he thinks he knows how to make me a nice, happy mother again. It's terrible, Jay, but I feel so lost. I don't know if I love Mitch anymore, I don't know if I want to be married, I don't know *anything*. I think that's why I wanted to come along on this trip so much—to get a little breathing space."

"Kids . . ." Jay winced. "Steven asked me about kids a few weeks ago." She looked out over the countryside. Mountains lined the horizon off in the distance to either side of the road and rose majestically ahead, as well. Every twist in the highway brought some new and wonderful scene into view; she wished she could concentrate on the scenery. She wished she hadn't mentioned Steven or that fateful conversation. "I always wanted them."

"I know." Sophie gave her a quirky little smile. "You used to talk about it a lot. I really expected you would end up with your own garage band, including backup singers."

"Me too."

Sophie sighed and repositioned herself on her bike saddle. She thumbed the shifter into a lower gear as the road beneath them began to rise; Jay did the same.

They rode in silence for a long while. Jay looked at the scenery and wished she didn't have to be alone with her thoughts. Then out of nowhere, Sophie said, "I have to know this . . . and I . . . haven't had a chance . . . to ask you . . . before . . . now." Sophie panted a bit from the uphill charge. "Why Glenraven?"

They reached the peak and Jayjay slipped into high gear for the downhill glide, then grinned over at her. She left the last glimpse of the broad Po Valley behind her as she did so. "I wish I knew. I found that book in the bookstore, and suddenly I had to do this. I had to."

"You had to." Sophie thought about that for a moment, then nodded as if it made perfect sense to her. "Just like me."

Jay signaled a right turn at a little mountain shop that said CAI on the door. The tiny parking lot was empty. "CAI is Club Alpinisti Italiani," she told Sophie. "It's the approved source for guides into the Alps. I booked our guide through this office."

"This place is an office?" Sophie got those little vertical lines between her eyebrows as she looked at the building.

Jayjay felt her stomach turn a bit when she looked at it. "This branch must not be too busy; the main office told me it didn't even exist, but here it is, right where the guidebook said it would be."

Their tires crunched through the gravel.

"I hope someone is home," Sophie said. She sounded doubtful.

"We have someone waiting for us." Jay pulled her paper out of her jeans pocket and studied the name. "Signi Tavisti Lestovru." She put down the kickstand on her bike. That kickstand. She chuckled, looking at it. She'd insisted on having the kickstand installed, in spite of the horrified expression the mountain bike salesman had given her when she'd told him what she wanted. High-end mountain bikes weren't supposed to have kickstands, but Jayjay didn't care. She didn't intend to lean her twelve-hundred-dollar bike against a wall or drop it on the ground when she wasn't using it. The salesman had reluctantly put the stand on for her, acting very much as if he felt he were painting a mustache on the Mona Lisa the whole time.

She waited for Sophie, who hadn't been quite so assertive, and who, consequently, was looking for some-place safe to prop her bike.

Sophie at last decided the tall grass wouldn't hurt the hardware too much, and carefully laid the bike on its side. "It doesn't look like anybody is here."

Sophie was right. The CAI office's windows were boarded shut, and its roof sagged precariously in the middle. "I called ahead this morning before we left the hotel to make sure the guide would be ready for us; I didn't talk with him, but I talked with the office clerk . . . I think."

Sophie started up the walk, then stopped. "This place is entirely too creepy."

Jayjay agreed, but she didn't intend to let that keep her from Glenraven. She opened the door and walked in.

The inside of the place in no way resembled the outside. It was brightly lit and if it was antiquated in design, with its old wooden display cabinets and low, heavy-beamed ceiling, it was nonetheless well stocked with mountaineering supplies both modern and old-fashioned. A tan, weathered young man, gaunt as a marathon champion, walked into the main showroom when the bell attached to the door rang. He smiled, displaying the worst teeth Jayjay had ever seen in someone so young. However, the smile on his face disappeared as he looked from one woman to the other, to be replaced by an expression of polite puzzlement.

In French, he asked, "May I help you?"

Jayjay smiled broadly. "But of course," she told him, also in French. "I am looking to meet my guide, one Signi Tavisti Lestovru—"

"I am Lestovru," he said. He looked, if possible, even more puzzled than before. "But you . . . you are per-haps looking for a guide to Saint Vincent or Breuil-Cervinia?"

Jayjay sighed. She had not talked with this man; she had talked with a very American-sounding woman who had been delighted to help her set everything up. She and the woman who took her call had discussed the odd fact that there was only one guide certified to lead parties to Glenraven. Frankly, Jay had been surprised to find any guides, considering the country had just opened up. But if the woman who took her call had made sure Lestovru was here to meet them, certainly he would be aware of their destination.

Sophie tapped her on the shoulder, and Jay turned to see what she wanted. "What's he saying?" Sophie whispered.

Jay translated quickly. Sophie had missed Jayjay's childhood experience as the daughter of anthropologist parents, and hadn't taken her Spanish classes seriously; she spoke only English. Jayjay, on the other hand, had learned a fair amount of French, some Spanish, a little Inuit, and enough Japanese to get herself into trouble, but not enough to talk her way back out.

Jay leaned forward. "Did not the woman who arranged our trip tell you we would be traveling to Glenraven?"

Lestovru paled and looked behind him, as if he thought someone might overhear. "Where?" he whispered.

Jay frowned. She pulled the Fodor's guide out of the inner pocket of her jacket and held it out with the title plainly showing. "Glenraven," she said, pointing at the title.

He stared at the book. "May I see that?"

Jay felt oddly proprietary about the guidebook. She was reluctant to let it out of her hands, but she passed it to him anyway.

The young guide hefted it from hand to hand, though he didn't open it or flip through the pages. He tipped his head to one side and squinted at it as though he had never seen a guidebook before. Then he nodded and passed the book back to her. "Do you have your travel passes?"

"Mine and hers." Jay pulled two archaic squares of

hand-quilled parchment from her document pouch. She had been amazed when they'd arrived in the mail only two days after she sent off for them. She couldn't read a word on either pass, or even make out the letters of the alphabet. They looked so . . . unofficial. She hoped Lestovru wouldn't be as shocked by their appearance as she'd been. She held them out to him.

He clicked his tongue as he looked at them, then shrugged. "So you are the ones. I would not have thought—" His demeanor changed then. He straightened and met her eye and smiled again, displaying his dreadful teeth. "Just so. You were not as I imagined." Jayjay wondered if he tried to imagine his other clients before he met them. It seemed an odd remark. Lestovru, though, was still talking. "My job is to get you there safely, and that I will do; after all, who am I to question?" After he offered this comment to thin air, he rubbed the palms of his hands together briskly and told her, "First, we must exchange currencies. Your money will not spend within . . . Glenraven . . ." His voice dropped to a whisper as he said the name. " . . . And nowhere within the country is there a facility that can easily exchange monies."

Jayjay had been prepared for this. Her Fodor's mentioned the difficulty of exchanging currency, and warned that only at the CAI office—before entering the country—could an exchange to spendable currency be made. In Glenraven no Mastercard, Visa, checks or traveler's checks were accepted; no Western Union existed to rescue out-of-cash travelers with money wired from home. "Coin of the realm and barter" were, the guide claimed, the two acceptable methods of payment.

She handed him her traveler's checks, and he exchanged them for the precious metal dachrras of Glenraven. When he pushed the pile of coins over to her, he said, "This is a great amount of money. Do you have something to carry it in?"

Jayjay had been warned by her handy guidebook about the weight of the money. She nodded. "A money belt."

"Use it." He stared into her eyes then, long enough that she began to grow uncomfortable. "Don't let anyone know how much you carry. For such an amount, even those otherwise inclined to treat you kindly would be tempted."

He exchanged Sophie's money, but didn't say anything to her at all. Instead, he looked from one woman to the other with a speculative expression in his eyes. "Now we go," he told them when they'd both tucked the coins into money belts under their sweatshirts. "We shall put your bicycles on the back of my car and drive as far as Bardonecchia. Beyond that point, we ride."

"We knew that. We enjoyed our ride here," Jay said. "We're looking forward to the trip to Glenraven."

He frowned. "Perhaps you are, though when you have been for a time in a place without the modern comforts, you will come to miss all of this." His gesture encompassed the outdated little store with its several bare lightbulbs dangling from the ceiling and its worn, sagging floors, as though it epitomized modern convenience.

She sighed. He'd decided she fit the stereotype of the spoiled American; someone who didn't know what it was like to bathe in a river or wash her clothes on a rock or live without electricity. Oh, well. She wasn't any more impressed with him than he seemed to be with her, but she wouldn't have to put up with him once she and Sophie reached Glenraven. They could dump him when they got to their first destination, and find somebody personable to guide them out on the trip back.

Once she got into Glenraven, everything would get better. She didn't know how she knew that, but she knew it.

Five

Jay gave one last look to the guide's car before she pushed her bike over to Sophie's side. They stood at the intersection of the main highway, S25, and an ancient stone road of possible Roman origins that headed into the valley off to their right. Bardonecchia was behind them, and according to Lestovru, considerable risk lay ahead of them. He had given them a brief lecture on the danger of travel through mountainous regions; he mentioned the possibility of sudden changes in the weather, of avalanches and flash floods, of dangerous animals, and of the difficulty of getting quick medical attention once they were well into the mountains, should it prove necessary. He seemed almost to hope that his dire warnings would convince Jay and Sophie to back down, but the only effect he had was to make Jay like him less than she had. She knew the dangers. She still wanted to go to Glenraven.

Lestovru used English once he discovered Sophie spoke no French. His English was accented, but then, Jay realized, his French had been, too. She found herself wondering what his first language had been. He told them, "You will follow behind me. Some portions of this ride are difficult, and we will have several traverses, but you must at no time permit yourselves to become separated from each other or from me; once separated, all dangers become greater."

They took off on the maybe-Roman road, and immediately found themselves cycling around missing stones, fallen pavement, and clumps of weed and grass that had overgrown the ancient highway. Jayjay could almost believe no one had trodden that road since Christopher Columbus.

At one of the few relatively smooth places, Sophie dropped back to Jay's side. "I don't like our guide."

"I don't like him, either." Jayjay noted a bad bit of pavement and jumped it. "But specifically what don't you like?"

"He seemed too interested in the amount of money I was carrying. He didn't say anything, but he sure looked. I don't like the idea of riding into the mountains with just the two of us and this man we don't know from Adam, when neither one of us has a weapon."

Jayjay nodded grimly. International travel made carrying even such defensive weapons as pepper gas a nightmare, so neither Jay nor Sophie carried anything more lethal than a bicycle wrench. "Not much we can do but watch him."

Sophie glanced quickly at Jay. "Fat lot of good that will do us if he's carrying a gun."

"He was certified by CAI. They're reputable. If they say we can trust him, I think we can."

Sophie didn't look mollified. "Maybe. Be a pity if they're wrong, though."

"He doesn't seem much like a guide, does he?" Jayjay made the comment because as soon as Lestovru finished warning them about all the dangers they faced in going through the mountain pass, he lapsed into silence. Sophie had asked him the origin of the road and Jay had wondered aloud about a couple of lovely plants that were growing by the side of it. He'd ignored those questions with a shrug of his narrow shoulders. Neither did he make any attempt to identify sites of interest along their route, though many existed. The ruin of some great stone tower squatted atop a knoll off to the right, and a gorgeous mountain stream chuckled in its bed on their left. The meadows through which the road wound were full of flowers, most of them foreign to Jayjay's eyes. Unfamiliar birds of all sorts flew by, and a lumbering marmot-looking beast sat up on its haunches and watched them pass. Jay would have loved to know the names of those creatures and flowers, but after Lestovru brushed off her first questions, she wasn't enthusiastic about asking more. Instead, he pushed their pace hard, concentrating on making progress, and beneath them the road rose steadily uphill in a moderate grade.

Jay lost interest in talking; she was in shape but between the thin mountain air and the hard work of pedaling and dodging potholes, she had little energy left to discuss things with Sophie. When the road narrowed, the three of them ended up riding single file; then no one said anything at all.

They traveled at an uncomfortably quick pace for perhaps an hour. Then Lestovru called a halt. He rested one foot on the ground and pointed ahead. "We approach the uphill now. You will perhaps wish to walk your bicycles?"

Uphill, Jay thought. What does he call what we've been doing? "We'll ride," Jay told him. "We can do it." She loathed the idea of showing weakness in front of the man. She didn't want him to connect the thoughts of her and weakness in any way. She was already uncomfortable about the calculating look he'd given the little hoard of coins she tucked into her hidden money belt.

The look he gave her said as clearly as words, I don't think you can do it, but he nodded. "Very well."

Jay gave the road ahead a harder look. The valley dead-ended as the hips of two mountains met, and the road went into a series of switchbacks to rise over the higher ground between them so that it looked like a snake in convulsions. Jay tried self-motivation; she told herself that her daily bike rides and the walking and light weight lifting she did to keep in shape would be enough to get her over those switchbacks. I can do this, she thought.

Sophie looked less certain. "We need a rest," she told Lestovru.

Jayjay glanced at her friend. She wasn't breathing any harder than Jay, and she didn't look particularly tired. Well, nowadays Sophie always seemed to be a little tired. Jay got off her bike and pushed it over beside Sophie, and the two of them sat down on the side of the road.

"What's wrong?" Jay asked her.

This time the problem wasn't tiredness. "We need to have a plan in case he pulls a gun on us," she said.

"We rush him together. With any luck, he'll only be able to kill one of us before the other one has had time to disarm him." Jay grinned when she said it, and for a miracle, Sophie smiled back at her.

The unspoken question hung between them: should they turn back? The situation felt wrong to both of them, and perhaps they could look around and find another guide to take them to Glenraven. Or they could spend the rest of the vacation in Italy. Or they could go home. If either one of them backed out, they were both going to have to; that fact hung in the air as well.

The question remained unspoken. Sophie said, "I guess we'll take our chances. If he kills us, the names of those intrepid explorers Sophie Ann Cortiss and Julie Jean Bennington Pfiester Tremont Smith will go down in history, right?" Sophie glanced sidelong at her, a wry half-smile on her lips.

The list of names hit Jay like a gut punch; she laughed, but the laughter was strained, and she caught the change of expression on Sophie's face that told her Sophie hadn't missed the reaction either.

They grabbed their bikes and waved to the guide that they were ready. He nodded and led off.

They struggled up one steep incline, caught their breath on the switchback, and started up again. Jay felt sweat popping out in beads on her forehead even though the air was quite cool. She thought, third time was supposed to be a charm. Steven was supposed to be the husband who made me forget the others; he was supposed to be the friend I got to live with. But he wasn't, and I know that now, so why am I dealing with it like this? She started to feel a stitch in her side, and the muscles in her legs burned. I'm running away when I should be sitting down with a lawyer and wrapping up the relationship. I should be holding my head up and going on with my life. This is running. This is hiding. Why am I doing this?

The switchbacks followed each other in a seemingly endless series; she found herself wondering how the writers of the Glenraven guide could have ever considered the route into the country a "pass." They weren't riding through a pass. They were mountain climbing on wheels.

When she thought of Glenraven, though, the tingle of excitement still fluttered in her gut.

Lestovru pedaled upward, keeping his lead and managing to look like he was riding across flatland. Jayjay loathed him for that.

They rounded another switchback. Ahead, Sophie groaned and gasped, "How much further?"

"We are nearer," Lestovru called back.

Nearer. That was vague.

The air grew colder, and the breeze became stiffer and more of an obstacle in its own right. They weren't high enough to suffer from lack of oxygen due to the thinning atmosphere. Yet.

Jayjay reached her lowest gear and still struggled, making creeping progress; she wished she had another gear or two below first.

How much longer can this bloody road go on? she wondered.

Then the road hit a plateau, and immediately took a sharp jag left and disappeared into a hole in the sheer stone face of a mountain.

"The lamps, please," Lestovru said. He was short of breath, but not as severely as either Sophie or Jayjay. He didn't smile at all, or congratulate them for reaching the top as most guides would have done. After his other failings, Jayjay was curious about precisely what qualifications he presented to have convinced someone to certify him as a guide for this region.

They switched on the bike headlights but stood for another moment, resting.

Jay began to breathe easier.

"Now, please," Lestovru said. "We still have some distance, and we don't want to arrive late."

Late? Late for what?

He slipped onto his bike saddle and took off into the tunnel. Sophie went next, and Jayjay followed, trying to remember any mention of a tunnel in the Fodor's. Her guidebook had said something about the road to Glenraven being in poor repair, but the book hadn't mentioned levitating on bicycles up cliff faces, and even with concentration, she recalled nothing about a tunnel. She hoped the writers of the guide hadn't forgotten other equally significant details.

The tunnel rose gradually and curved to the right. The gentle incline was still punishing after the mountain road. They quickly left any sign of daylight behind them. The inside of the mountain was warmer than pedaling up the outside of it had been, but certainly not warm. Jay guessed the temperature at about fifty-five degrees.

In front, Lestovru's light bobbled from side to side as he dodged obstacles on the tunnel floor. He had plenty of stamina, but he didn't ride the bicycle particularly well. To Jay that seemed as ominous a sign as his complete uninterest in the details of the local terrain; he had to be good at something to get a job as a guide, but she couldn't see any area in which he even met minimal expectations. So who was he? A thief? This seemed a hellish lot of work for the little money the two of them carried. Granted, if he wanted to rob them, the tunnel seemed to offer a nice location for it. He could leave their bodies lying in the darkness and it might be years before someone tripped over the skeletons. The dampness and the pervasive chill in the air added atmosphere to such thoughts; the flicker of the bicycle headlights along the rough-hewn stone walls and the grotesque shadows that darted ahead of them like madly pedaling demons began to oppress her spirit. She felt as if the mountain had swallowed her; even though she traveled uphill, she couldn't shake the sensation that she was sinking into the eternal blackness of the earth's stony mantle, never to see the light of day again.

Lestovru made a sharp right turn, and Jay heard the sound of tires swishing through a puddle. Sophie followed, and for a moment she felt alone, abandoned, as if she were in one of those nightmares where she ran endlessly, and never got anywhere. Then she rounded the corner and got their lights in sight again, and the oppressive solitude lightened.

But not much. They went around two more corners—a left and a right—and suddenly she realized one of those had been an intersection. The tunnel branched.

Unmarked, it branched. She wondered if she had missed other branches because she hadn't been looking for them. She imagined lurid scenarios of the three travelers riding on and on, while their lamplight grew weaker and yellower, until one by one the lanterns went out and she and Sophie and the unpleasant, taciturn Lestovru were left listening to the echoes of their own breathing and the maddening drip of water from the walls.

She tried to keep track of the time that passed; in the darkness, minutes stretched long and longer. They had been in the tunnel half an hour, she thought, trying not to let herself exaggerate, though it seemed half a day. She couldn't see her watch; the sleeve of her jacket covered it, and anyway, last in line as she was, she didn't have enough light to read the dial. But she wished she could. The longer the darkness persisted, the more certain she became that something had gone wrong; that the three of them had gotten off the path and were wandering through some minotaurian labyrinth.

Then Lestovru turned at another branch, and Sophie, too, moved out of sight. Jay heard her squeak; Sophie wasn't much of a squeaker in normal circumstances. Jay slowed and peered around the corner and down the branch before following. She saw Lestovru. She saw Sophie. No danger. No disasters. Nothing out of the ordinary.

Shrugging, she followed, and instantly her stomach felt like it had been turned simultaneously inside out and upside down. She gasped, started to fall forward over the edge of a cliff she couldn't see, and then both the queasiness and the dizziness passed, and she felt fine.

Sophie turned another corner. Her delighted, "Daylight!" echoed back through the tunnel, and Jayjay started; her attention snapped forward. She pumped the pedals to catch up, and as she went around that last curve, she saw ahead the first glimmer of light on a wall that was not cast by a headlight.

Jay murmured, "Oh, thank God!" and began to pump faster. Sophie already raced toward the exit. Even Lestovru was not immune to the draw of daylight; his pace picked up as well. The demon cyclists on the walls seemed to be hurrying to outstrip the light that devoured them; the image struck Jayjay with its air of futility, and then the sunlight at the tunnel mouth threw the shadows backward where she didn't have to see them, and Lestovru and Sophie and she burst out of the tunnel onto an overlook that clung to the side of the mountain through which they'd ridden.

They braked hard. All three sets of bike brakes squealed in unison.

Jayjay parked her bike and found a boulder at the edge of the overlook, and climbed onto it. Below her lay a vast green valley, dotted with the sapphire of glistening lakes; with the velvet rough of two great, uncut forests; with ethereal spires of impossibly tall, delicate castles that sat on hills and by rivers and on top of little mountains, all with tiny picture-book towns nestled inside their sprawling bailey walls. The whole, ringed by the greater wall of the Alps, looked like it had been lifted in one piece from a gentler terrain and tucked into this out-of-the-way nook for safekeeping. Jay thought she could willingly lose herself in that perfect miniature of a world.

The photo on the cover of Fodor's didn't do it justice.

Sophie climbed out onto the rock beside her. "Incredible," she whispered. "I can't quite believe it's here."

The sun beat down hot on Jayjay's face and the chill breeze blew against her skin, so that she was both hot and cold at once; the feeling was wonderful. She tingled and her heart raced with excitement. *Come*, the place whispered to her. She'd been waiting all her life to find herself in a fairy tale, and there it lay, before her. It tugged at her far more strongly than it had from a third of a world away. *Here*, an eager voice promised, *here you will find what you've been waiting for.*

What is that? she wondered. What have I been waiting for? She had only part of an answer.

Glenraven.

Six

I'm here, Sophie thought, staring down into the verdant, castle-dotted valley. She rubbed her hands along her knees and glanced at Jay, who was lost in rapt wonder. The place called to her, but its promise frightened her. *Here you will find rest and peace.* Its promise for her. Rest and peace.

She knew what that meant. She would never leave Glenraven. She would die down there. Glenraven would give her the road back to Karen, or perhaps the simple silence of nonexistence.

Rest and peace.

The wind blew through her hair; she heard its voice in the trees that grew not far below, and in the whispering of the mountain peaks far above. The wind picked up Glenraven's refrain. Rest and peace.

Perhaps I should have done a better job of saying good-bye to Mitch. Perhaps I should have tied up all my loose ends. Gone to see my parents. Double-checked my will.

Rest and peace.

She looked directly over the edge of the boulder. Straight down. Life doesn't hold on by much, she thought. Not much at all. One instant it's here, the next it's gone forever, and nothing and no one can make it last.

She looked at Lestovru, standing impatient and dour-faced by his bicycle, unimpressed by the beauty of the scene below. Jay still stared, spellbound.

Do I want peace and rest? Do I really?

And she thought, yes. I do. I want to sleep at night without seeing Karen on the ground in my dreams. I want to wake and breathe freely, without the weight of sorrow crushing me. I want so much.

Peace and rest would be enough.

Lestovru evidently tired of waiting for them to go; he said, "If we do not leave soon, we will miss the closing of the gate."

His voice snapped Sophie out of her gloomy reverie. Jay backed off the rock; Sophie followed. She would go on to Glenraven, even though something told her this would be her last chance to turn back. Maybe her last chance to do anything. She would go to Glenraven because it offered something she had been able to find nowhere else.

They were halfway down the twisting road that led to the border when Sophie realized Lestovru wore weapons. He had a crossbow slung across his back, and daggers strapped at both hips.

When had he done that? While they stopped at the mouth of the tunnel? She hadn't seen him, but then she'd been studying the panorama that lay beneath her.

The three of them cruised, not pedaling at all; the road down the mountain was nowhere near as steep as the road up had been. Sophie's fingertips touched her brakes from time to time, and every once in a while she reached up to be sure that her helmet was still tightly in place. However, as it had been impossible to talk riding up the mountain, so it was impossible to talk while gliding down. Too many gaping holes marred the ancient pavement; too many tree branches reached across the narrow road at head height.

Because she couldn't talk, she worried. She worried about Jay, and whatever had convinced her to take this trip. She worried about Lestovru and why she didn't feel she could trust him. Mostly, though, she worried about Glenraven. She had seen the guidebook, she had come out to find the little country, convinced such a place existed in spite of knowing better—in spite of knowing that Western Europe might have tucked Andorra, Monaco and Liechtenstein away in its borders, but those had all been where they were for a good long time. Nobody could have managed to sneak a new country into Western Europe past her, and Glenraven had never been there before. So why was it there now?

She worried at her willingness to travel to a place she knew didn't exist. It had something to do with associating with Jayjay, of course. People who hung around Jayjay for too long got to see the mountain walking to Mohammed more often than they cared to explain.

And here was Glenraven. The mountains were walking.

Behind a tree-covered knoll, before the road dropped for the final time into the valley, Lestovru braked to a halt and slid off his bike. He was frowning. "We must now stop, before we reach the gate," he told them. "You will have to change your clothing. I brought some clothing—" he shrugged a Gallic shrug, "but I expected men. You will have to wear what I brought for you. This is just as well for the riding, perhaps. The women's clothing, it is not made for bicycle travel and even less for riding the horses. And we do not have for you the carriage. We thought . . ." He shrugged again and smiled. "No matter."

"Excuse me," Jay said, "but what do you mean we have to change our clothing? We have on comfortable clothes."

"They are not appropriate for Glenraven. You will be too . . . observable? Is that the word?" He stared up and to his right as if he were reading a dictionary someone had left in the branches overhead. "No. *Conspicuous*. You will be too conspicuous."

"We're tourists," Sophie said, annoyance clear in her voice.

"There are no tourists in Glenraven," he told them. Sophie found that remark bizarre.

Jayjay and Sophie glanced at each other. Sophie could see uncertainty in her friend's eyes.

Lestovru reached into his own pack and pulled out two bundles of clothing, holding them out to Jay and Sophie.

Sophie shifted her pack on her shoulders. And what did horseback travel have to do with any of this? Why had they bothered with bicycles?

Jay finally nodded, stepped forward, and took the bundle he offered her. She watched him warily. "Where do you expect us to change?" she asked the guide. "We're not going to do it in front of you."

He shook his head. "Of course not. You will be safe enough here for a few moments . . . but please do not wander off. I will be down the road, behind those trees. Wait for me and I will return for you in a few moments, when you have finished dressing."

Sophie took her bundle from him. She could just see it. He hadn't needed to rob them in the tunnel. He'd planned the robbery for his own convenience. He'd wait until they were undressed; then he would jump out from behind a tree with his gun pointed at them, and take everything. Or worse. Maybe he didn't just have robbery in mind.

While she stood there worrying, he jumped on his bike and pedaled down the hill and around the curve in the road. When he was out of sight, she cleared her throat.

"This is weird, Jay."

Jayjay stood in the middle of the road, staring in the direction Lestovru had taken. "Weird," she murmured. "Yes. It is." She shook her bangs out of her face and frowned. "What do you think he's *doing*?"

"All of my guesses involve robbery, rape and murder."

"Mmm. That occurred to me, too." Jay turned to face her. "It's too late now, really. I don't think there's any way we could get ourselves back to Italy through that tunnel without a guide. But I'm wondering about something. You didn't trust Lestovru from the time you met him. You could have said, 'I don't think we should be doing this' at any time, and I would have turned back. Why didn't you?"

"Why didn't *you*?" Sophie asked. She'd been wondering the same thing, both about Jay, and about herself. She'd been doing something she knew was stupid and irresponsible and dangerous, and she *knew* she knew it, and she knew she ought to stop. Yet she'd kept going . . . and in a minute, she was going to change into the Glenraven clothes and wait for Lestovru to return. Stupid. Stupid. Why?

Jayjay nibbled on the inside of her cheek, eyes unfocused; she stood still for what seemed to Sophie like a very long time, but which was probably only thirty seconds. "This is going to sound ridiculous," she said at last. "It probably is. But there is something in Glenraven for me. I felt it the moment I saw the book, and I feel it even more now. I had to come here."

Sophie nodded. "I wish I could say that I didn't know what you mean. I do though." She didn't tell Jay what she thought she would find in Glenraven. Jayjay kept thinking she was going to pick herself up and brush off the pain of the past and move on. Like Mitch, she didn't understand.

"Still, I'd rather not make it easy for him," Jay said, and when Sophie frowned, she clarified. "I know what we're doing defies all logic . . . but I don't want to be an easy target. Let's take turns changing."

Sophie nodded. "Here," she said, stooping over. "This is a great rock. Now I have a weapon."

"He had a crossbow." Jay stripped off her shirt and jacket and pulled on the rich green, baggy-sleeved tunic and heavy woolen pullover Lestovru had given her.

"I noticed that. Knives, too."

Jay unlaced her boots and quickly kicked them off. "Hey! He gave me a dagger!" She unrolled a belt from inside a large folded square of brown leather. Sophie saw a scabbard and the protruding hilt of a narrow, straight-bladed knife. Jayjay shook out the leather square; it turned out to be a pair of brown leather pants. She pulled them on, hopping from leg to leg to get them up. They turned out to be snug around her hips. Jay tugged her boots back on and started lacing them. "Funny. Why did he give me a knife? Did he give you one?"

Sophie untied the string that bound her pack and rummaged through the clothing, which was identical to what Jay had been given. A knife belt and knife waited for her, too. "That doesn't make sense."

Jayjay pulled the knife out of its sheath and tested its edge with a thumb, a thoughtful expression on her face. "True. But what does?" She strapped the knife around her waist, then crouched down and dug through her pack until she found her travel document case. "By the way," she added, "you need this."

She handed a small parchment square to Sophie. The parchment was covered with writing . . . or maybe hieroglyphics. Sophie turned it over, studying the letter forms and trying to think of anything she'd ever seen that was similar. She came up empty. "What is it?"

"According to the Glenraven Travel Commission, it's

the local equivalent of a visa. We'll need it at Customs."
Jayjay stuck hers in a pocket of the woolen tunic.

Sophie changed her clothes and put on her own knife belt. "You aren't as worried by all of this as you ought to be, are you?"

Jay's grin was sheepish. "No. I'm excited. I've never had the chance to do anything like this before." Jayjay sat down on the edge of a boulder and looked around, a tiny smile on her face. Sophie thought she looked ten years younger than she had when they took their flight out of Atlanta.

"In spite of everything, you look better."

"I feel better," Jay admitted. After a reflective pause, she added, "I needed to get out of Peters for a while. You won't believe what's happened."

Seven

"Yemus? It's Signi. I have both of them. They aren't what we expected."

"If they were what we expected, they'd be what the Kin expected, too. Be grateful." There was a pause, followed by a cautious "Where are you?"

"I can't tell you. I think the Kin know I'm out here. They might have Watchers posted nearby."

Softly whispered profanity preceded another, longer pause. "Are you sure?"

"I can't be sure . . . but I've seen signs."

"Then you know what to do."

"Yes."

"Well, then . . . we'll watch for them. Good-bye, Signi."

"Good . . . good-bye."

Eight

"—So we got into this huge discussion about whether we were ready to have children or not, because he had suddenly decided he wanted a family right that minute. And I got upset and told him that he didn't spend enough time with me and where was he going to find time for kids and . . . and . . . that's when he told me he was gay." Jayjay glanced up from staring at her hands to see that Sophie's mouth had dropped open.

"Gay? Steven?" Sophie cleared her throat. "But . . . but we've known him since junior high. Jesus, you two have been married for three years. Didn't you ever suspect?" She shook her head. "What am I saying? I never suspected."

"I know." Jay looked down at her hands. "He said he figured since we were friends, we could get married and have kids together. He figured since I'd been married twice already, and since I was so down on men when the two of us got together, the 'relationship' part of the relationship wouldn't matter too much to me." She shrugged. "He figured we could help each other out financially . . . and he had someone he loved, and he wanted kids." She closed her eyes. "But he didn't want me. He never wanted me."

Sophie shook her head. "So he had this other woman that he loved and he wanted to have kids, but he married you instead?"

Jay smiled a bitter little smile. "Other man. He had a man he loved, that he'd loved for years, but his parents being who they are . . ." His parents owned half of Peters, and had hooks in the other half. Steven was their only child. They expected great things from him, and so far he'd been their golden boy.

"I can see where the mighty colonel would hate having his masculinity called into question by the presence of a gay son."

"Steven told me he figured they would disinherit him, and he's willing to work hard right now, but he doesn't want that to happen. He'll come into more than a few millions when they die."

"Lovely. So you were going to be his propriety shield."

"I was his cover story. He figured after Bill and Stacey, I'd be happy to have a man who left me alone."

"What the hell happened with them, anyway? You walked out and gave both of them everything you had at the time, and everyone in town figured they'd caught you cheating with somebody. You've never told anyone more than that 'things didn't work out.' Not even me, and I'm supposed to be your best friend."

"Yeah." Jay shrugged. She'd handled it in the way that seemed to make sense at the time. She'd refused to say anything bad about either one of them, figuring that the truth would come out on its own, and that when it did she wouldn't have spent years looking like some venomous bitch who'd done everything she could to ruin the reputations of two of Peters' well-liked men; and she didn't want to hear any of the catty remarks about her having been a golddigger out for their money, so she had left both marriages without anything but what she had earned and purchased herself.

Unfortunately, though, the truth didn't come out, and everyone figured she'd been a tramp who got caught sleeping around. "The truth," she murmured. "After all this time, I don't think anyone would believe me if I told it. My moment for vindication has passed."

"Try me. I know you."

Jayjay nodded. "You do. Okay. Bill drank, did drugs, dealt a little on the side. He never got caught; no one ever looked at good old Bill and said, 'There goes a scumbag cokehead.' He didn't look the part."

"He was an accountant, for Chrissake!" Sophie's eyes were huge.

"Yep. And he kept a very careful accounting of the money he poured up his nose. I couldn't deal with it. So I got out, and when Stacey moved into town, we liked each other and we had some fun. He was so free-spirited. After Bill . . . well, a free spirit was a new thing. I felt so much younger. But once we were married, he still attended his Saturday night poker games, and while he was there he drank till he floated, and if he lost much money, when the game was over he came home and beat the shit out of me."

Sophie sat there clenching and unclenching her fists. "And Steven is gay."

"I have a very special knack for picking the wrong men."

"I'd say. So what are you going to do?"

Jayjay laughed; the laugh sounded cold and hollow in her own ears. "Well, Steve told me he and Lee— that's this man he's madly in love with—wanted to share in bringing up kids. They both wanted to be parents, but Lee simply can't function with a woman at all. Steven can . . . but it isn't his thing. They wanted me to have the babies. Of course Steven wanted Lee to move in with us—"

"With *both* of you?!"

"Mmm-hmmm. So Lee wouldn't miss out on any of the wonders of parenting."

"Right." Sophie looked ready to go back to Peters and cook Steven for lunch. "What were you supposed to get out of this deal? Is he bi? Did he say he loved you, too?"

"No. He figured we were friends, and he decided since we both wanted kids and I obviously wasn't having great luck with men, he could stay married to me and all three of us could have the children we wanted. But until he started pushing hard for children, he forgot to mention that he was gay . . . even though he and Lee had planned this even before Steven proposed to me. I think Lee even had a hand in picking me out. The two of them figured I wasn't in a position to be picky, I guess. I, of course, was head over heels in love with Steven . . . like an idiot. When all of this came out, he said he had never loved me . . . but he *liked* me."

Sophie picked up a pine cone and started ripping it into tiny shreds. "He liked you. How special."

"Not quite the romance of the century." Jayjay shook her head ruefully.

Sophie growled, "No. Not quite. So I take it you aren't considering becoming a baby breeder for Steve and his true love."

"Ah . . . no." Jay didn't intend to admit to Sophie or anyone else that she had—briefly—considered it; that for one dark moment she had been desperate enough for a family, for someone to love who would love her back, that even such an empty relationship seemed possible. She wasn't the same person who felt that way anymore, so it seemed pointless to bring it up.

"Then what are you going to do?"

Jayjay grinned and spread her hands wide. "I'm doing it, Soph. I'm living. I'm moving on. I found a great travel guide, I planned a trip, I'm taking the trip. When

I go back to Peters I'll file for legal separation, and when my year is up I'll get a divorce."

"And next time find the right man, I hope."

Jay took a deep breath and stared down the road toward Glenraven. Her determination to be upbeat cracked. "No. I've had my three strikes. I'm out of the game now."

"You're going to be celibate?"

Jayjay glanced sidelong at Sophie. She couldn't help smiling a little. "Well . . . I'm going to be *single*."

Sophie chuckled. "So you aren't actually out of the game. You simply intend to pinch-hit."

Jayjay laughed, and this time her laughter sounded happier. "Not at all. I intend to be what you could call an 'interested spectator.' Nothing else."

Sophie chuckled, then glanced at her watch and frowned. "Damn . . . look at the time. Lestovru has been gone a lot longer than a couple of minutes."

She was right. The two of them had been sitting and talking so long the shadows of the trees had stretched across the road, and the air had gone from warm to chilly.

Jayjay stood and slung her pack onto her back. "He said he was going to be right around the bend."

Sophie stood, too. "He also said he'd be back in a minute. Let's go. I don't feel like sitting on a rock waiting while he's chatting on the phone with his girl-friend for hours."

Side by side, they pedaled down the slight grade and around the bend. The road could not have been emp-tier. Neither Lestovru nor his bike nor the phone kiosk Jayjay had been expecting waited for them. The road curved away again.

"Keep going?" Sophie asked.

Jay raised an eyebrow. "What are our choices?"

"Keep going, I guess. I sure as hell don't want to try going back the way we came."

Jay thought about that. "No. Besides, we have a great room at a terrific place waiting for us."

"But did our guide really ditch us?" Sophie was looking from side to side, from the ancient, gnarled trees to the rolling meadows to the ring of jagged mountains that bordered their horizons on every side.

"He decided we were more trouble than we were worth," she said, trying to make light of it. Jay suspected that Lestovru had run off to call a couple of disreputable friends, and that somewhere ahead, robbers lay in wait.

They kept riding, nervous as foxes who heard the hounds. Around the next bend, they didn't find Lestovru. They did find a gatehouse: an ancient sag-roofed stone shed. In front of it sat a man who looked like he might have been present when it was built. He glanced up as the two women rode up to him and squinted and spit on the ground beside him. He didn't bother to stand.

Jayjay swung off her bike and parked it. Once again she felt dizzy and light-headed, as if she were standing on the deck of a small boat in high seas and the deck was tossing. She held her breath until the feeling passed and somehow refrained from throwing up. I like that, she decided. "Refrained from throwing up." It sounded so in control.

As soon as she felt better, she rummaged through her pack for her guidebook. The old man watched her but didn't move. She said "hello"; he didn't move. She thumbed to the back, to the Galti Vocabulary section. The first phrase in the Useful Phrases section was "Do you speak English?"

She thought that seemed pretty useful. "Gesopodi ennlitch gwera?" she asked, hoping the pronunciation was close enough that she hadn't inadvertently told him his mother sucked rocks.

He shrugged and said nothing.

Jay glanced at Sophie. "Get out your visa . . . you know, the gate validation pass. Maybe he never talks."

She pulled the parchment square out of her pocket and started to hand it to the man, but halfway to him, it crumbled into dust and the dust, sparkling, blew away on the breeze. Beside her, Sophie muttered, "Omigawd." Jay turned to see the wind carrying off the last fragments of her visa, too.

The old man finally stood up. He held out his hand and pointed at her book. Puzzled, she handed it to him.

He held the book for a moment, then nodded. He squinted up at her and smiled. His teeth, she thought, were what Lestovru's were going to look like in a hundred and fifty years. It wasn't a pretty sight. "You verry late." He rolled his *r*'s so hard Jay almost expected him to cut his tongue on those teeth.

"We lost our guide," Jay told him, pronouncing each word distinctly so that he would understand her. "Signi Tavisti Lestovru. Have you seen him?"

"Signi you guide? No Signi here." He spat again. "Horses waiting, I waiting, and you late, late, late!"

Jayjay frowned. "We got here as fast as we could, but without a guide—"

"Horses?" Sophie asked.

"We were going to bike," Jay told the man. She patted the saddle of her bicycle.

He shook his head vehemently. "No. No bike. No bike in Glenraven. You take horses."

"Bikes," Sophie insisted.

The old man turned and shouted a string of gibberish, and two dark-haired peasant boys stepped through the door. One ambled up to Jay, smiled, removed her packs from the bike, smiled, lifted her bike in one massive fist, smiled, bowed, and walked away with her bike.

"Hey!" she yelled, and Sophie yelled something at

the same time. The other peasant had made off with her bike.

"Horses," the old man said with conviction.

"Horses, hell! I want my bike back," Jay yelled.

The old man shook his head. "They waiting when you back here. Nobody take. Nobody want."

"I don't—" Care, Jay had intended to say, before starting a tirade, but the same urgency that had dragged her across the world to Glenraven tugged at her again. *Take the horses*, it insisted. *You don't want the bikes. Not here. Not now.* She froze, bewildered, then glanced at Sophie. She, too, looked puzzled.

A moment later, the peasant boys came back leading a string of four good-looking horses. Two were already saddled for riding; the other two wore pack saddles. The horses were good, solid animals, straight-legged, straight-backed, and muscular. All of them bore a brand on the right flank: a sweeping curlicue with an inverted V slashed through the center and two dots below the point of the V.

"Rikes Gate close at sunset. After that—" The old man glared at both of them. "—you sitting in forest until morning; you still alive tomorrow, maybe someone let you in. Now—" He pointed a finger at Jayjay. "Horses there. You take."

Jay began trying to find her document case in her pack. "Do you need to see our passports? We had gate validation passes, but they—well, you saw what happened to them."

He stared at her blankly. Jayjay found his lack of official presence worrisome.

"I have a receipt proving that I paid for the passes. You'll at least need to see that, won't you?" She thought, Don't you need to see some proof of something, you bizarre little man?

He shook his head with an almost frantic vehemence.

"You not the right people, you not be here. Take horses and go. Go. You must hurry."

Jayjay stared at him. The fear he exuded when he talked about hurrying bothered her. "Why must we hurry?"

From the look in the old man's eyes, Jayjay wished she didn't need to know.

"Night coming," he told her as if that explained everything.

She waited, watching him. Surely that couldn't be the whole reason for the big rush. Night was, after all, something that happened every day.

He turned, found her still standing there, and his expression became purest exasperation. "City gates close at night, you. If you not to gates before dark, you sleeping in forest."

"Oh." Jayjay turned to Sophie. "I guess we'd better hurry."

Jay picked two horses, a dappled gray mare and a rangy bay gelding, and stowed her gear on the pack saddle of the mare, then mounted the gelding. Uneasiness twisted at her gut. Where the hell had Lestovru gone? The old guy hadn't seen him, or wasn't admitting it. Jay hadn't seen any phones— or phone lines, or power lines, or anything that smacked of the potential for rapid communication. Not even smoke signals, come to think of it. If Lestovru had called ahead to friends, how had he done it?

What was the deal with the horses?

What about their bikes?

And why was the old man so afraid of nightfall?

Sophie finished checking the horse supplies: grain, hoof picks, rope and other necessary paraphernalia. She frowned over at Jay. "Whoever outfitted us did a good job. Why couldn't we take bikes, though?" She didn't look at all happy about having to ride. Jay didn't blame her. She doubted Sophie had been on horseback since the accident.

"I don't know." She sighed. "I don't know anything."

Sophie mounted smoothly. "I feel like we need to be going," she told Jay.

"I know. I have the same feeling. Like we're racing a clock." Jayjay led off, unhappy about the uncanniness of the events that had transpired, and about her uncharacteristic acquiescence. They'd walked off with her bike, dammit; and she couldn't even find it in herself to feel upset about that.

What was the matter with her?

She and Sophie trotted out of sight of the kiosk and down the road, into a large clearing. The last of the day's sunlight sparkled in the meadow grasses to either side of the narrow paved path that served as a road, and birds flitted past. The castle behind the forest that lay to the left was invisible except for the spire with the golden ball on top. The gleaming stone walls of the castle that lay to the right had taken on a warm, amber glow in the lengthening light of day. It beckoned temptingly.

At the end of the meadow, the road branched. The right branch clearly lead toward that lovely, sunlit castle. The left branch vanished into the depths of an ancient wood. Jayjay frowned. She still saw no sign of Lestovru.

Sophie looked at the road, all traces of amusement gone from her face. "Now what?"

Jay had studied the map in the front of the guidebook, tracing out her itinerary, until she imagined she could do the route blindfolded.

"There's only one road into Glenraven; that's the road we're on right now," she told Sophie. "From here, the road to the right goes to Cotha Dramwyn, and the one to the left goes to Rikes Gate."

"The road to the right looks better to me."

Jayjay agreed, but she shook her head and tucked the guidebook into the front pocket of the pack, where she could reach it more easily. "Our reservations for tonight are in Rikes Gate."

"The old man mentioned Rikes Gate."

Jayjay paused, suddenly sick to her stomach. He had mentioned the place by name, hadn't he?

They had reservations in Rikes Gate, but only Lestovru should have known that. If the old man knew, then he must have talked to Lestovru. However, he said he hadn't even seen Lestovru. If he had talked to Lestovru but didn't want Jayjay and Sophie to know it, then he must have had a major reason. And it wasn't likely that the reason was good. Robbers really did wait for them on the road to Rikes Gate, she thought. So they couldn't go there. Cotha Dramwyn was a pretty destination, but seemed obvious. If Lestovru had put so much work into waylaying the two of them, then he might be willing to try to find them to take a second stab at them, so to speak.

They didn't dare travel to the two main destinations from their current location.

However, a third destination lay within reach. Jayjay considered possibilities, and pulled her guidebook out of the front pocket of her saddlebag. She double-checked the map. The tiny town of Inzo lay to the north, on a road marked "footpath" in the guide. She flipped to the section on Inzo.

"Three kilometers (1½ miles) north of the Glenraven/Italy border, nestled behind the easternmost arm of the Cavitarin Wood, Inzo is a tiny, primitive hamlet secluded from the rest of Glenraven. Its few inhabitants make their livings from farming, spinning and weaving, and cutting wood. Inzo burned in the Malduque Rebellion of 1040, and the besiegers reduced its once-proud castle to rubble. From that day forward, it has avoided the disputes that have marked Glenraven's long and disputatious history . . .

" . . . there is little here to interest the visitor; the time needed to find Inzo would be better spent in viewing other, more scenic venues . . ."

It didn't sound like much of a tourist haven; its last excitement in 1040, its inhabitants folks who made a profession of keeping their heads low. Nevertheless, to Jay it sounded like a good first destination; if Inzo didn't have anything that would draw tourists, then robbers wouldn't have much reason to search for them in that direction.

As for the reservations . . . well, if the inn at Inzo didn't have any available rooms, that's why they'd packed their tents.

She told Sophie, "I found another place in here I think we should try."

Sophie raised an eyebrow but said nothing.

"Yes?"

Sophie nodded. "Yes."

Nine

Lestovru pedaled faster, wishing he carried more than a crossbow. He could hear the trees breathing, the air was so still, and the eyes of the forest watched him.

He rode hard around the outskirts of tiny Inzo, heading toward the depths of the Cavitarin Wood beyond. He could not hope for survival; he could hope he would be a successful diversion—that his death would draw attention from the heroes who headed toward Rikes Gate and safety.

He pressed his lips together in a thin, hard line. Heroes. They were women; he was going to die for two women. Yemus had been wrong, as he had been wrong so often of late, and the salvation of the Machnan was not at hand. The Machnan had paid everything they had to bring in the heroes, and for their pain they were going to get nothing.

Women.

He pedaled harder. The pathetic hovels of Inzo lay behind him; the Wood around and above him watched. His machine would bring death to him; the outland metal and plastic and rubber would call forth Her Watchers from the Wood. They would sense its alienness and they would purge it from Glenraven with a fury that would destroy it and everything near it. When they finished with it—and with him—nothing would remain.

They would come.

They would come.

Before they finished him, he hoped to kill a few of them, to strike a dying blow for the doomed Machnan.

He heard the sound of their approach, the rustle of leaves through the branches of the windless Wood. He looked for someplace to make a stand, some opening free of underbrush that would block his field of fire. He did not know the Wood around Inzo; if such a place existed it would be luck for him, the first in long and longer. He would not ask for luck, not with his death growing green in the long grasping shadows. The Wood was no place for the luck of a Machnan.

Dead leaves tumbled across his path; above and behind him branches rattled. He shuddered. Coming. They were coming. Soon he would have to stop; he would have to fight them. He pedaled faster. The ground beneath his tires grew spongy and sucked at his wheels; the Wood itself conspired against him. Treetops rattled and swayed; the sweat that dripped down his forehead had nothing to do with his exertion. He reeked of fear.

Closer.

They were closer, closing, hurrying.

Coming. For him.

Away, he thought. He needed to lead them away; he prayed they would not discover he had not been alone. Let them believe he was a renegade; let them kill him quickly, never thinking to drag out of him the secrets he knew.

Let the heroes be real heroes, he prayed; his last prayer and then the time for prayer passed. He saw movement in the shadows, pacing him on either side.

The flickering of light, shimmering carpets of tiny lights that raced along the ground. Soft giggling whispers. The underbrush dragged at him with clawed and thorny fingers; he had no good place to stand and die, but he was Machnan, and they would bleed to take him.

He braked and slid off his bike, unslung the crossbow from his shoulder, shoved his back against a tree. Then Her Watchers, so long silent, chittered and snarled; the shadows and the lights moved nearer, though not so near he could name them. He told himself if Her Watchers rose up within his arm's reach, he had no guarantee he could name them.

Rumors. He had nothing but rumors, the speculations of living men on the manner of death of the dead.

Without a clear target, he aimed the crossbow and shot the first bolt. A flurry of movement, the flare of light, the swooping wings of darkness, the billowing of the shadows he could see; he could see nothing concrete, nothing definite. Only silence rewarded the flight of his bolt. Complete silence. They waited. Watched him. Silence.

Drawing, dragging silence, while he knew they moved closer, while he knew he was helpless to move at all.

Suddenly the wind roared around him, out of nowhere, and the lights that had flowed like water along the ground rose up and melded with the billowing shadows, and took shape. They moved toward him. Her Watchers. He saw them clearly for the first time then, and his mind refused to comprehend what he saw. His arms fell to his sides and the crossbow dropped to the ground; he felt it fall and didn't care. Instead, he smiled.

And death stepped out to meet him.

Ten

Aidris Akalan danced through the long, empty corridors, past the hollow-eyed portraits of her dead-and-gone family, with the blood burning in her veins, with her heart thudding powerfully, with her muscles burning from the joyous exertion. Her back was straight, her waist lithe, her joints limber.

She leapt into the air, spun, landed with the grace of a doe, pirouetted, laughed out at the crushed-rose sky and the stretching shadows.

For this, I would sentence them all to death again, she thought, rejoicing. She stopped in front of the portrait of her immediate family: father, mother, a single brother, two younger sisters. Her own face stared back at her from the ancient canvas, unchanged from the face that looked back at it. She gave her family and her past a mocking bow.

"You are dead and I live," she told them. "I *live*.

"And I will live as long as life."

Eleven

Sophie's mood had improved during the trip to Inzo. While she and Jay had been cautious, nothing bothered them. No one attacked them. In fact, they saw no one at all on the road to Inzo.

When they got there, Sophie could understand why. "My God, Jay, this place is unreal." She felt like she'd fallen through a time portal. The tiny stone cottages along the narrow, twisting dirt street huddled beneath steeply pitched split-shake roofs. Cows ambled down the center of the street, herded by a scrawny blond boy in leather shorts and knee socks. Young women in full-skirted, tight-waisted dresses stopped their field work to lean on their hoes and stare at the two mounted strangers who rode into town. The older women and the town's men came out of doorways and stood in the street, frankly staring, as she and Jayjay reined in.

"Oh, boy," Jayjay murmured.

Sophie counted fifteen houses in Inzo. If the village had any more than that, it hid them well. The rubble of a ruined castle glared down at the tiny hamlet from a hill at the edge of the forest; it had been a *long* time since that had been anything but a pile of stones. "I don't think they're going to have a hotel here, you know?"

Jay fumbled through her pack. "The guidebook said something about a place to stay in Inzo," she said. "Let me find the passage . . ." She flipped through pages wildly while Sophie tried to count the little kids hiding in their mothers' skirts. "Yeah! I found it." She put her finger on the page and read the entry. "'Retireti's. Family-run, with two available rooms in a quaint setting, it offers an up-close look at the lives of Glenraven's common folk. Cash or barter, primitive facilities. Inexpensive.'"

"Barter?" Sophie clicked her tongue. "Shucks. And here I am, fresh out of beads. I can just imagine what they mean by primitive facilities, too. I got a whiff of that when the wind shifted."

Jayjay raised an eyebrow and said in a voice that mocked only herself and the fact that she had brought the two of them to this place, "Where is your sense of adventure?"

"Waiting for a hot shower, madam."

"The natives look clean . . . mostly." Jayjay poked her nose into the guide again. "Okay . . . more Useful Phrases." She tried the phrase that had eventually worked at the border, asking if anyone spoke English.

She got nothing but blank looks.

Sophie wasn't surprised. "You could ask them how to reach the bus stop, and tell them you'd like a cocktail and caviar while you're at it." She studied the people of Inzo. The term "ignorant peasants," rude though it was, had never seemed to fit any group of people more.

Jayjay glanced down at them. "I guess finding an English speaker here was hoping for too much, huh? That's all right. This should do the trick. 'Where is . . .?' That's 'SAY-hoo something hay-LER-oh.' So I would ask 'Seihau Retireti heilero?'" Jay sighed. "The guidebook insists we can get rooms in Inzo."

"And authentic stir-fry at the five-star restaurant, too."

Jay snorted. "You are a pain in the ass sometimes, Soph." She cleared her throat. "Seihau Retireti heilero?" Sophie could tell Jayjay was trying to sound confident, mostly because she was trying too hard. The folks of Inzo didn't seem notice, though.

"Retireti," they said to each other, excited. They began to smile; Sophie noted a lot of bad teeth in the bunch and tried not to cringe. Even if Jay was right and they did bathe occasionally, the natives certainly hadn't discovered the wonders of fluoride. With a lot of hand waving and chattering, they pulled one of their number forward. He was an unprepossessing young man, rail thin and unkempt. His watery blue eyes peered out from beneath thick straggly eyebrows; his nose jutted over a chin notable only by its absence. If he'd had acne, Sophie thought, he would have looked like ninety percent of the Bob Dylan wannabes with whom she'd gone to college. He glared up at them sullenly; the rest of Inzo, which now included even the girls who had been working in the fields and young men who hadn't been apparent anywhere, looked—relieved.

Sophie frowned. Three lean farmer types held the young man in place, and they all looked pleased to have him in the spotlight. Odd.

Jayjay's nose was back in the book. "These useful phrases are only useful when you can find the one you want," she grumbled. Oblivious to the little drama being played out in front of her, she said, "I'd like a cigar, I'd like a map, I'd like the key to the ladies' room. Dammit, where is it?" Then she grinned. "Here! I'd like a room." She looked down at the captive Retireti and said something else in Galti.

Retireti's expression went from sullen to baffled. His smug neighbors stopped smiling and stared at each other. He babbled something lengthy and complicated, gesturing wildly as he did so; as if his life depended on his passionate speech. Sophie wished she knew what the hell he'd said; she was sure it would have been enlightening. But that was the trouble with guidebooks; they suggested all sorts of questions to ask, but didn't give any help with translating the answers. And Sophie had discovered that as soon as people heard a foreigner speak any three intelligible words in their language, they assumed that foreigner could, in fact, understand them.

Jayjay repeated her question, saying the words slowly and pronouncing them carefully.

The three farmers let Retireti go, and he smiled a little. That was the only thing other than acne that could have made him homelier than he already was. He answered briefly, and Jayjay said, "Yes. He said yes, he has rooms. That's what 'jen' means."

"Good. Now ask him if you only get a hot shower if you sleep in the barn under the cows, and if the beds do or do not come with hot and cold running parasites."

"If I didn't know better, I'd take you for a city girl." Jayjay seemed enormously cheerful since the two of them had found a room. The villagers were clearing a path, backing toward their homes with nervous glances at the two strangers on horseback and the suddenly happy and voluble Retireti.

Voluble—an adjective that sounded like the phenomenon it described. Sophie thought the syllables were a perfect mirror for the stream of liquid sounds the young villager poured out at them. He'd glanced from Jay to Sophie initially, but to Sophie, he might as well have been speaking pidgin Bantu, and she was sure her face reflected her total lack of comprehension. So he turned his attention completely toward Jayjay, who in Jayjayesque fashion nodded from time to time, thumbed through the back pages of her guide, and made little murmured "jens" and "niques." If Sophie hadn't known better, she would have thought her friend understood the conversation.

Who knew? On some subliminal level, maybe Jay did; getting the gist of a conversation in a language she didn't speak wouldn't be any stranger than some of the other oddball stunts she'd pulled off.

Finding Glenraven in the first place came immediately to Sophie's mind.

Retireti led them to a house that looked no different than the others in the village; its roof sagged, dead insects and dirt and mold stained its tiny oilcloth windows, scrawny dogs sprawled across the dirt pathway that led up to the narrow front door.

Retireti led them behind his house and helped them groom and stable and bed down all four of their horses in a grim little shed attached to the back, then led them around to the front again, and with wide, enthusiastic smiles welcomed them inside.

"Oh, my God," Sophie muttered under her breath. She nodded at Retireti and tried a smile, though it hurt her face to do it. "I thought the guidebook described this as quaint."

Even Jayjay seemed taken aback by the obvious poverty and squalor of the place. She cleared her throat. "Well," she managed at last, "I suppose in a certain light, this might be considered quaint."

Sophie studied the dirt floors, the low ceilings festooned with herbs and cobwebs, the chickens roosting in little shelves along one wall. She tried to avoid breathing; the stink of live chickens and garlic and primitive sanitation permeated everything. And she muttered, "In a certain light? Only in the dark."

Twelve

Jarenne and her three-year-old daughter Tayes and her six-year-old son Liendir lay in the dank, stinking straw in one tiny cell in a cold, dark dungeon. All three of them had been held prisoner for days; brigands— three rogue Kin-hera and their Kin leader—had stopped Jarenne's carriage on an isolated stretch of road as she and the children headed home from the Festival of the Watch. They killed her Machnan driver outright, and kidnapped her and both children, blindfolded, bound and gagged them, and dumped them here. Wherever here might be.

For the first time since she took vows, she found herself cut off from Dommis, her *eyra*. The walls of the cells were imbued with old magic, Aregen magic, that broke the otherwise unbreakable bonds of the Kin lifemates. Dommis would know she wasn't dead; if she had died, he would have died too. But he wouldn't know where she was, and although he would know what had happened, since he had still been linked to her when the attack occurred, he would have no way of finding her. The prison that severed the soul-bonds between them also hid her away. She imagined he must be frantic, trying to find her.

Jarenne wondered if she and the children were being held for money, wondered if he would have to pay to have her and their children safely returned to him. She had discussed the possibility with the woman in the cell to her left, a young and well-born Kin named Adeleth whose pregnancy had reached the fifteenth and final month and who mentioned frequently that she hoped to be home before she delivered her baby.

The warrag pair in the cell on the other side scoffed at the idea of ransom. They had, they said, no one who would care to ransom them; if their captors had wanted money, they would have killed them as soon as they found out who they were. At home the warrags had only their first litter of pups and the sister-cousin who was caring for them in their absence. The warrags became more certain every day that their absence would be permanent. They had been in their cell for three days when the brigands brought in Jarenne.

Though she did not want to admit to fear—fear was for others, not for Kin of the Old Line—the bloodstains in the straw and on the walls gave Jarenne nightmares. Something terrible had happened to someone in her cell before she'd been thrown into it. The other prisoners reported that their cells, all nine of them, bore the same grisly evidence.

The cells were ancient. They'd been built by the now-extinct Aregen to hold the Kin, back before Galira the Champion and her Heroes conquered them at the start of the Age of Heroes. Such Aregenish artifacts were supposed to have been destroyed in the Cleansing, when most of the Aregen oppressors were hunted down and killed. That one still existed indicated conniving on someone's part.

Jarenne had tried the locks with her magic, without success. She'd tried to bribe the guard, tried to make a tunnel, tried to slip her children through the bars so that they, at least, could escape. In the end, she had decided further attempts at escape were hopeless. She was going to have to wait; going to have to discover what her captors had in mind. Meanwhile, she kept her children entertained with a little of the magic that had otherwise let her down; she spun light for them with her fingertips, shaped it into little dancing characters that ran and tripped and fell across the makeshift stage of her arms. She let the shining little dancers race up her daughter's chubby legs, let them hop up her son's tummy, sent them sprawling headlong into the straw, while Tayes and Liendir laughed. When the children sang the songs they knew, she made her light-puppets spin and cavort in time to their music.

For their sake, she never showed fear. She told them Father would be coming to get the three of them soon, but that in the meantime they were to eat their meals and play and have a wonderful time together. They were to be happy.

Her children believed her. They were happy.

She sent the little light-dancers scurrying into her children's arms when she heard footsteps. The door at the end of the corridor between the rows of cells opened, and the brigand leader entered. Usually he came accompanied by at least one of the warrags who worked with him, but today a woman walked at his side. Jarenne stared for a moment, unable to believe what she saw. Then her heart leapt. Her friend Aidris Akalan stood staring up and down the corridors, looking into each of the cells.

Whoever had been holding them had been found out, and the Watchmistress had arrived to set things right. She came for us, Jarenne thought. Perhaps for some of these others, too; I'm not the only one here who is her friend. But certainly for us.

She breathed a quiet sigh of relief. Until her fear left her, Jarenne didn't know how fierce it had been.

She felt weak and even a little light-headed, knowing that she was going to live.

"Aidris," she called. "We're here."

Aidris's head came up, and her face broke into a smile. "You're not hurt, are you? Have they been treating you well?"

"Well enough. And if they hadn't, we are Kin, aren't we? We endure."

Aidris hurried down the corridor to her side. "Yes. You're so brave. And you and Tayes-Tayes and Liendir are all here, and all safe. Completely unhurt. I'm so glad. There has been so much speculation among our friends since you disappeared. Dommis has been completely mad, rushing about trying to find you and trying to understand how he couldn't hear your thoughts if you were still alive, and how he could still be alive if you were dead." She glanced at the pregnant girl. "And Kirlon's daughter Adeleth is here, and Shir, and . . ." She shook her head. "So many friends."

"What did they want, Aidris?"

"Who?"

"The brigands who captured us."

"Oh. Them." Aidris spread her arms, palms upward, and shrugged smoothly. "Who could possibly know what they want? It isn't important; I'm here now."

Aidris looked older. She usually looked younger than Jarenne; and at first Jarenne thought the dim light didn't flatter her friend. But the lines around Aidris's eyes, the slight wattling of skin at her throat, the swollen knuckles and mottled skin of her hands were not tricks of the light. Something had aged her since she and Jarenne stood by the fountain together during the Festival of the Watch and discussed the vagaries of the Watch Court.

Was Aidris ill? In the years that she and Jarenne had been friends, since the day Aidris had chosen Jarenne from among the highborn daughters of the Old Line Kin to sit in council with her, Aidris had never aged a day. While Jarenne grew up, found her *eyra*, and had her babies, Aidris stayed the same. She wasn't the same now.

"I'm glad to see you," Jarenne said. Her children had quit playing with their lights and now hid with their arms around her legs, their faces pressed into her skirts. "How did you arrange to get us out?"

Aidris's eyebrow rose.

Jarenne's stomach dropped in an inverse line to the movement of that eyebrow.

"Get you out?" Aidris asked. She still smiled. Something about that smile froze Jarenne's blood as quickly as if she'd been thrown into an icy mountain river in the dead of winter.

"Rescue us," Jarenne persisted, hoping that she was simply being dense, that Aidris was there to rescue her and her children and the others in the cells.

"I'm the reason you're here," Aidris told her, still smiling, and now that smile grew broader; hideously wide, horribly ugly. A fleshless, leering skull could not have grinned more broadly or with less compassion.

"Why?"

Aidris chuckled. The Kin brigand returned at that moment, carrying a large bucket and a huge spoon-tipped stirring stick. Aidris didn't speak to him; she only pointed to the bucket, and then to the ground at the door. He seemed to know what to do; he put the bucket and stir stick down and backed out of the door again.

He looked frightened, Jarenne realized. The brigand was frightened; the evil man who had killed her driver without any sign of remorse, who had imprisoned her and her children and these others in their cells; *he* was frightened.

Something ghastly was about to happen.

"Because living forever costs," Aidris said, turning her attention back to Jarenne. "Glenraven's magic fails daily.

It grows weaker, more anemic, less useful. It sputters like a candle that has burned to the end of its wick and now dies slowly. Living forever takes magic. And I intend to live forever."

Aidris walked down the corridor, picked up the bucket by its handle, and dipped the stir stick into the dull, red-brown liquid. She stirred for a moment, then lifted out a spoonful of whatever she had in there, turned, and flung the liquid on the powerfully built young Kin man who crouched in the first cell on the right. He jumped and shouted and tried to brush the spatters off of his clothes and skin. It didn't do any-thing to him. The liquid made a mess, but it didn't burn him or eat holes in his clothes. He couldn't rub it off, though; instead, it smeared and spread.

"What is this?" he yelled at Aidris.

"Blood." She stepped away from him when she said it, and raised her head, and gave a soft, penetrating cry.

Something ghastly . . .

Jarenne heard the whisper of wind. She would have sworn until that moment that the cell in which she'd been imprisoned lay deep underground, but the voice of the wind was unmistakable.

Wind where wind could not be. She heard it, growing louder, moving closer, and after a moment she felt it on her cheeks. It carried with it the faint but inescap-able scent of decay, of rot and ruin, of death. A soft breeze. Cool. Rank. Evil.

Aidris, carrying her bucket, walked down to stand in the corridor beside Jarenne. "For nearly a thousand years, I took my sacrifices from the Machnan, and, when I could catch them, from the Aregen."

Jarenne listened with only a small part of her atten-tion. *Nearly a thousand years.* She heard that phrase and it registered, and she realized the rumors of Aidris's almost unthinkable age weren't rumors after all. Nearly a thousand years, when a strong, healthy Kin could hope to see little more than his second century. Aidris had lived far beyond expectation. What a pity, Jarenne thought. The majority of her attention focused itself on the man in the corner cell by the door and the events that were taking place in his cell. The wind grew stronger and louder. Tiny lights began to flicker around him, touching the places where blood had struck his skin and clothes.

Tiny lights and wind. Innocuous. A soft breeze, but it carried the stink of death. Bright, beautiful firefly lights, but the blood drew them. Called them.

"These are my Watchers," Aidris said, looking at the men and women and children of Kin and Kin-hera descent. "Every Master or Mistress of the Watch has had Watchers. Luckily for me, mine do more than just watch."

Jarenne pulled her children close to her.

Aidris laughed.

Jarenne backed against the far wall and hid Tayes and Liendir beneath the wide, floor-length folds of her silk skirts.

Something ghastly.

"Do watch," Aidris said. "I so enjoy this part."

The blood spots on the man's skin began to glow. Pale, soft pink. Pretty. Even though she knew that what she was seeing was evil, Jarenne couldn't escape thinking that the light was so pretty. The man stared at his hands, his arms; he rubbed at the spots, and Jarenne realized he had begun moaning softly. Round-eyed, breathing harshly in the almost silent dungeon, he ripped a strip of cloth from his tunic and scrubbed at his skin with it. Every pair of eyes in the dungeon focused on him.

The spots grew brighter, redder. Light began to crawl in waving, wormlike lines under his skin. The light shone through his skin, brighter and brighter; the lines spread and connected, connected, spread, filling in the spaces faster and faster until his whole body glowed.

Red. Ruby red. Bloodred. His skin transparent now, brilliant glowing red; he was a living gemstone illuminated from within.

His moaning grew louder and changed in character; then became not moaning but desperate utterances, pleas for mercy; the pleas became wordless, panicked shouts; the shouts mutated into screams. He dug at his skin. Clawed at it, tore it. Clawed at his face, at his chest. Ripped off his clothing.

And then he began to swell. Transparent red skin stretched and ballooned, lifted away from his body, and under that skin, the light changed things; for a few moments Jarenne could see the outlines of his muscles. Beneath the terrible bloating he still bore the shape of a man. Then flesh melted into liquid, pooling in his legs and feet, and she could see only the sticklike forms of bones. The red light ate into those, too, so that only whatever it was that caused him to swell gave him shape. He toppled, his limbs flopping as his body bounced on the straw; he lay on his belly, blown up like a week-drowned corpse. Unmoving. But not silent. The scream that emanated from somewhere inside of him had become whistlelike, reedy, thin and quavering. Then it stopped, too, and Jarenne noticed cracks forming in his bloated skin—rips and rents where white light streamed out.

She wanted to look away, but she couldn't. She couldn't. She kept her babies tucked beneath her skirts and held her breath and watched the man's body deflate like a punctured pig bladder. The only sound came from the air that hissed through the rents and tears.

The light curled out of him like sparkling smoke rising from the embers of a fire, and when the last of it rose above him, his skin lay flat and crumpled on the filthy, packed straw, mired in a pool of his own blood and the liquefied remains of his body.

Aidris sighed, and Jarenne turned to find her smiling.

"The Aregen are extinct, save for one who casts auguries for me. They were richer in magic even than the Alfkindir, but I cannot hunt them now that they are gone. The Machnan never had a great deal of magic, but in the last few years, they have lost every bit of what they had," Aidris told her. "I have studied the problem, and I cannot puzzle out the reason why their magic is gone . . . but without it, they are useless to me. So while they remain plentiful and easy to catch and kill, they have no value to me beyond the amusement of watching them die. I have had to begin hunting among our kind."

Jarenne stared at the woman she'd thought she knew, the one she had thought was her friend. The lights surrounded Aidris, brushed against her skin, swirled rich warm red-gold against her flesh, and for a moment she began to glow as the man in the far cell had glowed. As the light bathed her, her skin smoothed a little. Her back straightened a bit. Years fell from her body. Still old, still with every evil she had committed etched into the lines of her face, she was nonetheless inarguably younger than she had been moments before.

She smiled at Jarenne. "It won't do you a bit of good to hide all the way over there. I can throw the blood that far." She scooped a dripping spoonful out of the bucket, stared at Jarenne, then flicked it sideways; it splattered on pregnant Adeleth.

The girl, shivering and crouching in the far corner of her cell, screamed like the spirits of a thousand restless dead.

Aidris's smile grew broad and happy; she shook her head, bemused. "The pregnant ones are always interesting to watch."

Jarenne turned her face away. She tried stopping her ears at the screams—the nightmarish screams. She knew, though, that sound would never leave her. She would die hearing that scream.

She lifted her head and stared straight at Aidris. "I don't care what you do to me, Aidris. I don't care. But please . . . please . . . let my children go. Let them go back to Dommis. Please."

Aidris laughed softly. "You think I brought them here accidentally? No. Tayes and Liendir are here because I want them here. They're such sweet little things." She tipped her head to one side. In that pose, she looked like an evil bird. Like a vulture. Like a grinning vulture. "So many things grow old and lose their charm in a thousand years, Jarenne," the Watchmistress told her. "You see the sun rise and the sun set with wearying regularity. You see every amusing sight, hear every story, grow endlessly weary of every song. Things pale, pall, become insignificant and dull and it becomes so hard . . . so terribly hard . . . to move through another day."

The screams of the pregnant girl had become soft and liquid and bubbling. Though Jarenne wished she hadn't been able to hear Aidris or the dying girl, both sounds reached her ears with awful clarity.

"My children don't mean anything to you," Jarenne said. "You don't need them. Let them go."

"It's true that they will contribute almost no life to me; they're far too little to have much magic. Neither I nor my Watchers can do more than taste them— you're right about that. But I do need them. I find, after all these years, that the only spectacle which never wearies me is the glorious spectacle of death. And your sweet babies will be wonderfully entertaining when they die." Aidris's smile was a mockery of the sunny, friendly smile Jarenne had always seen before. "As will you."

No more screaming. None. Adeleth was dead. Now in the dungeon Jarenne heard only a few voices begging mercy. Begging release.

Aidris dipped the spoon into the bucket of blood.

"Let them out of your skirts," Aidris said. "You don't want them to have to watch you die. Believe me, little mother, my dear friend, you will hurt less if you and your babies die all together."

Jarenne stared at Aidris. She tried to imagine her children trapped in the straw, watching her swell and scream and claw at her eyes. She wished she could die right then. She wished she could kill her children quickly and painlessly, and then destroy herself. She wanted to beg, to fall on her knees and plead with the implacable Watchmistress, to offer her anything, everything, if she would only spare the lives of her beloved children. She would have given anything; but she could see in Aidris's eyes that nothing would please her more than such a display. Jarenne was Kin—Old Line Kin. The Old Line persevered, they lived with their heads held high, and they died bravely. No mercy would flow from Aidris's hand. And the bitch was right. It would be better if the three of them died together.

She lifted her skirts and pulled Tayes and Liendir into her arms.

"Aren't you going to try to spare their lives? Send them to me," Aidris said. "Perhaps my little niece and nephew can convince me to let them live. Maybe they can tell me how much they love me." She pursed her lips and shrugged. "I would think you'd try."

"If I sent them to you, you would make me watch them die," Jarenne told her. "You wouldn't let them go."

Aidris laughed at that, sounding genuinely delighted. "Oh, you're right. You're so right. You aren't at all as stupid as you have always seemed."

Jarenne cradled both silent, frightened children closer and faced Aidris. "I gave you my friendship," she said coldly. "You didn't deserve it."

"I didn't need your friendship. Why would a lion befriend the lamb that was to become its dinner, except to amuse itself with the irony? Why would a bird befriend the worm? You are nothing to me but meat. That is all you have ever been."

Jarenne pulled her shoulders back. Her children clung to her neck; she could feel the racing of their hearts pounding against her chest and the soft, rapid rush of their exhalations. They were so frightened. She rubbed her cheeks against their faces and hugged them tightly to her. "Be brave. We're together," she told them. "I'm with you. I will always be with you." They were comforted at the sound of her voice, and she glanced up at Aidris. "You've been misled," she said. "You've failed to see which of us is the bird, and which the worm. My children and I have flown on falcons' wings. We know love and joy; we know the wonder of life. We've seen the sun, and the moon, and the stars. But for as long as you live, you will know nothing but slime and blindness and filth, hatred and ugliness, poison and villainy. You will never know happiness. Your long life will be nothing but a parade of miserable days and miserable nights."

Aidris snarled and flung the spoon of blood at her. "I'll live, though." The blood spattered against Jarenne's skin, cold and thick and stinking. It struck both children, who began to cry.

"I'll live, and you'll die."

The lights came. The pretty, pretty lights. Tayes stopped crying when she saw the lights, when they brushed against her downy cheeks, her silken hair. Tayes laughed.

Liendir loosened his grip on Jarenne's neck and whispered, "Look, Mamma. Oh, look."

The lights came. Soft and pale and beautiful, they swirled down like a hundred thousand stars transformed into snow. They touched skin and clothes, like butterflies landing.

And after them came the pain.

Thirteen

Jay's nightmares flowed together, eerie Daliesque jumbles that included blood and bones; a hunter, blue-gray-golden eyes and fangs and cat-clawed hands and an aching alien beauty; a dreadful stench; an overpowering feeling of searching malevolence that was both dark and light, both hideous and beautiful. And woven through it all, like the sign to Peter after he betrayed Christ, or like the voice of the oracle of some pagan temple, was the crowing of a cock.

A pinpoint of light touched her right eyelid, and something sharp and heavy scratched its way across her arm. Jayjay woke to find herself eye to eye with the skinniest, evilest chicken she'd ever seen. When she moved, it glared at her and the dirty black feathers around its neck stood out. It lowered its head and spread its wings.

She hated chickens.

"Hah!" she whispered, and flapped her arms at it. It took a peck at her, got a finger, drew blood, then withdrew when she yelped and flailed at it with hands and feet. Jay glared after the retreating fowl. "There seems to be some confusion over which of us is going to have the other for lunch, bird."

Behind her, Sophie laughed. "Impressive. I had no idea you had such a way with chickens."

Jay sucked on her bleeding finger and turned to find her friend awake and watching her. "You put it up to that, didn't you?"

Sophie grinned at her. "You bet. My way of thanking you for the bathrooms."

Jayjay winced. "Where might those be, incidentally?"

"Just guess."

"Uh-oh. Chamber pot?"

"Dear . . . a chamber pot would be high society compared to this."

Jay bit her lip. "Outhouse?"

"Did you *see* an outhouse when we got here?"

"No."

"Nor will you."

"Worse than an outhouse?"

Sophie pointed to the little square of oilskin that covered the window to the loft where they—and many chickens—had spent the night. "If we could see out the windows, I could show it to you." She bared her teeth in a smile that would have looked at home on a werewolf. "It's lovely. This little trench dug into the dirt over there near the trees. You put one foot on either side and—" She closed her eyes and shuddered. "—and you squat. And these lovely facilities aren't *in* the woods, where you might have a bit of cover . . . oh, no! They're simply *near* the woods."

"The guide did say that Inzo wasn't really recommended," Jayjay said. She felt guilty that Sophie wasn't having a lot of fun; she wanted her friend to get back to being herself again. She had hoped a wonderful vacation would do the trick. "The cities will be more exciting."

"I don't know how much more excitement I can stand." Sophie glared at another of the skinny, temperamental chickens. "Oh, yeah. And be sure to take a handful of leaves with you; I gather that none of Inzo's brilliant inventors have gotten around to toilet paper yet."

"Oh . . . wonderful."

Jayjay headed for the edge of the woods, recalling that mornings were not Sophie's best time. After discovering what passed for plumbing in Inzo, though, she found herself in agreement. The little ditch had nothing quaint about it.

She stood, feeling grungy and smelly. She would have paid good money for the use of a bathtub; and she would have bet the gold in her money belt no such thing existed in the village.

She sighed and looked over Inzo. In the daylight it was obviously more dusty and dirty and poor than it had been at night. She'd seen poor; the palm-leaf shacks in the mountain villages of Guatemala filled with naked, potbellied kids and men and women who were old and worn at thirty had clung to her memory for years. But even in those remote mountain villages, she'd seen television antennas. Power lines. A few cars. Even in the smallest of villages, not everybody had been poor.

In her entire life, she'd never seen the sort of poverty that existed in Inzo. These people had nothing.

This probably isn't the place I should have taken us first.

She hooked her thumbs into the belt of her tunic and turned her back on Inzo. The village sat on the fringe of forest; the fields through which she and Sophie had ridden the night before ended abruptly in a wall of trees. Fifty men could have held hands around the trunks of some of those venerable trees; Jayjay didn't doubt for an instant that the biggest of those weathered giants had been standing when Christopher Columbus sailed out of Portugal in search of his shortcut to the East Indies.

She stared through the green velvet shadows at a clearing some distance in; pencils of golden light slanted onto the inviting perch of a huge, moss-covered rock. Flashes of pale yellow and rich purple fluttered in and out of the light—butterflies of several varieties that drank nectar from clouds of tiny white flowers growing at the base of the boulder. Even from where she stood she could see the rainbow sparkles of light shimmering through the dew. It could have been Eden.

The feeling that she'd found her true home returned to her. She forgot the squalor and poverty of Inzo; the beauty of the ancient forest washed it all away. She vaguely recalled some comments about the forest from her Fodor's, mention that the wildlife in it still included a few creatures extinct in the rest of Western Europe—creatures that could kill humans. Wherever the big predators hunted, she couldn't imagine them being anywhere near that beautiful clearing.

How could Sophie have *missed* this? she wondered. That single vista made the scratchy straw-filled mattress thrown directly onto the hand-planed boards of the loft a nonissue. It made sleeping with chickens irrelevant. It made missing a hot bath . . . well, Jay still wanted a hot bath, but she figured she would live until she and Sophie got to Zearn or Rikes Gate.

She started into the trees, toward that clearing. She wanted to sit on the rock and watch the butterflies for a while before she and Sophie had to get back on horseback and ride to the next town. It would make up for missing the bath.

The feeling of home grew in her—the certainty that she had been waiting all her life to find this place. She stepped onto the deep humus of the forest floor with a happy sigh, and rested one hand against the trunk of an ancient tree. Light sparkled around her—the effect of a slight breeze moving the leaves in the canopy above, no doubt, but still an enchanting sight.

She thought, I could stay here forever, and she fancied the forest sighed a deep, contented "yes."

"JAY-JAAAYYYY!!!"

Sophie's voice, shrill and panicky, shattered her fantasy. Go away, Jay thought. The clearing and its dappled sunlight and dancing butterflies beckoned, promising lazy contentment. I'm on vacation and I want to relax. I want to forget. The little glade promised forgetfulness.

"Jay-*JAAAYYYY!!!* Where *are* you?"

Jay sighed and turned back toward Inzo. She was surprised to find herself so far from the cottages; the clearing must have been much further than it looked, for while she could no longer see any part of the little village, the clearing still looked no nearer. "I'm coming!"

"Where *are* you?" Sophie shouted again.

"I only walked into the woods for a minute." Jesus, I really walked into the woods, too. She trudged over logs and through thickets she hadn't remembered at all. How did I get through this? She looked at her arms, puzzled. Her forearms bore scratches, mute testimony to the fact that she had waded through thorns and thickets . . . oblivious.

She frowned, annoyed with herself. She frequently found bruises on her arms and legs, and had no idea where they'd come from. One of her facts of life; she concentrated so hard on whatever she was doing that little things like pain didn't get a chance to intrude.

Through the trees, she saw the roof of Retireti's cottage; behind her something growled. The hair on the back of her neck stood up and she shivered; that growl, nearby and angry, resonated in a sub-bass timbre that made her think the creature making it might have been a wolf. Maybe a grizzly. Or something bigger. What was bigger than a grizzly?

She didn't know, and she didn't want to find out. She fought her way through the thickets, praying.

"Are you going to tromp around in there all day?" Sophie sounded close, but Jayjay couldn't see her. Perhaps she stood behind one of the massive trees.

Jay pushed uphill through vicious briars, astounded that the last few yards of her retreat could be so hellish. She could not possibly have come in the same way she was leaving—she'd evidently gone in on a cleared path and come out off of it—but she couldn't remember seeing anything that rough looking when she'd admired the butterfly clearing.

Jayjay broke free of the forest.

"Oh, there you are!"

Sophie moved. She had been in plain view, standing next to a tree; why neither she nor Jay had seen each other, Jay couldn't understand.

"Here I am," she agreed. She gasped for breath and her heart thudded beneath her breastbone.

"Jesus, Jayjay, what happened to you?"

Sophie stared at her with disbelief in her eyes. Jay looked down at herself; her arms bled, her peasant clothes were rent in several places. "I went walking in the woods," she said, feeling the explanation was lame even as she gave it. "I got snagged in some thorns on my way back."

"Where?" Sophie looked into the forest, back along the route Jayjay had taken.

She turned and pointed. "Right—" *There*, she had meant to say. But the deep, placid woods behind her grew clear as a park, the leaf mold and humus making a rolling golden-brown carpet from which the great trees arched up like pillars in an Old World cathedral; the clearing with its butterflies lay near them, the way to it unobstructed by any underbrush. Jayjay frowned and studied the woods to either side of the clearing. They were as free from underbrush as the manicured grounds of a park. She looked for the slope she'd had to climb, but couldn't find that either.

She stared down at her arms. The gashes in them still welled with drops of bright red blood. She could still see her skin through the rips in her sleeves, too.

"What . . . *in* . . . the world . . . ?" She turned to Sophie and saw her own confusion reflected in her friend's face. "All I can tell you is, it's a lot rougher in there than it looks." She shook her head slowly, then shrugged and grinned.

"You always were like that," Sophie mused. "You would come in filthy from walking down to the end of the drive to get your mail; I remember your mother looking at you like she'd gotten you from Mars, and was thinking of sending you back."

Jayjay laughed. "Some things never change." She was not buying the "Jayjay from Mars" explanation to whatever had happened in the woods, but she didn't intend to make a big deal out of it in front of Sophie, either. The trip had already been pretty odd, and if it got any stranger, Sophie would decide to cancel Glenraven entirely and go to Spain or something. Jayjay refused to let that happen. Glenraven had been sitting in its little valley forever, waiting for the two of them to find it. Jay intended to make the most of her discovery, no matter how bewildering it might be.

Fourteen

"Did you see the look on his face when you gave him that one tiny coin? I thought his eyes were going to fall on the ground." Sophie shifted her weight in the saddle and twisted around to get at her canteen.

Jayjay's big bay gelding ambled beside hers. Jayjay slouched against the high cantle of her saddle; she rode only slightly more gracefully than a bag of bricks would have, but Sophie kept this opinion to herself.

Jayjay snapped out of her reverie. "Huh? Oh . . . yes. I think I overpaid for the room. When I looked in the Glenraven guide, I found out money goes a lot farther here than I'd thought."

Sophie sipped the water. It was already lukewarm and tasted of the metal canteen, of grit and mud and the tablet she'd dumped in it to rid it of anything noxious. She felt wonderful. They'd shaken off whatever trouble Lestovru had planned for them, and if Coke in a can would have tasted a million times better, so what? She couldn't have had that riding on a superlative horse through this undiscovered patch of God's own country. "Retireti certainly seemed happy. You gave him about five dollars for the two of us, didn't you?"

"Yes. That included the bean-soup breakfast."

About ten times what the accommodations were worth, Sophie thought; but that was uncharitable. Retireti hadn't been running an inn. She'd realized that when she saw the place. He'd been putting them up in his home—two uninvited strangers. He'd cooked them breakfast, carried on an endless chatty unintelligible conversation, kept his hands to himself. And he had been profoundly grateful for the lousy little five-buck coin Jayjay had pressed into his hand as they were leaving. He'd given them the best he had, and if that wasn't much, it also wasn't his fault.

She glanced over at Jay, who had tied her reins together and looped them over the low, flat pommel of her saddle, and who, still bricklike in the extreme, sat thumbing through the Glenraven guide.

"So what's next, O mighty explorer?"

"I'm debating." Jayjay didn't bother looking up from her pages. "We should come to the intersection any time now; then we can either go left to Rikes Gate or right to Zearn. The guide recommends both places. Rikes Gate has the Sarijann Castle. We had reservations to spend the night there."

"Castle? You booked us into a castle?"

Jay grinned over at her. "You bet. Sarijann is one of the highest-rated castles in Glenraven. I figured we deserved it. We're traveling first class."

"I would have believed you if I hadn't awakened with a chicken on my chest."

"That was an aberration. We were simply being cautious; I mean, you wouldn't have wanted to run into an ambush, would you?"

Sophie reconsidered the likelihood of an ambush; in the warm light of day, riding along the peaceful dirt road with cultivated fields to either side of her, she couldn't imagine why she had been so frightened the night before. She felt confident they would discover a logical explanation for the bizarre events of the previous night. But she nodded and, straight-faced, said, "Nope. I wouldn't have wanted to get ambushed."

Jay was still reading. "Rikes Gate also has an open-air market, some interesting little shops, a couple of taverns that come *highly* recommended, and the Walled Sector, which sounds cool. Zearn has something called an Aptogurria—I can't figure out from the description what it is exactly—and a mine and a lake and road-houses. And another open-air market; this one is supposed to have a lot of textiles. No castle, but it does have two fortresses—Kewimell and Doselt. Both are still in use, and the Fodor's says Kewimell has unique architecture. And we could rent a boat to go on the lake."

Sophie thought about the castle. She would have loved spending the night in a castle. "Any chance we could get a room at Sarijann Castle tonight, without reservations?"

Jayjay sighed. "I don't think so. Those reservations were hard to get. I do have us booked into another castle in a couple of days, though. That one is a pretty little castle built right in the middle of a lake in Dinnos. We're supposed to have a luxury suite. Rikes Gate would really be backtracking, anyway."

For as long as Sophie had known Jay, her philosophy had always seemed to boil down to the two-word maxim, *never backtrack*. Push ahead, forge on, keep moving. Never cover the same ground twice. Sophie didn't want to battle Jay's psychological momentum over the now-unlikely possibility of a night in a castle. "Let's go on to Zearn, then." She looked over at her friend, who'd finally put the book back in her pack. "I want to know something, Jay."

"What's that?" Jayjay grinned.

"Why didn't you ever tell me about Bill and Stacey and Steven?"

"I did tell you." Jay's grin vanished and she looked away. "I told you yesterday."

"That isn't what I mean. I knew you before you had front teeth, Jay. We shared classes and teachers and makeup. Jesus . . . we both kissed Bob Blatzmeir. I've known all three of your husbands through you. If I'd had something that big going on in my life, I would have told you."

Jay glanced sidelong at her and raised a single eyebrow, but she didn't say anything. The corner of her mouth curved up in a tiny half-smile.

Sophie looked away and swallowed hard; the lie stuck in her throat. She felt the heat rise to her cheeks and hoped she wasn't blushing. Did Jay know? From the look in her eyes, Sophie would almost think so, but how *could* Jay know? She took a deep breath. Or had Jayjay Bennington once again come up with the perfect way of sidetracking the conversation? That was most likely the explanation. "I really want an answer, Jayjay. If your husbands were awful, why didn't you say something? Maybe I could have helped."

For a long, uncomfortable moment, the horses plodded along the dirt road and Jay kept her silence. Then she cleared her throat and stared straight ahead. "Soph, there are people in this world who get a big thrill out of pity, but I'm not one of them. I never told you—I never told my folks—I never told anybody. I never wanted to have somebody whisper behind my back, 'Oh, poor Julie, she married such a shit . . . did you hear that he beat her?' I never wanted that." Jayjay's expression turned stubborn. "I figured it was better to be the goat than the sheep. So when my marriages went sour, I smiled and talked about made-up lurid affairs to people I knew couldn't keep secrets, and sooner or later the word got back to the husbands and . . . pfffftt! . . . Mr. I-Want-A-Divorce-You-Bitch came barreling through the door." Sophie found Jay's humorless smile unnerving.

"That hardly put you in the best light for a divorce settlement."

"I didn't want anything from either of them except out. I could take care of myself then, and I can take care of myself now." She turned in the saddle and looked at Sophie, her eyes ferocious. "I'm nobody's victim, and I won't be treated like I am."

Sophie remembered how Jay had left Bill with sole ownership of the house they'd bought together, not even taking a cash settlement on it, though she'd paid in half the money. And how she had walked away from her second marriage with less than she'd taken from the first. "I hope you'll be more sensible this time, Jay. You've lost a fortune giving them everything."

"About $300,000 total. Getting out would have been cheap at twice the price." Jayjay smiled off at nothing, her eyes still staring straight ahead. "I kept my computer, I kept my writing and my contracts, and I kept my sanity, though sometimes I thought I was going to lose that for sure. What else did I need?"

Sophie imagined leaving behind everything she had. The idea choked her. "But you are going to try for an equitable settlement with Steven, aren't you? You two have that big house and everything—"

"I figure I'm going to give him the keys and walk. Just like I did before."

"You'll be starting over again, Jay. You're thirty-five years old, and you'll have to reestablish your credit and maybe live in an apartment again and . . . Jesus . . . live on beans and macaroni."

Jay laughed. "It won't be that bad. At least I've learned to cook."

"You'd be better off if you learned to think."

"Just because you don't like the decisions I make doesn't mean I don't know how to think, Soph."

Sophie didn't know what to say to that. Jay did what she wanted; she always had. And she didn't want to hear about her stupid decisions either. Sophie figured the reason she'd never heard about Bill Pfiester's drugging or Stacey Tremont's battering was because Jayjay didn't want to admit she'd made a mistake.

Unlike everyone else in the world, Jayjay didn't make mistakes. *She* made *decisions*, and her decisions had complicated consequences. Sophie could hear the words running through her head in Jayjay's know-it-all voice. "Complicated Consequences"—words Owl would use to lecture Pooh.

Sophie felt like a Winnie-the-Pooh right then; told to mind her own business because she wasn't bright enough to offer useful advice. Head stuffed full of fluff, that's me.

I would have told you if Mitch had been a shit, she thought. She glared over at Jay, feeling sulky and left out. I would have asked for your advice, because that's what best friends are for.

But she'd been distant. Since Karen's death, she hadn't wanted to talk with Jay, because she figured Jay wouldn't understand the pain she felt. She hadn't wanted to associate much with the people who'd known her in better times.

And in fact, she hadn't managed to tell Jay about everything that was happening in her life.

She clucked her tongue and shifted her weight; her horses picked up her cues and trotted ahead of Jayjay. And Jayjay, being her usual obstinate self, refused to catch up.

Sophie watched the road and thought. She *hadn't* told Jay everything. She hadn't mentioned Lorin. It wasn't the same, of course. Sophie didn't really have anything to tell—yet. She might never. Nothing had happened. It might, but it hadn't so far.

You wake up one morning and look in the mirror and a stranger looks back. And no matter what you think you know about yourself, you find out in that moment that you're wrong. You are capable of inconceivable things.

I am capable of inconceivable things.

Fifteen

Aidris Akalan paid mocking tribute to the memory of her family and to her role as Watchmistress of Glenraven; she held court, as the Watchmistresses and Watchmasters had done since the beginning of the reign of the Kin. She sat in her simple chair on her low dais, acting the part of the woman who cared for the future of her people, acting as if she were one of them. As her parents had, as her brothers had. She amused herself with her role, welcomed in the petitioners with a steady smile, and watched how they blanched when they saw her as young and strong as she had ever been.

She knew, deep down, that was why they still came; not for any hope of justice at her hands, for at every turn she had crushed that hope. No. They hoped to see some sign of wear in her face, some weathering of her skin, some weakening of her bones that would tell them that some day death would touch her, too, and they would at last be free. None of them hoped for this miracle in their own lifetimes, she suspected. Not anymore. But some of them who had grown old under her rule—whose parents told stories of their parents who had spoken of her with bitterness—some of those hoped and prayed for a sign that their children's children would be born into a world that didn't contain her.

Aidris held court because she liked to grind their hope to powder the way a miller ground wheat to flour. Slowly and steadily, she crushed them beneath the stone of her will, missing not a grain, not an individual. Now, though some hoped that she would die, and she imagined that all wished her ill, they were broken. They would not rise against her even if someone strong and charismatic and determined tried to lead them. They knew they could never hope to win, and now they would not even try.

She smiled.

One young, strong, idealistic, charismatic Kin plotted treason. He hoped to stir the broken hearts of her people against her. He wanted to bring her down.

Matthiall. Matthiall of the single name, of the single desire. Matthiall, whose face she saw in her dreams.

She wasn't going to break him, though. She intended instead to let him break himself against the apathy and despair of his fellows. It would take as long as it took. When his eyes opened and he saw, as she did, that sheep existed only to be slaughtered, his idealism would die. Then she would claim him as her consort. Her mate and lover. He would never be her equal, but he would come to worship her for her power, her beauty, her wisdom.

He was only the second man she'd found herself wanting in the last thousand years. The first she had kept for half a century, until he tried to hire someone to assassinate her. Then she murdered him as they mated, and took great pleasure from both acts.

Some fool stood before her, rambling on about predators in the forest beyond his hovel, complaining about how they stole his food and his flock, and asking her to do something about them. After all, he kept mentioning, by the Watch accords, he had the right to ask. She let his voice roll past her without touching her, letting herself think about Matthiall instead. When the stupid bastard finished complaining, she would do what she always did. She would promise him relief, and then she would do nothing. He would receive no help, he would struggle against the forces that opposed him, and he would sink deeper into apathy. Meanwhile, she pretended to listen.

"A moment of your time, Watchmistress."

The voice buzzed in her ear, sharp and urgent, cutting through the ramblings of the farmer. "Hold, please," she told the man, and turned to face the badger-faced little monster who served her. Amused, she said, "Hultif, can't you see I'm busy?" When one of her servants interrupted her during court, she always pretended that she cared about the supplicant and his problem. Her servants knew better, of course.

Hultif played the game with her as she had taught him. "Yes, Watchmistress. I know how important this is to you . . . but this is a matter of dire need." The usual words. The usual words, but this time they stirred something in her gut. Hultif's black bead eyes gleamed uncharacteristically bright, and the line of black fur along his neck bristled erect. In him she saw fear or excitement, and definitely uncertainty.

For no reason, she felt uneasy. Damn. The phlegmatic Hultif had never shown excitement since the day she'd lifted him from the arms of his dead mother, when he'd been a child. Something had to be very wrong.

She turned and signaled to her corpsmen, who announced that court was closed for the day. The people still waiting turned and shuffled away, sighing, muttering, heads hanging. They expected no better. Not one voiced an audible complaint.

Pity. Had there been any complainers, she would have singled them out to be killed on their trips home.

When the room cleared, she turned to Hultif again. "What?"

"I can't tell you here. I have to show you."

She nodded. A few of the services Hultif performed for her were things no one else could know about. If she considered her power as a chain, then her need for Hultif and his special talents was one of the few weak links in it.

She followed him out of the Hearing Chamber, through the halls and down into the cellars of his workroom.

He liked clutter and darkness, the scents of mold and mildew and rotting leaves. These were all traits of his race, of which he was the last surviving member. She had made sure of that. He liked dirt walls and worms and other burrowing slimy things, and in his home, which he had dug for himself at the back of one of the wine cellars, he had a maze that gave him everything he liked.

He led her in—he'd made his front room taller for her convenience—and bade her be seated in the high, straight-backed chair he kept there for her. He lit a small lamp for her, another concession he made for her comfort.

Without preamble, he said, "The omens are bad, Mother." She'd taught him to call her Mother when they were alone. She had no offspring and never would; she had no intention of giving birth to her own replacements. One of them might turn out to be as clever and ambitious as she was. She wouldn't want that. When she considered how she had come to raise Hultif, and when she thought of what he would call her if he knew the truth, his unquestioning devotion to her well-being delighted her.

She nodded and waited.

Hultif stood watching her for a long, silent moment, head cocked to one side, ears flicking forward and back, forward and back. His wet black nose twitched and the squared nostrils flared rapidly. He tried hard to give the appearance of calm and control, but now that she had him alone, his agitation was clearer to her than before. Finally he sighed and lumbered over to the shelf where he kept his instruments. He brought back a bowl full of amber, acrid-smelling liquid, which he set on the table, being careful not to spill the contents. She waited. He could have had everything waiting for her when she arrived, but something in his nature preferred the heightened drama of making her wait while he demonstrated his magical skill.

She was patient. She had all the time in the world.

Next he brought out a round, wood-backed, black glass mirror. What he was doing was quite different from his usual procedure, which involved tracking the movements of worms or snails or ugly, thick-carapaced bugs through sand and reading the future in their tracks. She found that method amusing; she suspected him of eating his oracles when he was finished with them.

But this was different. She'd never seen the black mirror before, and though she couldn't define why, she didn't like it.

He settled the mirror onto the liquid. It didn't break the surface, but it did deform it, so that she could see the bulge of the amber meniscus rising around the mirror's rim. The smell of the liquid changed when the mirror touched it. For a moment it was sickeningly sweet, and then the stink of dead meat overlaid that sweetness. She did not let herself gag, but the smell became so thick she almost couldn't bear to breathe. Hultif seemed unbothered.

Her eyes and nose and mouth began to itch. She felt as if insects were landing on her face. She bore that, too. Hultif's magic no doubt had something to do with the itching, as it did with the hideous stink that he pretended not to notice and she refused to acknowledge.

He waited a moment, watching her. Curious. Expectant. He wanted a reaction to what had happened. She knew it. He evidently didn't see what he hoped to see in her eyes, though, because he sighed again and said, "Look into the glass and tell me what you see. Perhaps for you the omens will be better than they were when I read them for you."

She looked into the glass. She saw a dim reflection of her face. She frowned, and the lovely face frowned back at her. She smiled in spite of herself, and her reflection returned her smile. She looked up. Disappointed, she said, "I see nothing but myself."

"Really?" He seemed to brighten, as if this was unexpectedly good news. "How do you look?"

"I'm looking at my own reflection," she snapped, but as the words left her mouth, she wished she could take them back. Her reflection changed. The face in the mirror became still, where hers still moved. She tried to get it to reflect her smile, but the mouth went slack. The eyes ceased blinking. Then the face—my face, she thought—began to swell. Flies crawled in the eyes and nostrils and into the open mouth. Her mouth. Her eyes and nose. The flies laid their eggs and left, and after a short while maggots appeared, eating through her swelling, discolored flesh.

She looked away, sick, and found herself staring into the bright, eager eyes of Hultif, who asked, "What did you see? What did you see?"

"Only my own face," she told him. She stood, feeling weak and frightened and irrationally angry, as if he had created the omens he'd placed in front of her, when instead he had merely shown her what his own searching had revealed.

He smiled, sighed with obvious relief, and lifted the mirror out of its liquid bed. "Wonderful. I'd foreseen disaster, Mother. Disaster for you. I'm relieved that you did not see the same thing."

So he had not taken joy in the news he brought her. She'd thought from his odd demeanor that he might have. She decided to tell him the details of her vision, to find out how he reacted to that. "I saw my own face, but I was dead," she admitted.

He frowned at her words, and exhaled sharply. He looked away. "So. Not my imagination, then. Danger is coming. I saw two tall and shining heroes riding through the forest, armed with tremendous weapons and followed by all Glenraven's rabble. I saw battles and blood raining from the heavens. I saw darkness and plagues."

"Interesting," she said. "An indication, perhaps, that those who plot against me are not as ineffectual as they seem." She watched him, coldly curious. "What do we do to avert this fate?"

He sucked the whiskers on the right side of his face into his mouth and chewed on them. The long, hard digging claws of his right hand rested on the table, clicking nervously. He stared down at his bare, clawed feet, shaking his head. "Avert. Avert. That is the question; can we avert it? I will do what I can to find the danger, Mother. What I can. What happens then . . . who can tell?"

"It would be wise of you," she said softly, "to be prompt in finding your answer. Your value to me lies in your effectiveness. My . . . son."

Sixteen

Jayjay kept waiting for some sign of bandits or murderers among the increasing flow of peasants that joined her and Sophie on the road to Zearn. To her amazement, though, the trip took place without incident. She and Sophie drew a few looks and some carefully hushed whispers, but people didn't stare. The Glenraven costumes had been a good idea, she decided. No matter what his game had been, Lestovru had done the two of them a service with those costumes.

Zearn rose up in front of them, a white-stone-walled city with a cleared swath of closely cut grass all around the outside. The guards could see anything larger than a mouse approaching over that, she realized, and looked up at the battlements to find cold, appraising faces staring back at her. At *her*. Not merely at the mob of people in general, but at her and Soph in particular.

So maybe the costumes weren't foolproof.

A man in a gorgeous red and gold and blue uniform stepped out from the guard tower as the two of them rode up. He watched them but made no move to stop them. Jay nodded at him, and he bowed slightly to her, his eyes still narrowed and his entire air one of speculation. They rode past him, with Jay constantly expecting to hear his voice calling them back. But he didn't, and she decided that perhaps his reaction hadn't been important.

Inside Zearn, Jay found herself thrown into an astonishing tableau from the past, and surrounded by all the scents and sights and sounds of a prosperous and bustling medieval town.

Tall barracks leaned out over both sides of the narrow, twisting cobblestone street, and soldiers in the same gold and black and blue uniforms lounged in the doorways and leaned on narrow, stone-balustraded balconies overhead, calling to young women passing below and shouting to each other, their voices quick and hard and full of amusement, their words unintelligible.

They left the barracks behind and now passed little storefronts; signs carved in the shapes of the things found within hung over the street. The town had no walkways; riders and pedestrian traffic shared the same thoroughfare. Zearn was pretty and quaint, but the smell wasn't. It indicated sanitation held at a medieval level. Down alleys that pierced the otherwise unbroken wall of buildings, Jay spotted rats crawling through the darkness.

She'd considered the tiny, poverty-stricken village of Inzo an anomaly; she'd imagined that it was an odd relic in a world that would otherwise fit western conceptions of hygiene and civilization. But the smell of this city, highly recommended by the guidebook as a location of special interest, struck what was perhaps a racial memory in a primitive part of her brain. Glenraven ceased to seem to her like a Disney World model of a medieval city; the scent of raw sewage and smoky wood cooking fires and animal dung snapped her fully into a world where night began at sunset, where food spoiled unless it had been smoked or dried or salt-cured or kept in a springhouse, where children died because they'd never had inoculations for measles and mumps and diphtheria. She glanced at the faces in the streets around her. Some of them, both men and women, bore the deep disfigurations of pox scars. Probably smallpox. She shivered and stroked her sleeve over her right deltoid, feeling for her smallpox vaccine scar. Thank God for the sixties, when they still immunized for that. She realized this place was truly a holdover from ancient Europe, pinned in its primitive time like a formaldehyded butterfly to a board.

They came out of the close press of buildings at last, into a huge open square. In it, an open-air market fair was in full swing. Jayjay reined in and gaped at the madhouse that churned in front of her, and, as people noticed her interest, around her. A flock of fat, dark brown ducks charged quacking under her horse's hooves, and an instant later a black-and-white streak of collie came tearing out of an alley barking after them. Neither Jay's nor Sophie's horse startled, though Jayjay jumped. Women and men shouted at her and at each other, waved brightly colored swatches of cloth and handfuls of vegetables in her face, and pointed at their chickens and piglets and breads while no doubt lauding the quality of their wares. A couple of buskers—a flautist and a drummer—and a thin, pale-haired dancer plied their trades on the corner directly across from the near edge of the market square. Solemn-faced little girls dressed in hand-embroidered smocks carried baskets of eggs on their heads, while their mothers, with babies on hips and hiding behind their long, full skirts, carried larger baskets full of fruit, bread, beans and grains. Boys and young men herded long-horned goats and long-legged sheep or carried packs or huge sheaves of rushes. Old men and old women dickered at their stalls in the marketplace or watched the goings-on from narrow plank benches lined along the city walls. One man blew glass into

utilitarian shapes—pitchers and glasses and plates—
dipping and spinning his long metal rod while women
waited, calling out their orders. His assistant, a boy
of about six or seven, stacked the cooled wares and
counted out money. Tinkers hammered, leather work-
ers cut and tailors sewed.

That was only the near edge of the market. The stalls
were packed side to side all the way through the
square, with little paths between that made them inac-
cessible to riders on horseback, or even, Jay thought,
to claustrophobes. The smells of cookfires and roast-
ing meat and pastry and livestock and sweating people;
the din of shouts and laughter and the cacophony of
scattered bands of musicians all playing different songs;
the sight of fortresses and ancient houses and shops
and the pageantry of local costumes untouched by anything resembling clothing from the twentieth century;
the feel of thousands of people packed into a tight
space walled all around, thronging, surging like a tide.
Jay found those sensations overpowering; but the feeling of being *somewhere else*, of complete immersion
in another world, left her shivery and breathless.

Through the artful mayhem, two men appeared; they
cantered between the city gates, riding matched chest-
nuts with arching necks and fiery eyes. The men slowed
to a trot as they moved up the road, though they never
looked at the people in front of them. It didn't matter; the crowd parted before them like the waters
before Moses in a Metro-Goldwyn-Mayer epic, only
this was real. Voices grew hushed, hats came off of
heads and those heads ducked. No one hawked their
chickens or melons at either rider. The dancer stopped
dancing, the flute player and the drummer stopped
playing; the noise from the more distant parts of the
market only made the silence that fell where the men
passed more surreal.

But if the reactions of the townsfolk said more to

Jayjay about the two men than words ever could have, the actions of the riders said as much. Neither gave any indication that they saw the people who moved out of their path, who bowed, lowered their heads, doffed their caps; from what Jay could see, both men could have been riding alone in a field for all the attention they paid to the scene around them.

She wondered who they were. They wore clothing plainer than most of what she saw on the people around her. Their silk shirts were white and unadorned, their fitted black leather riding breeches showed signs of wear, and their mud-spattered riding boots were utilitarian, but not elegant. Yet they gave the impression of power, of wealth . . . and of danger. Why?

Were they soldiers? Tax collectors? She couldn't be sure, but from the looks in the eyes around her, she could tell they were to be avoided.

They drew nearer, and she got a better look at them. The nearer man was taller, older, and handsome. He had a rugged outdoorsman's face, tanned skin, broad shoulders. He'd pulled his sandy brown hair back into a short ponytail that only accented the rugged line of his jaw.

The angle of their approach hid the other man behind him until they were nearer. Then Jayjay could see that he was leaner and darker, with the pale skin and intense, ascetic look of a priest or a scholar.

Jayjay couldn't take her eyes off him. "Holy Mary mother of God," she whispered. "I know him."

Sophie had glanced over at her in time to see her lips move. "What did you say?"

The riders drew even with them, and Jay stared, then glanced away before she could get caught. She didn't recognize the fair-haired man, but the dark-haired one—well, he didn't wear glasses and his hair was tousled instead of combed straight and slicked down; and he didn't look the least bit prim. Or fussy.

Sophie poked her in the ribs and she jumped.

"What?"

"I asked you what you said. You got pale all of a sudden. Are you feeling sick?"

"No." Jay frowned after the two men until they rode around a street corner and out of sight. Then she shrugged. "For a minute, I thought I knew one of those men." She breathed deeply. "Everybody has a twin, I suppose. Still, I've never actually crossed paths with anyone's before."

"Really?" Sophie urged her horse forward again, and shouted over the crowd, which had gotten louder as soon as the men were out of sight. "There's a girl I ran into in Raleigh a couple of weeks ago who looks just like you. Well, you're a brunette and she's a redhead, but her hair is a dark red so it isn't so noticeable, and otherwise she looks just like you." Sophie nibbled at the corner of her lip and added, "Except younger. She's five years younger. Maybe ten."

Jay sighed. "And twenty pounds lighter."

Sophie laughed. "Not more than ten. She looks just like you did five or ten years ago."

"Except for red hair." Jayjay chuckled and shook her head. "I got you. But this is different. That dark-haired man looked identical to Amos Baldwell from Peters. You've been to the new bookstore on McDuffie Street, haven't you?"

Sophie shook her head. "I haven't been out book hunting in . . ." A coldness passed across her face, the briefest touch of death. "In a while."

"Well, the dark-haired guy was a perfect match."

"It happens. Considering where we are, I doubt he's related." Sophie changed the subject with a shrug. "Are you at all hungry? I think I'm going to starve if we don't stop someplace and get a bite to eat. Breakfast with Retireti wasn't enough."

Jay looked in the direction the two men had disappeared. Their arrival had felt important to her.

Momentous. But the feeling passed, and now she wasn't sure if the second man really had looked like Amos; more important, she couldn't imagine why she had thought it important that she thought he did. Sophie was right. Everyone had a twin.

Lunch felt much more important at that moment.

Jayjay pulled out her Fodor's and flipped through pages until she found Zearn. "We've arrived right at the beginning of the Gootspralle Fair. The guide says the fair is dedicated to the spirit of the Machnan troops who heroically defeated the Alfkindir oppressors in Zearn during this, the month of Spralle, winning the town for the Machnan for all time."

"The month of Spralle?"

"Obviously they haven't adopted the Gregorian calendar yet. Not a surprise, considering . . ." She read down the page. It went on in the same historical vein for about two paragraphs, all "brave Machnan" and "evil Alfkindir," but it didn't say anything about lunch, so she skipped to the useful information. "What counts is that the fair will be going on for about three weeks, and it only started yesterday. We need to get our room early or we won't have a place to sleep." She glanced over Zearn's offerings, then told Sophie, "The Beuslattar and Slattar ong Gwaltmet are the two most highly recommended inns in the reasonable price range." She compared the names with locations on the map. Then she compared the map with her current location. "Okay. Slattar ong Gwaltmet is the closest one. It sound all right to you?"

"What does the guide say about the place?"

"'Slattar ong Gwaltmet. This delightful old half-timbered inn sits in the heart of the oldest portion of Zearn, across from the Temple of the Iron Heart and only two blocks from Zearn's thriving open-air market. The charming rooms are spacious and the excellent service commends itself."

Sophie arched an eyebrow. "Charming, huh? We had 'charming' last night, didn't we?"

Jayjay laughed. "Um, no. Last night we had 'quaint.'"

Sophie narrowed her eyes and smiled a toothy smile. "Do they use the word 'charming' to describe . . . what was it? Bugslatter?"

"Beuslattar." Jay checked the entry. "Nope. It's 'vintage.'"

"Oooh. *Vintage*. I'll betcha 'charming' and 'vintage' are related to 'quaint,' whattaya think?"

"I think you're a cynic."

"I think I am, too . . . but I'm not waking up face-to-face with fowl again. How does Fodor's describe the outrageously expensive places?"

"Well, Wethquerin Zearn gets Fodor's star for best ridiculously overpriced digs in town." She read down the entry. " . . . ancient ancestral home of the Sarijanns . . . sumptuous furnishings . . . stunning view . . ." She paused, then looked up and gave Sophie a conspiratorial grin. "All *right!*"

Sophie leaned forward in her saddle. "What?"

"Hot baths."

"Hot damn, let's go. Which way?"

"Thattaway."

Jay didn't even worry about lunch. If she could just have a hot bath, she would willingly live with her hunger for a while.

Seventeen

"My God, it's breathtaking." Sophie tipped her head back so that she could see the steep slate roofs that towered over her. Narrow, tall stained-glass windows glinted out of Wethquerin Zearn's white stone walls, rough-quarried but smoothed by time. A master crafts-man had carved the deep bas-reliefs of fierce wolves and slender winged lions into the wooden surface of the brass-bound door. The knocker was a nearly life-sized brass wolf's head that snarled evilly; the metal knocker ran through his upper teeth but didn't quite reach his lower teeth, so that the person who wished to knock on the door had to stick a hand in the wolf's mouth.

"Bet that gives the door-to-door salesmen second thoughts," Jay said. She laughed and brushed her hair out of her eyes. "That is incredibly cool."

"Not precisely a symbol of hospitality, though."

Jayjay didn't seem to be in the least disconcerted. "Nah. This place offers rooms to tourists now, but according to the book, it started out being sort of the county seat for the local nobility."

Sophie loved the place, but she found it intimidat-ing. "I wish we had reservations."

111

"The only places I could find in the whole country that took reservations were the castle I had us lined up to stay at in Rikes Gate and the one in Dinnos. Every place else, it's first come, first served."

"I wonder why that is?"

Jayjay shrugged. "No phones, I guess. Bit tough to call in reservations without them."

Sophie nodded. "That makes sense."

Jayjay reached her hand into the wolf's mouth and knocked. The knocker crashed down like thunder, and Jay dropped it and yanked her hand back. She looked wide-eyed in Sophie's direction and shook her head. "Yeesh! That's pretty dramatic for a lousy knocker."

"A little electricity and a doorbell would be a real improvement, wouldn't it?"

Jay tipped her head and studied the door. "In this case, yes. I do hear someone coming, though, so at least it works."

One half of the massive door swung open on well-oiled hinges and a plump little man in a dramatic red, blue, and gold tabard, black silk doublets and black tights stood before them. His eyes flicked from Jay to Sophie, clearly sizing them both up. He stared at their horses, then back at the two of them again, plainly not liking what he saw. One eyebrow arched and his nose went into the air. He asked a question in short, rapid syllables.

Jay sighed, flipped to the back of her guidebook, and put her index finger beside a line. "Teh-HOO-thin RO-sal eff-EL-due dim-YAH?" Sophie heard the uncertainty in her friend's voice, and realized how intimidated Jay had to be. She usually managed to give the impression that she was completely at home in the most uncomfortable situations.

The little man's nose came down out of the air and his eyes, briefly, showed startlement. Then he pursed his lips and stared from them to the horses and back again. He held out one hand, palm up, in an unmistakable gesture.

"Bribe him, Jay," Sophie said. "Evidently we don't look rich enough to be here."

Jay fumbled through her pockets and came up with two silver coins. She held them out, but the man only frowned and pointed to her guidebook.

"You want this?" Jay stiffened and looked at Sophie. Sophie knew how she felt. That book was their lifeline, and if the man decided to keep it, they were going to be in real trouble. At last, though, she handed it to him.

He held it in both hands, not bothering to open it, and Sophie saw his skin pale. A fine sheen of perspiration broke out on his forehead, and he looked up at the two of them, wearing an expression Sophie had last seen on the deer she caught in her headlights and almost ran down. He shuddered and handed the book back to Jay. "What are you doing here?" he asked the two of them in English, and Sophie first thought he was questioning their right to be at the front door. Then she realized he hadn't said, "What are *you* doing here," but instead, "What are you doing *here*," as if he expected them, but not where they were.

Sophie and Jay exchanged glances. "We're looking for a room," Sophie told him, repeating in English what she hoped Jay had said in Galti.

His eyebrow rose again, and he pursed his lips. "You seek lodging for the night? Here? Don't you have a room?"

"No. We don't," Sophie said. "And her guidebook says this is the best place to stay in all of Zearn."

His nod said no one was questioning that. "Since you've come, you shall have a room. Lucky the master arrived earlier. I suppose there's been a mix-up, but he'll explain it, I'm sure."

Sophie noticed that when the doorman talked, he

looked like one of those poor actors in a Godzilla movie whose lines had been badly dubbed. His English was flawless, unaccented and colloquial, not even having the stiffness she'd heard in people who had learned the language well but late in life. It lacked the perfection and precision of the fluent nonnative speaker. He sounded American. But she couldn't figure out how he spoke; his lips formed shapes that bore no relationship to the sounds that came out.

The man stepped outside the door and whistled. After a moment, a boy came running; the child was perhaps nine years old, certainly no more than eleven.

The doorman gave him quick instructions—in English, Sophie noted—though the boy nodded and grinned and chattered back in Galti. He looked over at the horses with bright eyes and held out his hands for the reins.

The doorman turned to both women. "He will take your horses for you."

Jay handed hers over without a quibble. Sophie held on to her reins, however, and looked down at the child waiting to receive them. She hadn't enjoyed riding horseback; the memories it had brought back to her had been almost too bitter to bear. She'd done it at first because she hadn't been able to think of anything else to do, and then because as transportation went it was better than walking. Half a day in the saddle had not inured her to the act of riding, but it had made her appreciate the willing, well-trained horse she rode, and the equally good animal that carried her gear. Even though she would not get in a saddle again if given her choice, she still thought the horses deserved better care than they would get from a small, busy boy. She gave the doorman an apologetic smile. "I'm sure he would do a good job," she lied, "but I would prefer to take care of my own horses. I'm particular about their care."

The doorman smiled at her as if he found her unspeakably eccentric. "I know the owners of the animals will appreciate your concern, madam, but all four of these horses are *ours*. You see the brand on the flank?" Sophie nodded. She'd wondered about the brand since they'd obtained the horses. "That is the Sarijann mark. They come from the Rikes Gate stable instead of the Zearn one . . . but they are nonetheless Sarijann beasts. And I promise you we will not mistreat them."

Sophie felt her cheeks grow hot. "I'm sorry," she murmured. "I didn't know." What were she and Jay doing with horses that belonged to the royal family, or what seemed to pass for it in these parts? Her previous uneasiness worsened.

The boy led the horses off and the doorman beckoned with a finger. "This way."

They followed him into the enormous entry hall. This isn't your standard bed-and-breakfast, Sophie thought. Light streamed through harlequin-patterned stained glass onto gorgeous room-sized tapestries of hunters chasing stags and bears and armor-clad warriors spearing each other and dying in pools of crimson gore. Spears and shields hung above the tapestries, right below a balcony that ran the circumference of the room. Above the balcony, stuffed heads of dead animals hung in rows.

It wasn't a room; it was an adventure.

"The inn testosterone decorated," Jayjay said, wrinkling her nose.

Sophie nodded, speechless. She couldn't quit staring at all those heads on the walls; she recognized wolves and deer and bear and some sort of giant elk without difficulty, but she didn't know what to make of an entire row of beasts with greyhound faces and curling, tufted ears and close-set, almost-human eyes.

She stopped and stared into those faces, and bile rose

in the back of her throat. She gagged and swallowed and turned away, not knowing what the creatures were or why seeing them on the walls made her feel sick.

Jayjay didn't show any signs of a similar response. She had stopped a few yards ahead and was staring at one vividly colored tapestry that glinted with bits of gold thread woven in among the rich reds and blues and dull yellows and browns. "Wow! That's a dramatic tapestry!" Jayjay said. The hanging ran most of the length of the stone hall. "Look—the armies aren't the same. The guys with the red, blue and gold shields are men, but what in the world are those things on the other side?"

Sophie looked where Jayjay pointed, and caught a quick glimpse of the details she'd mentioned; men in battle lined up against a foe that looked like it had come straight from hell. Great shaggy brutes in armor stood next to creatures with horns and fangs, and demons riding giant lizards charged down a mountainside with hideous clawed dogs at their sides.

"Allegory?" Sophie suggested, as the doorman hurried them down the hall and into another corridor. "Glenraveners take on Satan's host?"

Jayjay shrugged, her attention already focused on the armor helms sitting atop posts on both sides of the present corridor. Sophie watched her glancing from one coat of arms to the next. Jayjay, for all her strengths as a friend, sometimes had the attention span of a three-year-old.

A detail clicked in the back of her mind. That tapestry had shown creatures that resembled the canine things whose heads hung on the walls. Those hideous giant clawed dogs who had ranged down out of the hills with the rest of the hosts of Hell.

Odd.

What did that mean?

Their guide led them through the doorway at the end

of the corridor into what had to be the dining room. Two rough trestle tables ran down the sides of the room with benches against the wall. The center of the floor was clear, which probably made serving convenient. A third table at the end of the room connected the trestle tables; it sat on a dais three feet above everything else. Sophie studied the setup and decided maybe seventy-five or a hundred people could eat in there at the same time. She wondered how often the place filled to capacity.

"Does this place have a restaurant?" Jay asked. "I didn't notice one being mentioned in the guide."

The doorman pondered the question for a moment. "We all eat here," he said at last. "The midday meal will be served shortly. You will be expected to arrive in appropriate attire."

"This is what we have," Sophie told him, thinking that wasn't entirely true, but that he was likely to find Jayjay's Banana Republic wardrobe even less appropriate to the situation than the Robin Hood suits Lestovru had given them.

The doorman's nose tilted into the air again, and he sniffed. "Thus comes the salvation of the Machnan," he murmured, then glanced at them. "I'll see that you are provided with something appropriate."

Several side doors led out of the dining room, and the guide picked one. Sophie stepped into a dark, narrow hall crammed with people, all of whom were heading someplace in a hurry. Well, different someplaces. They all wore variations on the outfit the doorman wore—red, blue and gold over black.

The doorman led them through a maze of stone corridors, down long halls and up a circular staircase, through stark, cold rooms, and all Sophie could think was that she was never, never going to be able to find her way out of that place; she would never remember her way to the dining room or to the garden in the center of the building, and she could very easily spend the rest of her life wandering through the corridors and up and down twisting staircases, looking for a door that led out.

"Your room," their guide said suddenly, and stopped in front of the two of them and opened a door that looked like every other door in the place. No number identified it, no cute little theme-related sign—nothing. It was just a plain brass-bound wooden door, big and solid and ancient.

"How are we going to find anything in here?" Jayjay asked, and Sophie could have hugged her for not being embarrassed about being lost in a hotel.

"Pull the bellcord. Someone will come and take you where you need to go. I'll have the chambermaid bring each of you something suitable to wear when she comes to pour your baths." He eyed their clothes with evident distaste. "If you need anything else, tell her; she'll be able to get it."

"Does she speak English?" Sophie asked.

The doorman gave her a blank stare and said, "Does anyone?"

"My senior English teacher in high school used to make remarks like that," Jay said, watching the doorman walk away. Every time he graded papers, I think the answer he came up with was 'No.'"

Sophie looked around the room. A massive hand-carved canopy bed took up much of the space. Rich red brocade hangings were drawn back and tied, but Sophie saw dark wood rings along the top that would permit them to slide forward. In drafty old places like this, those bed curtains would make an intolerable room warm enough for sleep. A writing desk took up one corner; unlike the bed, its style was simple and unadorned. A chair and musical instruments waited in the other corner. French doors led onto a balcony; Sophie walked over to them and looked out to the courtyard garden one story below. A fire had been laid in the fireplace, but not lit.

She stared out through the small, uneven diamonds of glass, not seeing anything in front of her. A host of unrelated images flashed through her mind. Karen lying on the ground, gray-skinned and still; the old man at Glenraven's border studying them with an expression of worry; the highway robbers they'd eluded—maybe; the badly dubbed doorman; the yellow-eyed dog heads hanging on the walls and the way her stomach flipped when she looked at them. The tapestry. Her feeling when she had first seen Glenraven that she had come there to die.

The horses. Something about the horses bothered her.

Jayjay shouted, "Here's the bathroom!" After a short pause, she added, "Sort of."

Sophie pulled herself away from the French doors. Jayjay had opened one of the room's side doors and gone in. Sophie leaned through the open door and sighed. "Sort of?"

Jayjay crouched beside the toilet, looking for a mechanism to make it work. "At least they have indoor plumbing here. After the ditch in Inzo and the side of the road, I was afraid we'd have chamber pots here." She tapped the pipes, and with an expression of sheer frustration, thumped the tiles on the wall behind the toilet with the palm of her hand.

Sophie chuckled. "While you're figuring out the plumbing, I'm going to lie down for a few minutes. I'm tired and my butt hurts. Whoever made that saddle didn't do it with women in mind."

Jay waved her away, and Sophie sprawled out on the bed. The hard mattress felt good after a night on a wood floor and half a day in the torture saddle. And the room certainly seemed luxurious enough.

She closed her eyes, and when she did, her worries

about the situation in which she found herself faded, replaced by bigger, more confusing worries. She saw Lorin the way she'd first seen her—bending down on the road in front of Sophie's house, a hoof pick in hand and her mount's left front foreleg tucked under her left arm while she probed for a stone. Lorin had pulled her hair back in a ponytail, and the light coming through the trees that overgrew the road had turned it to gold. She'd looked up and grinned when Sophie came down the walk, flicked the stone out with one final tug, and put the hoof back on the ground. She straightened and brushed her hands off on her jeans; short, sharp movements at odds with her tall, grace-ful frame. "Hey, there. He picked up a stone in his frog, and I had to get it loose," she'd said in a cool, vaguely southern drawl, and Sophie had nodded her understanding.

"This part of the road is a bad spot for them. It was pitch-and-run until they paved it last summer. You'd be surprised how much of that gravel is still in the grass on the side."

Small talk. She hadn't been able to figure out why she'd spoken. She'd just wanted to pick up her mail, and she definitely didn't want to discuss horses with anyone ever again; but Lorin hadn't talked about horses. And in Lorin Sophie sensed the same sadness she felt in herself.

They'd talked. Small talk, really. The weather. What Lorin thought of Peters, because she wasn't from there. What Sophie thought of Tennessee, which was where Lorin came from—though Sophie had only been there once and hadn't much to contribute. Peters' complete lack of the cultural attractions Lorin had enjoyed in Knoxville; Sophie's dry commentary about the Junior Club Fall Fashion Fling and the Jaycees Fair being the height of culture in the town. Both women had laughed at that.

And Sophie had gotten her mail and walked back to the house feeling good.

That had started it. Lorin dropped by when she was riding past, and Sophie walked over to her house after Lorin told her where it was. The two women became friends; they went to lunch together once or twice a week in one or another of the little cafes in Peters, sat in each other's living rooms on Sundays when Mitch was out mowing the lawn, chatted about their dreams and their ambitions and their lives.

Lorin had described herself as "between relation-ships" and Sophie had tried to avoid what she instinc-tively knew was a painful subject. Neither of them had talked about children, neither had talked about men. And then one day Lorin had remarked how hard it was to be alone and how much she missed her parents and her brother and sister, people with whom she'd had a falling-out but who she still loved. And she talked about a lover long gone, who had left her for a younger woman, who had moved out without even saying good-bye.

And over lunch, Sophie found herself talking about Mitch for the first time, wistfully recalling the days when things between them had been good. She'd talked about Karen, too, and about how her death had changed everything. She told Lorin about her restless feeling, her hunger for something she couldn't quite describe. A need to leave the past behind, to be some-one new. To walk away from the unending pain.

Lorin smiled sadly. "It hurts to love."

"It does. Maybe that's the problem. Maybe what Mitch and I have left doesn't hurt enough." Sophie rested her chin in her hands and sighed. "I wish I knew that I still loved him . . . but I don't know that I do. I think maybe I'm ready to move on to something else."

Lorin's face got serious, and she rested a hand on Sophie's elbow. Her sad eyes stared into Sophie's, and she whispered, "If you are, do you think you could move on to me?"

Sophie opened her eyes and stared at the canopy overhead.

Do you think you could move on to me? The question hung in her memory, as fresh and burning as it had been the moment Lorin asked.

Karen's death had broken so many things inside of her. She knew she would never want to have children again. She would never want the risk of giving birth and loving and losing another child, as she had loved and lost Karen. And she had lost the part of her that could take joy from Mitch, too. She saw him more as a reminder of what she had lost than the man with whom she'd dreamed of building a future.

Restless, Sophie rolled from side to side, trying to find a comfortable position. Trying to find escape from her thoughts.

Of course, if her premonition were correct, she wouldn't have to worry anymore. If she died in Glenraven, the problems of her life would cease to exist.

She smiled wearily up at the canopy and considered the few and painful merits of leaving her troubles far behind.

Eighteen

In the castle of Cotha Maest, buried deep in the Faldan Woods, darkness knit itself tightly to everything on the brightest of days. The Alfkindir designers disliked daylight, but found it necessary to keep a firm grip on their diurnal Machnan subjects, so they built Maest aboveground in concession to that need. They built most of the immense castle within the shadows of the forest, though, and where windows were necessary, abutments and carved stone trees and other clever devices cast shade at all hours. Just past midday, most of Cotha Maest already squatted in tenacious gloom.

Aidris Akalan wanted to be alone, however. Therefore, she settled herself into the Wizard's Bell at the top of the tallest tower, the only point in the massive building where light ever poured into the windows. From that height, with the glaring unfiltered sunlight streaming around her, she could sit undisturbed in only slight discomfort; neither lesser Kin nor Kin-hera would risk the painful daylight brilliance to disturb her thoughts with problems.

She wanted to consider Hultif and his omens. She didn't doubt the validity of his magic. Too many times before he had demonstrated his accuracy. She had to believe him when he said that death stalked her in spite of her pact with her Watchers, her hellspawn summoned from beyond the Rift. Their power could keep her young and strong until the last magic-wielding creature breathed its last breath; and all they asked in exchange was the opportunity to feed on Glenraven's creatures. Still, they did not protect her. She had to do that herself. Virtual immortality belonged to her—if she could hold on to it.

Her face in the black glass had been the face of the dead. She had not admitted she could die for easily a hundred years; she hadn't faced anything in that long that threatened her. Now she felt the pressure of her own mortality, and she didn't like it. Something—or someone—challenged her; something that wanted her dead also had the wherewithal to make his wish come true.

Perhaps the omen portended Matthiall's unlikely success.

Maybe she ought to kill him, simply on principle. She would rather have him as a broken slave . . . but she didn't see much point in dying for the pleasure of trying to break him.

Matthiall wasn't the only possibility, of course. The list of people who wished she were dead had to be almost the same as the list of people who lived in Glenraven. Among them, there might be one or two with the backbone to go after her.

Well.

She sat in the sunlight, staring out the window at the verdant canopy of the Faldan Woods.

I was born to rule, she thought. Destiny smiles on me. There is no threat that I cannot overcome.

Hultif would make himself useful. He would locate the source of the threat. When he did, she would take care of it.

And she would do it in the most horrible manner she could contrive.

Nineteen

Jayjay hadn't thought Sophie was ever going to wake up. She'd been sound asleep and snoring lightly—a little cat purr of a snore—when the chambermaid brought both of them new outfits. The girl had given her a gold silk shirt and a full green silk skirt that went to her calves and a thick belt that started right below her breasts and hugged her waist and cinched tight, and a pair of rawhide moccasins that wrapped at her knees; she'd carried in a similar outfit in different loud colors for Sophie. Jay looked at herself in the tiny brass hand mirror and tried to decide if she looked like a gypsy or if she only thought she did.

Jayjay recalled a Dilbert and Dogbert cartoon she'd once seen, where Dilbert and Dogbert, having arrived at a restaurant without the required jackets, were forced to wear the establishment's dreadful jackets, clown feet, and something that she recalled looking like platypuses on their heads. She had to wonder if she was wearing the Wethquerin Zearn equivalent of a platypus hat.

Sophie was in the bathroom at the moment, soaking in the tub; Jay hoped when she came out she would be a little brighter. She'd been quiet during the day, and Jayjay had seen the telltale signs that she was obsessing over her daughter's death again. Jay empathized, but she kept hoping something about their adventure would finally get through to her friend and bring her out of the worst of the pain.

Sophie came out fiddling with her skirt. "Do I look as idiotic as I feel?" she asked.

"You look terrific." Jay decided if she looked in her outfit the way Sophie did in hers, she probably didn't look like a gypsy after all. She probably looked like a silk-swathed manic-depressive bag lady in her manic phase. And from the cautious smile Sophie gave her when assessing the clothing Jay wore, she figured her worst fears had been realized.

"This stuff is sort of . . . frilly . . . isn't it?"

Jay thought wistfully of her beloved Banana Republic photographer's vest and wrinkle-resistant khaki pants. She would have given almost anything to wear those to dinner. And through the rest of her trip, too. "Yeah," she agreed.

Sophie frowned down at her skirt, a full circle of ruby red silk padded out with rainbow layers of slips. "You suppose we really have to wear this?"

"We'll try it. If every other woman there is wearing an elegant little black dress, though, I'm not staying."

"I'll stay." Sophie sighed deeply. "I'm starving. Right now if the doorman said we had to go to dinner naked in order to be served, I'd at least consider it."

"Yeah. You're right. Even if everyone else looks gorgeous, I'll put up with having people laugh at me." Jay glanced at her watch and realized she and Sophie had been waiting in their room for well over an hour. Enough was enough. She walked over to the bellpull and gave it a good hard yank.

The chambermaid appeared at the door. She didn't speak English, but she'd been patient when Jay had wanted to know if everyone at dinner would wear such colorful clothing. Jay decided to try the girl's patience once more.

Jayjay dragged out her guidebook and used the phrasebook in the back to try to explain that she and Sophie were going to positively die of starvation if they didn't get something to eat soon. She went over the guidebook phrase three times, while the girl repeated the words after her, eyes getting wider and wider with each repetition. Then the chambermaid threw one hand over her mouth, gave a little yelp, and raced away, skirts flying behind her.

"Nice going, O mighty explorer." Sophie leaned against the French doors, a smile on her face. "What in the world did you say to her?"

Jayjay stared into the empty hall and sighed. "I wish I knew."

"Do you think she'll ever come back?"

"Depends. If I threatened her life or her virtue, probably not."

Jayjay stared down at the Fodor's guide, noticing again the tingle she got in her fingertips merely from holding it. She'd quit thinking about that—the sensation really didn't amount to much—but her fingers insisted the tingling had become stronger. Silly of Fodor's to use a coated paper that carried such a static charge.

Sophie had settled down on the side of the bed with a Ziploc bag full of trail mix. "Want some, or would you rather wander around in the halls hoping we can find the dining room on our own?"

Jay sat down on the bed beside her. "Gimme."

Moments later, as the two of them sat in their silk dresses on the edge of the canopied bed stuffing their faces with granola bits and peanuts and chocolate chips and tasteless dried bananas, the doorman burst through their door, short of breath and red-faced. "She said one of you was dying," he gasped, and looked from Jay to Sophie, then back to Jay. As he took in the two of them sitting there, eating and obviously fine, his expression flashed from fear to bewilderment to relief to annoyance. "You are not dying," he said, pointing a finger at Jay. "And you are not dying." He pointed at Sophie.

The poor chambermaid arrived at that moment, sobbing and wringing her hands, and the doorman lit into her with a stream of invective hot enough to melt the stones around them all. Oddly enough, he was shouting at the girl in English. She hadn't understood a word of the English Jay had tried on her, but she seemed to understand very clearly what he was saying.

"Excuse me," Jayjay said.

The doorman kept shouting.

Jayjay tapped him on the shoulder. "Excuse me."

The doorman turned and caught his breath. "My apologies for sending you this stupid girl—"

"She isn't a stupid girl," Jayjay told him. "I tried to tell her what I wanted but my Galti is terrible. I tried to tell her that we were starving, and I probably told her we were dying."

"Starving?" The doorman turned from the chambermaid and stared at Jay. "You told her you were starving?"

"Yes. We had breakfast a long time ago, and we rode from Inzo to Zearn, and we're hungry. But the useful phrases included, 'We're starving,' so I used that instead. Because we're really, really hungry."

The chambermaid sniffled and wiped her eyes with a sleeve.

The doorman glowered and lifted his chin so that he could look down his nose at them, in spite of being shorter than either. "*Starving.* I thought you needed help."

"Look. Just tell us where we can find the nearest restaurant . . . well, tavern or inn or whatever. We don't care. We'd love to eat here, but we want to eat now."

He stared at her as if two dragon heads had sprouted

from her neck. For a moment, he sputtered. Then he said, "You would stay under the master's roof and refuse the hospitality of his table?" His tone made it clear that he believed people who would consider such an atrocity would be capable of any crime. Jay knew she'd become a psychotic ax murderer in his eyes.

"No, we wouldn't do anything of the sort," Sophie said, smiling and doing her best to soothe the poor man.

He sniffed and glowered some more, then said, "I will come back for you when it is time." He snapped an order at the chambermaid, who scurried off like a mouse chased by a cat; then he stalked away, too.

"And still no food," Sophie mourned.

Jayjay looked down the long, many-doored hallway after him.

"That's the way it goes." Sophie leaned against the wall beside the door and looked at Jayjay, her expression quizzical. "Did your guide really tell you how to say 'I'm starving'?"

Jay nodded.

"That's a weird phrase to stick in a guidebook."

Jayjay stood there and considered Sophie's remark for a moment. It *was* a weird phrase to find in a Fodor's, come to think of it. Fodor's guides never included slang or colloquialisms. They told the tourist how to ask prices and directions and how to find a bathroom or a newspaper in the most inoffensive way possible. They were made by people who knew how easy it was to say the wrong thing, by people who had gone out of their way to make sure that untraveled neophytes from North Carolina or Nebraska or New York wouldn't cause an international incident by saying something printed in one of their guides.

Yet when Jayjay had looked in the book, she'd been looking for a way to tell the chambermaid she was starving—and right in the back on page 546 under

Useful Phrases, there it had been. *I'm starving. Ag dru gemmondlier. ach troo je-MOAN-dlee-air.* Three neat little columns: the English, the Galti, and the pronunciation guide.

She could still see it on the page, right underneath *I don't understand* and *I am American.*

But she'd been using Fodor's guides for years, and she'd never seen anything like that in there before. Jayjay flipped to the back of the book. Page 546, Useful Phrases. She ran her finger down the left-hand column.

> *I don't understand. I'm American.*
> *What's your name?*

Not *I'm starving,* but *What's your name.* She took a deep breath and let it out slowly. She read the entries in the column. Statements about speaking Galti and not speaking Galti, asking what time it was and where she could find medical help, stables, post offices, banks. She found the separate entry Fodor's always had for *Where are the restrooms*; that question had a little section marked off for itself in every Fodor's Jay had ever used. The most essential words in any language, she guessed.

Nowhere in there did it tell tourists how to say they were starved. The book had, though. It had, and she had used the phrase, and the chambermaid had understood her, but had taken her literally. She had not heard Jayjay say *I'm really hungry* but *I'm dying of starvation,* and she had gone to get help.

"I can't find it now." Jayjay put the book on the bed and crossed her arms. She paced beside the bed. "It isn't in there."

"It was in there before," Sophie said. Ever the voice of reason, that Sophie. "It sure didn't go anywhere."

"Okay. You find it."

Sophie grinned. "Maybe looking will keep my mind off the fact that I'm still starving." She sauntered over to the bed, flopped down on it, and picked up the Fodor's. A funny expression crossed her face, and for a moment she held the guide. "I felt that the first time I picked it up, too."

"What?"

"Exactly that sort of electric shock. I figured static electricity, but . . ." She shook her head and flipped to the back of the guide. "It's really evident sometimes, isn't it?" She ran a finger along the entries, reading. She looked annoyed.

Jay watched her.

"Yeah, yeah," Sophie muttered. "I am American, I do not understand, I am an international buffoon with oatmeal for brains and I cannot find the potty."

Jayjay snickered.

Sophie did nasal. "What is it? Why? Who? Where is the carriage house? Where is the post office? What should I do about . . ."

She stopped, and Jayjay caught a change in her expression. Bewilderment and fear flashed across her face and the color leached out of her skin until she was white as death.

Jayjay felt the shivers run down her spine. She took the book from Sophie's unresisting hand, and looked at the page, at the left-hand column.

> *Where is the carriage house?*
> *Where is the post office?*
> *What should I do about Lorin?*

"What should I do about *Lorin*?" Jay held her place in the Fodor's with a thumb and rubbed her temples with her other hand. She felt a headache coming on, and she suspected aspirin would be a tough find in Glenraven. She wanted her little stash in the emergency kit to last as long as it could, though, so she didn't want to take any unless she absolutely had to. "Who the hell is Lorin, and what is useful about that phrase?"

Sophie, still the color of bleached linen, slumped on the bed as if someone had taken the bones out of her.

"Soph? You okay?"

Sophie didn't say anything.

Jayjay walked over to her friend and crouched down so they were eye to eye. "Soph. Snap out of it. C'mon, Sophie. Talk to me. What's wrong—and what does that question mean? Lorin . . . who's Lorin?"

Sophie rolled onto her back and drew her knees to her chest. She stared at the canopy with flat, blank eyes; when Jayjay finally turned away, deciding that Sophie had gone into shock and she needed to find help, Sophie whispered, "How did it know?"

Jay looked down at the sentence again, and the air hissed out of her lungs.

> *Where is the carriage house?*
> *Where is the post office?*
> *Welcome, heroes. We have awaited the day of your arrival for a very long time.*

Jay dropped the book on the floor and stood there shaking, staring at it.

What the hell was going on? Heroes? What heroes? And who had waited?

She crouched down and touched the book again. That little electric "zing" tingled through her fingertip; stronger now that she was looking for it, but dammit, she should have gotten spooked by that the first time she picked the book up. And she should have put it down.

She should have listened to Amos when he tried to trade the Glenraven Fodor's for a Spain Fodor's. Spain wasn't all that bad an idea. People had heard of Spain. Spain had plumbing and electricity and an air of cosmopolitan elegance that Jay was sure she would adore.

The forests in Spain probably looked the same on the inside as they did from the outside. And books in Spain wouldn't send their own private messages.

Bells began ringing from somewhere in the Wethquerin Zearn Inn and out in Zearn itself. The city came alive with the sound. Jayjay raised her head, then stood, drawn by the joyous music. She opened one of the French doors and it poured into the room; she heard the richness and variety of hundreds of bells pealing up and down the valley, echoing off the mountains. The inn's bell tower was straight across the garden from their room. Somewhere in the distance, a bell ringer played an exuberant melody; at each pause, the untuned bells of the rest of the city created an accidental but perfect antiphony. Home, the bells sang. This is home. Welcome home.

Spain didn't have bells like that, either, she'd bet anything.

Which didn't make Glenraven home. That was still Peters. Home was pain, and Glenraven was impossible—but at least it was impossible in a good way. In Glenraven, a book called her a hero and welcomed her. Things like that didn't happen in Peters.

They didn't happen anywhere, did they?

Sophie was sitting up, biting at her bottom lip, looking distraught. Lorin, Jay thought. Lorin. Who the hell was Lorin, to make her friend become so ill? The question mattered—just as the remark about heroes mattered—but Jay decided while Sophie's skin was still gray under her faint tan and while her eyes still bore their haunted, hunted look, she wouldn't ask.

Meanwhile she had to consider the import of the book that was more than a book. What could cause a book to change its print to suit the person who read it? A brilliant bit of microelectronic technology? She would welcome such an idea, but the *Fodor's Guide to Glenraven* consisted of paper and ink; a glued-on cover of glossy paper cover stock, pages of a good-quality smooth paper, black ink that smelled like the ink in a paperback book. No place for a microchip existed, and even if it had, how could it induce ink on paper to change and reform to spell out new words? She was comfortable with the idea of technology, of course. If the cover hummed a bit beneath her fingertips, she could pretend that it was part of the technology that made the book work. But comfortable as such an explanation might have been, she wouldn't allow her mind to accept it. The lazy mind forced every unexplained phenomenon into the molds of things already known and experienced. The lazy mind, confronted with the seemingly impossible situation in which a book changed its print by itself, soothed itself with the thought that those whiz kids in the basement at Microsoft had been hard at work. Electronic paper. What will they think of next?

But for all the flaws she admitted in herself, Julie Jean Bennington would not admit the flaw of a lazy mind. The book was not a modern-day miracle of technology. The book had done something she knew to be impossible, and yet, because it had happened, what she knew to be impossible was not impossible. Highly unlikely, but unlikely and impossible were different animals altogether.

She stroked the book's cover. Not technology. Not the safe thing, not the known thing, not the reassuring thing. Instead, something that reeked of voodoo drums, of midnight rituals, of superstition and fantasy and fear and trembling, shimmering, breathless wonder.

Magic.

Her mind reflexively scoffed at the thought, but she slammed the reflex out of the way.

Magic.

How easy to close her eyes, to ignore the unlikeliness

of this trip to a place she didn't really think could exist. To deny the fact that the book had called to her. To refuse to see the impossibility of this place out of time, untouched by modernization, unaware of industrialization, of mechanization, of electronic miniaturization.

Insisting always that there had to be a logical explanation was a form of blindness. She'd partaken of that blindness as long as she dared. But no more.

"Sometimes," she whispered to the book in her hands, "there is no logical explanation."

The book hummed and sang against her palms, purred like a cat. She sensed that it was content for the moment. It had made its point.

The bells stopped swinging almost at the same instant, and the last of the echoes died away, and behind her someone cleared his throat.

She turned. The doorman was back, waiting. "Now," he said, "is the time to eat."

Back they went through the mazes of corridors, and arrived at last in the great dining hall they'd seen earlier. Now, however, people filled it from one side to the other and spilled out the doors; servants in the Wethquerin Zearn livery ran in and out, carrying bowls and platters and shouting to each other, while men and women sat around the long tables, shoving food in their mouths and talking and laughing; the cleared central space between the tables held a troupe of entertainers; a lute player and someone with an almost-violin, a flautist, a drummer, and several dancers who clapped and stomped and leapt their way through a lively circle jig. The seated crowd were well dressed in colors as bright as those Jay and Sophie wore, and they all looked well fed, as did the liveried servants; the entertainers looked dusty and seedy and thin.

The doorman tapped the shoulders of two men at the lower table, and whispered something. The men flashed smiles and scooted down on the bench, making room for Jayjay and Sophie if they didn't mind being cozy. The food smelled delicious, and Jayjay would have put up with a lot more than crowded eating conditions to get some of it. Sophie, with faraway eyes, settled into her seat and began filling the wooden bowl in front of her.

The chef had provided quite a bounty; venison and pig and stuffed fowl and baked fish and several types of bread and fruit. He'd not included a single vegetable, however. That's right, Jay recalled. Vegetables were animal fodder in the Middle Ages; meats, grains, and fruit in season were *it*. She looked at the table; spread in front of her was the Upper Class Gout Diet. She sighed. Oh, well—she only had to eat it for three weeks. Three weeks of fatty foods and no greenery wouldn't kill her.

She loaded her own bowl, then glanced up. She'd felt for a moment that she was being watched. Casually she let her gaze wander up and down the table, as if looking for something else to eat. And there he was, Amos Baldwell's identical twin. Staring at her.

She looked down at her food and gave Sophie's shin a good, hard kick.

"Ow!"

"Don't look up," Jay murmured. "You know that guy I told you about in the market this afternoon? The one who looked familiar?"

"I remember. What does that have to do with you kicking my shin to pulp?"

"He's sitting at the other end of the table from us, and staring this way."

Sophie kept her eyes fixed on her bowl and speared chunks of meat onto the tip of her knife; forks and spoons being noticeably absent, the knife was the only silverware she had. "Why shouldn't I look?" she asked under her breath.

"Because I'm not sure whether that is Amos or not, and if it is, I'm not sure whether we want to recognize him or not." Jayjay frowned into her dinner. "I got the book from him and the book is doing impossible things, and he's here, and that's way more strangeness than I'm willing to pass off to coincidence."

Sophie glanced sidelong at her and smiled slowly. "Okay. So if you want to pretend you don't see him, why did you bother to point him out?"

Jayjay forgot what she intended to say as, out of the corner of her eye, she saw Amos, still staring steadily at her, rise from his seat and motion to the two human gorillas who sat one on either side of him to stay where they were. Her stomach flipped; if he was Amos Baldwell, what was he doing in Glenraven? And if he wasn't Amos, what was he doing watching her?

Magic, she thought. It's all tied together and wrapped up in one big, incomprehensible package of magic.

She watched him work his way through the milling crowd of servants and retainers and entertainers and hangers-on; she kept her head down and pretended to eat. Should she run out of the room before he worked his way past the dance troupe and the mob of waiters and maids, or sit tight and find out what he wanted? She decided to sit tight. He couldn't very well do something to her in full view of everyone. And since at the moment she knew nothing, if he gave her information of any sort, she would be ahead.

Meanwhile, she ate steadily. When his hand dropped onto her shoulder, she didn't even have to pretend to jump.

"Julie Bennington!" The voice was Amos's . . . but not quite. Some of the stiffness and prissiness was gone.

She looked up at him and smiled brightly. "Amos?"

"Of course!" He smiled and the smile, too, was familiar but not quite right. It was too easy, too broad and confident. "Who else could I be?"

She tilted her chin up and looked at him out of narrowed eyes. "Someone who looked like Amos but who knew how to ride a horse," she said coolly.

He blanched, then hid his response with a laugh. "If you saw me earlier, why didn't you stop me and say hello?" He smiled again, that broad, too friendly, too-happy-to-see-her smile, and nodded toward Sophie. "Who is your friend?"

Sophie looked up and gave him a polite half-smile.

Jayjay sighed. "Sophie Cortiss, my best friend. This is Amos Baldwell, who had a bookstore in Peters and who sold me the interesting book we have."

"I hope you're enjoying your visit." He tapped the shoulder of the man next to Jay and gestured for space; the man nodded and immediately all but shoved himself into the lap of the man beside him. "I cannot believe I ran into you here! Mind if I join you?"

Since he'd already stepped over the bench and was halfway seated, Jay said, "Of course, not at all." She rested her elbow on the table and leaned her jaw into her hand. "What are you doing here in Glenraven?"

His grin broadened. "Quite a coincidence, isn't it?"

"I don't believe in coincidences." Jay didn't bother to smile, but Amos seemed oblivious.

"My brother and I decided to take a vacation. We're touring the country for the next month."

"I see." Jay found something reptilian about him—something she had never noticed in her brief encounters with him in the bookstore. His cheerful smile and bright enthusiasm did nothing to conceal the coldness and calculation in his lying eyes. She could see that he wasn't at all the person he'd portrayed himself to be. He was a user, a manipulative, lying bastard, and he wanted something from her. He wanted something, and she didn't doubt for an instant that what he wanted would be trouble for her. Or maybe she was just projecting her feelings about Steven onto this stranger. He started talking about the sights he and his brother visited, and Jayjay let his voice wash over her without taking in any of the words.

Magic. He's tied up with the book, and because of his connection with the book, I'm somehow bound to him.

Maybe she was projecting. She still didn't like it.

" . . . wonderful . . . I'm so glad you agree!" he said. Something in his voice alerted her that she had just missed something important. Jayjay realized she'd lost him; she'd been nodding along politely, but she hadn't been listening, and now she'd said the wrong thing.

"I'll tell my brother you've said yes; he'll be delighted to spend the day in such lovely company, and we'll take in all the sights and try out one or two of the restaurants."

Jay realized she'd agreed to spend the day with him. She wouldn't, though.

He'd paused for breath, waiting for a reaction from her.

"Well—" She stared up at the ceiling, to discover that the heads of more dead animals stared down at her with worried eyes. Damn right, she thought. Somebody lopped their heads off and nailed them to the wall. That would make anybody look worried. She smiled at Amos. "We've spent the whole day riding, and more than anything we wanted to sleep in until noon. Then we were planning on heading to the market to see what sort of fabrics were there. I shouldn't have agreed so quickly. Why don't we make it another day?"

Amos looked disappointed. "I'm afraid if we don't go tomorrow, we won't get to."

"We're planning on spending a couple of days here," Jay lied.

"We are?" Sophie sounded surprised. Jay hadn't realized she was even paying attention.

"Of course we are," Jayjay said, kicking her in the shin again. What a lousy time for Sophie to join in the conversation. "We have to make time to see the Aptogurria and the fortresses, especially Kewimell. And we wanted to rent a boat to go out onto the lake day after tomorrow."

"I can get you into the Aptogurria," he said. "The inside is quite a bit more interesting than the outside, but you have to know who to ask to be permitted in."

"Are we going to have time for all of that?" Sophie asked, missing Jayjay's cue.

"Yes." Jay glared murderously at her and mouthed the word, "No!"

"Oh," Sophie said, and nodded. "You're right. We'll have time for all of that." She smiled vaguely and returned to her meal.

But Amos was going to be insistent. "Really, it would be such a waste to have you here at the same time we are and not spend the day with you."

"We can't give you a whole day," Jay said, firm. An idea occurred to her. "But why don't we meet you here late in the afternoon? Four o'clock?"

Amos smiled. "Marvelous. I think it would be criminal of us to waste such a lovely opportunity. So I'll see you at four. If I don't run into you both in the market before then, of course." His smile grew broader, making Jayjay think he intended to do just that. "I await tomorrow, then." He rose. Across the room, the two human gorillas tracked him with their eyes.

"We'll have a wonderful time, I'm sure," Jay told him.

He stepped over the bench and seemed about to walk away; at the last instant he turned. "Incidentally, where are you staying?"

"Here." Jay didn't like admitting that, but she couldn't think of a convenient lie fast enough.

"Yes, obviously. You wouldn't be eating here if you

weren't staying here as well. The dining room isn't open. But what rooms are you in?"

Jayjay and Sophie exchanged glances; Jay noted wariness in Sophie's eyes, too. "I haven't the foggiest idea," she told him. "Some little guy took us through a maze to get there, and told us if we needed help to ring the bell. I don't think I could find my way back . . . or out, for that matter . . . if my life depended on it." She grinned. "I have a lousy sense of direction."

He chuckled; Jay saw a satisfaction in his smug smile that she didn't like at all. "So I guess I'll have to wait until tomorrow to see you."

She shrugged and gave him the best "I-am-an-airhead" smile she could manage. "I guess so."

He left, and Jay leaned over and whispered in Sophie's ear, "Do you have a pen or a marker or anything on you?"

Sophie watched Amos strolling back to his seat; her eyes were narrowed and she'd pressed her lips into a thin, distrustful line. "Mmmm-hmmmm." When he sat down, she rummaged in the leather travel pack she wore around her waist. After a moment, she came out with a blue felt-tip marker, a green felt-tip marker, a soft-lead pencil with a plastic cover to protect the point, two roller-ball ink pens, both in black, and a piece of pale yellow chalk.

Jay stared. "Wow. What else do you have in there?"

"A little bit of everything." Sophie looked smug.

"I believe you."

Sophie turned her attention to her food. She kept her head down and her voice low, and said, "So what do you want with them? Something sneaky, I presume."

Jay took her cue from Sophie and pretended to be engrossed in her meal. "Yep. Going to make sure I leave us a trail of bread crumbs to follow back to the front door," she said. "I figure we can be a long way from here by four P.M. tomorrow if we get out of town at dawn."

Sophie inclined her head by the tiniest amount. "Sounds like an exceptional idea to me. I didn't care much for your . . . friend."

"He's a creep and a liar. I didn't know it in Peters. In fact, I liked him a lot when I met him in Peters. But he's lying now."

"But it is the same guy?"

"Absolutely. And he's tied up in this, and every instinct I have says he's trouble."

Sophie looked at her solemnly. "Our instincts agree."

Twenty

Hultif sat in the deepest part of his tunnel, watching Herself. She was engrossed in plotting, the fiend. Up in the Wizard's Bell, she could keep track of so much. If she chose to spy on him, he would be dead between one beat of his heart and the next. She wasn't looking in his direction, however, and he didn't think she would. Not for a while, anyway. He had given her too much else to think about.

He longed for a return to the days when the Aregen ruled Glenraven. When that day came, he would crush her, as she had crushed his family, the majority of his potential mates, and his rightful future.

He double-checked his chart of omens and actions. Change approached, the massive, complete change that could send the corrupt Watchmistress and all her Alfkindir cronies to their deaths, or make them so strong nothing would wedge them from their places for another thousand years. Coming, coming, sure as a storm when thunderheads filled the valleys . . . but the change wasn't guaranteed to fall in the favor of Hultif and the few remaining Aregen, who had bowed beneath oppression since they fell from the Watch, and who now hid themselves away, awaiting a shift in the prevailing winds. This change was only potentially an ally.

He stared a moment longer at her cold, hated face, and then with one claw he tapped the rim of the flat metal viewing bell that hung on its rack on his table. Light flashed across the metal surface, light red as fire and blood, and when that light cleared, his mentor stared back at him.

"You're taking a risk, calling me."

Hultif nodded. "Yes. But I have the information you needed. The field shifts and tears and becomes more unreliable every day, but I think these predictions should serve you." He held the pages up to the bell one by one, and his fellow conspirator on the other end copied them rapidly.

When the other finished, he nodded. "News this good is worth a risk—but we can't lose our chance here, boy. Can't. You and I won't live to get another, and if we die, the Aregen bloodlines die with us."

"I know." Hultif sighed. "She doesn't suspect me yet, but she'll have to realize what I'm doing sooner or later. When can I leave my post here?"

The other growled, irritated. "When she takes the bait, boy. Only when she takes it."

Twenty-one

"I see the next one." Jayjay flicked the pencil beam of the pocket light onto a little x of yellow chalk yards away, then slipped down a corridor, her finger smudging out the last x as she went. Sophie hurried behind her, listening for any sign that their departure had been discovered.

"How much farther can it be?"

Jay shrugged. "I don't know. It's taking forever to get where we're going, but it *was* a long way to the room."

It had been. Sophie couldn't deny that. The awful feeling that their luck was going to run out at any time and that they were going to get caught weighed on her.

Will it be here? she wondered. Is this the moment the premonition warned me about? Will I die this morning?

If someone did come along and questioned their presence in the halls, they had an alibi. The two of them intended to say they were going out to visit the Aptogurria. But this seemed so much more dangerous than simply sneaking out of a bed-and-breakfast. Sophie hoped she and Jay were being ridiculous, and that Amos was simply a nice, if pushy, bookseller who meant well. She'd love to think her presence in Glenraven was linked to nothing more sinister than a tourism board's decision to open the place up. But she and Jay had talked long into the night, discussing Jay's discoveries with the book and bouncing hypotheses off each other until, weary of speculation, they'd dropped into exhausted sleep.

Sophie didn't like the idea of magic, she certainly didn't intend to be anyone's hero, and some little part of her was beginning to insist that things back home weren't as bad as she'd led herself to believe. That maybe disappearing into the wilds hadn't been her brightest idea.

"Yes!" Jay looked back and grinned; her teeth looked very white in the predawn gloom. "The dining room."

"We're almost out of here." Sophie shivered, reacting to fear as much as to cold.

They slipped into the dining room, and immediately heard voices through the door that led to the foyer. One of the voices sounded a lot like the man Jayjay had introduced her to the night before; it had been a rich, vibrant baritone that Sophie would have thought unique. She glanced at Jayjay to see if her expression revealed anything, then glanced back at the door. The voices got louder.

"They're coming this way," she whispered.

Jayjay sucked in a quick, nervous breath and looked around the room. "Under the table."

It wouldn't provide much cover, but if no one looked directly at for them, it might be sufficient.

Sophie dove under the table and tucked herself toward the inside of the "U," crouching beneath the ledge of the little bench. She thought it a pity the Glenraveners didn't cover those massive trestle tables with cloths of some sort; she and Jay could have hidden indefinitely then.

Jayjay crouched in front of her, down on hands and knees. Both of them held still; Sophie prayed.

The door opened, and Amos Baldwell walked in, accompanied by several men wearing the livery of the Wethquerin Zearn and carrying weapons. Amos spoke to the men in the sharp tones of command, and Sophie became aware that though she heard his meaning as English, he spoke Galti. That killed any last hope that he was merely a bookseller from back home. Or a tourist. Or benign.

She crouched lower and held her breath. Please don't see us, she thought. Please, please don't look down.

Leather boots with jangling spurs stomped past, inches from her left hand, two pairs, then four, then eight, then twelve.

" . . . eadennil nrembe ta doshi Julie Bennington ve Sophie Cortiss besho terdelo meh. Condesheldil trehota ve berdo becco . . ."

The boots were past them then, and the voices faded quickly.

Sophie didn't care. One of the men with Amos had mentioned both of them by name. Jay glanced back at her. "We were right," she whispered.

Sophie nodded.

Jayjay crawled out from under the table and reached a hand down to pull Sophie up. "We're in real trouble. Lestovru and Amos and the book and the magic . . ." She glanced around for any signs of further danger, her face pale in the darkness.

They opened the door into the entryway carefully; it swung back silently to reveal the empty, dreadfully decorated hallway beyond.

"Nobody in any of that armor, is there?" Sophie whispered.

"I hope not. If there is, we're done for."

A premonition flashed across Sophie's field of vision—both of them dead, in nameless open graves in the midden behind a foreign castle. And no matter how hard her friends or her husband looked for her, they would never find anything to tell them what had become of her. Glenraven wouldn't open its doors for them as it had for her. It would devour her, devour Jay, and they would have ceased to exist without even a footprint to mark their passage. Sophie followed her friend down the hallway and out the massive front door, which opened without difficulty.

"Which way were the stables?" Jay asked.

Sophie pointed. "Back there . . . the kid took the horses that way."

They kept close to the side of the building, staying in the darker shadows. The sky was beginning to gray, and Sophie wished the two of them had managed to sneak out the door an hour or two earlier. If they had, they wouldn't have heard Amos's mastery of the local language, but they didn't really have to have their suspicions confirmed, and they would have been well away from the Wethquerin Zearn before the sky brightened enough to make them easy targets. As things stood, by the time they retrieved their horses and tack and got everything together, they were going to be parading out of the courtyard in front of God and everybody.

The stables lay straight ahead, slightly downhill from the main building and in a pool of darkness. No sound yet came from them; Sophie wondered how much longer she and Jay had before the stable hands came out to begin cleaning and feeding their animals.

"Run straight across the clearing and keep low," Jay said, pointing out the route she'd picked. "Through the darkest of the shadows right there."

Sophie nodded and followed; she knew horses, but Jay, with her odd childhood history of hunting and hiking and wandering in the remote reaches of God-only-knew-where with her parents, had a good feel for cover.

They skulked across the clearing, over the fence, and into the stables; no one cried out, no dogs barked, no grinning workmen rose up out of the darkness to bar their way. The stable doors were open; the sweet smell of hay and feed and horse rolled out, and for an instant Sophie felt tears well up, felt her throat tighten. They were Karen smells.

Those smells almost took the fight out of her. What was the use? She'd go back home, but her little girl wouldn't be there. She thought longingly of quitting, giving up, giving in to whatever disaster stalked them and plotted after them. She could embrace the night.

But Jay would be alone, and Jay wasn't ready to quit. One of them would have much less chance of surviving than two—and she couldn't abandon Jay. She couldn't give in. She would keep trying a little longer. For Jay. Just until she knew Jay was safe. That's what friends were for.

Jayjay leaned against a stall, breathing hard. "Now all we need to do is get our horses and get the hell out of here."

Sophie said, "If they're all from the same stable anyway, let's take the closest four."

"In this part of the world, they probably hang horse thieves."

"That's the least of our worries," Sophie said, and after considering it for an instant, Jay agreed.

"Time does matter more right now. Horse thieves it is."

Jayjay brought the first horse out and hooked two holding ropes into his halter. She ran into the tack room and came out with saddle and saddle blanket, tossed the blanket across his withers and adjusted it, then dropped the peculiar high-cantled saddle into place and tightened the girth. Sophie saw the horse suck in a big gulp of air; his belly distended. Jayjay didn't appear to notice.

"Walk him and retighten that girth before you get into the saddle," Sophie said.

Jay, who had gone for the bridle, turned. "Why?"

"That one has decided he wants his belt loose for the trip . . . and you probably don't."

Jayjay glared at the horse. "Most of the time I'd rather have a bicycle to ride and see you guys cooking over the campfire." The horse flicked an ear in her direction and regarded her with one huge, contemptuous brown eye.

Sophie had her mount's hooves checked and had him saddled and bridled, the girth tightened and double-checked, and the saddlebags loaded, balanced and in place before Jayjay got *her* mount to accept the bit. Jay looked up to find Sophie leading out her choice for spare horse, and blew out her breath in a snort that could as easily have come from one of the animals.

"I'm sorry about this, Sophie. I never would have considered you coming with me if I'd known about the horses."

"I know," Sophie said. She looped the lead for her spare horse into one of the metal rings worked into the back of the cantle and knotted it securely. "I know. It isn't your fault. I invited myself, and I'm dealing with the horse part of this well enough." That wasn't particularly true, but Jay didn't need anything else to worry about. Sophie sighed and went to help Jayjay get her spare horse ready, since she was still struggling with her saddlebags.

A few minutes later, they waited, mounted and still, in the doorway of the stables. Liveried men moved out in the courtyard, blocking the route to the road and freedom.

"How are we going to get out of here?" Sophie felt heartsick. If they'd only been a few minutes faster, they could have gotten away before the day at Wethquerin Zearn began. Now, though, the pink promise of daylight glowed across the rocky eastern horizon and people moved in the courtyard, down the road, up the road. . . .

The bells began to ring through the little city. Somewhere nearby, an all-male choir began a mournful contrapuntal song, voices soaring. And the liveried men in the courtyard, still shouting at each other, ran for the doors into the main house, and breakfast.

Jay managed a tiny smile. "Saved by the bell."

Sophie groaned.

They trotted out the stable door and across the temporarily empty courtyard—and then down the road.

Twenty-two

Hultif followed the serving wench into Aidris's morning room. Aidris glanced up at him and smiled, content. He would have what she wanted; if he didn't, he wouldn't have dared present himself at her door.

Aidris took the tray the scrawny Machnan girl offered and chased the child out of the room. She set the food on the table in front of her and lifted the silver dome. Ripe berries, hard brown bread and crumbling cheese, wine, meat served nearly raw. It looked lovely. Evidently the disappearance of one complaining cook had done wonders for the efficiency of the kitchen help. She sawed off a large slab of bread with her dagger and crumbled some of the cheese onto it. Only then did she bother to turn back to the patient, subservient Hultif. "What have you found?"

Hultif squatted at her feet and briefly rested his muzzle in her hand. The gesture came from his childhood, when he had run to her for comfort. That he should regress in such a fashion now, that he should feel the childish need for her comfort after so many years, unnerved her far more than seeing a vision of her face reduced to bone in the black mirror the day before.

"Death rides two horses, Mother," he told her softly, his face still buried in her hand. The words came out muffled. "It rides in from a place beyond the known, and it brings devastation to you and all yours."

"Speak plainly."

"Wizards. Machnan wizards, powerful beyond words, ride here to destroy you now."

"You're certain?"

"These are the truest and strongest of omens. I have never been more sure of anything than I am of what I tell you now."

"Wizards." She stabbed the meat with her dagger, lifted the entire slab to her mouth, and ripped a bite away. The flavor was superb, but the meat itself was tough. She'd insisted that her morning meat come only from Machnan children less than ten years of age. This meat surely came from a boy grown far past that. The muscle was dense and a bit fibrous. Perhaps she needed to emphasize her point more clearly to her Machnan cooks. She was certain she could make them understand.

She considered Hultif's concern over the wizards. "Glenraven's magic weakens daily. While my own power remains constant—perhaps even grows—the magic of my enemies dwindles until now I sense none who can hope to stand against me." She frowned, tapping thoughtfully on her front teeth with one claw. "Your worries would seem exaggerated, yet your omens suggest the danger is real. How can this be?"

"These two are fresh somehow. They've found a new source of magic. They are strong enough to destroy you."

"Well." She closed her eyes, considering. Her Watchers stripped Glenraven of its magic when they fed. They didn't need the magic—they desired only the souls of those they hunted—so what magic they stripped from their victims, they stored and fed to her.

"You've identified the problem. Have you also identified our solution?"

"The omens are very bad. We may have no solution. Our hope is thinner than a spider's silk." He looked up at her and added, in a voice so soft that she almost couldn't make out his words, "But spider's silk is strong, Mother, and we might yet cling to this faint hope, too."

She nodded, irrationally annoyed at his melodramatic presentation. He had managed to send a tiny knife of fear into her gut, in spite of the fact that she knew she was stronger than anything that could attack her. She didn't like feeling fear. So that he wouldn't suspect that he had unnerved her even a little, she tore off another bite of meat and washed it down with a swig of wine. "Tell me what you have discovered without decorating the facts." She was pleased to hear that the edge in her voice sounded like nothing more than annoyance.

"Send your hunters to bring the wizards here to you, where you may study and later destroy them. The omens are clear. You must seek out these avatars of your destruction and win them over as your allies."

"And how are my hunters to find them?"

"I will tell you the exact moment and direction the omens dictate. Just have your hunters ready."

"I'll have Bewul put together a party immediately."

But Hultif shook his head. "No. No, no, no. Mother—you must send the traitor Matthiall after them. You must pretend to trust him, and you must elevate him over even Bewul. For the time, make him your favorite. Only his actions can bring the wizards to you and deliver him into your hands at the same time."

Aidris frowned at Hultif. "Pretend to trust Matthiall. I don't like that. Matthiall is so . . . unpredictable." She sighed. Hultif gave good advice. "Very well. Matthiall will head this hunting party. What else?"

"Nothing else. Only have them ready to leave in an instant. I will monitor the omens constantly, and notify you the second they are most propitious for your success."

"You've done well, dear child." She smiled at Hultif even as she considered giving him to her Watchers and taking his magic for herself. His omen reading served her well, but he alone was aware that she was in some way vulnerable. If he ever determined some way to make use of that information, he could hurt her. Better to destroy him before he had the chance. "When you leave, send me Matthiall and Bewul. I shall inform them of my great pleasure in Matthiall, and of my decision to honor him with a command."

He bowed and brushed his muzzle against her hand again, obviously touched that she called him her child when she had not done so in years. "You are our one true hope, Mother." He smiled up at her, his lipless mouth stretched back along his muzzle clear to his knife-edged molars.

She dismissed him, still smiling, thinking, The moment this threat is over, I'll grind the bones of your ugly grinning face into flour, little monster.

Twenty-three

Jay felt better. Getting out of Zearn proved ridiculously easy compared to getting out of the Wethquerin Zearn. Unwatched, unquestioned, she and Sophie rode down the road they'd come in on, through the market where vendors set out their goods and called half-heartedly after the two of them as they passed; past the barracks where now no men leaned out of balconies; past the fields on either side of the road outside of the walls where more soldiers practiced fighting each other on horseback and on the ground, using swords and pikes, where they practiced formations; through the cool dew-laden morning air that was not the blessing it could have been. The stillness before the day warmed held into the walled city the miasma borne of rotting garbage and raw sewage and smoky early morning cookfires, and the stink followed them out and clung in Jay's nostrils far past the point where she believed she could still really smell the place.

They traveled against traffic; most of the people on the road headed toward the city. Many of the peasants carried vegetables or heavy, anonymously lumpish bags. They herded their children, who toiled along with them under the burden of the things they brought to sell at the market, or they herded livestock. Their bodies, their clothing, their faces, spoke eloquently of the grinding poverty, sickness and disease and shortened life spans that were their lot. They chatted with each other as they traveled, they laughed and shouted, they evidenced the excitement that travel to a market fair and a day away from the routine of their lives engendered, but when Jayjay looked into their eyes, she saw hunger and poorly healed grief and the same fear she'd seen in the faces of the men and women and children of Inzo.

Their faces were a slap to the comfortable notions she'd held about the goodness of life prior to what she had considered the dehumanizing effects of mechanization and industrialization and progress. Life in the Middle Ages hadn't been full of pageantry and chivalry for the great mass of people. These peasants who trudged by her were the great masses, and they were stoop-shouldered and gray-faced and rotten-toothed and gaunt. They shared their homes with livestock and rats, pissed in trenches, bathed rarely, ate when their crops survived the rats and the birds and the late frosts and the early snows and went hungry when the crops didn't. Their children died in droves. So did they.

She wanted to find Glenraven's leaders and shake them until their brains rattled. How could they keep their people trapped in such misery? All her guidebook's enchanting descriptions of this last untouched medieval paradise failed to mention the completely modern pain it rode upon.

She felt the bitter taste of helpless rage. Why didn't someone do something?

They reached the end of the guarded road that led to Zearn. It branched off into a main road then, heading south toward the gate back to the world they knew, and north, deeper into Glenraven.

Jay, riding first, turned right. The road to the right

led south. Back to the gate. Back toward home, and safety, and the troubles they both knew and understood. Sophie had said she didn't think she was going to make it home, that she'd had a premonition she was going to die in Glenraven; the faintly bemused, almost grateful expression on her face when she'd told Jay that had scared Jayjay silly.

"I want you to get back, though. You aren't ready to die."

They left the fields behind; left the soft droning of bees from an apiary they could see near a small, isolated farmhouse; the weeds and wildflowers of the ground lying fallow between the crops of wheat and barley and millet, the hide-and-seek light of the sun as it dropped behind little, fat clouds and slid back out again. They moved into forest, and the weight of the air around them changed. As they moved into the tunnel of cool green overhanging boughs that wove a roof over the road, the sun didn't just hide. It lost its potency, gave over its dominance of the day to a tenebrous, watching twilight that crouched, hushbreathed and waiting. Waiting for what?

"Jay?"

Sophie's voice breaking the silence like that sent superstitious little shivers down Jay's spine. "What?"

"They're going to come after us."

Jay didn't say anything for a long time. She didn't need to ask who Sophie was talking about. "I know," she admitted at last. "I know. I simply don't know why. Why do you think we ran into Amos? Why did our guide disappear? What do they want from us? Do you have any theories?"

Sophie shook her head and looked down the road. "No. But I have a bad feeling about the way we're going. They'll look for us this way, because this is the shortest route to the gate. I can feel it. My heart is racing and my throat is dry and I have this itch between my shoulder blades that is giving me the creeps."

Jayjay nodded. "I'm a little edgy, too." A few peasants passed, but the gloom in front of her was so deep she couldn't tell if any more followed. And she hated the way the forest swallowed sounds, so that mere moments after the people moved by her, their chattered conversation muffled into silence. She and Sophie and their four borrowed horses seemed all alone in the world.

"Maybe we should have taken the road from Zearn to Inzo, and then back to the gate," Sophie suggested. "That route avoided this forest."

"There's a road here," Jay argued, but without much feeling. "It's dirt, but it's kept up. It's the shortest way to get where we're going." The forest ate her words so that even to herself she seemed to be whispering.

Sophie didn't answer, and Jay couldn't think of anything else to say. They rode for a long while, while gloom bore down on Jay and Sophie's premonition gnawed at her. Then Jay caught a sound in the distance, and reined her horse to a stop. "Sophie? Listen!"

Sophie came to a halt, too, and the two of them strained to hear. Sophie's face froze, and, spine rigid, she turned the horse back the way they'd come. "That way . . . horses, Jay. A lot of them, coming fast."

"So soon?"

"So soon. I'd hoped they wouldn't notice we were gone for a little while yet."

Jayjay looked at the woods around them. The hard dirt road beneath their horses' hooves showed little sign of their passage. A troop on horseback would obliterate that, if they rode past fast enough to miss the point where the freshest prints stopped. If they didn't, she and Sophie could at least give them a run for their money before being captured.

"Into the woods," she said. "We'll wait until they've gone by, then decide what we ought to do next."

Sophie nodded.

The huge trees grew far apart, and their vast canopies were so dense little underbrush grew beneath them. The forest had an almost parklike appearance, though Jay couldn't help thinking of the park as being one Vlad the Impaler might have found homey, but it provided little cover. "We're going to have to go in deep," she said.

The soft humus covering the forest floor killed even the dull clop-clop their horses had made on the packed dirt road. Now the only sounds Jay could hear were the sounds of her breathing, the soft snorts of the horses, and the occasional creak of the leather saddles. The wide spaces between the trees and the smooth ground permitted them to urge their horses to a trot. They moved steadily away from the road, trying to get deep enough into the darkness of the forest that they would be effectively invisible—far enough that if their horses whinnied greeting to the troop pursuing them, humans wouldn't be able to hear the sound.

Jayjay looked over her shoulder and noticed they reached a place in the woods where the road was a series of pale tan squares peeking between massed trees. "Sophie," she said, "This will do, I think. We'll still be able to see them ride by from here, and maybe tell if they're looking for us. But I don't think they'll be able to see us."

Sophie slipped out of her saddle and dropped lightly to the ground. Jay decided to wait in the saddle, watching from sixteen hands' height. If they watched from different vantage points, they stood a better chance of not missing anything. They could no longer hear the thundering hooves of the approaching horses; the trees muffled the sound. The gentle susurrations of wind through the leaves overhead did the rest; that tiny nearby whisper would have drowned the noises of a war.

They waited. They waited a long time. The riders must have been farther off than they had sounded. Did that mean there were more of them? Jayjay wondered. Possibly. Probably.

Sophie pointed left, and Jay squinted through the trees. She caught movement, a flash of something red, bits of blue, dull gold. Then more red, and lots of gleaming black—men in uniform, galloping horses. Jay couldn't begin to guess how many, but the line of moving color streamed from the place where she could first see the road to the place where the last of it disappeared behind trees, rolling over the road like a river that had overflowed its banks. At its height, she and Sophie could once again hear the hoofbeats. They sounded almost as loud as the pounding of her pulse.

"Jesus."

Jay looked over to find Sophie's eyes wide and round and horrified.

Her friend murmured, "So many? After us?"

The flow of the human river broke, became a trickle heading left, then vanished at last into silence. Jayjay shivered. "What have we gotten ourselves into?"

"Trouble." Sophie's frown said more than her single word. It said, *Maybe my premonition didn't tell me everything. Maybe neither one of us is going to make it out of here.*

Jayjay lifted her chin and forced herself to give Sophie a reassuring smile. "We're going to walk away from this."

"Right." Flat, emotionless, Sophie's single uttered syllable sent a wave of nausea through Jay. *I'm not,* it said.

They were, though. Sophie had been through enough. Jay was going to get her back home alive. If she couldn't make Sophie believe that—hell, if she couldn't even make herself believe it—that didn't mean she couldn't make it happen. All she had to do was keep going.

"Let's wait a few more minutes until we head back to the road. If they realize they've passed us and turn around, I don't want to be standing out there waiting for them. Once we know what to expect, we'll get out of here."

"Fine." Sophie settled her back against a tree, her mount's reins loosely looped around her fingers.

Sophie wasn't buying into Jay's false confidence. Jay only had so much to spare; she decided to wait in silence, and settled into her saddle, letting herself slouch back into the cantle. It might be a long wait.

Insects buzzed and chirped around them, busy in the cool, dark forest. The leaves whispered wordless stories. Jayjay listened to the calls of birds. She recognized the sound of starlings, the hoot of an owl up past his bedtime.

The space between her shoulder blades began to itch.

She shivered again and listened hard, focusing on the sounds behind her; she heard nothing out of place, all four horses were completely calm, the normal forest noises did not suddenly fall silent. Yet she felt compelled to turn around; she was certain something watched her. She refused to give in to the compulsion.

I'm being ridiculous, she told herself. *I'm acting silly. Danger hunts us on the road. This is the safe place.*

The hairs on the back of her neck and on her arms stood up, not reassured by her logic. Sophie glanced up at her. Fear radiated from her; she breathed quickly and her eyes stared, wide and white-rimmed. She felt it, too.

Behind me. All I have to do is look behind me.

For an instant she was eight years old, crouched under the sheet on her bed with her head under her pillow, the cool night breeze touching her through the thin cotton; for an instant, she was eight and she knew something watched her from above her bed. A ghost. White mist and a woman shape, with terrible teeth and glowing eyes. Waiting.

And then she wasn't eight anymore; she was thirty-five, and she refused to be intimidated. She turned slowly, telling herself there would be nothing behind her but trees.

She was right. The woods sat quiet on the dark, dank earth; the gentle breeze still stirred, the insects still hummed. Nothing. She should have felt better but she didn't; she waited, instead, for the something that hid behind the parklike facade, the something that watched from just beyond the outside edge of her field of vision.

"Jayjay?"

Jay tried to answer, and though her mouth opened, the sounds would not come. She looked at Sophie, scared, and found Sophie back in the saddle with fear settled on her shoulders and in her eyes.

"We need to get out of here," Sophie said.

Jayjay nodded. The cold clammy touch of dread stroked the back of her neck—stupid fear, sitting in an old woods in the early morning, safely hidden from the danger that chased after her, with nothing in sight but trees, without any reason to be afraid. She feared, but feared nothing real. It didn't matter. "Yes. Let's." She cleared her throat, trying to force the words to come easier. "We can travel slowly and listen for the soldiers."

"That sounds fine to me."

They trotted out of the woods. Jay would have urged her horses to a canter if that hadn't felt like an out-and-out retreat, like something shameful.

Once they traveled on the road for a while, the fear boiled off until it became only a tiny knot in her stomach, not much bother at all. Not gone, but not devouring, either. She felt better . . . but she didn't want to think about Glenraven anymore. She glanced at Sophie, whose face was once again composed.

Sophie noticed her attention and turned to her. "Why were we so frightened back there?"

Jay sighed. "Why does my Fodor's guide ask its own questions, Soph? I don't know." She fell silent and rode, listening to the slow plodding of hooves on dirt. Then she added, "I don't think I want to know. I can't help myself for feeling that something terrible waited back there, looking us over and trying to decide what to do with us. I'm probably being an idiot, but I want to get the hell out of here. I'm sorry I brought us."

They rode along together, neither speaking, companionably.

After a while, Jay drifted into reverie, and she realized she did want to talk about one thing, desperately—and that one thing had nothing to do with Glenraven.

She cleared her throat. "Sophie?"

Sophie's "Hmmm?" had the drowsy buzz of bees in a field of wildflowers.

"What's been bothering you?"

"Oh . . . nothing much. The usual."

Jayjay frowned. "It's more than that. It has to do with this person Lorin, doesn't it? The one the guidebook asked you about."

Sophie smiled—an enigmatic Mona Lisa smile—and nodded.

"I don't want to pry, but I'm worried about you, Soph. You talked about dying here as if that weren't such a bad thing. What's going on?"

"I'm feeling lost about this. I'm not sure that I want to discuss it, that I can make you understand something I'm not certain about myself. I always thought I knew myself pretty well; I mean, Mitch and I loved each other and we both loved Karen. We were such happy parents. But that became most of what we had with each other—Karen and her accomplishments and the fun we had doing things with her and watching her grow. Now Karen's gone and Mitch thinks if we had another baby, things could be the way they were. For us. Between us. But there are days when I can't stand to be in the same house with him, because he looks so much like her, and because he laughs the same way, and because every time I see him, I bleed." She twisted the leather reins between the fingers of her left hand and stared off into space. "I keep thinking the only way I'm going to breathe again is if I get rid of everything that I ever was. Become someone new.

"And this other person . . . well, there wouldn't ever be any question of another child. I'd never have reminders of the person I was before. Still, the whole situation has me thinking I've never really known myself, and I don't like that." Sophie fell silent. It was the sort of uncomfortable silence that made the muffled creak of the saddles sound like screams. Then Sophie sighed deeply and bit the corner of her lip.

"He might want kids," Jay said. "Men change so much after you marry them. Or they don't, but after you're married you find out who they really are."

"I don't know what you're going to think of me if I tell you this."

Jay frowned. "You're my best friend. Nothing you say could change that."

"Right." That flat affirmative that was really denial again. Sophie shrugged. "Oh, well. If we do survive this, and if I do make it back to Peters, you'll hear." She sighed. "Lorin is a woman."

Sophie couldn't have blindsided her more effectively if she'd hit her between the eyes with a brick. "You want to become a lesbian?" she yelped.

Sophie, startled, burst out laughing. She laughed for a long time, and when she finished, she wiped tears from her cheeks and sighed. "Jesus, Jayjay . . . that's what I love about you. You're all tact."

"Lorin, huh?"

"Lorin. Talsach."

Jay didn't know what to say. Finally she spread her arms wide and shrugged her shoulders. "This is going to sound trite, but, God . . . I hope it works out. Whatever working out means."

Sophie smiled, but she didn't say anything. Jay read the look in her eyes, the one that said, *Maybe this is what* working out *means.*

Twenty-four

Yemus Sarijann, who had invented the persona of Amos Baldwell for Jayjay Bennington, waved his hand to bring the army to a halt. He snarled and stared at the little metal ball affixed in a wire cage to the pommel of his saddle. A reassuring light glowed from it, the same steady golden light that had glowed there from the time he and his men headed down the Rikes Gate road. Jayjay's damned book called to the little globe the way a lodestone called to iron filings. His locator globe should have glowed brighter as he drew nearer the talisman; it should have dimmed to a dull, guttering red as he wandered astray. The damned book should have led him right to his heroes.

He snarled. Heroes. Lestovru, a decent man and a good soldier, had died on his orders to cover the entrance of these two heroes into Glenraven. The saviors of the Machnan, the saviors of magic; the book had declared both of them this by choosing them. The damned book had taken him to Peters, North Carolina, far outside his world. It had absorbed the magic from the lives of all of his people, had cost them everything they could afford to give. The Machnan had given willingly, because they were dying, magic was dying,

167

their world was dying, and they would offer everything they had to save it.

He'd spun the spell carefully. He'd woven it of his people's desire to live, of their hunger for the return of magic, of their love of Glenraven—and of their hatred for Aidris Akalan, the foul Alfkindir Watchmistress, and her monstrous Watchers. The spell had created an artifact that had taken the incomprehensible shape of an unreadable book, so he had spun in a language spell with the last of his magic and discovered that his spell had formed itself into a travel guide for tourists. It told him what he had to do from there. He had to take it out of Glenraven and across the seas. He had to find a place to display it. It would tell him when he'd found the place. He had to set it on a shelf, where it promptly disguised itself as another, different book, and there it languished. And he languished with it. Waiting. Knowing that in the world he'd left behind, time passed, friends died, and the magic seeped away.

When finally the damned book had chosen its unlikely heroes, he'd hurried home, knowing the book could carry on without him. At home, everything had changed, and nothing for the better. His father was dead, his mother imprisoned by Aidris Akalan for treason; his brother, Torrin, who had been a stripling youth when he left, had grown tall and powerful and bitter. Torrin looked into his returned brother's eyes and said, "Where were you when they took her away? If you hadn't sold our birthright for your dream of victory, we would have had the magic to save her."

And now it looked as if Torrin had been right. The book played games with him. It hid its location. It played with his locator stone. It taunted him.

He wondered if it had been taunting him all along, if Glenraven's magic had soured against the Machnan and had betrayed them in favor of the powerful

Alfkindir. He wondered if his "heroes" had come to destroy him utterly.

"Go back," he said. "We'll go slowly and look for tracks leading into the forest. They can't have come this far, but something has jinxed the stone."

A few of his men kissed amulets that hung around their necks. A few more looked up and murmured muffled prayers. The rest sat their horses stoically. None, though, begged to check some other route. He said the heroes had come this way, and they would follow him into the very embrace of the Watchers if they could just get them back. These men had ridden down the road through the Watchers' Wood knowing where they traveled. But they also knew they pursued the last hope of the Machnan. They wouldn't falter.

Twenty-five

One of the horses whinnied, and Sophie heard an answering whinny from the road ahead. She and Jay glanced from one another into the leafy, expectant darkness ahead. "Someone coming."

"Them?"

"Maybe."

"Back into the woods." Jayjay looked into the depths of the forest and Sophie saw her shiver.

"We don't have much choice." Sophie frowned, feeling sick inside.

They rode single file, urging their horses to a trot. Sophie almost believed that she would prefer to face the men who hunted after them than to go back under the silent watchful hush of the deep forest. The very trees seemed to watch; they waited; and the forest's inhabitants lurked in the long shadows, merely looking for a signal to leap out and devour her. But she could convince herself that her dread regarding the forest came from her imagination; she knew the soldiers were real.

Behind her, a man shouted, his voice harsh with excitement. Other voices took up the cry. Sophie and Jayjay both looked behind them. Vivid splashes of blue and red and gold moved through the trees toward them.

"Shit," Jay yelped.

That pretty much said it all. Sophie kicked her mount into a canter and passed Jay. She was the better rider of the two, after all, with years of trail and hunt experience. If both of them hoped to elude the hunters without breaking their necks or their horses' legs, she would have to take the lead. "After me, Jay," she growled as she swung past.

She submerged her concentration into the terrain, willing the rest of the world away. Her determined focus paid dividends. She and Jay negotiated the maze of trees and uneven ground without mishap. Most of the time they traveled at a canter, though twice the ground broke up and they found themselves reduced to a cautious, step-at-a-time walk. Behind them, their pursuers lost ground. In fact, Sophie was surprised at the speed with which she and Jayjay pulled ahead; she would have expected the soldiers to take advantage of the fact that they were on their own home ground, but if they had such an advantage, they didn't use it. Sophie began to think she and Jay would get away; then the ground descended abruptly into nasty, thorny, tightly grown underbrush that sprang up everywhere. The canopy overhead broke, but not into cultivated land. Jay found what looked like a deer trail and the two of them followed that. The trail led them at an easy angle down to the banks of a swiftly flowing stream. It was past midday. Sophie hadn't realized so much time had passed until she and Jay rode out into sunlight again and felt the dank chill of the forest replaced by the cozy warmth. She would have loved to find a place to hide in the thicket. The sunshine on her skin felt wonderful and welcoming, and the horrible feeling that she was being watched, a feeling that hadn't passed even in the heat of the pursuit, now left her entirely.

"They'll be right behind us," Jay said. She sat looking up and down the stream while her horses sipped from the stream.

Sophie looked back the way they'd come. The soldiers were still far behind them, but growing nearer. Sophie let her horses drink, too. She was risking the animals getting colic because she hadn't cooled them down before watering them, but she didn't know when she and Jayjay would find clean water again. Once they escaped, they would cool the horses properly.

She pulled both animals away from the stream before they had a chance to drink their fill. Later, she kept thinking, you can drink more later . . . if we're still alive.

"Sophie?" Jay's voice held a note of panic that stopped Sophie cold. "What is that?"

Sophie looked where Jay was looking—back the way they had come. She didn't see anything, but then she realized Jay wasn't referring to something she saw. Behind them, the sounds in the forest had changed. She could no longer hear the approach of the soldiers who hunted her. She heard men's voices, but they sounded farther away than they had been. And frightened. And over the sounds of their desperately shouted commands, she heard . . .

"Wind," Sophie said. She frowned. "In the forest."

Not even the faintest breeze brushed past her; yet in the trees, in the forest, wind moved. That didn't make sense. Wind moved over open ground; the shelter of the forest would stop it. *Should* stop it.

The wind in the forest blew harder, the soughing through the branches of the ancient trees now punctuated by hard gusts. Moaning.

A man screamed.

The horses shifted and stared toward the forest they'd left, their eyes rolling and their ears laid back.

Whatever was going on behind them disturbed the horses, too. That was a bad sign.

"I think we should get moving," Jay said.

Sophie agreed. Then she noticed a swirl of firefly lights moving through the trees, perhaps head-high or maybe a little higher; a *layer* of fireflies, like a floating carpet of them, beautiful to behold, sparkling gold and soft pale green and white through the darkness, stars fallen from the sky and brought to life and she wanted, wanted, wanted to move toward them, to go to them, to see, to touch, to experience—

A hand like a talon grabbed her arm and she snapped back to herself. "We need to get moving *now*," Jay said.

Sophie, still feeling the pull of those trembling, bewitching lights, nodded sadly. She felt as if she were being pulled away from a glorious, wonderful dream into the dark and ugly confines of reality. But when Jayjay pointed to the stream and urged her horses down into the fast, shallow water and rode away from the light and the wind, Sophie followed.

Behind them, a moment later, the screaming started in earnest. Not just one man screamed, but dozens. They howled and sobbed, and some of them laughed. Laughed—crazy, wondering, happy laughter—with the laughter cut off by shrieks, too. Sophie knew she was hearing men die. Those bubbling, tearing, wordless howls of pain that clung to the afternoon air and filled it with hellish darkness could not possibly have led to any other end. Those screaming men would not walk away, would not crawl away from whatever had found them in the forest.

Light—light as lovely as the sparkling trail of magic that poured from Cinderella's fairy godmother's wand— that light that had bewitched her and seduced her, that would have killed her.

She and Jay splashed along the pebbled bed of the stream as fast as they dared, and the screaming faded.

Faded. Finally stopped.

Sophie caught up with Jay and looked into her eyes; found in them a reflection of the haunted fearfulness she felt inside herself. Neither woman said anything. They kept riding, heading upstream. They kept their silence, listening for a breeze, and they watched through the dark stands of trees on either side of the water for any sign that a river of light flowed toward them through the air.

Will whatever killed the soldiers back there be what kills me? Sophie shivered. The idea of ceasing to exist hadn't seemed so bad to her when she'd first thought of it. She hadn't welcomed the thought of death; she had, instead, welcomed the idea of release of her grief and pain. But she had heard those men die. Her stomach knotted just thinking about it. While she still could not look at life with any joy, she could no longer view her impending death with equanimity.

Twenty-six

Yemus counted the men who had survived the retreat. Thirty-two. Out of one hundred seventy-eight men chosen for their skill, their ferocity, their ability to obey orders, their fearlessness . . . thirty-two remained. He could not let himself think of friends lost. Devoured by . . .

He couldn't think. His mind inched toward the images it held of what he'd seen, of Her Watchers, and it recoiled. His mind refused the nightmare reality, refused to let him examine the horrifying deaths his men had suffered. He could bring himself right up to the edge of the disaster, right to the point where his men, who had been frightened, lost their fear and started laughing. Started riding toward instead of away from the formless numberless hellspawn that pursued them. Thirty-two men had followed orders. Had dug their spurs into their horses' flanks and had refused to look back. Had run.

Like cowards. All of us, he thought. We abandoned our friends, our brothers, to that . . . that . . .

But they would have died. Every last one of them. Outside the forest, Yemus and his men had turned and waited, had prayed that some who had not followed immediately might still escape. No one else joined them. They waited an hour, calling. And an hour past that. Praying.

And then they had turned away. Ridden to Zearn.

To report his continuing failure to Torrin.

"They've joined the Kin," Torrin snarled. "Your *heroes* have joined the Kin. They're in league with *Her*, and with Her Watchers. We gave you our souls, all of us, every man and woman and child in Glenraven. We gave you our magic, and you brought us traitors."

"We don't know that the heroes didn't die, too. After all, they were in the forest, somewhat ahead of us. They could have been taken first."

"Then our souls, our magic, your talisman, might even now be in the hands of the Kin? In her hands? Should all of us then bend our necks and await our deaths?"

Torrin had forced Yemus to leave his chambers. Yemus, climbing the stairs to the Wizard's Bell in the Aptogurria, thought, I was going to bring them up here. I was going to tell them how much we needed them, how they were supposed to help us find a way to overthrow the Watchmistress and her Watchers. I was going to tell them everything.

What if they are in league with the Kin?

His logical side told him to be reasonable. How could they be Aidris Akalan's minions? Jayjay Bennington and Sophie Cortiss had been in Glenraven only one night when he found them. Granted, he didn't know where they had spent that night, but it wasn't likely that Aidris and her Watchers had picked them up as soon as they diverged from their itinerary, discerned not only that they were outlanders but that they were the outlanders who would bring down her rotten regime, turned them *and* the artifact to her own uses, and got them back out the door in time to plant them at his dinner table the next day.

The side of him that had lost most of his best men,

the men who would have spearheaded the final attack against Her, insisted otherwise.

He reached the top of the stairs and stepped into his Wizard's Bell. The late afternoon sunshine gleamed on the gilt top half of the sphere, and the mirrors angled outside of each window to catch and reflect that golden light threw it onto the blackwood diviner inlaid on the pale yew floor.

He settled himself in the center of the diviner and rested his hands on the smooth points of the ideogram of searching. The hands of all the wizards before him—both the Kin wizards whose people had built the Aptogurria and the Machnan whose heroes at last took it away from them—had worn the ideogram into the floor. Countless thousands of ghostly touches reached forward through time, binding Yemus to those other wizards as gently and invisibly, but as firmly, as the spirit of the earth bound his feet to the ground.

We have always been searching, he thought. Searching for answers we fear we'll never get. Searching for courage, for hope, for a promise of life better than this life. All of us search, until we would wear the very bones of the earth thin as hairs . . . and for all this searching, we do precious little finding.

He wondered if they were searching for answers to the wrong questions.

He pictured Jayjay and Sophie, closed his eyes, forced his doubts and fears out of his mind. Jayjay and Sophie. Jayjay and Sophie.

After a moment, a vision grew in front of him. The two of them riding up a shallow stream bed between sloping, brush-covered banks. On either side, forest. Endless, unbroken forest. He knew the stream, realized the two women had fled up it when he and his men were pursuing them. They'd stuck to it.

He couldn't have asked for more damning proof that his brother was right. Not only had they lived—he could have forgiven them that if somehow he had been able to see that they were still his heroes—but they lived, and that the two of them rode unmolested into the very heart of Her domain, through the hunting ground of Her Watchers, straight to her. *Untouched.* Any man who could see *that* and not realize the depth of treachery and disaster he faced deserved the death that would surely come his way.

He had to get the book back. He hoped he could recover Jayjay and Sophie, too, so that he could have them executed for treason to the Machnan. But if they gave the artifact to her, she could—*would*, why mince words?—destroy the Machnan utterly.

Twenty-seven

Sophie and Jay rode. East, east and south, east, east and north. Moving, moving, keeping themselves in motion, making some sort of progress, though they needed to be heading steadily southeast if they hoped to make the gate by nightfall.

They rode.

Their shadows rolled ahead of them in ever-lengthening lines. Trouble, Sophie realized. They should have passed a road, come to a bridge, seen a house or a planted field . . . something. But in the whole time they'd ridden along that stream, they had seen no sign at all that another human being existed on the planet. Not even a jet had overflown them, leaving its friendly white contrail in its wake.

Darkness pursued them. Night. Night, when people hid behind their walled cities and their locked doors while something unspeakable, something deadly, hunted the places they controlled with such confidence during the day.

Jayjay reined to a stop.

"What's the matter?" Sophie caught up with her and reined in, too.

"We're running out of time."

"We haven't found a place to spend the night." Sophie had been hoping they would find the gate and be out of Glenraven before dark, but she could tell that wasn't going to happen. She still hoped they would find a hotel where they could rent a room for the night. All she wanted was a single room with a lock on the door and shutters over the windows. She wasn't picky. She didn't care if she had to spend the night with live-stock, or fleas. But she wanted to be able to see other people, to feel that she might find some safety in numbers.

Jayjay looked miserable. "We can't keep hoping we're going to find a place indoors. And we're losing our light; if we keep moving, we'll end up trying to set up camp in the dark, and we'll have to make our preparations without being able to see what we're doing."

"What kind of preparations?"

"I don't know. It would be great to think we'd have time to build some booby traps, but I imagine all we'll be able to do is gather enough firewood to keep a fire going all night."

Sophie nodded. Jayjay was being logical. Practical. They were in trouble, neither of them had seen any signs that they were going to get *out* of trouble any time soon, and they needed to do whatever they could to protect themselves and minimize their risks before they lost what little chance they had.

Where there's life, there's hope, Sophie thought, and right on the heels of that she remembered that she hadn't believed in hope since Karen's death.

Maybe I believe a little bit, she thought.

The hellish sense of being watched returned, stronger as night drew near. They found a place on the opposite side of the bank from the side where they had seen the lights. It wasn't a clearing, but the trees were so huge and ancient and the overhead canopy of leaves so dense that the ground was clear in a space large enough to tether the horses, set up camp, and build a fire. They dropped their bags where they would pitch the tent and tied down their still-saddled horses; then, as the pressure of her fear became a physical weight, she and Jay went scavenging for firewood.

The horses were weary. They needed to be rubbed down, groomed, fed and given a good rest before they had to do anything else. Under normal circumstances, Sophie would have seen to their comfort before her own. Under normal circumstances. The invisible eyes of the forest threatened, though. The horses would wait. They would have to.

She and Jayjay stayed close to each other, gathering deadwood in a tight circle near their chosen campsite. Neither spoke. Sophie found the sound of her own voice frightened her, or perhaps what frightened her was the way the forest again swallowed sound.

They found several armloads of deadwood apiece. They stacked it next to their chosen tent site. Sophie suggested, and Jayjay agreed, that neither of them were going to want to walk away from tent and fire to get more wood.

They were scavenging for a fourth load when a soft breeze brushed against Sophie's cheeks. She froze, heart thudding in her throat; she felt as if she'd walked through a spiderweb and the sticky tangling silk clung to her skin and covered her nose and mouth and eyes.

"Breeze, Jay," she whispered.

Jay's head came up and she stared all around the campsite, through the forest, toward the stream, back the way they had come. Darkness sucked the last of the color out of the day, falling hard and fast, leeching life out of the clinging rim of twilight to the west, and Jay's face looked ghost pale, her eyes like two smudged black sockets in a death's-head. She cleared her throat—a nervous cough, a strangled sound. "It might be nothing more than a breeze," she said. "Maybe we left behind whatever killed the soldiers."

"Maybe."

"Still, I don't think we'd better get any more wood. We need to start the fire."

"Now," Sophie agreed. They scuttled back to the center of their camp, arms full of deadwood.

Sophie dug a firepit and filled it with wood; Jayjay hunted for and found the matches. Sophie located one of the quick-light tinder blocks she'd brought with her. She hated struggling with fires when she was hungry, and she'd decided those would come in handy; never in her life had she been more grateful for a bit of foresight. Between the two of them, they had a blazing fire going in just under ten minutes. The ruddy light flickered and grew bold, and the darkness danced back from the circle of flame. Sophie drew a slow, shaky breath. The pressure of fear eased up as she stared into that warm, reassuring light. Not gone, but better.

"Set up camp?" Jay asked.

"I'll take care of the horses if you'll get the tent."

Jay nodded. "We could use some water for cooking."

"We can eat cold food." The stream was very close, but Sophie didn't care. After that single puff of air, the breeze had died again, but it didn't matter; neither water nor food nor the promise of instant wealth could have drawn her from the dubious protection of the campfire. She removed the tack from the horses and stacked it in a neat pile to one side of the camp, brushed all four animals, cleaned their hooves, rubbed them down. They'd been able to drink from the stream at will for the last few hours. They were going to have to do without water for the night. She had nothing in which to carry water to them, and she had no intention of walking them one by one down to the banks of the stream for a drink. She had nosebags for each of them; she filled these with grain and slipped them into place, attaching them to the halters.

By the time she'd finished, Jay had the tent up, the gear stowed, and was sitting with their aluminum camp skillet on her lap, slicing slabs of Spam into it.

"Spam?" Sophie asked.

"A treat."

"Those cans weigh a ton."

"I only brought one. And one can of smoked salmon. I figured there might come a time when we wanted the comforts of home, and I couldn't think of any way to bring a Subway Sub Shop with me."

"But *Spam*?"

Jay shrugged. "I like it. So sue me."

She and Jay sat in front of the tent, watching the fire, smelling the mouthwatering ham scent of the cooking Spam as it sizzled on its metal tripod to one side of the fire. Sophie had a big supply of dried fruit and oatmeal-raisin cookies to add to the meal. They each had their canteens. They sat quietly, eating and staring into the dancing flames, looking for an omen. And waiting.

The strip of sky to the west over the stream glittered with stars. In the east, it paled with the luminous leading edge of the rising moon. Sophie heard owls hooting and insects droning, the *plish-shirr* of the stream as it hurried over its stony bed. No breeze stirred the still, sweet night air. No unidentifiable lights flickered through the forest.

The horses stood with their heads hanging, nose to tail, unconcerned.

"One of us ought to sleep," Jay said.

Sophie had been concentrating so hard on the faint sounds outside the circle of light that Jay's voice was as startling as a shotgun blast would have been, and she jumped. She glanced over at her friend. "Jesus, you scared me."

"Sorry. I was just thinking."

Sophie felt her heart stop racing, and she drew a deep breath. "I know. One of us needs to tend the fire and keep an eye on the horses. And, um, everything."

"So do you want first watch? I can take it."

Sophie snorted. "After that little burst of adrenaline, I don't think I'll be going to sleep any time soon. So I might as well take the first watch. Go ahead and get some sleep."

Jay's smile was grateful, and genuine. Sophie watched her crawl into the tent, and listened as she wrestled with her sleeping bag. Jayjay, the ultimate morning person, needed her eight hours of sleep at night more than anyone Sophie had ever known. She would be able to take her turn at watch . . . eventually. Sophie figured she would do well to wake her up at two A.M. That was morning, sort of. Jay could be a morning person then.

Sophie got her own rolled sleeping bag out of the tent and propped it behind her. She sat on the ground with her knees tucked to her chest, her arms wrapped around them. She rested her chin on her knees and watched the fire.

She didn't want to think about the night noises, about her on-again/off-again feeling that the forest watched her. As long as the horses were calm, she probably didn't need to worry. They would sense danger approaching long before she did. Night birds flew over, silent, their silhouettes blacker against the deep black of the trees, the velvet blue of the sky. Bats flicked past. The horses dozed, the fire crackled comfortingly.

Sophie put more deadwood on; it caught with little crackles and sputters, then burned with a rhythmically pulsing red-gold light. For a moment, she could imagine Karen and Mitch sitting across from her; smiling and chatting while they cooked marshmallows and sang ridiculous camp songs about the frog who went a-courting and the old woman who swallowed the fly. She smiled. She hadn't thought of that trip in a long time. She could see Karen sitting on a log, ten years old, front teeth outsized and crooked before she got started on braces, bright eyes laughing and mouth wide open as she bellowed, "I don't know WHYYYYYY she SUH-WALLOWED that fly—I guesss sheeee'll DIIIIEE!" Off-key. Karen couldn't carry a tune in a bucket; no . . . she couldn't carry a tune in sealed Tupperware. Karen . . . and Mitch . . . and her.

Sophie and Mitch toasted their marshmallows to a pale golden brown. Karen caught hers on fire, watched them burn, then sucked the liquid centers out from between cracks in the charcoal, insisting that they tasted better that way than anything else on earth. And Mitch sat there and let her feed the awful things to him, and got smears of charcoal all over his face. And Sophie laughed at him, and because she laughed, he tackled her and kissed her and smeared the charcoal on his face all over hers. And Karen sat there laughing like a wild thing, egging them on.

The horses' ears twitched in their sleep. Their tails flicked lazily back and forth, across each other's faces. Sophie put more wood on the fire.

They had a food fight. Got up the next morning, went fishing. Karen had put the worms on her own hooks, and took the fish off herself, gently removing the tines from the cartilage mouths, not rubbing the slime off the fishes' sides. Letting the little ones go, and one of the two bigger ones she caught. The other she gave to Mitch, informing him that was what she wanted for breakfast. By the time the sun was fully up and the mist burned off, she sat next to the fire eating a breakfast she'd earned.

So proud of herself. Ten.

At least Karen always knew how much she meant to us.

One of the horses snorted and twitched, raised his

head, looked around with nostrils dilated, ears swiveling in all directions. Sophie leaned forward, listening too. She heard nothing, and felt no breeze, and the horse, for all his alert concentration, didn't seem spooked. Just . . . curious. She decided that she didn't need to wake Jayjay up.

Still, because she was feeling paranoid, she threw more wood on the fire. It burned brighter, and the cheerful glow helped dispel some of her anxiety.

The horse grew bored with whatever he thought he heard. He whickered softly, and gradually his head dropped lower and he fell back to sleep. Sophie watched, grateful for the horses' presence. They made good watchdogs; defensively they would be worthless, but the fact that they were prey animals kept them cautious. If anything dangerous was out there, they would warn her in time for her to be ready.

She leaned back and watched the flickering patterns in the firelight, watched Karen's face, Mitch's face. Karen. Mitch. Karen . . .

A sharp, frightened whinny woke her, and with horror she realized she had drifted off while on watch. Her neck and back throbbed. She'd slept sitting. And she'd slept for a long time. The fire, so bright and comforting earlier, had nearly burned out. A few flames licked along the ends of pieces of wood at the periphery of the fire pit, and the embers still glowed red. But a coating of white ash filled most of the pit where in the center even the good-sized branches had burned to nothing.

The horses milled on their tethers, rearing and tossing their heads, stamping fitfully at the ground. The forest moved in around her, encroaching on the tiny, shrinking circle of light, watching with gloating eyes. She heard wind rustling through the tops of the trees, rattling the branches. The little patches of sky she could see proved the night was still clear, yet the wind whistled, growled, whispered.

A shiver crawled down her spine and nibbled at the hairs on the back of her neck. Now that it touched her, she felt this wind and knew it wasn't wind at all. It was the thing that had watched her and Jay as they rode down the road. Watched as they entered the forest to hide. Watched. Waited. It was hatred. Evil.

Hungry.

The fire, she thought. I have to build up the fire.

"Jay!" she yelled, but she didn't unzip the tent. She grabbed the smallest twigs she could find and scraped the few still-burning pieces of wood into the center of the fire pit.

"Jay!" She fumbled with her pack and came out with another of the tinder blocks.

"JAY! Wake up!" She shoved the twigs in among them, and watched with relief as they caught.

"Jesus, Jayjay, wake up! It's coming!"

She heard the sound of the zipper as she put bigger logs on top of the smaller ones. The fire was still tiny, still a dim light. Out over the stream, the brighter light of the moon competed with it.

Jayjay crawled out of the tent, bleary eyed. "What?" she murmured. She was still more than half asleep.

The wind began to howl. The horses panicked; rearing and plunging, they fought against the ropes that tied them. If they didn't calm down, they were going to break loose.

"Oh, my God!" Jayjay shouted. Sophie looked over at her long enough to ascertain that she'd awakened completely.

"Come help me with the horses!"

The horses were more than spooked. They were wild. Even as Sophie and Jay ran toward them, one of the animals broke its lead rope and galloped into the darkness. The other three screamed, and kept rearing and plunging.

Sophie moved to the two closest, hoping she would

be able to calm them. She approached slowly, making soothing noises. Both horses laid their ears flat against their skulls. One reared and struck at her with his hooves. The other kept fighting with the rope.

"Sophie—" Jay backed away from the horse she'd been trying to calm. "Soph, get to the fire. Now!"

Sophie heard the terror in Jayjay's voice. She backed away from the horses and moved immediately to the questionable safety of the edge of the fire pit. Again the horses were going to end up taking second place in her priorities.

Jayjay pointed out into the dark. Sparkles of light circled around the periphery of the camp. They weren't in a flattened cloud as they had been when she'd seen them streaming through the forest.

Jayjay made torches out of two of the good-sized branches and handed one to Sophie. "Better than nothing."

"Yeah." Sophie held the burning branch and tried not to shiver. The howling of the wind increased in volume; in its currents she heard eerie, ululating, trembling calls that wavered and sang; in every gust she heard a hundred discordant voices . . . or a thousand. What good would her torch do against such wind-borne death? What possible good?

Another horse broke free and charged out of the circle, into the darkness.

Sophie saw a tentacle of beautiful, glittering light coalesce in the direction in which the horse had fled. Whatever it was out there, it didn't only want people. It would take horses, too. The horse didn't have much chance. She bit her lip. She and the horses would probably share the same fate.

She didn't get long to worry about it. The wind worsened overhead by an order of magnitude; from the hard wind of a thunderstorm, it mutated into the screaming banshee of a tornado. It slammed down out of the treetops in a fierce howling, roaring, angry spiral, and now she saw the firefly lights en masse, a streaming spinning starfield of them, pouring down through the center of the funnel, illuminating it from the inside.

The tip of the tornado touched down in the center of the fire pit and sucked wood, embers and flames up in its twisting center. The insane babble of voices grew louder, louder than the tornado winds, but softer, too. Sophie realized she could hear the voices inside her head even more clearly than she heard them outside. They pounded on her skull from the inside until her head felt like it would shatter outward in an explosion as full of violent power as the impossible tornado that hung in front of her. She could feel the voices, and though the words were meaningless, she felt the hunger and rage and all-encompassing hatred that poured out of the source of them.

Jayjay dropped her torch and pressed her hands to her temples. Eyes squinted shut, she screamed. Sophie saw what she did only for an instant, before the pain became so intense that her own feeble torch dropped from her fingers—whiteblinding brilliant diamond-edged pain like a knife or a hundred knives, a thousand knives carving their way out of her skull at the same time—and she collapsed onto the soft leaf mold ground and vomited.

Somebody help us, she thought. Help us, please. I don't want to die like this.

Twenty-eight

Matthiall stalked along the Kin-road through the moon-bathed night, with the bitch's handpicked Kin and Kin-hera behind him. The worst of his enemies except for Her, the bastard Bewul trailed at the very back of the "hunting party," muttering to his friends.

Matthiall expected trouble from Bewul's contingent; they'd protested bitterly when Aidris Akalan declared him her much-beloved choice to lead the search for two deadly invaders that she insisted planned to destroy the Kin, and even more bitterly when she made a point of putting Bewul, until now Matthiall's equal, under his command. Matthiall would have protested, too. He hadn't made any secret of his hatred for the Watch-mistress and all she stood for, but he hoped that by acquiescing without complaint to her "promotion," he would startle her enough that he would get some insight into what she was really after.

It hadn't worked. He found himself still hunting through the darkness as the night wore on, waiting for something to happen, and he still had no idea what she really wanted. He couldn't even begin to imagine, and that bothered him. He'd always been able to see at least some design in her machinations before.

Perhaps she hoped that once the hunting party, twenty strong, got far enough into the forest, Bewul would turn on him and kill him, and that the rest of her loyal followers would help, or at least not interfere. The more he considered this, the more he thought it likely. How could the Watchmistress expect him to believe that two Machnan were heading toward Cotha Maest through the Alfkindir forest, past her vile Watchers, and that they actually posed a threat to her regime? How could Aidris hope he would believe *she* believed that?

One of his outrunners trilled a long low note; before they'd set out, Matthiall had designated this as the sign the invaders had been located. Now that he heard it, though, he braced himself, figuring that Bewul and his men had decided the time had come to kill him.

Then off to his left, he saw the flicker of light where no light should be, and he broke into a run, racing for the disturbance. Her Watchers—they'd hunted down something. And if for once Aidris was not lying, he should find the two Machnan wizards who were coming to destroy the Kin.

Twenty-nine

Jayjay had been dreaming of an underground world, of petrified forests and diamond rivers and uncounted impossible creatures with wings and fangs and wolf-ish slanting eyes, and she had been almost unable to shake the dream when Sophie tried to wake her. Even as she fought off the screaming voices in the back of her head, even as she faced her last few minutes of life, that dream wouldn't leave her.

Something is coming, she thought, though it was a stupid thought. Something was already there. Anything coming behind the trouble that had already arrived would be redundant . . . and entirely too late.

As the wind continued to scream, both remaining horses freed themselves. One broke the branch to which it was tied; the other managed somehow to pull out of the halter. The horses galloped away together, biting and slashing as they ran at things that kept themselves hidden from the torches' light. The terror of the horses' screams faded into a middle distance, became suddenly worse—more gut-wrenching—then died into abrupt, shocking silence.

The wind vanished as if it had never been. A shimmering cataract of the firefly lights coalesced out of the illuminated pillar that had filled the center of the tornado. Jay watched it, sick dread carving a hollow in her belly.

Sophie dragged herself to her feet and rested a hand on Jay's arm. "Now it's down to us."

"We could use a miracle."

Sophie managed a wavery laugh. She moved closer to Jay and asked, "You have any last thoughts here on how we might get out of this?"

"Sure. I am a veritable fountain of brilliant escape ideas."

"We aren't getting out of this, are we?" Sophie sounded resigned.

"Nope." Jayjay swallowed hard. "I think we've hit the end of the road here." She lifted her chin and pulled her shoulders back. If my life has been lacking in grace, she thought, at least I'll go out with a little style.

Beside her, Sophie wiped the back of one hand across her cheek, sniffled once, and nodded.

"You've been one hell of a friend," Jayjay told her, hoping she would have enough time to say what she wanted to say. "I really hoped this trip would help you . . . that it would help me, too, I guess. I'm sorry it didn't."

"I keep telling myself now maybe I'll get to see Karen again . . ." Sophie wiped her eyes harder than she had before.

"I know."

"But what if there isn't anything else?"

"I don't know."

They stood in the dead and terrible silence, and in front of them the lights pulled in tighter, moved together until Jay could make out the distinct three-dimensional forms of arms and legs, hips and full breasts, a face that grew more beautiful as it grew clearer—a woman of light as tall as a three-story building.

The woman of light smiled at them, the gentle smile a mother gave to her children. She knelt on one knee, then held out her arms to them. Jay heard the thing's voice as a crowd of whispers inside of her head.

> Come
>> come to me
> us we want
>> love desire
> want *want* you
>> love you we can give
> give you peace
>>> peace rest
>> silence
> love
> come

No, Jay thought. I don't think so. Not today.

"She's what the men saw, isn't she?" Sophie asked.

"Probably. Probably why some of them sounded happy at first." She backed up a step, and then another, moving cautiously away from the thing.

> you we you
>> need us
> need
>> I
> we can give
>> what you want
>>> everything
> *everything!*

The thing was more tempting than it had any business being. Jay didn't desire peace and silence and release from the troubles of the world. In spite of that, she found herself wanting to go to it. Wanting. She didn't want what it offered, but some traitorous part of her acted as if she did.

Sophie had taken the first two backward steps with her, but when Jayjay took a third, Sophie didn't follow.

Instead, she cocked her head as if listening. She held very still for a moment. "Oh," Sophie whispered. "Yes." She stepped forward.

Jayjay grabbed her. "No, Sophie. Bad idea. Bad idea, Soph. I don't know what it's telling you, but don't listen to it."

"Karen," she said softly. "She can take me to Karen."

"No she can't." Jay moved forward, locked both arms around Sophie's waist, and started backing. "She's lying."

"You don't know that."

Which was true, Jay reflected, tugging. She didn't know. The odds that the woman of light was telling the truth, however, seemed small enough to fit comfortably under the lens of an electron microscope, if electron microscopes had lenses.

Sophie pulled against her. Jay struggled, but they moved forward anyway; Sophie wanted this desperately, and her strength because of that was enormously greater than Jay's. Jay reflected that she didn't want anything.

Yes, I do, though. I want my friend to live.

She pulled harder.

The woman beckoned, still smiling.

Sophie gained another step, dragging Jay with her. Shit.

How could she stop Sophie? The flashlight clipped to her belt? Worth a try, anyway. Anything was worth a try. She hung on with one arm, lost another two steps to Sophie's forward momentum, got the flashlight free and with a prayer that she wouldn't do any permanent damage, and that they would live long enough for it to matter, brought it down on the back of Sophie's head in one smooth overhand arc.

Sophie groaned once and dropped like a felled ox, collapsing into Jay. Dead meat.

The beautiful face snarled. The woman of light rose

to her feet and screamed a many-tongued banshee scream.

"Oh, God," Jay whispered. She linked her arms under Sophie's armpits and started dragging her backward.

The woman took a step toward her, covering a lot of ground.

I'm going to die going to die going to die to die to die die die die . . .

Her brain screamed; her body kept moving. Hopeless. Back and back and back, and the thing took another slow step and its face mutated into something hideous, the light forming and shaping into a snouted dragonish visage complete with horns and forked tongue and teeth as long as Jay's arm.

Keep moving. Keep moving—

And suddenly pain slammed up from behind her and devoured her in ribbons and sheets of invisible, cool fire. Flung her into the air, away from the woman of light, flung her into the darkness. She heard screams and thought at first that Sophie had come around, and then realized the sounds poured from her mouth.

She stayed airborne forever, for hours and days while the world beneath her froze. Then her body smashed into a tree and crashed to the ground. Lights spun crazily behind her closed eyelids, and pain pressed down on her chest; she tried to breathe and discovered she didn't remember how. She lay gasping for air with her chest, her ribs, her back on fire, certain she was dying, or that if she wasn't, she wished she were.

She heard the woman of light scream, and then she heard something that unburied every atavistic fear she'd ever known. From all around and all at once, she heard a low keening; the sound started as a nearly inaudible sensation at the back of her mind, but quickly rose to a cacophony that was nothing less than madness given voice. Madness given *many* voices. Her skin prickled, and her mouth went dry.

Nearby, something rustled over dried leaves, moving fast. Suddenly, a huge form leapt over her, silhouetted for an instant against the moon-paled sky. Four-legged. This beast was four-legged, hairy and dark and with nothing of light about it. Whatever this was, it didn't stop. She wondered if the creature thought she was dead and intended to come back and devour her once it finished off Sophie. It landed silent as a shadow and was gone.

A painful, frightened moment passed while she marveled at the fact that she was still alive; the pain began to recede and she found she could breathe again. She drank in the cool night air with greedy gasps.

The howling grew closer and louder, and the voices of men joined it. Light filled the forest for an instant, green lightning without any thunder, without the crack of electricity or the whiff of ozone; a brief, blinding flash, then darkness. She tipped her head to see the place where the woman of light had stood, and she saw the myriad lights dissipating, scattering on the still night air, floating away like sparks from a campfire.

Howling, keening, shouting; the muddled blended insane whispers of the light-creature; a babble, a cacophony.

Then silence.

Cut off as cleanly as if it had been severed by a giant cleaver; one moment noise, the next silence, and into the silence slowly crept the sounds of the night forest. Water gurgling in the stream, the splash of a jumping fish, birds, insects.

I'm alive, Jay thought. She stared up at the sky, grinning like a fool, and she felt all her aches and pains, and she was grateful for them.

"I'm alive," she whispered. "Alive."

A hard, ugly thought caught her, worried at her. What about Sophie?

Jay tried to get up. The pain, bearable when she lay

still, tore through her back and legs, through her ribs, through her arms, and through her skull at her first movement. She didn't remember which part of her body had hit the tree. She felt as if all of it had. She gently lay flat again. Maybe she'd broken something. That would be bad news. She lifted her head. She could move it, but the pain grew so horrible she feared she would faint. Then she would be fair game for whatever it was that had thrown her.

Jayjay lay in agony, trying not to make any noise when she breathed, waiting for the four-legged nightmare to come back and rip her apart with its claws and its long, yellow fangs.

Then she heard Sophie moan, "Jay?"

Sophie sounded close. And she was still alive—for the moment, anyway. If she made noise again, though, Jay was afraid that whatever was out there now would kill her for sure.

Jay rolled over, which sent blinding white-hot arrows of pain from her back and ribs down her legs and out her arms. She gritted her teeth and kept moving.

I have to save her. I have to do something, dammit. Something, but I don't know what.

"Jay . . . Jay?" Sophie was going to get herself killed.

Shut up, you idiot, Jay thought; but thinking angry thoughts at Sophie wasn't going to save her life. Dammit!

Faster. Got to get to her. Got to. Now!

She dug her fingers into the crevasses in the bark of the tree she'd hit, and used them to pull herself to her feet.

Pain scattered tiny red flares across her eyes. She hung her head down, breathing deeply; the pain receded enough that she thought she would be able to totter without screaming. Maybe she hadn't broken anything . . . at least not anything important. She hoped.

She thought Sophie's whispered call had come from the little clearing.

She started out in the direction of Sophie's voice, then stopped, breath caught in her throat. Something flitted through that beam of light; it was slightly bigger than a bat, slower moving, and in the silvery light, it looked like nothing she had ever seen before. Translucent batlike wings, trailing gossamer membranes, a knobby, ropy, split tail. When it moved away from her, apparently unsuspecting that it had been watched, she sagged against the trunk and let out the breath she didn't realize she'd been holding. She still had a chance. Quickly, she headed toward Sophie.

Behind her, something growled; the sound stabbed through her blood, through her lungs, through her heart.

She stiffened and managed not to scream. She feared that if she screamed, whatever crouched behind her would attack. She hadn't a prayer of climbing the tree; the lowest limbs were fifty feet above her head. She turned. Slowly. Tried to think, but thoughts fled. She wanted to flee, too, even before she saw it. Before she saw . . . what the hell was it?

It stood man-high, but on four legs. She made out the rough edges of an animal silhouette. The faint moonlight that made its way through breaks in the trees overhead didn't offer much detail, though. She couldn't be sure what she faced. Wolf, she guessed first, but then, no—not a wolf, either. It stood tall as a bear. The animal took a step toward her. One step. And growled. Soft. Low.

Her heart fluttered—a bird in a cage, beating wings futilely. She smelled the hunter's breath, smelled the stink of carrion, of death. Felt the heat of its breath wash over her face.

Not my night, she thought, her mind being funny at her body's expense.

Standing on all four legs, it was eye to eye with her, and its eyes glowed pale, cold green in the silver moonlight. She didn't dare run because it would pounce if she ran; she knew that. Oh, God, but if she didn't run, what difference would that make? What was it? What could be as tall as she was on four legs; what predator stood that high?

It keened, a knife-edged caterwaul that ripped through the night, through the silence. Her nerve broke and she shouted and ran.

In a single bound, it caught her; it knocked her down with sharp-clawed paws pressed hard into her back. A combination of enormous strength and massive weight held her still, and the animal's muzzle dropped down next to her head—that stinking breath, that heat—and she shoved her head down into the mulching topsoil of the forest; she tasted dirt and leaves.

Jayjay closed her eyes tight, anticipating dagger teeth in powerful jaws crushing her skull, or ripping through her vertebrae; anticipating death, feeling as a mouse must feel that had been pinned by a cat. Dirt and leaves rotting on her tongue, she would join them, become part of them and no one would ever find her. No one would ever know.

In her ear, the predator chuckled.

Her mind raced. A chuckle? No. It hadn't been a chuckle. It had been some sort of growl, some animal call; it had been anything at all but what she thought she heard.

Then from nearby, a cool, amused voice cut through the darkness, urbane and civilized and faintly mocking. "Did you find her, then?"

The four-legged beast chuckled in her ear again, and growled, "Of course . . . the little rabbit. I like her. She would taste good."

"I would taste terrible."

The beast laughed outright. "Let's find out, shall we?

I'll take a little nibble, and tell you what I think. If I'm right, I'll eat you. If you're right, I'll let you go."

The urbane voice sighed. "Lovely experiment. But you can't have her, Grah. You can't have her at all."

"Aidris Akalan won't miss this rabbit. She wants a wizard."

"Yes, but we must take her and her rabbit friend to *Matthiall*," that last word said with bitterest scorn, "so that he can take them both to the Watchmistress. Maybe she'll let you eat both of them when she finds out they aren't who she hoped they would be."

Jay was having a hard time listening to their cheerful banter. Not simply because she was the butt of their jokes, but for some other reason as well. Something she couldn't quite pinpoint was bothering her.

She considered, frowning. English, she realized. The beast speaks English, as does whatever it's talking to. They haven't said a thing in Galti.

The beckoning light; the hideous bat-winged creature; this English-speaking monster on her back. She had a real sympathy for Dorothy when she found herself in Oz.

"I know the Watchmistress gets them," Grah said. Its growling voice still held a hint of amusement. "But I pleasure myself to think of if she did not."

"Pleasure yourself later. Let her up, and let's take her, shall we?"

The pressure on Jayjay's back vanished. She lay still, trying to make sense of what was happening to her, but events refused to untangle into anything but a mess.

"Up, you." The voice that had been so suave and urbane a moment before turned gruff. "Now. Morning will be here soon."

Jayjay rose, hurting. If she lived long enough, she ought to have interesting bruises to show for this night. She spat out the dirt in her mouth, and waited. No place to run. If they weren't going to kill her immediately, at least she'd gained some time in exchange for her pain.

"Follow me," the voice that did not belong to Grah said.

This other was a man. He stayed out of the direct moonlight, so she couldn't see him clearly. But he was only a man; two arms and two legs in the normal places, a head and hands and feet. He scared her, though; scared her as much as the talking dog. She had the feeling he would have watched Grah devour her without saying anything—or perhaps he would even have encouraged him—if it hadn't been for these two wizards they'd been looking for. "Follow you?" she asked. "Where? Where are we going?"

"Move," Grah snarled from behind her.

"But what just happened here?"

Grah butted her in the small of the back with his head, and she staggered forward a step. "Follow Bewul."

Just because they weren't going to kill her, it didn't follow that they would be kind to her. All they had to do was be sure she was still alive when they got her wherever they were going. She shut up and followed, limping and feeling the aches that would undoubtedly get worse for the next two or three days.

Bewul led her back to the clearing; the first thing Jayjay noticed was that the tent was gone. The second was that Sophie wasn't. Jayjay limped to Sophie's side. They hugged.

"You're still alive," Sophie said at last.

"At least for a while. Do you know what's going on?"

"Maybe. Several of our rescuers helped me pack our belongings while I was waiting for the rest of them to find you after they chased off the Watcher."

"Our *rescuers*?" Now Jayjay felt really lost.

Sophie looked around, making sure no one was listening. "That's the story. They were out hunting and they came across the Watcher that was attacking us. Several of the hunters and their dogs chased off the thing . . . not before the horses were dead, but they saved *our* lives."

"What do you think?"

"I think they were hunting for something they don't want to admit. Us, maybe. Or the men who chased us into the woods yesterday morning."

Jay nodded. "I heard one of the two tell us that they were supposed to take us to . . . their . . ." She thought a moment. "Their Watchmistress. He didn't think they'd found the right people, but they were definitely looking for someone."

"When they find out that we aren't who they were looking for, do you think they'll let us go?"

Jay thought of Grah's paw pressing her facedown into the dirt, of his speculation on how tasty she would be. "No."

"Me, either. I think if we see a chance to run, we'd better take it."

One of the hunters approached. "Get your belongings, please. We must hurry." His voice was gorgeous. Rich and deep. Sexy. It so startled Jay that for a moment she forgot to worry about the trouble she was in. She had a sudden overwhelming urge to take her flashlight and shine it in his face.

"Where are you taking us?" Voice or no voice, Jay remained suspicious.

"Home. Don't ask questions now." He sounded annoyed. "We're in a hurry; her Watchers might decide they want you more than they want to obey their Mistress."

She didn't want another run-in with the lights. She grabbed her pack and swung it onto her shoulders. She hated leaving the saddles and bridles and horse supplies in the woods to rot, but she couldn't carry them. Sophie stood beside her.

The men surrounded her and Sophie, their weapons out. They started marching, talking rarely, but always speaking in English, even to each other. What were English-speaking hunters and their English-speaking dogs doing in the middle of the great forests of Glenraven? And what did they want with her?

She marched through the moon-silvered darkness, hoping for a chance to run and figuring she wasn't going to get it. She wondered what the Watchmistress wanted from her. She wondered why she was in Glenraven at all, but she didn't let herself think too long about that. Some questions were better left unanswered.

Thirty

Yemus sat next to his brother, Torrin, in a secret meeting of the Machnan elite. Dressed in the clothing of commoners, the hoods with which they had hidden their faces thrown back for the time being, nearly a hundred of the most powerful men and women in Glenraven stared at each other with worried looks, waiting in silence.

A stout, red-bearded man burst through the door, flung back his hood, and bowed briefly to Torrin. "Lord Wethquerin," he murmured, and found a seat on one of the long, crowded benches.

"Lord Smeachwykke." Torrin nodded back.

Haddis Falin, Lord Smeachwykke, was a genial man most times, but Yemus sensed suppressed fury in him at that moment. Yemus suspected he'd had some rumor regarding the purpose of this emergency meeting. Or perhaps he had a natural bent to pessimism that Yemus had never noticed before. In any case, the leader of the northern hold of Smeachwykke looked around at the silent men and women who glared at Yemus, then cleared his throat. "I rode a horse to death getting here," he said. "One of my best. What's happened, and why all the secrecy?"

Torrin looked at Yemus, disdain in his eyes. "Utter disaster has happened," he said bitterly. "But had you all come racing here openly, you would have tipped off the Alfkindir that we are aware of their coup. We believe that we have no hope of salvaging the situation, but perhaps, with the element of surprise in our favor, when they take us down we won't go down alone."

Yemus felt the weight of a hundred hostile stares fall on him.

Torrin turned to him. "Tell them what has happened. Tell them the outcome of this perfect plan of yours, this plan in which we have all invested our lives."

Yemus swallowed hard. "The heroes came, but somehow the Kin found out about them and subverted them. They escaped here yesterday morning, having learned whatever it was they had hoped to learn, and though the Wethquerin Special Guard and I chased them, they eluded us by hiding in the Faldan Woods." He heard the gasps around the room, and nodded, grim and heartsick. "We pursued them into the Faldan Woods, and as a result, the Watchers decimated the Special Guard. Those few of us who survived retreated to regroup. Meanwhile, according to my auguries, our 'heroes' continued into the heart of the Faldan Woods, and met up with their contacts among the Kin only moments before you began arriving. The artifact is in the hands of the Kin now."

Stunned silence greeted his statement.

He watched the people, many of them his friends, most of them men and women he'd known since childhood. They were people who had put their lives and the lives of their loved ones, their husbands and wives and children and parents, into his hands because he had believed he could set them free from Aidris Akalan and her Watchers and the Alfkindir overlords who were draining the lifeblood from their Machnan subjects.

Stunned silence. He saw men turn their suddenly tear-streaked faces from him, saw women stare down at their hands or up at the ceiling, breathing hard, swallowing convulsively. He saw two enemies from rival villages turn to each other, rest hands on each other's shoulders, and weep.

Smeachwykke stood and stared him straight in the eye. "It's over then."

"At their whim, yes." Yemus clasped his hands in front of him and nodded slowly.

The lord sucked his bottom lip into his mouth, nibbled on the flesh until Yemus saw a trickle of blood well up beneath his teeth. "I suppose the only question is, shall we execute you now, while all of us can watch you die, or shall we let you live so that when the Kin destroy the artifact and us with it, you will be left utterly alone?"

Yemus nodded. He'd expected the question; his brother had asked him the same thing.

"Wall him into his tower," Bekka Shaita, Lady Dinnos, suggested. "Feed him, take him water . . . and let him ponder the effects of what he's done. And when we are gone, he'll know it, because no one will come to his window again. That way we will die with the comfort of knowing the one who killed us will die, too, but that he will suffer first in a suitable manner."

Yemus saw Torrin glance around the table, taking rough count of the nodding heads. At last he said, "So be it. Most of you are agreed—"

"I want to stand in front of him and watch a sword run through him. I want to watch his blood pour onto the ground," one of the lesser lords of Zearn said. Yemus remembered that the man had three daughters and two sons, all of them still young, and he understood how the man felt.

Torrin shook his head. "We will wall him into the Aptogurria. That way he can work toward a solution that will save us from the Kin. If he succeeds, we all live. If he fails, he dies with us."

Torrin nodded to the Special Guards who stood at the doorway to the assembly room. "Take him. Wake two masons, and have them construct the wall immediately. Kill anyone who approaches the wall, whether they wish to kill him or to offer him comfort. One of the Special Guard will be designated to take him food. That man must never utter a word to him, nor make any sign in response to anything he says, except to bring me should he ask for me."

Torrin stared into Yemus's eyes. "The Aptogurria has water. Leave that as it is. Better he dies slowly of hunger: hunger for food, hunger for friends."

Better he dies slowly.

Yemus didn't fight the men who led him away, though as the only Machnan who still wielded magic, he didn't doubt that he could have escaped them. The truth was that he didn't want to escape. He wanted to die.

He wished they would have executed him immediately; he couldn't argue, though, with the fairness of their decision. He had consigned every one of them and all their families and friends to an early and probably horrible death. They had every right to decide the method by which he died.

In his little apartment in the Aptogurria, listening to the soft "click-click" as the stonemasons walled up the door and most of the lower window, his brother's words kept running through his mind.

Better he dies slowly.

Better I was never born at all, Yemus thought.

Thirty-one

The ground twisted under Sophie's feet. It was the third, possibly the fourth time she'd felt the phenomenon. For an instant she felt she was falling forward . . . and then, before she could catch herself, she wasn't falling anymore. The sensation reminded her of something. She puzzled while she walked; then it clicked. Cycling through the tunnel on the way to Glenraven, when she had turned that last corner before they came out of the tunnel, she'd had the same shifting feeling.

"What *was* that?" she asked the shadowed form next to her.

"What?"

"The ground shifting. Didn't you feel it?"

"The ground didn't shift." The voice belonged to Matthiall, the one who'd captured her. "Perhaps you're ill."

"I'm about to be." Sophie turned to Jay. "Did *you* feel it?"

"Did I feel the earth move under my feet?" Jayjay groaned. "Yes."

"What do you suppose it was?"

"A very quiet earthquake."

At first, Sophie had been grateful she'd been captured; after all, she and Jayjay were minutes, maybe even seconds, away from death when their captors arrived. But the longer she walked between their circle of drawn weapons, listening to them talk to each other, the more flatly terrified she became, and the more certain she became that her captors were something she'd never encountered before. With the giant talking dogs, of course, that was obvious. But something about the men frightened her even worse.

She'd never seen one of their faces, never gotten a good look at any of them. From their silhouettes, they seemed normal enough, and the few times one had walked through a patch of moonlight, he had looked like a man. Their voices were clear enough, too, but something about them struck Sophie as wrong. Perhaps it was a musicality of tone she'd never heard in anyone's voice before, or maybe it was the little burr at the back of her skull that tickled every time one of them spoke.

She wanted to take a hard look at them. It wouldn't be long before she could. She noticed a slight grayness along the horizon to her right. Dawn coming.

The trees thinned out, and through them Sophie managed to discern the hulking outlines of towers and battlements; they had come upon a massive outpost in the middle of dense forest.

"Day comes," one of the hunters muttered. "Quickly!" Another put a curved horn to his lips and blew a rippling arpeggio.

That guy could give Winton Marsalis a run for his money, Sophie thought. He got the attention of whoever ran the gate, too; in the next instant, chains rumbled and a drawbridge lowered rapidly to the ground.

"Inside!" shouted the hunter who'd noted the coming of dawn.

Everyone obeyed, including Sophie and Jay, since they were in the center of the circle. The whole weary crew trotted across the bridge. She figured between the people and the dogs, more than twenty living beings ran over the wood planks at the same time. Yet Sophie noticed uncomfortably that she and Jay were the only two runners whose footsteps she heard.

Then they were through the gate and behind the battlement walls. Sophie looked up, expecting to see the sky. Instead she saw a low stone ceiling and a corridor that ran off to right and left; little spheres of light placed irregularly along the inner walls made the corridor about as bright as outdoors at late twilight. Sophie had never seen any place so poorly lighted. Nor had she ever seen a fortress that didn't include inner and outer baileys to protect the main keep.

The men stayed away from the lights.

"So, are you going to drag these two up to her now? Going to tell her you've captured her wizards?" Sophie recognized the mocking voice as one of the three she could put a name to. Bewul. Jay had told her his name, and what she'd thought of him.

She recognized the second voice, too. Matthiall. "No. I want to be sure of them. I think I'm right about them, but what you said has given me something to consider. I'll take them to her when I'm sure I'm right."

Bewul laughed. "Then she'll be waiting a long time to see them. Feed them to your friend Grah, why don't you. Save yourself the humiliation you'll get if you take them to her." Still laughing, Bewul strode away, followed by most of the men and dogs.

Matthiall sighed. One of the giant dogs growled. "He will take the news straight to her, Matthiall. He'll take word of your failure."

"I know, Grah."

"Why don't you go to her, let her know that you haven't failed, and that these are the people she wants?"

"Do you think they are?" Matthiall sounded surprised.

There was a pause. "I have no opinion on the matter at all. I merely assumed that you must think so, since you brought them here."

"She told me I would find two people in the forest, and that these two people would be powerful Machnan wizards. I found two people in the forest. But I confess, old friend, the longer I walked beside them, the more certain I became that they were not wizards at all."

"So what will you do with them?"

"I don't know. I'll lock them away for a time, until I've decided."

Grah chuckled; Sophie didn't like that sound at all. "Shall I come with you? Maybe I can help you with them."

"When I've decided what I must do, you can assist me. But for now, I'll take them alone."

"What if they escape you?"

Matthiall laughed softly. "They can't get out of here. All they can do is run through the labyrinths. If they're stupid enough to do that, you and the other warrags can catch them and eat them. You haven't had Machnan in a while, have you?"

"It's been far too long."

"Well, Grah, if they try to run, it won't be much longer."

"I'll take that happy thought with me," the warrag said. He trotted away.

As far as Sophie could tell, she and Jay and Matthiall were alone.

"You heard what I said to Grah?" Matthiall asked.

Sophie said, "Yes."

After a moment, Jay agreed.

"I wasn't exaggerating. If you run from me, the kindest death you'll find is at the teeth and claws of the warrags." Sophie heard him sigh. "Come with me."

He didn't sound cruel, as Bewul had sounded. Sophie dared to ask him, "Where are we?"

"Inside the main gate."

"The main gate of what?"

"Oh. This is Cotha Maest."

Jayjay said, "And where is Cotha Maest? I haven't heard of it."

Sophie heard Matthiall inhale—one sharp, short breath. "No more questions," he said. "No more words until I tell you that you may speak again." When he said that, she would have expected anger in his voice . . . but instead, she thought she detected fear.

Matthiall led the two of them past empty twilit rooms and through long meandering halls, down and ever farther down beneath the surface of the earth. Silver shimmered on the cold stone walls, falling in pale shining curtains of metal like frozen waterfalls. The silence of the upper levels gave way to voices echoing from far off as the three of them traveled downward, and as they reached level passageways at last, those voices resolved into singing and laughter, high and tinkling, as if it, too, were made of silver. The stone hallways changed; rough and crude in the upper levels, they had seemed to melt as she and Jayjay descended until the tiny puddles of light revealed that both walls and columns curved in graceful fluted lines; stone carved so beautifully it almost seemed to live. Sophie touched a pillar, curious, and her fingers told her it was still stone—still hard and cold and faintly damp—but it rested, feeling so sinuous and almost muscled beneath her fingers, that she could have believed it would move.

They walked on, and the floor beneath her boots grew soft; she bent down and touched the ground with her fingertips, and discovered with a thrill of disbelief that she walked on grass. A sigh swirled around her, and seemed to breathe through the halls. She looked up, startled, and saw that Matthiall had stopped. She guessed he looked at her, though she could make out nothing of his face.

"I have heard nothing like that in time out of mind," he whispered. "You summon life to these ancient stones, fair guest."

He didn't say she or Jay could speak, so she didn't say anything.

They came around a curve in the stone passageway, and the darkness of the halls opened into the interior of an enormous dome, hung about with thousands of tiny lights that mimicked the twinkling of stars. Fireflies flickered, warm yellow in the near dark. The rich blue of twilight where sky would have been and the dew-and-grass scent of meadow, the sounds of whippoorwills and katydids and the bright chirping of little frogs brought a lump to Sophie's throat and tears to her eyes. For a moment, she felt like an eight-year-old again, in the long evening of summer, out on the lawn with her parents. The pang of the loss of both of them, and a wistful ache to return to childhood, caught at her with startling tenacity.

I feel I could be barefoot and running around with a Mason jar, she thought, full of wonder. Like I still weighed sixty-five pounds, like I was still all skinny legs and knobby knees. Like summer was going to last forever, like Mom and Dad were going to be around forever.

One hot tear burned down her cheek. She swallowed and sniffed.

"My God," Jayjay said slowly. "Do you know how much this reminds me of the park behind our houses when we were kids?"

"Yes." Sophie wiped the tear from her cheek, grateful no one could see it in the dark. "Something about the smells and the sounds."

"Yeah." Jayjay sighed. "I haven't thought about that place in years."

"I still go there sometimes," Sophie said. "It's beautiful, but I'm not eight anymore. You know?"

"I took my very first real date there when I was sixteen, ostensibly to go fishing." Jayjay laughed. "Instead, he and I necked alongside one of the hiking trails, and the little shit gave me my very first kiss . . . and my very first hickey. I nearly swore off kissing right then."

Sophie smiled. She remembered catching fireflies; Jay remembered a boy. It figured. Then she frowned. "You got your first kiss at sixteen?"

"I was a slow starter."

Matthiall hadn't stopped them from talking. Instead, he'd listened.

A rushing fountain gurgled off somewhere in the distance. Instantly Sophie felt hot and tired and thirsty and filthy. She wanted to wash the tear streaks from her face, and drink cold, clear water until she put the memory of the happy past safely away. She headed toward the sound, but Matthiall saw her wander from him and caught her elbow.

"Follow me. You don't want to get lost here."

Sophie sighed. Nearby, she heard bursts of song and laughter so high and giddy it could only have belonged to children. But she saw no one.

Then the faintest hint of movement caught her attention. She looked hard, and discerned the lumpish outlines of a huge dark mass piled against one of those beautiful carved pillars. She wondered at first if someone had left boulders sitting there, or bags of potatoes, or something equally ungainly. She couldn't see what had moved on that pile, until the boulders themselves shifted forward slowly, terribly slowly, with a sound of rock grinding on rock, and Sophie realized they were alive. *It* was alive. The enormous creature sniffed the air as she and Jayjay and Matthiall drew nearer. The giant misshapen boulder that was in fact the creature's head turned, and two tiny glowing red eyes searched myopically in Sophie's general direction, swung back and forth past her, then focused on her. The thing growled—a rumble like an earthslide—and the sound shocked Sophie into stillness.

"Keep moving," Matthiall snapped. "He's slow and stupid, but if you stand there and tempt him, he'll come after you."

"What in God's name is that?" Jayjay asked. Sophie could hear her voice shake.

"The gods had no hand in him. Only the Aregen," Matthiall said, hurrying past. "If you stay well away from him, he won't bother you."

"But I want to know," Jay insisted.

Matthiall stopped and turned, and Sophie got the impression that he stared at Jayjay. His gorgeous voice dropped to a low, ominous growl. "If you want to know so badly, why don't you walk over and ask him?"

Jayjay dropped back to Sophie's side and said nothing else as they walked through the grass, under arches that had been carved to look like trees, along a stream that ran through the middle of the enormous, many-vaulted dome, and at last into another hallway that ran to a series of little grottolike rooms.

"You'll be here until I decide what to do with you."

"If we aren't the people you were looking for, why don't you let us go?" Jay asked.

"You *are* the people we were looking for," Matthiall said. The way he said it made Sophie's stomach twist. "I simply don't know yet whether that's good for me, or whether it's bad for me. I'll be back when I've figured it out." He growled something Sophie couldn't hear, then added, "In the meantime, no one will find you here." With that remark, he hurried away.

Sophie and Jay stood perfectly still in the nearly lightless grotto for only a moment. Then Jay said, "We're going from bad to worse. We have to get out of here."

"Back the way we came," Sophie agreed. "I still have some markers so that we can keep track of our path. You still have your flashlight?"

"Yes. Right here." Sophie heard a soft click, and a muddy brown circle of light appeared on the grass. "Great," Jayjay muttered. "Give me a chance to change the batteries . . . I have some in here . . ."

Sophie heard her digging through her pack.

While she waited for Jay, she stepped forward, nervous but determined to at least take a look down the passageway outside the grotto. When they ran, she didn't want to walk into the talking dogs—no, the warrags—or the red-eyed stone monster or any other horror hidden within the bowels of Cotha Maest. Her right foot swung toward the invisible line that separated the inside of the grotto from the passageway . . . and stopped. Sophie tripped, flung out her arms, and bounced off of nothing. She landed hard on her backside in the grass and sat staring at the doorway.

What in the world—?

She crawled forward and reached out a hand. Nothing stopped her. She crawled a bit further and stuck her head out into the passageway. No resistance. She crawled further; both shoulders went through with no problem. Had she imagined a barrier? Had she simply tripped over her own feet, or slipped on the grass?

She had her waist in the passageway, and suddenly she couldn't go further. She moved both legs; they worked fine. She pulled with her arms and shoulders; nothing wrong with them either. But when she tried to put everything together and get out the door, she . . . couldn't.

More magic. She felt a coldness in that invisible, intangible barrier; a coldness that seeped into the marrow of her bones. It was nothing natural—nothing that belonged in the real world. It resonated of infinity, of an evil time lost and misplaced and forgotten and suddenly resurrected, brought from its dank cell into a world where it had never been meant to exist.

She backed up and drew her knees tight against her

chest and shivered. Wrongness. When she'd felt the forest watch her, when she'd felt the ground shifting beneath her feet, that had been imbued with the same feel. But this was worse. Whereas she had been able to rationalize the feel of the forest and the ground, this was clearly magic. When she'd read the Fodor's guide, she had seen proof of magic, of course, but it had felt small and human and somehow accessible. With the act of trying to go through that empty doorway, she touched another kind of magic, an enormous cold magic that made her realize in the universal scheme of things, she was no more significant than an ant.

"There!" Jay said, and suddenly a circle of brilliant white light illuminated the grotto. "Much better."

Sophie turned to Jay. "We can't go anywhere. Look at this." She demonstrated the arcane properties of the invisible barrier, pulling away quickly after she did. That invisible barrier had the coldness and the stillness of a serpent waiting for prey to fall into its jaws. It felt watchful, malign. Something about it sucked at the soul, reaching in and touching hope and turning it into despair. Sophie couldn't stand the coldness on her skin, and this second time, she had to wait much longer before the ice thawed in her blood.

"That explains why Matthiall didn't worry about us wandering off, doesn't it?" She flashed the light over the opening, then stepped forward. Her right leg swung out, caught in midair on nothing, and bounced back. Jay pushed her hands through the invisible barrier, then pulled away as if she'd been burned. She pushed one finger back into the barrier, stood there for a moment wearing an expression of intense concentration, then jerked her hand back again. "Christ," she said, rubbing her arms and shivering, "that's evil."

"So now we wait?"

"Yes. I wish we knew for what."

Thirty-two

Hultif's black mirror reflected the faces of the two captives. They weren't at all what he'd imagined; they were women, tallish, slender, older than they looked. They hadn't been bent by the weary physical labor and endless childbearing that broke Machnan women by the time they reached thirty.

Matthiall had hidden them deep within the ancient labyrinth, in a section and level that had been sparsely populated when there had been enough inhabitants, Kin and Kin-hera, to fill the Cotha to overflowing. Now, for a while, the success of the Aregen plans depended on Matthiall's actions, and Hultif was helpless to influence those actions. Matthiall could never suspect that his actions served anyone but himself. If Hultif and the omens had done a good enough job of choosing this unknowing agent, though, the rebirth of the Aregen would soon drive Alfkindir and Machnan into their old bondage, and Hultif and the few survivors of his kind would stand free on the surface of the earth for the first time in his life.

Hultif smiled. He'd done a good job. He knew he had. Through his cat's-paw, he was about to destroy Aidris Akalan for killing his family, and most of his kind.

219

"Rise, Aregen, and retake your throne," he whispered. "Paint it with the blood of your enemies. Build new cothas from their toil and sweat, and triumph."

He smiled. He hoped he would have the chance to rip the arteries from Aidris Akalan's throat himself. "Mother," he whispered, his grin stretching wider. "I'm coming for you, Mother."

Thirty-three

Jayjay paced through the dark room, staring at the flashlight that grew dimmer by the minute. Eight hours and twenty minutes. She'd rested, paced, rested again, but she avoided sleep. Since she'd arrived in Glenraven, nightmares punctuated her sleep. She preferred being awake. She was weary of the darkness, weary of the pale pretense of light that the false stars in the ceiling scattered down into the room. She chafed at the confinement, at not knowing what would happen to her next.

Being in the forest had been better. Not good, but better; at least she'd been able to act. They couldn't act anymore. All they could do was wait.

If something happens to Matthiall, we'll be trapped in here until we die, Jay thought. As soon as she thought it, she wished she hadn't.

Sophie rested next to the stream that ran through the grotto; running water, cool and sweet, with a little hot spring that bubbled up off to one side and drained out through a hole in the wall. The same sort of barrier that blocked the door blocked the ingress and egress of the stream. As prison cells went, it was comfortable. Fresh water, a self-flushing toilet of arcane design hidden behind a lush stand of head-high, plumed grass. Soft grass to lie on. But human beings weren't meant to spend their lives in perpetual gloom. They needed some sunlight.

"God, I wish it was brighter in here," she said.

For a moment she didn't realize anything had changed. Then she noticed that she could see details of Sophie's face, even though she was on the other side of the grotto. The false stars that shimmered on the ceiling began to grow brighter. And brighter. And brighter. Shadows sprouted beneath her feet, and grew sharp, hard edges. The room became sunny and warm, and the grass beneath Jay's feet waved slowly back and forth in a breeze she didn't feel. At the first touch of bright light, the delicate petals of pale white flowers curled shut with the slow sensuousness of a cat stretching. They were night bloomers, she supposed. After a few moments, other flowers began to dot the grass; little yellow and red blooms opened and waved on slender stalks.

"The room is a little too bright," Jay announced, watching for a reaction.

She got one. The stars dimmed fractionally.

"Halfway between this brightness and the previous one will be perfect."

The stars glowed brighter.

Well. That was impressive.

Sophie sat straight up as the lights brightened, staring around the room. Now she stood. "Do you suppose if we asked the door to open for us, it would?"

"Maybe."

"We need to leave," Sophie said, walking toward the door. She tried to step through, hit the invisible barrier, and bounced back. "We need to go home," she amended.

The barrier remained impermeable.

"Open, sesame."

Nothing.

"Damn," Sophie said.

"It was worth a try."

"There's no telling what else this room would do if we could only figure it out."

Jayjay nodded. "Pity it doesn't come with an operator's manual."

A thoughtful expression crossed Sophie's face. "We need an operator's manual for this room."

Again, nothing happened.

"Maybe," Jay said, "the only thing the room does is brighten and dim its lights." But the idea of the operator's manual got her thinking. She pulled out the Fodor's guide. She hadn't put Cotha Maest on her itinerary, so she hadn't bothered to read much about it. Now she thought she could stand to know more about her enemies, what they were likely to want, why they would capture her and Sophie in the first place.

She flipped to the entry for Cotha Maest.

"Always an Alfkindir stronghold, Cotha Maest dates from the beginning of the Kin's Age of Mastery. It is the primary citadel of Aidris Akalan, Hereditary Watch-mistress of the Alfkindir. Unexplored and unmapped by humans . . ."

Hello, Jay thought. Unexplored by *humans*? What do the writers mean by that? What about the ones who brought us here?

" . . . Cotha Maest has been rumored to contain passageways that connect it magically to the other Kin territories, and to places beyond the Timeless Realms."

Jay knew the guidebook hadn't said anything about magic when she'd first read through it. So this was another example of its self-editing. She frowned and started reading again.

"Not that the history of the place is going to be of any use to you now. If you don't end up dead, it's going to be a miracle. Aidris Akalan will figure out that you're here to bring her down, and she'll kill you the instant she's sure of it.

Here you are, summoned to be Glenraven's heroes, destined to bring freedom to the Timeless Realm's enslaved people . . . and you, our rescuers, need to be rescued instead.

Idiots."

Jay closed the book, holding her place with one thumb, and took a deep breath. She couldn't decide which upset her more—that the news was so bad, or that the book was so obnoxious in delivering it.

"Soph." Sophie looked up. "Read this and tell me what you think."

Sophie took the book. She looked down at the page Jay indicated and sat reading. When she finished she looked up and made a face. "Charming." Sophie handed the guide back. "Let's take a page from ancient history and kill the bearer of bad news, shall we?"

Jay laughed in spite of herself. "What do you have in mind?"

"Throw the book in the water. Set it on fire. Rip it to shreds."

"All those ideas have their appeal, but it might still be useful for something. Besides, I'm getting the head-ache from Hell. Why don't we both take a nap? Maybe things will look better when we wake up."

Sophie nodded. "Sounds good. Maybe when I wake up, I'll discover this has all been a dream."

Jayjay sighed. "A dream. That would be almost perfect. Wake up back in Peters to discover that I was twenty years old and that I merely dreamed all three husbands into existence. Yeah, I could live with that." She sprawled on her stomach and pillowed her head against one arm. Amazingly, the ground seemed to give beneath her, to cradle her and support her, to float and conform to her body. Better than an expensive water-bed, she thought.

Then she was walking. I'm dreaming, she thought. Dreaming about walking. Not going to get much rest . . .

Walking.

No details at first. Just her legs moving, moving, moving, and for a minute she figured she was going to trip on something and wake herself up. She hated that. But no, she kept on walking, and suddenly realized she wasn't walking aimlessly; she headed toward something. Noise. Water. Yes, the sound of falling water, and something light and airy. Laughter. Children's laughter; but not quite children, either. In her sleep, she felt suddenly that she was walking in a place she had no business being, in a world where she did not belong. She had the sudden urge to keep quiet, to keep to the shadows, to hide.

And a chill passed over her, through her, and she began to notice details. Light, shimmering little pin-points of light—rainbow-colored—that flickered, floated, spun dizzily. She followed them, for they went in the same direction she wished to go. They went toward the laughter. She walked, hurrying, suddenly aware that her feet never touched the ground.

One part of her mind, drolly amused, noted that it would be harder to trip that way. The rest, though, focused on keeping quiet, making no sound. She knew, without knowing how she knew, that she headed into terrible danger. Toward death. And yet she could not turn back. She was going where she had to go.

The lights spun and swirled, fanned out in a thousand

directions at once like a chrysanthemum rocket on the Fourth of July, and she moved to a place where darkness met twilight.

Everything is twilight around here, even in my dreams, she thought, annoyed. *You would think in my dreams I could at least manage better lighting. A bright hot golden sun. Summer breezes. If I have to walk into trouble, why can't I do it in the sunshine?*

But the purple haze remained, and she realized that at least she could see well in it. She found herself in a beautiful grove where the trunks of trees were stone carved by a genius; they curved up to arch against the ceiling, where leaves of silver and gold hung in strands on tiny wires and chimed with every passing breeze. Ahead of her, through that stone forest, shapes moved toward a dull yellow light. She followed them, keeping herself behind the trees, sliding forward almost afraid to breathe.

As she drew closer, her fear grew. The light came from a ball of clear crystal that sat atop a short carved tripod of some dark, glossy wood. She would have been unimpressed; after all, how thrilling could a lightbulb be? But she felt power radiate from that crystal sphere. She knew with inexplicable certainty that the light it gave off represented nothing but an irrelevant by-product of enormous and ancient magic. She didn't know how she was so sure of this. She felt she could almost see the artifact's age, as if it radiated the weight of time along with its cold white light.

Its light reflected off faces and forms—creatures at home in the realm of nightmare—gathering around it. Tiny fang-mouthed fliers with bat wings and women's bodies fluttered and laughed, swirling in elegant silks at odds with their black wings and death-white faces. Theirs was the laughter Jayjay had thought so childish. *They flew with the hunters,* she realized. *I thought they were a sort of split-tailed bat.* Beasts with lean greyhound muzzles, curling, tufted ears and close-set almost-human eyes sat talking to each other, their voices deep and rough. They too wore clothing of a sort; leather harnesses hung with tools and weapons. She recognized their appearance. They were of the same species as the unidentified heads that had hung on the walls of Wethquerin Zearn. But she also recognized their bodies and their voices; they were the almost-dogs that had hunted through the woods with her "rescuers." *Warrags*. Like Grah. Not dogs, not wolves—something else entirely. She stared at their hands, long-fingered, coarse-jointed and claw-tipped; hands designed with thick, hard palms made to be run on and with fingers so double-jointed they looked like the legs of particularly hairy tarantulas, fingers that stuck up and arched out above those thick dog-pad palms.

"Oh, let's go out and save some more Machnan," one of them said, and laughed at its companion.

"Shall we save them? Shall we, Grah? I'll save mine for lunch if you'll save yours for dinner," the other one answered, gravel-voiced. Both laughed wickedly.

Jay felt that chill of fear run through her again. That *was* Grah—the one who had found her and caught her, who had played with her like prey. She didn't like Grah.

With a shiver, she turned her attention elsewhere. The giant, lumpish monstrosity she had mistaken for a pile of rocks leaned against one of the tree pillars at the outside edge of the circle of light, its eyes blood-bright and hungry. Rhinoceros-hided, hideously wrinkled, it grinned with rows of shark teeth. Incongruously, it wore a glorious gown of velvet, embroidered with gold and silver, glittering with gems.

Other, more terrifying creatures lurked beside it at the edge of the light, whispering in the shadows. Scaled or furred or slick with slime, dressed in beautiful raiment, like sycophants from the court of a medieval king transformed by a psychopath's nightmare, they all had in common that they frightened Jay. Their whispers made her think of fingernails on a blackboard, of stepping on a grave at midnight, of everything she had ever seen out of the corner of an eye that vanished when she looked for it again. They scared her worse than anything she'd feared as a child, worse than the worst nightmare she'd ever had.

A man stepped out from among the most terrifying of them and moved within the circle of light, and the joking and laughing stopped. But no, he wasn't a man after all. His eyes were pale blue-gray, gold-kissed; his sharp, straight nose stood out boldly above a perfect mouth, a mouth with lips arched at the center, curled upward at the corners. His golden hair, close-cropped, gleamed like precious metal above his high brow. He radiated a sexual appeal so compelling Jayjay found herself walking toward him before she managed to stop herself and hide behind the trees. His very presence called to her; seeing him, she wanted him, and didn't know how she could be so sure he was what she wanted. Seeing him, she wanted to touch him, to taste him, to feel him touch her.

But he smiled, and when he smiled, Jayjay saw long, sharp canines. And when he reached out and put one hand on the top of the sphere of light, she noted that his fingers were tipped with retractable claws. Her desire burned undiminished, but now fear curled beside it.

"Matthiall," Grah said, "why did you not let us devour them?"

Matthiall? What game was her mind playing on her? She had walked beside him in the darkness for hours. Beside him. *Him.* She had never felt anything but that he was human. Human . . . but whatever this thing was, she could see he was not human. It's a dream, she told herself. Oh. Silly of me. I'm dreaming.

But it was a good dream. Seeing him took her breath away. He . . . man, male, magical golden creature . . . turned to look at the beast, and she realized his ears peaked slightly. Neat, small ears, perfectly formed, but pointed. "I am curious," Matthiall said in a velvet voice that gave her goose bumps. "They do not belong here . . . and yet they do. I sense things about them that touch on old magic, but how can this be?"

Grah lifted one lip in a snarl. "I thought you had decided they weren't Aidris Akalan's precious magicians. I thought you believed the bitch's future killers were still free." It chuckled—that same rough sound Jayjay had heard before. "I thought you were going to give these two Machnan to me to eat."

Matthiall shrugged. "I told you that when Bewul was listening, Grah. I don't know what they are. They aren't wizards. But they're something. They're something . . . impossible." He sighed and frowned, staring straight at Jay, straight through her. "I simply don't know what."

"If they're dead, they can't be a threat," the red-eyed monstrosity at the edge of the darkness whispered. "And you could blame their deaths on Bewul; you could tell Aidris Akalan that he killed them but that they *were* the magicians she sought. Then the magicians would be able to attack her unhindered, and we would be unburdened of whatever those creatures are that you found."

"I think they are what she was looking for. I don't think she knows what they are, either."

The red-eyed rock creature shook its head, the gesture accompanied by the sound of grinding stone. "So you're going to hide them from her. What if Bewul finds a way to turn all of this against you?"

Matthiall turned and glared at the monster. "No matter what we do with them, Bewul will complain about us to her. Bewul eats at Aidris's feet as if he were her lapdog. If she told him to crawl on his belly and lick her toes, he would do it and thank her." The golden-haired not-man stared off into nothingness, his eyes fierce and cold. "I am no one's lapdog, Hagrall." His voice dropped to a low, ominous rumble. "Especially not hers."

Grah pulled the corners of his mouth back in an ugly grin and laughed. "And when tomorrow comes, and Bewul tells her you have captured two women who do not belong here, and that you are keeping them instead of killing them or giving them to her, she'll serve you your balls in a silver bowl, and watch you eat them. And what of our revolution then, old friend?"

"That's why Bewul won't tell her that." Matthiall shifted his other hand to cover the sphere. Jayjay noticed he was careful to slide one palm along the surface while he moved the other off, so that the top part remained covered at all times.

One of the hideous bat-winged women flitted up to his face and hovered there. "And how do you think to prevent him? You think you call us here and tell us you want to keep two Machnan, and we will take this to him and somehow convince him to lie to *her*? He is not one of us. He would betray us to her in an instant if he knew of us."

Matthiall's face became an expressionless mask. "No. I want you to find me two Machnan women's bodies; I will need fresh bones. Send the diggers, perhaps, to pull two who are newly dead down through their graves, and let the pakherries eat away the flesh so they can't be identified. If they find no young women freshly dead—" He hung his head and sighed. "—Then send them beneath the walls of Sinon after dark and find two who are not yet dead, and bring *their* bones to me."

All heads snapped up. All eyes fixed on him.

Jayjay felt sick. He would kill two innocent women

to hide the fact that she and Sophie were his prisoners, and not dead?

"Break the pact? For those two? Why?" Hagrall spoke.

Matthiall frowned. "I don't know. I only know that we need them."

Grah laid his ears flat against his skull. "If they die our hope of revolution dies with them? I had no idea they were so valuable."

"I believe they are the key we've waited for. But don't worry. They are well hidden, safe even from Bewul. When we give him bones to take to Aidris, he will be satisfied; and when Aidris reads the bones and finds nothing extraordinary about them, she will believe me when I tell her the outsiders were of no value, so I fed them to you for sport."

He stared down at his hand on the glowing sphere— glared at it as if it were his enemy. "In the meantime, perhaps," he whispered, "I will find the way to solve the puzzle these strangers pose to our overthrow of Aidris Akalan."

Grah whispered something to the others of his kind, then growled. "We did not realize our futures depended on these creatures we found. We wish to set guards, to protect them from harm until they achieve their destiny."

Matthiall showed his fangs in a slow smile. "Well spoken, Grah. Hanarl already guards them."

Grah nodded and grinned. "Good. Our future is safe with Hanarl. If you'll tell me where he waits, I'll relieve him at the end of his shift. Nothing will get past me."

"Thank you. With you there, our rebellion can breathe easier."

Jayjay felt herself starting to slip backward. Rather, she felt as if she were receding, like a tide, inexorably. One of the warrags asked a question she wanted very much to hear, and she saw Matthiall's lips move, saw him smile slowly, heard the faintest whisper of his laugh, but she floated away from him, faster and faster, back through the dark corridors and winding passage- ways, back through silence, back and back and back, seeing only where she had been and not where she was going.

With a start, she jerked awake. Shaking. She was shaking or someone was shaking her—

Sophie said, "You got restless, started thrashing and making whimpering noises. I figured you were having a nightmare. Are you all right?"

Jayjay sat up. She felt wearier than when she'd dropped off to sleep. "Another weird dream." She recounted the whole thing to Sophie, even the part about her inexplicable attraction to the dream-Matthiall.

Sophie nodded. "I understand the part about Mat- thiall. Your subconscious is fantasizing a replacement for Steven. Someone powerful and wild and irresist- ible. The rest of your dream was pretty bizarre, though."

"It didn't feel that way . . . like a dream, I mean. It felt so real."

"You ever been psychic before?"

"No."

Sophie's shrug dismissed the nightmare as irrelevant. "Let's concentrate on getting ourselves out of here."

Jay sighed. "Okay. We'll plan our great escape." She didn't say anything else about her dream, but she kept it in her thoughts. She didn't intend to let it go, because she wanted to believe that the dream had been a message from Glenraven. A promise that her life was changing, that she had something important to do here in this world where magic worked, and where she— a woman who had spent most of her life observing others taking chances and making risks pay off, while she wrote about what they had done—would have a chance to matter on a larger scale.

Thirty-four

Hultif waited behind the curtain; Aidris Akalan dismissed Bewul. Only when the Kin stalked out of the room and closed the door behind him did she turn to face the curtain.

"You heard what he said?"

Hultif, carrying the bowl and the black mirror with him, came out from behind the curtain and bowed to the Watchmistress. "I heard all that he said."

"Is he correct? Did Matthiall capture the wrong two people? And if he did, why did you recommend to me that he be put in charge of the search party?"

How like Aidris. She willingly passed blame for everything to anyone who was near her, but claimed responsibility for every success, no matter who engineered it.

"Matthiall did bring the wrong people," Hultif told her. "But somehow, that works to your benefit, too. Look. Study the omens."

He pushed the bowl at her and she took it and dropped gracefully to the floor, cross-legged. She stared for several long moments into her reflection in the black glass, her long pale hair falling forward, like curtains on either side of her face. Then she looked

233

up at him and smiled; her white fangs glowed like pearls against the deep copper of her face. Her honey-gold eyes narrowed as she grinned. They, too, seemed possessed of an eerie glow. "Yes, Hultif. This *is* much better. I don't simply defeat the Machnan—I destroy them utterly. These are wonderful omens."

Hultif knew they were. He'd fabricated every aspect of the vision she saw in the glass; he had made it as mysterious and complex as any real vision the oracle would have presented to her. He had formed every image to reflect power, conquest, success. Everything she saw encouraged her to believe that Matthiall, by doing the wrong thing, had done the right thing for her—that she was not merely safe, but that she was about to achieve complete control of every faction in Glenraven, and all without sending a single soldier into battle.

There was an enormous advantage in always telling the truth, Hultif thought. When at last you told a monstrous lie, who would suspect it?

Thirty-five

Sophie closed her eyes and let the waterfall in their grotto pool pound down onto her neck. It gave a wonderful massage. Didn't do a thing for her thought processes, though. She might as well have disconnected her brain.

Sophie looked at her fingers and realized she'd shriveled into a prune. With a sigh, she pulled the Glenravener outfit out of the stream and spread it on the boulders next to Jayjay's. Then she climbed out, dried off, and pulled on clean underwear and jeans and a polo shirt; she and Jayjay had finally decided the filthy Glenravener clothes had to come off for a wash. Her own comfortable, worn cotton felt wonderful. She was going to miss it when she had to go back to the leather and linen. When she finished dressing, she joined Jayjay on the other side of the grotto. "Have you thought of a way to save us yet?"

Jayjay, who had taken the first bath and who now wore her favorite outfit—khaki pants, a khaki shirt, and the infamous Banana Republic photographer's vest—had been staring off into space. When Sophie spoke, she jumped slightly and looked up. "What?"

"Have you thought of a way to save us?" Sophie

repeated, managing to keep her voice patient. "Have you come up with anything? Five Best Ways to Escape an Invisible Wall; Three Easiest Techniques for Overcoming Guards—like that."

"Oh. Not so you'd notice."

The grass felt like strands of heavy silk beneath Sophie's bare feet. She hated having to put on shoes and socks, but if they came up with something, she wanted to be able to act quickly. She sat down near Jay and regretfully began to tug on a clean pair of socks. "Okay. So you've failed to be brilliant. Have you been moderately bright?"

"Would you be satisfied with 'not entirely stupid'?"

"If it got us out of here, I'd settle for Jerry Lewis dumb. What did you come up with?"

Jay pointed at the tall grass that hid the low, angular toilet. "We can take a couple of good-sized rocks from the little wall there. We can hide behind the grass, and make a lot of noise until somebody comes in. We can watch how he gets in, then hit him over the head with our rocks and run."

Sophie stared at her friend. "You're right. That lacks almost everything a good plan needs. How do we make sure only one person shows up? If only one person shows up, how can we be sure we'll see how he gets in? If getting in and getting out are the same, and we do manage to overcome our theoretical responder and we get out, how do we find our way through the maze? And even supposing we find our way out of the maze, how the hell are we supposed to get across the drawbridge?"

Jay wrinkled her nose. "I know it isn't great. What's your plan?"

"I still haven't come up with anything."

"Nothing?"

"Nope." Sophie didn't mention the hypnotic power of the waterfall. She felt a million times better for having had a bath, but the joy of being clean wasn't going to set them free.

"But you don't want to try my great escape?"

Sophie jammed her hands into her jeans pockets and nestled her back into the stone wall, which, like the ground beneath her, conformed until it fit her comfortably. "Well . . . let's just say I'd like to see the bugs worked out of it first."

"Escape plans are unnecessary," a voice growled from the door.

Jay and Sophie jumped to their feet and turned to face the door. A heavily furred, vaguely lupine creature the size of a Shetland pony sauntered into the room, whiplike tail lashing. He walked on four legs, but the unusual bulges at his hip and shoulder joints made Sophie think he could probably stand erect briefly; he had hands, though they bore obvious traces of an evolutionary heritage from paws.

His face and coat were stained with bright red blood. He was breathing hard.

Jay whispered. "One of the warrags."

Sophie realized she was facing a creature she had been visualizing for the last eight or ten hours as a talking dog. The nightmare creature had little of the dog about it. It was lean and glossy and beautiful in a frighteningly predatory way, and when it looked at her, she felt it was assessing her for her suitability as a snack. She wondered why it was so bloody. She swallowed hard.

The creature ducked his head in a slight bow. "I am indeed a warrag," he said. He evidently had acute hearing. "You may call me Grah."

Jayjay nodded, frowning. "You're the one who found me. And you're Matthiall's coconspirator, aren't you?"

Grah chuffed and tipped his head to one side, managing to look both quizzical and deadly. He said, "You seem ever so well informed. Did Matthiall mention me to you when he brought you down here?"

"No." Jayjay said. "I simply have good access to information."

"Fair access, anyway," Grah said. He looked from Jay to Sophie. "And who are you?"

Jay inclined her head in imitation of his tiny bow. "Julie Bennington."

"And I'm Sophie." Sophie's voice cracked; nerves made her sound like a teenage boy. She, too, ducked her head.

"Sophie—Juliebennington. You grace us with your presence."

Sophie wasn't sure what the warrag would consider polite and what it would consider insufferably rude, but she couldn't stand not knowing anymore. She asked, "Why are you so bloody? Did someone attack you? Did someone try to get past your guard to attack *us*?"

"In a manner of speaking." The warrag's smile grew broader. "Someone attacked your guard, my dear friend Hanarl . . . and killed him, poor Hanarl. He died trying to protect you." Grah laughed, a hideous sound, and said, "It's a pity he failed."

Jay paled visibly. "What do you mean by that? Aren't you here to guard us?"

Grah cocked his head and grinned, a happy doggish smile. "I'm here to kill you. I don't hold with the ideals of the rebellion. You're trouble for the way things are. Aidris Akalan believes it, and so does that traitor Matthiall."

"But Matthiall trusted you," Jay protested.

"Everyone makes mistakes."

"We aren't anyone important. We can't hurt you."

The warrag sighed. "I am inclined to believe that; you look worthless to me. But when both my Mistress and the traitor agree that you are important, I would rather not take chances. I don't want change."

Jay backed up a step and crouched. Sophie couldn't see what she was doing, but Grah could.

"Poor silly Juliebennington. I'll eat you before you can hurt me with your little rock," he said.

Sophie turned to look just as Jay snapped an underhand fastball pitch—one of her softball specialties. Jay didn't have the ninety-mile-per-hour pitch that could have made her a star, but she'd been clocked at seventy-five a couple of times, and she was accurate as hell.

She pitched a strike that time, too, and caught Grah solidly on the left eye. The warrag staggered, but he didn't fall. Instead he stepped forward, growling.

Jay pitched another rock into the strike zone, and Sophie turned and grabbed a rock of her own. The warrag looked from one to the other, and went straight for Jayjay, teeth bared and fingers flexed, claws outstretched.

Sophie acted on reflex. She flung herself onto the warrag's back and started bashing his skull with her rock. He howled and thrashed, trying to buck Sophie from his back, but years of horseback riding came to her rescue. She locked her feet around the warrag's chest. She shifted with his movements the way she would have with a horse. And she kept hitting with the rock, landing her blows on the same spot.

Jay got to her feet and struck with her own rock, though she couldn't throw it because Sophie was in the way. Grah howled again, and this time Sophie heard someone shout, "I'll be right there!" The warrag growled softly and spun; Sophie could almost make out what he said. Almost. It was threat, or maybe promise; whatever it was, it portended yet more trouble. With Sophie still on his back, Grah ran for the doorway.

The man who'd shouted charged into the room from the corridor as Grah reached the doorway. Man and warrag collided, both crashed to the ground, and the warrag's fall threw Sophie into the rock wall. The rock didn't have time to conform to her presence as it had when she sat against it; when her head hit it, red and white light flashed across the backs of her eyeballs and pain so intense it had weight and sound and taste and smell screamed along the top and back of her head. She dropped onto the grassy floor, stunned. Her skull throbbed in time with her pulse and her nose felt like someone was running white-hot needles into it. She ran her tongue around her teeth; a few of them felt loose, but none had come out or broken off. That was good; she had a real phobia about having her teeth knocked out.

The warrag was first to his feet. He disappeared into the darkness of the hall as Sophie rolled herself onto her hands and knees and scrabbled around for her rock. She braced for an attack from the newcomer.

Jayjay wiped blood from her face with the corner of her shirt and stared at the man; Sophie wasn't sure whether all that blood had come from Jay or Grah. Jayjay cocked her head to one side and asked, "Matthiall?"

Sophie had only an instant in which to study this newcomer. He had fangs. Claws. Pointed ears. Jayjay's description had been flawless. When he stood, he turned his back on them. "Yes," he said. "Matthiall." Evidently he didn't consider Jay and her a threat. Sophie didn't know if he was a threat, though, and wondered if she ought to brain him with the rock on principle, so the two of them could run. She decided not to. At the moment they needed an ally desperately—desperately enough that she was willing to consider chancing her life to an enemy in the hopes of finding one. Since Jay held on to her rock, too, and waited, Sophie suspected she'd reached the same conclusion.

He stared down the dark corridor where Grah had disappeared. "Grah attacked you, didn't he?" he asked without turning around.

Jayjay wiped more blood from her face. Sophie realized a lot of it was coming from a laceration right at her hairline. "He wanted to kill us," Jay told him.

Sophie's glance moved from Jay back to the stranger. She watched his face in profile. The points of his ears unnerved her, and the fangs that flashed briefly when he spoke frightened her all out of proportion to what they were. Teeth, she told herself. They're only teeth. Cats and dogs have teeth just like them. But years of indoctrination from television, movies and books drew comparisons between those fangs and the similar-appearing teeth of the werewolves and vampires of fantasy, and her mind refused to be comforted.

Matthiall said, "I knew one of my . . . associates . . ." He frowned. "One of my fellow conspirators . . . also worked for Aidris Akalan. I thought I knew who it was." Matthiall still peered into the gloom of the corridor. "I didn't think it was Grah. He and I were friends. We've been friends all our lives." Matthiall turned to face them and shook his head. "He's going to be back before too long. He'll come with Bewul and Aidris Akalan and a pack of Kin hungry for our blood. If they find us here, they'll get what they came for."

"Are you on our side?" Jay asked him.

He turned and smiled wryly; his eyebrows rose. "The important question is, are you on mine?" He shrugged. "We'll have to find that out as we go, though. You're important somehow, to someone; I haven't the time to figure out to whom . . . or why. And I don't dare leave you behind; Aidris will kill you if she finds you, and if you are potential allies, I won't stand for that."

"And if we're enemies?" Sophie asked.

Matthiall nodded to her, polite acknowledgment of either the question or the courage it had taken to ask it. "Then you'll kill me, or I'll kill you. For now, though, I suggest we flee . . . and live."

"That was what we had in mind," Sophie said.

Matthiall glanced at Sophie, then at Jay. The instant they looked into each other's eyes, Sophie saw both of them stiffen. The current that passed between them was electric, and so palpable she could almost see it. Both Jay and Matthiall seemed to stop breathing. Sophie saw Jay's pupils dilate and when she looked at the Alfkindir, Matthiall, the centers of his pale blue-gold eyes had grown huge as well. Sophie felt she might as well have become invisible; the two of them obviously had forgotten her presence.

Jay dreamed this, too, she thought. Dreamed that she would find herself drawn to Matthiall, dreamed that he wasn't human, dreamed that Matthiall had set a guard to protect us. So Jay hadn't really dreamed at all. What had she done?

No time for that. No time to think, only to act. Both Matthiall and Jay had broken eye contact; Jay picked up her pack and slung it over her shoulders while Matthiall stared down the corridor again.

"Where are we going?" Jay asked.

"I have another ally—someone Aidris Akalan believes long dead. We'll take several weapons I've been saving for this day, and run for his hideaway." He shook his head. "If Fate favors us, we'll survive the journey. Of course, Fate hasn't shown me much favor lately."

Sophie finished settling her pack onto her back. Matthiall said, "Lights down," and the room responded, plunging all three of them into darkness. "Tell me when you can see."

Sophie's eyes took several minutes to adjust. "Now," she said. A few seconds later, Jay said, "Okay. Me, too."

"Then stay with me. Let's go."

Thirty-six

Matthiall led Jayjay and Sophie at a run through back corridors and twisting passageways, toward the place where he had hidden the Blindstone, the tool by which he hoped to escape the careful searching magic and numerous hunting parties Aidris Akalan would certainly send out after him. He took the women by the fastest route, all the while praying to the oldest gods he could name that Grah would not get to help in time to find the three of them.

In spite of his fear, he could only keep part of his mind focused on caution.

The woman Jayjay fascinated him—drew him. The moment he looked into her eyes, he felt he'd known her forever, though of course that was impossible. He rarely associated with Machnan, and certainly he had never seen her. But something about her resonated inside of him, as if he were a bell and she the mallet that struck him. Her animated voice, the set of her shoulders and the thrust of her jaw when she stood there holding her rock, trying to decide whether he was friend or enemy, the flash of her eyes; he knew— *knew*—each of those characteristics as if it were a part of him.

And even though he was not watching her at the moment, he could feel her presence as a pressure at his back, as steady and sure as the touch of a lover's hand.

Who was she? How had she come to him?

And what did her presence mean?

Thirty-seven

A magical surge of energy flowed into Yemus as he lay on the narrow cot, staring across the room at the single sunbeam that fell through the tiny slot of a window the stonemasons had left him. He sat up, and the surge intensified; it shivered through him and left his heart pounding and his mouth dry in its wake. Something had happened. Something had changed—something good. He could not remember the last time he had felt Glenraven's ambient power increase instead of decrease.

"What's happening?" he whispered, and hurried to that single window he'd been left when they walled him in. He raised himself up on his toes and stared out, hoping he would see something that clarified the situation.

The Aptogurria fronted on a quiet street well away from the busy center of town. Wizards since Zearn had been in the hands of the Kin had found the calm of the neighborhood conducive to their work. Now, though, Yemus loathed that quiet. It cut him off from participating in life even to the extent of experiencing it vicariously by watching the lives of others. And it eliminated any hope that he could discover news of the world that had closed him away.

The street lay almost empty. A bony, gangling dog lay on the cobblestones in a location that would have invited disaster on a busier street. Well away from Yemus, a child sat on the stone stoop of his house, bouncing a jointed wooden dancer on the board he held on his lap; the silence of midday was so complete Yemus could hear the clack of the wood.

Nothing. Nothing, nothing, nothing. For all the evidence Yemus had, he and the child might have been the last two living Machnan in the world. Yemus refused to let himself despair, however. He could see nothing useful, but he could still feel. And he had felt Glenraven's long-dying heart stir slightly. He hadn't the evidence that his world would live, but suddenly he had hope.

There were times, he thought, when hope was more sustaining than the best of food and drink or the most congenial of companions. This was one of those times.

Thirty-eight

Jayjay followed Sophie, who followed Matthiall; he led them by back ways and through forgotten tunnels where the grass had either died or never lived, where dust lay thick on the stone shelves, where the false stars had long ago died of neglect and Jayjay had to slow her pace long enough to fumble her flashlight out of her pack. Beautiful carved stone formed the corridors and the arches, but from the dust, from the cobwebs, she could feel the aching emptiness of the years that had passed since anyone had cared for the place. The desolation bore down on her, heavy with the smell of dust and neglect, while the bouncing light of her flashlight threw shadows that looked frighteningly alive.

They ran; stopped and hid when the echoing voices of searchers reverberated through the long winding tunnels of stone; ran again. Matthiall stopped at last in a stone cul-de-sac. "Through here." He slid his hand along a branch of one of the stone trees. Jay heard a soft click, then saw a strip of blackness appear in the beam of her flashlight. The maw expanded and she realized the stone wall was sliding away to one side, but it moved in absolute silence. She tried to imagine the craftsmanship that could accomplish such a feat;

that could build an invisible door and have it still soundless and perfect after uncounted years of disuse.

When she considered this miracle more fully, she decided perhaps it wasn't so astonishing after all. Maybe Matthiall had done work on it in a better time, preparing for what he feared might lie ahead.

The three of them stepped through into the darkness, and Matthiall stopped at another tree pillar. He tapped it with a claw, and Jay turned the light back the way they'd come to watch the door slide into place.

False stars flickered to life in the center of the huge room. Jay turned off her flashlight. "We'll only be here a moment," Matthiall said while he reached up into the branches of a stone tree and pulled down a leather pack. "I feared this day would come, and I made preparations against its arrival." He strapped the pack on his back. It was bulkier than the packs she and Sophie carried, and made of leather; it looked to her like it had seen a lot of hard use. "I have dry rations for two weeks, along with the Blindstone. We'll find that more useful than anything else I have in here. I did not expect to have company in hiding, though, so the rations won't hold up well. I have extra weapons; I can give each of you a dagger and a sword. Here, at least for the moment, we're safe, so catch your breath."

While Jay and Sophie stood panting and trying to rest, Matthiall gathered the rest of his supplies; then he brought each of them a sword and a dagger. He helped Jay belt her scabbard on and showed her how to fit the two buckles to speed her draw, and as he did so, he paused from time to time to look into her eyes.

Again she felt his gaze as if it were a touch, a caress—just like in the grotto, just like in the dream. She pulled away, stiffening her back and averting her face so that he could not mistake her distaste for him. Still, her breath quickened and she felt the heat rise to burn her cheeks. Her body was a traitor to her mind, to her well-being. It always had been.

Matthiall smiled a tiny smile with lips that trembled; he looked in that instant so uncertain. Disarming, somehow. Compelling. She glanced at him in spite of her determination not to, and felt the electric shock of his nearness. She could imagine him kissing her, touching her, their hands sliding along each other's skin, their breath warm on each other's flesh. She felt herself flowing against him, moving with him, his fingers circling her breasts, his thighs between her thighs, the ecstatic moment when their two bodies joined and became one—

"No," she whispered.

"No?" he asked in a whisper softer than hers.

She risked a glance at him, and was startled to find him wide-eyed and pale, breathing hard. She looked away again. His every gaze was a touch, and when he looked so vulnerable, she could not look and still resist.

"No." She meant to sound confident and a little fierce, but the single syllable betrayed her by quavering at the end.

Wonderingly, he asked her, "How did you do that?"

"Do what?" She felt weak and helpless standing there, mere inches from him, surrounded by the heat of his body. She didn't want to admit feeling anything. She feared the power such an admission would give him over her.

"You felt it, too. I can see it in your eyes. How did you do that to me, little Machnan?"

"I'm not Machnan, and I didn't do anything."

Out of the corner of her eye, she saw him shake his head. "No. I would have no reaction to you, and you would hold no attraction for me, unless you were something that you cannot be. *Machnan.*" He invested that word with a bitterness almost as dark as that which filled Jay's soul. "*I cannot desire; I cannot have anyone. I am last and alone of my straba*—the sole survivor of my line; I am and will be always alone."

He pulled back from her, putting physical space between them to match the emotional wall he summoned. Jayjay watched him, furious about the wash of feelings she had for him—overwhelming feelings that came from nowhere, for no reason. Try as she would, she could not deny them and she could not make them go away.

Jayjay stared at her hands; they shook. Something inside of her stirred, something she'd never felt before. She could not put a name to it, she could barely describe it to herself. She ached and a heavy burning emptiness spread through her, and a weight settled on her shoulders that pressed the air from her lungs.

It's psychological, she told herself. Some perverse desire for self-destruction. I'm thirty-five years old and I've screwed up three times in the men I chose, and some twisted part of me wants to see me finish the job and break myself entirely.

Matthiall went to assist Sophie, watching as she strapped on her sword and dagger. Sophie asked him whether or not she should fight since she didn't actually know how to use a sword.

"If someone comes at you and I can't reach you—and you don't want to die—I suggest you fight."

Jay laughed in spite of herself. Matthiall seemed to be a smartass; she'd always liked that in a man. Not one of her three husbands had had a decent sense of humor.

Matthiall glanced her way, frowning, then turned back to Sophie. "Don't be afraid to hurt someone; don't hesitate to kill if you get an opening. It isn't likely you'll do well if it comes to that, but who knows? Desperation breeds strange champions."

Doesn't it, though? Jayjay shook her head, bemused.

And suddenly thought she caught a sound from the right side of the room.

The false stars gave too little light at the periphery for her to see if anything was there. She pulled her flashlight out of her pack and pointed the light toward the sound. The beam threw dancing shadows on the walls from the eerily twisted shapes of the carved stone trees. She thought she saw movement, but when she flashed the light toward it, she saw nothing. She shivered. The unrelieved darkness and the pregnant silence wore at her nerves. She hated imagining things. She needed to get out into the sunlight, or at least into the honest darkness of night under an open sky.

"Would it be too much to ask if we might leave now?"

Both Matthiall and Sophie glanced at her.

"This room is well hidden. We'll probably be safe here for a short while." Matthiall shifted his pack and began to slide his sword into its sheath.

Jay felt like a fool, but she said, "Probably, but I thought I heard something move along the wall, and out of the corner of my eye, I thought I saw it. I know I'm being ridiculous, but—"

Something chittered. A fingernails-on-blackboard sound, a metal knife blade dragged across a mirror, a wrong and terrible noise.

Matthiall's head came up and his lips stretched back in a terrifying snarl. "To me, quickly!" he snapped, and drew his sword.

"Oh, shit," Sophie said, and drew hers.

"You have to be kidding," Jay muttered. She tried to pull her blade out of the scabbard while running and nearly tripped herself. She stopped long enough to yank it free, then bolted toward Matthiall; the unfamiliar weight in one hand threw off her stride.

From the corner of her eye, she saw movement again, this time coming straight at her. She started to turn to face it, and Matthiall shouted, "Don't stop! To me! To *me*!" She kept running.

"That way," he shouted, pointing. "Kill anything that crosses your path. Don't let them touch you!" He dropped behind as they ran. "I'll guard the sides and back!" Sophie took the left, Jay the right. Black shapes boiled out at them from both sides, coming fast.

"Shit!" Jayjay yelled. "I want my pepper gas!"

One of the creatures materialized in front of Sophie, leapt at her throat with dagger teeth flashing. Swinging the sword like a baseball bat, Sophie drove straight through its neck. The head separated and the mouth opened in an agonized silent pantomime of a scream. Sophie growled, "*I* want a machine gun!"

In the dark, Jay couldn't see the creatures clearly—they were no bigger than terriers, they were fast, they launched themselves out of the darkness straight at her throat. She tried Sophie's baseball bat grip, concentrating on following through with the tip the way she had when she'd played on a softball team. The blade felt awkward; it didn't balance like a bat. It was heavier and springier, and when she connected, she didn't get the clean, solid shock she got hitting a softball. Instead, the hilt relayed to her hands the wet, sickening give of flesh, followed by a quick jar as the metal cut into bone. And her blade caught. It didn't go through cleanly. Blood spattered on her, on Sophie; the thing flopped to the ground. She swung the blade back to free it, then lifted it to strike again. And she kept running, kept running.

Another one, teeth coming at her like the mouth of a shark in her nightmares after she watched *Jaws*. In the dark, all she saw was the teeth. She swung, hit meat and bone. Felt the warm spatter of blood. Another one, jumping at her, hissing. Jay backhanded it with the dull edge, felt its weight connect as a jarring shock through her arms and elbows and the muscles of her back. And the thing came at her again. This time, two attacked. She kept moving forward, managed to dispatch one, but the other leapt from her right side, and she couldn't free the blade fast enough. The sharp white-hot flash of pain. Her sleeve ripped, its teeth dragged through her flesh, and suddenly her sword arm bled heavily from deep, ugly gashes. Left-handed, she drew her dagger. Pain—burning, searing pain—and then a warm sensation. Numbness. She swiped feebly with her sword; her fingers lost their hold and she hit her attacker with the flat of the blade. The sword dropped from fingers she could no longer feel. The thing jumped again, this time latching onto her arm and hanging there—a weight that dragged at her, but painless. Painless. She came in up and under with the dagger, left-handed, and felt the warm slick weight of intestines slide down her left hand and wrist and she smelled the stink of offal.

The thing fell away; her foot slipped in the wetness, in the tangle of guts, and she cried out. Went to one knee. Braced her arms to catch herself, landed on the right. The arm gave as if it wasn't even there; it buckled and she pitched face first into uneven stone floor and dead animals. Pain, nausea, and even worse pain as sudden weight landed on the back of her knee, and slammed down onto her. Matthiall, tripped by her fall; and more teeth coming at her face, at him trying to shake off the blow of the fall. Jaws from hell going for him. Another one, another one. And her left hand flashed out, shot straight into the thing's mouth, dagger piercing through mouth, spine. And the feel of those teeth around her left wrist, top and bottom. But Matthiall moved, rolled to his feet, pulled her to hers.

She couldn't get her balance, staggered as she tried to run. The numbness, the numbness. Right arm and left arm and now her whole body, warm and tingling, begging rest.

In her ear, Matthiall's urgent voice: "Don't give up now. Not now. We're almost there."

She found strength in her legs to run again, to stagger, and Matthiall stayed beside her, and Sophie on the other side kept swinging, kept swinging—batting a thousand, Jay thought, but Jay's batting average had been better in the league, why was Sophie doing better?

Dizzy, drowsy, let me sleep, let me sleep, and her legs lead weights that dragged forward against her will because of Matthiall's arm around her.

He stopped for an instant, hit something on the wall. She sagged, falling, and had the curious feeling that the cave caught fire, that the underground lit up in one incandescent ball, and that the fire burned the monsters; they were all screaming, screaming, and she wanted to laugh, wanted to cheer.

And then the fire went out.

Thirty-nine

I didn't care whether I lived or died, Sophie thought, and I lived. Jay *wanted* to live, and look at her now.

Sophie wished she could look away from her friend for a moment; Jayjay lay in the tall grass where Sophie and Matthiall had carried her—dead white, unconscious, soaked in blood, panting like a dying animal. Sophie didn't look away, though; she kept her fingers pressed against the tear in Jay's right wrist that spurted blood, and prayed that Jay wouldn't bleed to death before her would-be rescuers could treat her wounds.

Matthiall, the creature who had been both their captor and their rescuer, squinted against the glare of the late-afternoon sun and finished mopping the blood off Jay's left wrist, revealing more small, chewed lacerations.

"They don't look as bad as this one."

"The little ones are worse. The heavy bleeding would at least clean the wound. Voragels are poisonous," Matthiall said. "A tiny bite can do a lot of damage. She's taken several; she'll be full of poison."

Sophie felt momentarily light-headed. "Will she live?"

Matthiall finally looked up at Sophie. His face bore no expression. "Probably not," he said, and turned his attention back to Jayjay.

Sophie increased the pressure on the torn artery. Live, dammit, she thought. You have to. You can't leave me here alone.

Sophie could taste the bitter stink of sweat and the iron tang of blood at the back of her throat when she breathed; her fingers slid in Jay's blood, blood that formed golf-ball-sized clots, that soaked Jay's khaki shirt and pants almost black. Sophie tried not to think about the blood, tried not to think about Jay's husband Steven and Steven's friend Lee, tried not to let herself consider the possibility, however faint, of slow and wasting death by AIDS. Modern plague. Such diseases had no place in Glenraven.

Matthiall rummaged through her emergency kit, and through his pack. He didn't find what he was looking for in her kit, and when he pulled a couple of dingy brown skin-wrapped packets out of his supplies, she shuddered.

Sophie said, "The wraps in the emergency kit are sterile. We can make a pressure bandage."

"Not good enough. A bandage will not stop the bleeding, only slow it. We have to close the wound." He unwrapped the tie around one of his little packets and removed a curved silver needle, and from the other one he drew out some brown, twisted thread; lumpish thread that looked like he'd rolled it through the dirt.

"My God," Sophie said. "You can't intend to sew her arm with that. It'll rot off!"

Matthiall glanced at her, and she winced at the coldness of his eyes. "This is fine, twisted-gut thread. Do you have something better?"

Sophie didn't have any suture. She shook her head.

"I've done this before. Not often, but enough to know what I'm doing. If she lives, it will be the grace of the gods, but if she dies, it won't be because of my gut thread."

Sophie thought of the poison and bit her lip. "When will we know if she'll live?"

His jaw set. "Shortly."

Sophie cleaned the skin around the laceration with alcohol pads and poured peroxide into the wounds. Then she got out a roll of white cloth gauze.

Matthiall nodded. "Very good. You know to clean a wound before treating it. That is not common knowledge among the Machnan."

"It is among *North Carolinians*." She didn't like the Kin's condescending tone.

He glanced up at her from under his long, pale lashes, and she saw his eyebrows flick upward. "My apologies," he said, then turned his attention back to Jay.

Sophie mopped fresh blood out of the wound with a couple of gauze pads. She held pressure both above and below the torn artery, and managed to keep the wound from refilling before Matthiall found the spot he wanted. He located the torn ends of the artery, jabbed the curved needle through the ripped flesh, and pulled gently.

Matthiall took his time, making small, neat stitches, mopping the blood away before each one. The bleeding slowed down. Then it stopped.

He ran a line of suture through the skin above the torn artery, and lastly, he sewed the lips of the wound together.

Sophie watched, impressed in spite of herself. She would never have imagined that those claw-tipped fingers could be so dexterous.

While she bandaged over the cross-shaped line of stitches, he started on the other wounds, which, because they didn't involve bleeding from arteries, didn't require her assistance.

He broke the silence with a question. "You have known her long?" He kept his head down, his eyes on his work. The hands moved slowly, steadily, carefully. Sophie heard an edge to his voice that belied the steadiness of his hands, though.

"Most of my life."

"What sort of person is she?"

"Why do you care?"

"I'm not certain. This matters to me, though."

Sophie looked up at his face, at the sweat on his forehead and the shimmering beads of it on his upper lip; at his fierce attention to the work he did. He cared what happened to Jay; she couldn't imagine why he cared, but she believed that he did.

"She's a good friend. Loyal. Brave. She does what she thinks is right, no matter what it costs her. She isn't very good at taking advice, but she doesn't offer a lot of it, either. To the best of my knowledge, she has never told a secret that someone else told her." Sophie held Jay's limp, hot, dry hand and wished she could feel some life in it—some movement.

Matthiall nodded. "She has a lover . . . a mate? Children?"

Sophie studied Matthiall's face, but his expression gave away nothing. She thought of Steven, and sighed. "No. No one. Not anymore."

"She did once?"

Sophie wondered how much Jay would want her to tell this creature who was working so hard to save her life. She decided that, since Jay hadn't been particularly secretive about the men in her past, she needn't be, either. "She had three different husbands. None of them was worth the powder to blow him up."

Matthiall's forehead crinkled in puzzlement. "Powder? To blow?"

"All three of them were bad men. Users. Trouble."

"Ahh."

The second wound was ready for her bandaging. She waited, though, because it was close to the third bite, and she didn't want to get in his way. She didn't want to get next to him, either. Not really.

His stitching slowed down, and for an instant he stopped altogether. His shoulders tensed, and his claws flexed and retracted. "Three men and all three bad men." For an instant his upper lip curled back in a snarl that showed his fangs clearly. He looked at Sophie, and sighed, and the snarl vanished. "I see something in her that I do not understand. Something I believe is impossible . . . and yet I see it."

"What?"

He sighed again and resumed stitching. "It's only a dream. Nothing more than a dream. And impossible dreams are better left unspoken." He finished sewing the third wound.

Sophie watched him. He took Jay's hand in his own, and held his other hand beside hers. He sat staring at them, a slight frown marking his face. He's comparing, Sophie thought. Why, though? And what impossible dreams did he dream when he looked at their hands?

Matthiall lay Jayjay's hand across her chest, then packed the needle back in its wrapper and sprinkled a little powder on it. While he put his supplies away, Sophie bandaged the other two wounds.

When she was finished, Matthiall, his pack already on his back, crouched by Jay's side and scooped her into his arms. He stood easily and looked down at Sophie. "We need to put distance between us and this place before sunset. While day is on our side, my people will not follow us, but they can easily outstrip you and me if we aren't hidden once night falls. We need to create a safe camp while we have daylight."

Sophie stood and picked up her pack and Jay's. He led off across the field, heading for a nearby copse of trees. She asked, "Why will your people only follow us after dark?"

"The Kin and their associates are burned by sunlight

to varying degrees. None of us enjoy it, but it kills most of us."

"Why not you?" Sophie realized how rude that sounded, and cleared her throat. "Not that I would want it to, you understand. I just wondered."

"First, I'm a Kintari—a wizard. That confers some protection. Second, I'm old. With age comes strength."

Sophie laughed. "Yeah. You're ancient. You have to be . . . what? Twenty-five. Twenty-eight, tops?"

"Two hundred and ten."

"Is that in dog years?" Sophie blurted.

"Dog years?"

She sighed. "Never mind. I was wondering how you measured a year."

He glanced sidelong at her and smiled wryly. "The same way you do, I imagine. One rotation of the earth around the sun. Or are North Carolinians like Machnan? Do they still believe the sun circles the earth as the moon does?"

Sophie laughed.

"No? You're very forward thinking." He smiled a tiny smile that vanished when he looked down at Jay, lying limp in his arms.

He glanced at the sun, already low in the sky, and picked up his pace. His sense of urgency conveyed itself clearly to Sophie; though no danger showed itself at that moment, something terrible—something deadly, fearful even to him—pursued them.

Forty

Aidris Akalan sat alone in her audience chamber, facing her chief of guards, Terth. He stood in front of her, pale and sweating, his fists clenching and unclenching, but he held his head high and his eyes met hers.

"Why is Hultif not with you?"

The guard said, "His burrow has been abandoned. His clothing, the paraphernalia with which he did his magic, his books and notes—all are gone. He isn't here anymore."

Aidris tapped a finger on the armrest of her chair. "That isn't what I asked you, Terth. What did I ask you?"

Terth swallowed; she could see his Adam's apple bob in his throat. He glanced up and to his right, frowning, then looked back to her. "You asked me why he wasn't with me?"

"Yes."

"He's gone, Watchmistress. Completely gone."

She smiled, and watched the remaining color drain from his face. "My question was not where Hultif was. My question was why he wasn't with *you*. This is your last chance to give me an acceptable answer. If you don't, you will not like what happens next."

Terth nodded and stared down at his feet. His breathing grew rapid, and the sweat ran down his cheeks and dripped off of his chin and his eyelashes and the end of his nose. His skin was a bloodless gray. He was as near dead from fright as one of the Alfkindir could be. Finally, he faced her again. He said, "He is not with me because I could not find him."

"You looked for him?"

Terth nodded.

"But you could not find him."

Terth nodded again.

"I see." She smiled, and her chief of guards returned a tentative smile. She continued, still smiling. "That's the wrong answer, Terth. Do you know what the right answer would have been?" Terth made no response, but she didn't expect one. She continued as if he had answered in the affirmative. "The right answer would have been, 'He is not with me because I killed him . . . but I can bring you his head if you would like to have it.' Do you see that that would have been a good answer?"

He nodded slowly and licked his lips. His eyes, white-rimmed, looked like they would pop out of his skull at any moment and flee of their own accord.

"Good," she said. "I would hate to punish you without knowing that you understood why you were being punished. That would be unreasonable, wouldn't it?"

He didn't even nod. He didn't dare.

She let her smile grow broader. "I wouldn't want to be unreasonable, Terth. No one ever says I'm unreasonable, do they?"

He shook his head. "No . . . Watchmistress," he whispered.

"Good." She rested the tip of her index finger on her lips and studied the soldier, changing her expression from smiling to thoughtful as she did so. "I think a small punishment will be sufficient." She stood, tipped her head to one side, and made her face friendly and open. "Don't you agree?"

She saw wariness in his eyes, but also hope—hope that she would not make him suffer too much for his failure, hope that he would not have to bear the brunt of her awful rage. He nodded his head so slightly that if she hadn't been looking for the response, she would never have seen the movement.

"You do agree. How wonderful." She stared into his eyes, this time doing more than looking. "Come here," she told him.

He stiffened as if she had slapped him. He tried to look away from her but she didn't let him. He tried to control his own muscles, but she didn't let him do that, either. She held him firmly with her gaze, with her power; she was strong, as if she had been half a dozen of her own top soldiers. While she looked into his eyes, he did not breathe except by her wish that he continue to do so. He took a step forward. It was so funny to watch his leg lift and step toward her while the rest of his body fought it. She needed a little humor, a little comedy. She had a serious problem, a terrible problem that would tax her enormously, but Terth was not that problem. He was easy to fix.

His other leg lifted and stepped, and he made a strangled little cry as it did. She could feel him fighting her. She laughed.

Another step.

Another.

"Kneel," she told him.

His muscles locked, his back went rigid, he shoved his fists against the fronts of his thighs to strengthen his resistance. He screamed; the sound he made was the shrill, whistling scream of a dying rabbit. Lovely. She heard the crunch of bone and the popping of cartilage as his knees gave way. He dropped in front of her. His strangled breathing gurgled and he sobbed. His gaze, though, never left hers.

"Something small," she said in a soft, gentle voice. "Something so simple that you can do it yourself to show me how much you regret failing me. That would be best, don't you agree?"

He didn't answer. Of course.

"Something reasonable. Something fair. Let me see . . . you didn't look hard enough for Hultif. He's out there somewhere. If you had looked hard enough, you would have found him. No one can hide so completely that he can't be found . . . but you know that, don't you?"

"Ple-e-e-e-ase," Terth whispered. "Oh, please . . ."

"You didn't look hard enough . . ." She smiled down at him. "Of course. This is fair, simple and fitting."

"No," he begged.

"Take your eyes out for me, please."

"No . . . oh, please . . . no!" Even as he begged mercy, his hands moved toward his eyes. "No . . . Watchmistress . . . not my eyes . . ."

She smiled as his thumbs gouged into the corners of his eyes. She laughed happily as he began to scream in earnest, as his thumbs vanished up to the first joint into the sockets. Wordless bubbling pleading, shrieking despair, hopelessness . . . and all the while, his hands acted on her command, doing what she told them to do, and when he was finished, when his hands had done what she told them to do, those hands calmly held out the eyeballs that they had ripped from Terth's bleeding sockets; held them up to her in offering while the man himself tried to collapse and faint from pain and terror, though she would not let him.

"Dear Terth. How thoughtful of you. You may keep your eyes, though," she told him. "I wouldn't want to be unreasonable, and I have no use for them."

She let him go then. She broke off the link that had

controlled him, and when she did, he collapsed like a marionette with cut strings. He slammed to the stone floor and lay there bleeding and screaming.

She called in his second-in-command, who had been standing in the anteroom to her chamber, waiting while she decided Terth's fate.

The second came in, as pale as his commander had been.

Aidris settled back in her chair and crossed her legs, adjusting her silk skirt so that it showed off her exquisite ankles. "Your name is Dallue, isn't it?" she asked him as he walked toward her, trying hard not to stare at the lump of writhing flesh on her floor.

"Yes, Watchmistress."

"Very good, Dallue. This is a lucky day for you. You have succeeded Terth as my chief of guards. Please remove him from my chamber, then find Hultif and bring him to me. Alive if you can, but dead if you must. Do see that you don't fail me as your predecessor did."

"Yes, Watchmistress." Dallue's eyes kept flicking toward Terth, then back to her. She could see him trembling while he waited for her dismissal. She kept him standing there a good long time, while she stared at him and smiled and slowly licked her lips.

Finally she sighed. "You may go, Dallue."

Dallue picked Terth up and slung the man over his shoulder and hurried out of her chamber like a cockroach surprised by sudden light. He feared her. That was good; perhaps he feared her enough to be effective.

Aidris Akalan settled back into her seat. So much for simple entertainment. Her hunters had not yet brought in Matthiall and the two Machnan wizards; she had to face the possibility that they would fail her as Terth had. She had to plan for that eventuality.

Matthiall had to die, as did the wizards he had stolen from her. He was strong—a powerful Kintari—but he wasn't as strong as she was. If her hunters didn't find the fugitives, she could send the Watchers after them, though in order to do that, she had to know exactly where they were and she had to disable Matthiall. He was strong enough to fight the Watchers off. If she could create conditions exactly to her liking, she could kill them herself, from a distance. If the Machnan really were powerful wizards, it wasn't likely she could set up those perfect conditions.

Or she could kill them up close.

She had plenty of options. She didn't think that she had much time. She could destroy them in any number of wonderful ways, but however she did it, she had to do it quickly. She dared not disbelieve Hultif's presaging of her death.

She intended to live forever, no matter what the omens said. The future could be changed; she would act quickly to change it.

Forty-one

Jayjay felt light in his arms. Her skin was hot silk against his fingertips. Matthiall tried to ignore the magnetic sensations as he carried her; he tried pointlessly. Her body fit against his as if she'd been made for him. And his heart, terribly aware, raced faster than his forced pace could explain.

This is impossible. I'm deluding myself out of desperation, out of loneliness. There can be no one for me, ever. She isn't even Kin, and if she were Kin it wouldn't matter; Aidris Akalan killed all of my *straba* except for me.

I will be alone until I die.

But his body called his mind a liar. He touched her and his blood coursed through his veins with the warmth of sunlight—and she was sunlight that did not wound, that did not burn. When he looked into her eyes, he felt something inside of him open; he felt as if at that moment he drew the first breath of his life.

What if she were what she seemed to be?

Then he had more reason for bitterness against his fate, for he would have found her only to lose her. She died in his arms. She was dying slowly—much more slowly than he would have expected, yet she still died.

He closed his eyes. If she was what she seemed, what he hoped she was, what he had waited his entire life for—impossible as he knew that hope to be—he could save her. If she was the woman born to be his *eyra*, his other half, he could give her part of his strength, part of his life, he could bind them together. If she died, he would die. If she lived, he would live.

He watched Sophie set up a tent at the edge of the clearing, away from the deep and deadly shadows of the forest.

He let himself consider the incredible possibility that had leapt at him when his eyes first met Jay's. He let himself play with the thought that she might be his one mate, his soul, his life. Machnan and Alfkindir did not mix, but she wasn't truly Machnan. She looked Machnan, but she was an outsider. Outside . . . the very idea of life outside of the borders of Glenraven almost stole the breath from his lungs. Outside the guarded borders of Glenraven, life would have no Aidris Akalan. No dying magic. No shattered world. Outside of Glenraven, life would be different.

The price he would have to pay to attempt to save Jayjay's life would be extraordinarily high. If she was what he hoped, what he dreamed, what he would get in return would repay every sacrifice.

And if she isn't what you wish, you fool—if she is not your *eyra*, and the song of your *straba* sings not in her blood but only in your imagination, you will try to save her life by binding yourself to her—and she will die, and you will spill your life into the dust, and your revolution will wither into nothingness, and Aidris Akalan will proceed with her destruction of Glenraven unchecked.

He held the unconscious Jayjay in his arms, and closed his eyes, and felt her heart beating in his own veins.

What price my soul? he wondered. What price my world?

Forty-two

Sophie looked up from hammering in a tent stake when Matthiall lay Jayjay on the grass beside her.

"What's going on?" she asked, and then she looked at Jay and she didn't need his answer. "Oh, Jesus, Jayjay," she whispered, reaching out to touch her friend's forehead with the inside of her wrist. "Jay . . . you have to live. You can't die now."

Jay panted in shallow little gasps; Sophie counted almost fifty in a minute. Her skin was transparent and beaded with a fine sheen of perspiration, her dry lips had cracked, her tongue looked swollen, and her partly open eyes didn't blink—didn't follow anything. Nothing was left of Jayjay but a feverish, dying body, and in a few minutes the spark of life she still held on to would be gone as well.

Sophie couldn't stop the tears; she didn't try. She gripped her friend's hand and whispered, "You can't die here, Jay. I could, maybe, but not you. You can't let the bastards win, Jay. If you die, they'll have beaten you. You can't give up. You can't quit fighting. You have to keep on, keep moving forward." She choked on her tears, and scrubbed at her face with the back of one sleeve. She took a deep breath and said, "Remember what you keep telling me. Life is forward motion, Jay. No matter how bad things get, life never backs up . . . and you can't either."

She realized Matthiall was saying something—was repeating her name, over and over, his tone urgent.

"*Sophie.*"

She looked up at him. "What?"

"I think I may be able to save her. But if I am to have any chance at all, there are things you will have to do. I've set a spell with the Blindstone so that Aidris Akalan should not be able to track us here, and placed wards around this campsite to keep us hidden from the eyes and spells of my people. We are far enough off the road and close enough to twilight that the Machnan should be hurrying toward the safety of their cities; none of them should venture this far from the road. Still, you are going to have to stand watch."

"What are you going to do?"

"I cannot explain it. We don't have time. You will have to trust me, Sophie. You will have to trust me to take her into your tent, to stay there with her all night. You will not be able to speak to either of us, to look in on us, to permit anything to interfere with us. This is vital. *Vital.* We will either both live or both die." He shivered as he said that, and stared into her eyes as intently as if he were trying to read her mind. She stared back at him, wishing she could read his. "You will have to trust me, Sophie. If you cannot promise me that you will trust me and do as I say, then I will not try to save her, because if you do not do exactly as I ask, I *will* die."

"Why?"

"That is the way the magic works. I can save her life only if I offer my own, and if other special conditions are met."

Sophie shook her head. "That's not what I meant. Why would you risk your life for her? Because we're these 'heroes' you and the book and everyone have been waiting for?"

"No."

"No." Sophie clenched her fists. Everything was out of control, and this inhuman creature was asking her to trust him with her best friend . . . her helpless, unconscious, dying best friend. "Why, dammit?"

"Ask me tomorrow, if I'm alive when the sun rises. It is a long story."

Jay wasn't going to last much longer. Sophie was going to have to make this decision for her friend, because Jay wouldn't survive to make it herself. And really, Sophie had no options. She could trust Matthiall, or she could let Jay die. "Go," she said. "Anything that gets to you will have to come through me to get there." She drew her sword; its blade gleamed golden in the light of the setting sun.

He nodded. "Trace out the edges of the wards. You'll find them easily enough. Do nothing unless something passes into the circle you mark. If that happens, fight for your life. And I pray we both see you tomorrow morning." He scooped Jayjay up in his arms and hurried toward the tent. Sophie watched him go.

Just before he ducked under the flap, he stopped. "If we both die, the road is that way." He pointed toward the west with his head. "Stay out of the forests at all costs; find a city as soon as you can."

Before she could answer, before she could even think about what he'd said, he and Jay vanished into the tent. She heard him fumbling with the zipper to the bug screen. Resolutely, she turned her back—turned to face the setting sun.

My watch again, she thought. My watch. Last time I had the watch, I did a job of it, didn't I? I don't know if I could have done any worse than I did. Delivered us into the hands of our enemies by falling asleep; and now I get another chance. Great.

She began to pace. Matthiall said he'd set wards. She assumed that she wouldn't be able to see what he'd done. But she wondered how far out his wards extended, and how much space she had to patrol. She walked a tight circle around the tent, facing away from it. Inside, everything was silent except for the sound of Jay's raspy, rapid breathing, and Matthiall's soft murmuring.

"Forward motion," she whispered. "Life is forward motion; life never backs up."

She kept pacing, treaded the second circle outside of the first. She couldn't feel anything different. She extended her third circle outside the range of the second.

No wood for a fire, she thought. Not that I'd go anywhere near those trees to get some. Not if it were a hundred degrees below zero, which the way my luck is running it might become any minute now.

"I was right when I told her that. I was right. Good advice, and if she didn't hear me, at least I was listening to myself for once. Those are life's rules: never let the bastards win; never back up; never give in."

Another circle, wider. She stepped over her pack and Jay's. Matthiall evidently took his bag in with him, though she hadn't actually noticed him doing so. She kept pacing out her circles, slowly, carefully, looking for anything out of the ordinary, any little clumps of voodoo feathers or amulets or whatever. She didn't know what to expect, so she expected anything.

"I've been backing up. Haven't been taking my own advice. I've been too willing to lay down and die; I've been too willing to let silence and darkness and nothingness be an answer for a problem that demands life. Forward motion."

The meadow grass lay flat when she stepped on it and didn't spring back up. Dry, she thought, and then looked back the way they'd come. Very, very dry. She could still see a clear path beaten into the grasses where the two of them had walked. It was a trail an idiot could follow, and she was sure when anyone came looking for her and Jay and the Kin, they wouldn't be idiots.

And here I am, pacing out crop circles. Geez.

Forward motion. Do something. Do anything. Don't be paralyzed by fear of mistakes.

She kept going. She wanted to find the wards if she could. She needed to know where they were; she wouldn't know what they were, or what they did, but if she could identify them, she would feel better.

Another circle.

Another. She guessed she'd moved about ten feet from the tent—about a foot each time.

Another.

When she hit the wards, she almost shrieked. Her skin tingled and she had a terrifying urge to flee, to run across the fields until she couldn't run anymore. Instead, she sat down and shivered. *That* was a ward. She saw nothing. She reached out a finger, and felt nothing until that finger crossed whatever barrier Matthiall had set. The fear screamed into her skull again and she flung herself backward.

Damn! Those wards hurt. They would keep out small trouble, anyway. She didn't have to worry about attacks of marauding chipmunks. Or people. She didn't know whether it would be enough to keep the Alfkindir at bay.

She studied the circles she'd marked out, and told herself, "That's life. Put up your wards, pace out your circle, fight like hell to keep your head up and your skin intact. And never lie down and give up. Never, never let the bastards win."

She walked around the circle one last time, poking outward at random and jerking her hand back the instant she felt anything. The exercise reminded her of sticking her finger onto the hot burner of a stove; every time she did it, it got less fun. She completed her final circuit, though, and sighed, relieved. If Matthiall had left holes in his ward, she hadn't found them.

She circled closer to the tent, her sword still drawn. She heard Jay's breathing. It didn't sound any better, but it didn't sound any worse, either. She turned her back on the tent.

Leave it alone, Sophie. Just leave it alone. Don't be afraid to trust. Sometimes trust is the only hope you have. Guard them, pray . . . and wait.

Forty-three

"Blood," Aidris Akalan whispered to the swirling specks of light in which the Watchers manifested. "Bring me the wizards' still-beating hearts, and you can have their blood. Bring me Matthiall unharmed, though. I want to destroy him myself." She stared into the sparkling curtain of death and smiled. "When I've finished with him, I will give you his blood."

Blood, blood
>we want—

Do you promise
>—his blood all of his blood
>*we want to drink him dry*
>>Do you swear

I want to hurt him,
>you, you, you, do you swear
swear you will give us his blood?
>>She won't she won't she won't—

Aidris snarled, "Enough! I'll give you his blood. I said I would, didn't I? Have I ever broken a promise to you? I'll give you anything you want—I swear it. But don't bother me with that. Go now, and bring him to me quickly. And bring the hearts of the wizards he stole from me."

The Watchers coalesced into a single face that floated just above the floor and terminated a handbreadth below the ceiling. The face's eyes began to glow—dull red, bloodred, ruby red—growing brighter and more intense. Aidris had never seen the hunters form a single unified shape before; she had not realized that her minions could act in such complete unison. They'd created a beautiful face; except for those hungry, terrible eyes, it was a face that would have suited a goddess.

"We'll have our blood," that face said, speaking in a single voice—in her voice—and then she recognized that the face the Watchers had created was a replica of *her* face.

She smiled, flattered by their demonstration of subservience. "Yes," she told them. "We'll have our blood."

Her illuminated face smiled back at her, and the smile it gave her was hard, cruel. Then her Watchers dissipated into motes of light and streamed out of the Wizard's Bell through the window, a rapidly retreating magical ribbon of light.

She hoped the Watchers would reform their image of her face when they caught Matthiall and killed the Machnan wizards. She wanted him to know precisely who had sent his death. She wanted him to taste despair.

With the Watchers gone, she turned her attention to a relic she'd stolen from one of the last of the Aregen lords before she'd killed the little monster. It was a viewing bell, and because she wasn't Aregen, she should not have been able to use it. She'd discovered, however, that if she coated her hands with some of the blood of an Aregen just before she tapped the rim, the bell would listen to her and she could direct it to show her the things she wished to see. She'd drained the blood from every Aregen she slaughtered after that, and had a little Machnan flunky dry it and powder it for her. Now hundreds of vials of the dark brown powder lined one wall of her work space.

She took a bit of the powder, sprinkled it into a mortar, and used her spittle to moisten it. She'd experimented until she found that spittle formed the fluid most like fresh blood; she got the best results that way, and results mattered to her.

She smeared the brown, stinking fluid on her palms and, while it was still wet, tapped the rim of the flat silver bell. It rang softly and light shimmered out from the center. By concentrating, she guided the bell toward her hunting parties that slipped through the darkness, outward in a slow, spreading circle from Cotha Maest. She watched the black hulks of trees streaming past, the glow of moonlight reflected in water, and suddenly she was upon her line of hunters. She watched, moving from Kin to Kin-hera, studying each of her people and making sure that none of them failed in their duty. She wanted no mistakes. There would be no last-minute mercy, no bribes taken and cleverly hidden. She would be satisfied with nothing less than the destruction of her enemies. And she was taking no chances in making sure she got what she wanted.

When she had looked in on her hunters and satisfied herself that they searched diligently, she turned her attention to finding her Watchers. She ranged farther afield, seeking them by using the telltale feel of their magic and the light they gave off. She couldn't find them; not at all. She frowned, puzzled. Even when she couldn't see them, she had tracked them down by trailing their magic, so that she could have the pleasure of watching them destroy their victims. But now they seemed to be gone.

For a moment she panicked. Perhaps they had abandoned her, or returned to their Rift.

Then she considered: they hunted Matthiall, who was a Kintari strong enough to fight them off. If they had a way to hide their presence, they would surely use it.

She thought about that for a while and decided her Watchers were only exercising the intelligent caution that would bring them to their quarry faster, and that would give her what she wanted all the sooner.

She would be satisfied to wait.

She cleared the viewing bell and rinsed her hands. She intended to be well rested when Matthiall came in. No one had ever betrayed her so fully before; no one had successfully put her in jeopardy in centuries. She wanted to enjoy his contrition, and when he had groveled and begged for his life, when he had sufficiently abased himself, she would force him to become her consort. Or she would savor his death. Either way, his life belonged to her.

Forty-four

Matthiall laid Jayjay on the floor of the tent, on top of the bedroll her friend had put out. He stripped his own shirt off, then carefully removed hers. The bizarre garment underneath he left in place, uncertain of its purpose or the method by which he might effect its removal. He knelt beside her, not touching her. She was so near death—so very near.

Was she his *eyra*?

The Kin could have only one mate in a lifetime. One *eyra*, one soul. Every soul had a song that it shared with only one other; and from the moment Matthiall had found Jayjay in the woods, under attack by Aidris Akalan's Watchers, he had heard that song. Impossible as it seemed to him, impossible as it should have been, for he was Kin and she was, if not Machnan, then something very like Machnan, she appeared to be the other half of him.

Was she? Was she?

Lying there dying, she could not answer his questions. She could not look into his eyes and promise to love him, could not take eternal vows; she could not sit in silence and let her soul respond to his without words. Lying there dying, she could give him no answer to his question; and still he could hear and feel and touch the maddening elusive magical song of her soul.

If she was not his *eyra* and he tried to claim her, he would die. That was the bargain he would have to make to take the chance. He didn't want to die, but for the chance of discovering that they were *eyra* to each other, when he had believed all his life that there was no one for him, that there never would be, he would risk more than death.

He took his dagger from his belt and pressed the flat of the blade to his forehead.

He pulled his shoulders back and took a deep breath. Still kneeling, he held the dagger aloft in his right hand, and said softly, "Hear me now. I call upon the forces of earth and sky, of wind and water, of the hot white fire of day and the cold black fire of night. I summon as witnesses the spirits of my *straba* that have gone before to note the promises I make and bind me to them." He paused and took another deep breath. Resolved, he continued. "I offer my life to this woman," he whispered. "I offer my blood." He nicked his finger with the point of the blade, and when the dark red drop welled up, pressed the drop of blood to Jayjay's forehead. "I offer my breath." He inhaled slowly, and pressed his lips to hers, and slowly, gently, exhaled.

"I offer my heart." He sat cross-legged beside her and lifted her up, positioning her with some difficulty so that her legs went around his waist and her chest pressed against his. He felt the terrible racing pace of her heartbeat, the weakness of her pulse, the way her arms hung limply at her sides and the way her head lolled against his neck.

He paused for a moment, considering whether he should bind her to him as he had bound himself to her. He should, he thought. If he gave her his health and strength and half of his life, if he took the poison from her blood and bore it in his, he should have the right to take for her the vows she was unable to take for herself. If he was offering his life to save hers, he ought to know that when she woke, she would not be able to reject him.

But he wanted her love to be love. Not duty and obligation and a magical binding, not compulsion. Perhaps he would feel no difference between the two states . . . but he would *know* the difference existed.

He wanted her to choose him as he chose her.

What fools we are for love, he thought. What utter fools.

If she rejected him, if she refused to take the vows he had taken, if she left him, then he would die as surely as he would if she were not his one true *eyra*. He didn't want to die. He didn't want to live alone.

But he would not coerce her love.

"Because she cannot offer her promises of her own free will, I release her from them, and bear these oaths alone. I declare us *eyra*, and I declare my soul insepa-rable from hers.

"I am one half of her."

He stilled himself and focused on the rhythm of her breathing. Gently, he followed the path he had drawn between them into her lungs. He became her breath; they breathed together. He willed himself deeper into the trance, and felt the pounding of her heart against his chest, and felt his blood coursing through his own veins. Then slowly he *became* his blood and his heart. He found the bond between them, the bond he had created with his oaths, and again traced the path, becoming *her* heart, *her* blood.

He knew her pain, the fire of poison in her veins, the agony of the visions that tormented her mind. He knew her wish to be free from the pain, to escape the torture of the cage her body had become. He felt with her the hunger for death, for silence, for respite.

The part of him that was her begged that release,

and while her breath filled his lungs and her blood coursed through his veins, he yearned to grant it to her—to give her release. But his own blood and his own breath called out to him to live, to fight death as the enemy, to rejoice in blood and breath and the pounding dance of his heart, her heart.

Through the currents that sang between them, he called out, I have found you! I have found you! You are me! My soul, my soul, wake and know me. I will share your pain. I will carry your hurts. Share my love, and let it fill you.

He breathed her breath, she breathed his breath—sucked in air like fire that devoured everything it touched. Their hearts galloped, thundered, and the pain screamed, lashed, howled through their veins—and yes, Matthiall prayed, yes, let me share all your pain. Let it come to me.

The poison burned in his veins, dulled his sensations, made him numb. He fought the numbness, for the voragel poison was not her only pain. Memories washed over him—pictures he didn't understand. A lean man, pale-eyed and handsome, in a bed with a woman who didn't belong there. He felt her flinch back; she'd felt the pain as a stab to her heart, ran with her when she turned and fled. A blur, a flash, and then another picture—a dark-haired man, his fist raised in fury, and that fist smashing into her face. Matthiall felt his own body stiffen, felt himself trying to tear that man limb from limb, but he couldn't change the memory. She lay screaming, curled on a cold hard floor while a foot slammed into her stomach again and again. Blood, too much blood, and she wept. She had been with child, and her child was suddenly gone.

Matthiall felt her anguish as his own, her loss as his. It became darkness, but he fought it off and faced the vision of another man, another bed, another stranger with him, but this time when the one Jay knew and loved rose to greet her, the stranger beneath him was also a man. The men laughed, shrugged; one of them opened his arms and beckoned to her, and again she turned and fled, her soul torn by loss, betrayal, confusion, the pain of shame. And then there were more pictures, flashes, glimpses. Faces, faces on street corners and in a multitude of rooms, faces that stared at her with cold, hostile eyes. She felt their censure. He felt it with her.

So much pain.

Matthiall carried the pain, but he couldn't ease all of it. The memories flooded over him, dark and harsh and ugly, until the poison began to sing to him, to call him to come to the silence, to the peace where there was no joy, but also no pain.

He breathed with her.

He breathed for her.

Live, he said. Pain tires of itself; it grows dull and weak. We can bear this pain. We can bear it, we can overcome it, we can put it behind us. I am you, you are me. We are not alone. You are with me and I love you and you will never be alone again.

As you to me, so I to you.

My soul, my love.

His breath, her breath, all one. It steadied.

Yours, he told her. I am yours. I am yours.

He felt a stirring of consciousness within her then. He exulted. Breathe my breath, he urged her. Let my heart beat for you, let my blood feed you.

He felt her confusion, but her soul moved to his and embraced him. The fire of her life burned inside of him; the wonder of her flowed through him, and he felt whole. A part of her wakening self sought life. She let him catch their runaway breathing and carry it down, slowly, gently down, let him make it deeper and bigger and richer, each breath dragging in and holding cool clear air, each long, slow breath washing out the fire.

Her tortured coma lifted, and she drifted without waking into the healthier realm of deep, weary sleep.

They still lived. She was his *eyra*, and he was hers.

My love, his soul whispered into her dreams, *where have you been for so long? Oh my soul . . .*

Forty-five

Sophie stretched and paced, trying to stay awake and alert. The silence of the night was restful rather than ominous. Matthiall's voice, soft and deep and somehow desperate, had become silent perhaps half an hour earlier, and since then, she had heard nothing beyond the night noises of insects and animals and the wind in the grass. There had been, in the last few moments that she'd heard him talking—or possibly praying—a joy in his voice that Sophie thought boded well for Jay's survival.

Be all right, Jay, she thought. Please be all right.

She made a circuit around the perimeter of their camp, full of hope; hope that Jay would survive, that the night would remain peaceful and safe, that she and Jay would leave Glenraven alive.

As she came around to the front of the tent, she noticed that Jayjay's backpack had begun to glow. Sophie frowned. It hadn't been glowing before. She drew her sword, and cautiously stepped nearer. The glow was warm and inviting, like light from the windows of home on a cold and rainy night. It wasn't doing anything—changing shape or color, making noise, moving. It was mere light, nothing more, and it glowed through the nylon of the backpack almost like light through stained glass, and shone out around the edges, beckoning her closer.

She flipped the bag open with the tip of her sword. The light streamed upward like a beacon to heaven, and Sophie found herself hoping no one was out there to see that light. Still nothing attacked, nothing moved, nothing changed.

Holding her breath, she poked inside the backpack with the sword and stirred the contents.

Nothing happened.

Well, she thought, I can't very well start fishing things out with the sword. That would take all night. And I can't leave this alone without knowing what it is.

That left sticking her hand into the backpack.

She hated Glenraven. Things like this simply didn't happen back home.

She moved nearer, and, with her blood pounding in her ears and her mouth dry as a drought-stricken field, she fumbled around until she found the object that glowed so brilliantly. When her hand touched it, it dimmed to a soft, gentle yellow light, still glowing, but no longer so bright that she feared it would lead trouble to her. She pulled it out.

The book. Jay's *Fodor's Guide to Glenraven.*

She should have known. After all, that was the book that had started all this trouble. She opened it up, and was surprised to find that the pages were blank. Glowing, blank.

What does *that* mean? she wondered.

Words appeared on the page she held open; not as if they were being written, but all at once.

"The first condition has been met."

"What first condition?" she blurted.

The words vanished, and a block of text replaced them.

"You, Glenraven's chosen heroes, move one step closer to fulfilling your destiny, and freeing Glenraven from oppression and annihilation. Two conditions remain to be fulfilled. Have courage."

"Wrong. I'm not having courage, and I'm not fulfilling any damned destiny. Glenraven survived just fine without me until now, and it will survive without me when I'm gone. I'm taking Jayjay and the two of us are going to get out of here."

The words of encouragement vanished. The page remained blank for a long moment, and then the book said:

"The first condition has been met."

Sophie glared at the printed words, then asked, "Okay—what are the other two conditions you think Jay and I are going to meet? Unless the first of them is leaving this dump, you're going to be disappointed."

The page cleared again. She waited even longer for a response. Then:

"You know what you need to know. The first condition has been met."

Sophie hated anything that was intentionally cryptic. She said, "What is going to happen? Answer, or you're going into the campfire."

The page went blank for so long she thought the book had decided not to answer her. But then it gave her its message.

"You're going to be a hero. Wait and see."

The light went out of the pages. End of interview, evidently, and she had no idea what the damned book had been talking about. She frowned and tossed the Fodor's back into Jay's pack and pulled the flap over it. If it decided to glow again, she didn't want those searchlight beams getting out.

As she was resheathing her sword, she heard a faint grumbling, growling sound that might have been thunder had the sky been clouded over. She froze and listened, and when she'd located the noise, turned to face it.

By the pale light of a thin, cloud-splotched moon, misshapen forms approached—the creatures of the Alfkindir. Sophie watched them skulking toward her; she listened to the preternatural rumbling of their voices, to the swish of their legs through the dry grass; as they moved nearer she felt the thud of feet so heavy they shook the ground beneath her.

Sophie drew her blade again and stared into the face of impending doom; the taste of bile and adrenaline burned at the back of her throat. She recognized several of the shapes as creatures Matthiall referred to as Kin-hera—warrags and fliers. She couldn't make out their numbers nor could she identify the varieties of the creatures who walked in the center of their group. In the moonlight the Kin-hera were silvered and huge and somehow fitting to the night and the field, to their hunting and their intended evil. They moved along the clear path she and Matthiall had left; the fliers quartered back and forth through the air in front of the main group—hell's own hunting dogs given wings. They were still too far for her to make out their words, but every step brought them closer.

She wanted to call to Matthiall for help. She didn't want to stand and face those oncoming terrors alone. If Jayjay were to have her chance at life, though, Sophie knew she would have to hold them off.

Matthiall had faith in his Blindstone, but Sophie could see it didn't hide the clear trail they'd left. And no matter how good the artifact was at casting confusion, she couldn't imagine that the creatures stalking the three of them across the plain would be fooled when the path ended in a bubble of fear. Could they see her? She didn't think so; that at least gave her some comfort. If they had been able to see her, she felt certain they would have run straight at her. The Blindstone and Matthiall's wards were effective to a degree.

Did they do enough?

With both hands clenched around the hilt of her sword, she waited and hoped.

The first clear words carried to her ears. "The trail is still two people, one Kin and one Machnan. I tell you, I think they've set a trap for us. The other Machnan has circled round and even now closes in behind us." The voice that delivered this statement sounded childlike. It had to be one of the fliers, Sophie thought.

"Then fly back and see, if you're so sure." That was a midrange voice—male, annoyed.

"I don't want to go alone."

"We aren't splitting up. If they're hunting us, we'll fight them better if we stay in our group than if we let them pick off stragglers one at a time."

Something rumbled like the shift of tectonic plates in an earthquake. It took Sophie an instant to realize that sound, too, was the voice of a Kin creature, or rather, its laugh.

"Matthiall runs with two Machnan women, or maybe one. No other Kin run with him. And the Machnan women are nothing. What do you fear?"

"Aidris Akalan said they were wizards."

"I was with Matthiall and Bewul the night we brought them in. They aren't wizards. They're nothing."

They were close enough that she could finally make out details—that the deep-voiced creature, as gaudily dressed as all the Kin creatures she'd seen except the warrags, shambled bearlike on four legs, but had skin as hairless as a human's; that several warrags loped at either side of it, grinning; that a dozen fliers looped and dove in a circle that scouted front, back and sides of the hunting party. She counted fifteen and wasn't sure she'd gotten all of the fliers. She couldn't hope to fend off so many, nor to survive a concerted attack.

She glanced back at the tent. It was a dark, still shape, a lump behind her.

I may fight and die, never knowing if I fought for nothing. They might both be dead.

Then again, they might not.

Sophie turned and faced the oncoming monsters. The wire wrap of the sword's hilt dug into her hands. She realized the muscles of her forearms already ached from holding the weapon so tightly. She tried to relax.

The first of the flying Kin flitted within ten feet of the wards. It hissed and veered to the right, and the next two fliers followed it.

"Their trail doesn't go that way," one of the warrags growled.

"I touched an unhallowed spot," the lead flier called. "Go around and pick their trail up on the other side."

"Un-*hal*-lowed spot! Hah!" the same warrag muttered, and kept his path aimed straight for Sophie.

She swallowed; her mouth tasted like chalk, it was so dry. She aimed the point of the blade so it would skewer the warrag as he stepped through the ward. But then the warrag whimpered and backed up a step; he sat down on his haunches with a "woof" and growled. The hunting party came to a complete halt.

"What is it?" The bearish horror swaggered across the line the warrag had found and deep into the ward. But not through; it backed up so fast its scrabbling claws threw out little clods of dirt and grass. When it backed even with the warrag, it shook its head, and sat with a thud beside the smaller monster.

The two of them were at most ten feet away from her—close enough that she could smell them. She looked straight at them, and they looked right *through* her. They didn't see her; she felt certain of this. But they weren't leaving, either. The fliers came whipping around the periphery of Matthiall's wards, back to their comrades' sides.

"Unchancy," the bear thing said.

"Foul," the first warrag agreed.

"What do you think, Hmarrg? This feels to me like a warning set by her Watchers." The bearish Kin-hera leaned back and lifted a massive club-fingered hand to scratch its belly.

Another warrag stuck his nose into the ward, pulled it back, and shuddered. His hackles rose. "I don't think so. She said she told them to leave us alone—that we were to be given free passage."

The bearish Kin-hera puffed and chugged. Sophie realized it was laughing. "And if she made her bargain with them, does that mean they'll keep it for us? Not if they're hungry. If they're hungry, they'll suck us dry and throw our bloodless bodies in a heap, and she won't do a thing to stop them."

"You're only guessing it's her Watchers. The unhallowed spot could be something Matthiall did." Hmarrg stood and stared at Sophie, his eyes focused *on* her for an instant. She had the horrible feeling that he could see through Matthiall's wards straight to her. But then his gaze shifted slightly and he drew his lips back from his fangs in a snarl.

"Patience, Hmarrg. Next time we find Matthiall, we'll kill him," the ursine Kin-hera drawled. "We were going to do that anyway. I *still* think this stinks of Watchers."

"Doesn't matter. We have to go through." The warrag Hmarrg turned and looked coldly at each of the other Kin-hera. "If we go around, we show whoever did this that we can be frightened."

"If the Watchers set it, I *am* frightened," one of the little Kin-hera said. It fluttered around the warrags, landing at last on the back of one.

The bearish Kin-hera stood.

Hmarrg followed suit. The warrag growled, "Who takes the honor of first in line?"

Shit, Sophie thought. Shit, shit, shit! Going around was a *good* idea.

The moon came fully out from behind the clouds for a moment—a thin sliver that cast more light than it had any business doing. The bearish Kin-hera stood straight up on its hind legs and sniffed the air. "Can't smell Machnan, can't smell Kin or Kin-hera except for us, can't smell Watchers. Nothing on the air tonight but coming rain."

Hmarrg cocked his head and grinned. "Which means you want to go first, or you will let me have the honor? Come now, Tethger. Which will it be?"

"I smell no danger that would make it an honor." Tethger chuckled again. "If you think it will gain you some glory, Hmarrg, by all means go first."

"Nicely spoken," the warrag said.

Sophie saw Hmarrg turn to the wards and stiffen. Then, fur bristling, he took one slow step toward her. And another. And another. She aimed the sword at his open, panting mouth and steeled herself to run at him the instant she could tell he saw her. He began growling, and his head lowered, and his tail stuck out like a bristle brush. Another step.

Turn back, she thought. Turn back, turn back.

Another.

One more would put him into the circle with her. She caught her breath, clenched both fists around the sword, and lunged. His eyes focused on her at that same instant, and he leapt. She'd aimed the sword well. It went into his mouth and part of the way down his gullet and out through his back, shoved as much by his forward momentum as by hers.

But his teeth still snapped as his jaws slid up the blade at her hands, and his weight bore her down to the ground, and his almost-human hands wrapped around her throat with a ferocious strength that stopped the air to her lungs and brought the roar of her own blood to her ears. Pinned to the ground with him on top of her, she tucked her knees up to her chest and slammed her feet upward and back, toward the tender gut below the barrel of his ribs.

Hmarrg coughed and retched, spattering blood and bile and worse over her face and hands and chest. She kicked again, and his grip loosened. She could see his eyes beginning to glaze, but the field of her own vision began to dim, too. He renewed his death grip on her throat; he wasn't yet dead. Not dead enough.

She fought for air, shoved harder with the sword, felt the cold sharp points of his teeth against her hands. Felt pressure on one wrist as he tried to bite around the crosspiece. She refused to make a sound. She still feared those outside the circle could hear her even if they couldn't see her; then she jammed her feet into his gut again.

Hmarrg collapsed onto her, crushing her into the ground. He gave an eerie, gurgling cry and went limp.

He weighed entirely too much.

Sophie lay underneath him for a moment, trying to catch her breath. His fingers, still around her throat, no longer choked her, but she still struggled to breathe. His dead weight crushed her, his hot blood coated her skin, his bowels and bladder released and soaked her in stinking excrement. She braced her legs far apart and twisted her body to one side. The dry grass poked through the back of her shirt and scraped her skin; chaff clung to her sweat-drenched neck. She paused, inhaled, held that breath, and tried again. By shoving her shoulders along the ground and twisting her hips, she managed to get out from under the warrag.

She pulled the tail of her shirt loose from her jeans and used it to wipe the blood and mess off of her face. Instead, she managed to smear it around worse, and to bring the stink of his bowels right to her nose. The smell, held in place by the stillness of the night or perhaps by Matthiall's wards, proved too much for Sophie. She dropped to hands and knees and retched, trying not to make any noise and failing badly. When her stomach was empty, she wiped her face and hands on handfuls of dry grass, then turned to look at the other Kin-hera who waited outside the wards.

One of the fliers flitted around to the other side of the enchanted circle, then back. "He still hasn't come out," she chirped.

Another of the warrags sniffed the air and howled. "Death scent! Death scent! They've killed Hmarrg!"

"Watchers," Tethger said. "Nothing else would kill him soundlessly."

"We should revenge him," the same warrag said, pacing in a tight circle.

The bearish Kin-hera turned its head and huffed. "You want to cross their line and do it?"

No, Sophie thought. You don't. Really. You want to go home.

The first fight had left her so exhausted she almost couldn't stand. If she had to try to kill the remaining warrags and the giant Tethger and all the nasty, bat-winged little fliers, she wouldn't live to see the dawn. One of them would kill her, and that would be it for her, for Jayjay, and even for Matthiall.

The warrag glowered at the invisible barrier in front of him. "We should have brought one of the Kintari with us. He could have given us a spell to get through the Watchers' wall."

Tethger dropped to all fours and snorted. "He could

have, possibly. But the wards might be Kintari wards. Matthiall is a Kintari. He could have made them."

The warrags growled among themselves, and one of them spoke. "If we consider that a possibility, we have to go in." He paused, and Tethger sat down with a snort, nodding slowly. "But I think you'll agree, those wards don't feel anything like Kintari magic. They feel like the work of the Watchers, and that is something only the highest of the Kintari can deal with. We will have to send an emissary to speak with the Watch-mistress."

Tethger sighed. "Yes. An emissary. Someone . . . expendable."

The warrags' hackles rose and their tails lashed back and forth like the tails of angry tigers.

"None of you," Tethger said. "None of them." He nodded at the fliers. "I'll find someone."

"Then we return?" a flier asked.

Yes, Sophie thought. You return. You want to return. Really.

Tethger sighed. "We can expect Aidris Akalan's dis-approval, but yes. We return."

Sophie smiled and sagged to the ground. Safe, she thought. God, we're safe—for a while, anyway. She glanced at the dead warrag.

I won, she told herself. I lived.

She rested her sword across her thighs and prayed the adventure she'd faced would be the only one the night held in store.

Forty-six

The tiny simulacrums on the table, little figures that looked very much like the absent heroes Jayjay Bennington and Sophie Cortiss, ran through their scenario one more time. Yemus watched them, clenching his fists together, almost afraid to breathe. "Win this time," he urged, but in their conflict with Aidris Akalan, both of them crumpled to the tabletop and lay still. Dead. Defeated.

He'd watched the same scenario three times without changing anything, hoping that variables besides Machnan intervention would sway the outcome of their fight in Glenraven's favor. But each time, Aidris Akalan destroyed both heroes and everyone with them. With the heroes dead and the Machnan talisman in her possession, Aidris Akalan marched unchecked against the Machnan and destroyed them, too.

The simulacrum method of predicting the outcomes of known events was not infallible, but it was very good. Yemus trusted it; he'd trusted it when formulating the plan that would bring the heroes in the first place, and although that had appeared to be a complete failure, every omen he could test pointed to the possibility that Jayjay and Sophie could be completely successful.

If the Machnan fought beside them. Only if.

Yemus faced ugly reality; the Machnan had risked everything once on his word—on his promise that he could deliver victory against Aidris Akalan without destroying Glenraven in the process. They'd trusted him with their magic; with their futures and their lives and their hope. They'd paid the price for their magicless existence in diseases, in plagues, in early death, in bone-breaking labor and the loss of every comfort they had known, and they had borne their suffering in silence, waiting only for the day when the heroes would come and lead them into victory against their hated oppressor. Their heroes had finally come, not days . . . not months . . . but years after they'd been expected, and when they arrived and word circulated among the waiting Machnan, people had prepared themselves for battle, for one final sacrifice that might not give them freedom, but that would guarantee it for their children. And after all of that, the heroes had slipped away, had gone straight to the Alfkindir and into Aidris Akalan's stronghold, Cotha Maest, and had temporarily vanished.

When Yemus told his people that he'd failed them, and that in failing them he had left them defenseless against the Watchmistress and her hated Watchers, he destroyed all the hope they had and crushed them. They weren't going to want to trust him again.

But he had to try.

He went to the walled-over window and called out to the guard who stood nearby. "Hey! Drastu! Bring my brother here. Please. It's urgent." The guard, once a friend of his, ignored him completely.

"Drastu! I have good news. But I need to speak with Torrin." Yemus put his arm out the slit and waved it. "Drastu . . . please. I was wrong about the heroes. They aren't helping Aidris. They are working for her downfall . . . but we will have to help them if they are to have a chance; I have to tell my brother. He said you were supposed to bring him to me if I asked."

The guard didn't move. He didn't look up or respond in any way.

Yemus went back to his table and stood staring at his simulacrums as they enacted their defeat again. If he'd kept his mouth shut, if he'd said Jayjay and Sophie were doing what they were supposed to do—that they were infiltrating the Alfkindir cotha, by the gods—everything would now be fine. The Machnan would be waiting for the sign that meant attack, the heroes would be safe, and the future would be secure.

I did this, Yemus thought. I alone have brought us to this desperate moment; we face failure and annihilation because I lost my nerve. I have to do something to fix everything.

But what?

Forty-seven

The low roll of thunder woke Jayjay, and she shifted back into arms that wrapped around her and cradled her. Rain drummed on nylon above her head, and even the dull light of the rainy day was transmuted by the vibrant yellow of the tent roof into a delicious mimicry of sunlight. For a moment, confused, she thought she had been dreaming and had awakened beside Steven . . . but first, she and Steven had never gone camping, and second, even if they had he had never held her with such tenderness.

She opened her eyes and looked down at the hand that pressed against her belly—a powerful hand, muscular yet elegant, with strong fingers terminating in needle claws. Matthiall.

Yes. That made a sort of sense. It fit within the parameters of a dream she'd had, a marvelous, terrifying-yet-wonderful dream that still clung to the edges of her mind. Something had happened. Vague, glorious memories . . .

Something *had* happened. What?

She pulled away from Matthiall. She felt as if she ought to stay with him, to wake him and touch him and . . . love him? Yes. She felt she ought to love

him . . . her heart insisted she already did. Her head,
however, reminded her that she was a three-time
loser where love was concerned and that, no matter how she felt, she would be best off getting out
of the tent before she did something she regretted.
If she hadn't already.

God, he was beautiful lying there. His face, serene
in sleep, called out to her.

She longed to answer that inexplicable call, but she
didn't let herself. She wouldn't. She couldn't. She
couldn't love him, no matter how she felt. She couldn't
love *anyone*, and certainly not someone who wasn't
human.

How had she come to be in the tent with him? Why
was she there? And where was Sophie, and what part
had she had in Jay's night spent sleeping with Matthiall?

Confused memories flashed through Jay's mind,
memories of a beautiful promise but underlying that
promise nightmares and terrible pain; vaguely, she
recalled attacking animals and floating in a cold and
dark place far above her body, very near death; she
recalled scenes of her husbands and their various bru-
talities and betrayals. And Matthiall walking through
the minefields of her dreams, touching them and taking
away some of the ugliness.

I love him, the voice in her heart insisted, and she
silenced that thought before it could cause her more
trouble than she already had.

She sat up and stretched; the morning chill invaded
the tent and wrapped itself around her like the wet,
clinging tentacles of an octopus. She shivered and
rubbed vigorously at the goose bumps, and when she
did, she noted the pale silver lines of old, healed scars
around both of her wrists and a long, ugly cross that
ran from the inside of her right wrist, around and up
her forearm. She frowned. She'd never had scars there
before. A few cigarette burns on her back from her

second marital mistake. One scar on her ankle from a run-in with a stray shard of glass when she was nine. *Nothing* on her wrists. Where had those silvered lines come from?

And what made her so certain she'd danced with death the previous night?

She looked back to Matthiall. To the fierce angles and proud lines of his face, repose added a gentleness that caught her breath in her throat and made her want to touch him.

She reached out a hand to stroke his lips and stopped herself. She pulled back, stared, and after a moment reached over and shook his shoulder. "Wake up."

His eyes opened, and he looked up at her and smiled—a smile of breathtaking beauty, of unbounded joy.

"Oh my soul," he whispered.

No one had ever looked at her that way. No one. She had always dreamed someone would, but in the face of reality, she pulled back. He was not human. Not human. She stared at him, feeling her mouth go dry, feeling her pulse begin to pound in her temples; she licked her lips and shook her head in slow, uncertain denial. "No. Not me. I don't know what happened, but I can't be your soul." She swallowed hard. Her eyes filled, but she blinked away the tears and said, "I can't be anyone's soul."

He sat watching her, silent. She felt his pain at her rejection, and she tried to cover it with talk. "I dreamed of terrible things last night . . . and I don't remember how I got here . . . I'm sure there's a logical explanation, but you have to know I'm not the kind of woman who climbs into a tent with a stranger . . ." She felt like an idiot; her mouth was spouting words her heart didn't believe. She belonged with him—belonged, dammit—and she was sitting there lying and pretending she didn't; she was pretending she didn't know something magical had happened between the two of them, and even though she knew she was acting like an idiot, she couldn't make herself stop. Fear. This was what fear did. "I mean, you're a complete stranger—"

"We've never been strangers, but I won't insist on that point. Last night you were dying. I knew a way to save your life, so I did."

She nodded and swallowed hard again. "And I want to thank you . . . and before I go back to the United States, I'm sure I'll find a way . . . my God, I'll make sure I repay you . . . but . . . well . . . this isn't where I need to be. I'm sure you understand that. It looks so . . . well . . . none of my friends would understand—"

Matthiall watched her with his sad, knowing eyes, and when she finally ran out of stupid things to say, he nodded slowly, and smiled the smile of a man who was gallantly conceding defeat. "I understand, Jay." He spread his hands in front of him and flexed the fingers so the tips of the black needle claws peeked out from the fleshy folds. "I do understand." He sighed, and Jay thought she saw brightness in his eyes, but he blinked rapidly and when he looked up at her, she decided she had imagined all of it. "Whatever you want me to do, I'll do it. If you want my help in getting you home, then that's what you will have." He tried to smile again, but it didn't come off well at all.

"I appreciate that," she told him, starting to back toward the tent flap. "I do. God, you've been great, saving us from the Watchers and getting us out of Cotha Maest and then saving my life, too. I wish I'd met you before I screwed up my life . . ." And then she started to cry, and she backed out of the tent before he could see.

Forty-eight

Sophie, huddled under her inadequate rain poncho, heard the tent unzip. She turned to see Jay crawl out and blink as rain hit her face. Jay looked drawn and pale but she was inarguably alive. Sophie stretched and tucked her sword into its sheath, then hurried to her friend's side.

"You're alive!" Sophie hugged her.

Jay nodded, biting her lip and not saying anything. Sophie wondered if she'd been crying but in the dismal gray pissing rain, she couldn't tell. Then Jay took a second, hard look at her, and whatever she'd been feeling before vanished beneath an expression of pure shock. "My God, Soph . . . what happened to you?"

Sophie had let the rain wash away the warrag's blood. It hadn't done a particularly good job, but her skin was now neither sticky nor cracked, and the smell of dried blood and excrement and urine had lessened; she could still see blood on her hands, however, so she probably had even more on her face. Worse, her wet clothing clung to her body with uncomfortable intimacy, heavy and cold. She would have loved to wear warm, dry clothes, but she hadn't taken the time to change, fearing that any lapse of her attention would create the window of opportunity the Alfkindir hunters needed. She pointed at the warrag. "We had company . . . but I'm okay. How do you feel?"

Jay kept staring at the warrag, her expression impressed. "Tired," she said. "Kind of confused. I don't remember anything after we started running in that cave."

"You don't want to remember. It was bad. I was sure I'd never see you again." Sophie shook her head and looked at the dead warrag. She sighed. "I was sure none of us would survive the night."

Jay walked toward the warrag, shaking her head. "I'm surprised you could kill that thing. Three of us couldn't destroy the first one."

"We didn't think Grah was going to hurt us. I knew this hunter wanted us dead. And besides, this time I had a sword. We're lucky he was the only one who attacked. His friends were waiting outside the wards to find out what happened to him. When he didn't come back, they decided to go get stronger help."

Jay's eyes communicated her blank bewilderment. "Wards? What are wards?"

Sophie nodded. "Something Matthiall put up around our camp. You can't see them, but you can sure feel them." She shrugged. "It was magic." Then she glanced down at Jayjay's arms and gasped. Jayjay wore the evidence of even more of Matthiall's magic. The voragel bites were nothing but thin, healed scars. Sophie touched Jay's right wrist. "My God, how did he do that?"

Matthiall came out of the tent at that moment, and both Jay and Sophie turned to face him. His eyes bore silent testimony to suffering and exhaustion. They were hollow and sunken and the skin beneath them was so dark it looked bruised. "I took her pain. I took her wounds." His voice sounded ragged, as if he had only that moment crossed the finish line of a marathon. "I gave her my strength. The poison that was deadly for her only weakened me. Now we'll both live."

"How did you do that?" Sophie asked.

The Kin glanced at Jayjay and Sophie saw longing in his eyes—longing and pain and suppressed desire kept in check, or perhaps denied. "I . . . discovered that she and I have . . . similarities; they allowed me to make a . . . sort of sacrifice." He pointed at the dead warrag. "They found us last night?"

"Yes. A large party of them. They ran across the wards, and stopped outside of them. Several of them kept mentioning Watchers," Sophie told him. "Only this one came through, and I killed him as quickly as I could." She felt sick reliving the struggle through her words. She cut her explanation short. "They said they would come back tonight with a . . ." She considered the conversation she'd heard the night before. " . . . a *kindari. Kindeli.* Something like that."

"Kintari?" Matthiall suggested.

"That was the word."

"Then we have to leave right now. If the Kintari they recruit is old or powerful, they won't have to wait until tonight. A Kintari will travel in daylight without difficulty, and in this rain, some of the stronger Kin-hera will be able to travel, too. Even if they can't, they'll be able to give him adequate directions for finding this place." Matthiall sighed. "And perhaps Aidris Akalan will hear what the Kin-hera have to say and find the trip worth making in person. If that happens, and if she reaches us before we reach my friend's domain, we'll die."

As they began packing up the camp, fighting the cold dreary, ugly storm, hastily shoving things into backpacks and trying to erase signs of their passage, Sophie thought of Jay's *Fodor's Guide to Glenraven.* Sophie thought she probably ought to mention the book's unnerving behavior of the night before—both the message it had given and the brilliant light it had set off—but she was afraid if she did, she would be creating a delay that could mean their deaths. If the three of them survived to reach Matthiall's friend's house— or domain, as he had called it—she could bring up the subject of the magical travel guide and its smug predictions of heroism.

When everything was packed, Matthiall went to stand beside the corpse of the dead warrag. He raised his hands above it and chanted softly, and as he did, light curled from his splayed fingertips and glowed across the warrag's fur, flickering like fire in the rainy morning.

"Dust you were, dust you shall become," he said, finishing his impromptu funeral service.

The light grew brighter, and to Sophie's astonishment, it began to devour the warrag. It did so without mess, without smoke, without spilling blood or gore, and, she realized after a moment, without leaving even the slightest trace to indicate that there had indeed been a dead warrag lying on that spot.

Matthiall glanced up to find her watching him. Jayjay had turned to watch, too.

"I don't want them to be sure of how he died. The Watchers frequently disintegrate their victims when they've finished taking everything they want. Further, I'll leave a little surprise beneath the wards. Whoever finds this hiding place will wish he hadn't."

Sophie wondered what kind of surprise he intended to leave. Something explosive, perhaps. Maybe something worse. She'd seen enough of the real Glenraven to believe deadly magical surprises were not only possible, but probable. In these circumstances, she hoped she was right.

Forty-nine

Aidris listened with growing frustration to the tale of ineptitude spun for her by her servants. "You found them, but only Hmarrg attacked? Only Hmarrg?" She stared from warrag to tiny flying tesbit to enormous cold-eyed dagreth, and considered that these three idiots were only representatives of the large group that had located Matthiall and the wizards.

"We still don't know that we found them. We still believe we may have come across a place marked by your Watchers, Mistress." The dagreth shifted and wouldn't meet her eyes. "If they were your Watchers, we didn't want to disturb them."

"And the magic of the place was so strong, even if it came from your targets, we felt sure only a Kintari could overcome it," the tesbit shrilled. It fluttered over the dagreth's head, red eyes glowing like beacons in the darkened room.

"So you let Hmarrg go into this warded barrier by himself to test your theory that something dangerous hid inside, and when he failed to come out, you decided you had better come back for help."

They nodded.

"Even though," she continued, "if you had all rushed

in together, you could probably have overcome whatever you found inside, and certainly you could have overcome one Kin and two Machnan women."

The warrag cleared his throat. "That isn't the way you described our prey to us, Mistress," he said, managing to appear diffident even as he corrected her. "You described the two Machnan women as the mightiest and most deadly of wizards. We didn't need a description of Matthiall. We know how dangerous he is. If all of us rushed in together, perhaps all of us would have perished, and then no one could have come to tell you that we found them."

"At least so you convinced yourselves." Aidris wanted to kill the three of them right there, the lying cowards; then she wished she could round up the others who had accompanied this hunting party and destroy them, too.

She wouldn't do that, however. She would have them take her to the place where they had found their invisible, warded barrier. She would take the Watchers with her. And once she had fed the wizards to her Watchers, she would allow them to devour the pitiful hunters, too.

"Take me to where you left them," she said.

"Daylight—" the warrag protested, but Aidris silenced him with a wave of her hand. "I will summon darkness through which you can travel safely. The day already leans toward the dark. Bringing on the blackness of night will not strain me overmuch."

She watched the three hunters glance nervously at each other. Inside she smiled, though her smile never touched her lips. They were wise to fear her. They had simply not feared her enough when it could have saved them.

She debated calling the Watchers to her right then, but thought better of it. They grew restless and hungry and unpredictable if forced to stay among what they saw as food for any length of time without reward. They might tire of traveling and devour Aidris's hunting party before she was ready to have them devoured. And besides, they were hidden from her; they were still someplace beyond the reach of every magic she could muster. She didn't give that fact much thought. If she did, she might begin to suspect betrayal, and if she were to live forever, her Watchers could never betray her.

She decided instead to wait until she reached Matthiall's hiding place, then call them and let them have their fun.

She said, "Wait here," and went from the window-less meeting room up the twisting stairs to her wizard's bell. She stared out at a pounding, miserable rain that bent the tops of the trees around the cotha and drummed on the metal-clad bell roof and hissed down the glass. Disgusting, cold rain. She felt a creeping, damp draft curl around her ankles and without thinking about it, traced the draft back to its source and blocked it with a tiny touch of magic.

Then she lifted a hand and reached toward the sky, and drew the clouds together tighter, feeling power flowing through her like a river. Between the particles of water, she spun webs of blackness. This was an unnat-ural darkness and costly for her to maintain, but even if the rain ceased it would hold out the searching bril-liance of the sun. Then she linked the darkness to herself; now the sprawling blackness would follow her, and those who traveled with her would not die from the steady beating of sunlight on their skins.

She smiled, considering how they would die.

Then she thought further. She would do best to travel with her army. She didn't think Matthiall and his two Machnan magicians would be a match for her and her Watchers, but overconfidence had destroyed mighty empires. She wouldn't let it, or anything else, destroy her.

She closed her eyes, took a deep breath, and harnessed the river of magic once more. She used it to send out an order her troops received immediately— a compulsion to meet her at the gate of Cotha Maest. While she was preparing a few necessities, they would gather below. With her troops and her Watchers and her power, Matthiall, his wizards, and the threat they posed to her eternal rule would die.

Fifty

They wouldn't listen and they wouldn't come. Yemus punched his fist into the simulacrum board, scattering the moving images of disaster into rainbow shards of light that smeared across the walls and disappeared. Not even his own brother Torrin would listen; Yemus had formed an image of himself and had humbled himself in front of his brother and begged him to listen. Torrin had told him to writhe in shame for eternity.

They all thought the solitary confinement had cracked him, made him desperate. They didn't understand and they wouldn't try.

Yemus stared out the slit window at his home. His people. Glenraven. He could save them; he could redeem them. Except no one would listen.

Fifty men would turn the tide. A mere fifty. Just enough to do . . . something. Yemus couldn't quite see what they were going to do against Aidris Akalan, but fifty of them could do it successfully. And he couldn't get one.

He grabbed at a tapestry on the wall and tried to rip it with his bare hands. It resisted, and he had the feeling it would resist longer than he could try; he wasn't a strong man, nor a fast one. He couldn't fight, he couldn't cast destructive spells. He could finagle a bit of information from the recalcitrant future if it felt like cooperating. He could create some damned fine artifacts, but never deadly ones. He could do a few entertaining little tricks to amuse Torrin's guests at festivals. He was clever.

But cleverness wouldn't stop Aidris Akalan. And he couldn't summon out of thin air the fifty fighters that would.

Something snagged at his thoughts. A pattern of things that he could do. Artifacts. Festival tricks. Cleverness.

No, he thought. I need fifty men. I need someone to listen to me. But the idea persisted.

Cleverness.

Festival tricks.

Yes.

It won't work, he thought. And then he thought it might.

Festival tricks and cleverness. An artifact.

A little light, a little magic, a tiny little deception. He began to smile. Maybe he could summon those fifty men after all. Maybe Glenraven wasn't lost. Hope was a funny thing. Suddenly he had energy; he was in a hurry; he had a thousand things to do and a thousand details to consider and minutes in which to set his deception going.

Fifty-one

Andu, charged for the next two bells with keeping everyone away from the wizard's tower, jumped at the sound of the explosion. He stared from the smoke that poured out of the shadowed wall to the dark figure who retreated from the Aptogurria, and felt his commission slipping away as he did.

"Halt!" he bellowed, but he didn't expect the bastard Yemus to listen . . . and Yemus didn't disappoint him. "Halt! Traitor!"

The Aptogurria was supposed to be proof against all magic, he thought as he ran after the fleeing man. The damned tower was supposed to be wizardproof; that was why wizards worked inside such places. Nothing they did would get out, nothing anybody else did would get in. But the wall was gone and the traitor Yemus was getting away.

False security we've had all these years, he thought. No telling what the bastard and his experiments could have dumped on us. Maybe what he *did* dump on us. Could be where the poxes came from; might have been what caused the plague; might even have been the reason the old folks got so sick in winter and started coughing while their chests bubbled and whistled, until

313

they wasted away and died. Lies and more lies, wizard lies: *this tower protects the townsfolk and gives me someplace safe to work.*

A liar *and* a traitor. Torrin's brother had fallen far from his family's tree. Well, when they caught him, they would hang him from the branches and tidy things up.

Yemus raced toward the outskirts of Zearn. The guard shouted for help as he ran, and soldiers saw who he was, and saw the ruins of the Aptogurria; alarm bells sounded, and armed men poured into the street. Climbing onto horseback. Summoning others. Following the traitor.

Somehow Yemus commandeered a horse; on horseback, he shot down the cobblestone street and raced out of the guard's sight. Others were on his trail by then, but the guard found himself a horse and followed the growing pack; he wanted a piece of the action when they ran the traitor to ground. Whenever they found Yemus, wherever they found him, Andu intended to be there.

Fifty-two

Yemus peeked out the stone slit at the broken glass ball that lay on the ground outside his window. The illusion he'd built into it still held. It would hold for a full day, though the wizard expected someone to come along and run a hand along the place where there should be rubble and find solid stone sometime before then. If he were lucky, though, the men who had run off in pursuit of him would be out of reach by then—too far to call back without difficulty.

He focused on his doppelganger; formed of nothing but a trick of the light, it could elude any of the men who pursued it. It would cast no shadow, however. And the horse doppelganger would leave no hoofprints. As long as the day remained rainy and miserable, and he kept it close enough to the pursuers that they wouldn't have to look at the ground to track it, Yemus thought he would be all right. He concentrated hard on the location where he sensed the disaster would strike, and guided his double toward that place in the most direct route he could manage.

Fifty-three

The rain had soaked through to Jayjay's skin; her
teeth chattered as she walked. The path she and Sophie
and Matthiall followed gave way to another meadow,
and the meadow to another stretch of forest. The sky
grew darker, then darker yet; at just past noon, the
unnatural night felt as cold to Jayjay as the chilling rain,
and far more ominous.

"We need to move faster. She's coming," Matthiall
said, looking at the sky.

Jayjay looked over at him. "Who?"

"Aidris Akalan. It means our death if she finds us."

Jay slipped and staggered into a thornbush; she
returned her attention to the path and where she put
her feet. "How do you know it's her and not one of
the Kintari?"

"I can feel her magic. I *know* her. I recognize her
touch in this false night."

"She caused this darkness?" Sophie, who looked as
sodden and miserable as Jay felt, glanced up at the sky
and pulled her poncho tighter around her. Jay wished
she could see her friend's face well enough to get an
idea of what Sophie was thinking.

Matthiall nodded. "It will allow her to move her

hunters after us during the daytime. She doesn't need the darkness for herself."

"So she isn't coming alone."

"No. I imagine if she is using the energy it takes to conjure the night, she has a full army after us."

"How close is she?" Jay watched the blanket of night extend past the three of them, moving steadily . . . and quickly.

"I have no way of knowing that. The larger the circle of darkness she creates, the more effort she will have to expend and the less time she will be able to maintain it. So if we assume she is being practical, we also have to assume she's close."

"How much further do we have to go?"

"To the edge of Callion's domain, we have perhaps half an hour of travel if we hurry."

Jay nodded. She wished she and Sophie hadn't lost their horses. They could have moved so much faster on them.

But if wishes were horses . . .

Matthiall began to run slowly, as if he were pacing himself, or possibly holding back so that she and Sophie could keep up. The blanket of darkness occluded the last of the daylight, and Jay struggled to keep Matthiall in sight and avoid the obstacles on the ground that had abruptly become invisible to her.

A question occurred to her. "Who is Callion?" she asked, running a few steps behind him.

"An old friend. A fellow conspirator. Someone who wants the same things I want." He sighed again, or maybe he was breathing heavier because he'd picked up the pace. "I don't think any of us are going to get what we want, though."

He grew silent after that comment, and Jay, who felt she was responsible for his unhappiness even if she wasn't sure why, didn't ask anything else. They ran, picking up speed when the ground permitted and they dared, and slowing when they had no choice. Time passed slowly, but it passed.

Matthiall stopped as the three fugitives reached the black wall of a forest edge, and for a moment he said nothing. In the quiet, Jay thought she heard voices coming from behind them. They were distant cries, and faint, and the sound of the rain made her unsure that she heard anything at all. She didn't say anything. She waited for Matthiall, who studied the trees, searching for something. Jay suspected his friend Callion had marked his domain with some subtle sign; she imagined broken twigs or notches in branches. Whatever he had been looking for, Matthiall quickly found, but he didn't point it out to either Jay or Sophie. "This way," he said, and led them into the woods. The steady pounding of rain on Jay's face dwindled to a cold and dreary trickle.

They walked. Jayjay wanted desperately to run. Above the steady white noise of the storm, she had for a moment been certain she heard a clear shout. Neither Sophie nor Matthiall had reacted to it, but she felt sure her ears hadn't deceived her. Matthiall led them over deadfalls and once walked along the length of a fallen tree, balancing carefully; he insisted that Jay and Sophie follow his route precisely. Jay did so, feeling queasy creeping along the enormous, rain-slicked trunk, arms out to balance herself. Sophie followed her. Jay heard one voice clearly. It yelled "That way!" and though it was distant, it wasn't distant enough. Neither Sophie nor Matthiall reacted; Jay realized they had probably heard the pursuers at about the same time she had, but what was the point in saying anything?

Walking . . . walking . . . with the voices coming closer every minute. Walking . . . walking . . . following some path that didn't appear to be any sort of path at all to Jay. And yet she got a feeling of *pattern* from Matthiall's chosen route. A sort of inward, clockwise spiral. Walking . . . and she wanted to bolt, and she wanted to scream, and she wanted to cry, and she did none of those things. She kept walking. Following Matthiall, who followed his crooked path.

Matthiall slowed further and began dragging his hand along individual trees, muttering as he went. "No . . . no . . . not this one . . . no . . ."

Jay wanted to scream at Matthiall, Do *something*! *Do* something! She knew he was doing something, but it didn't look like much. The warrags began to howl.

"Yes. Here," Matthiall murmured. He stopped in front of a huge old tree and rested his palms on its trunk. He pressed his forehead against the bark, whispered something, then stepped back. For a moment nothing happened. Then the surface of the tree began to glitter, and a dry, icy breeze sprang out of nowhere. The tree faded and the center of the trunk began to bulge outward at the sides and melt away in the center until the one tree became two enormous, weathered trees that grew from the same patch of ground. The glittering light illuminated the surface of the trees but didn't go past them. The rest of the forest remained dark, and no light shone on Sophie's face or Matthiall's. She could see the weird trees well enough, however. One of them was pale and smooth-barked, the other dark and rough. At their bases they had merged, their mismatched wood overlapping and bulging, grown together through time and proximity and at least some compatibility until, over the course of what must have been centuries, they had come to form a single two-toned trunk that, about two feet above the ground, split into two limbless trunks that curved upward and away from each other; their arcs reunited twenty feet in the air and twined around each other. For another ten feet, the pale and dark trunks spiraled upward, dancing a slow waltz of centuries together. Only above that smooth spiral did the first branches fan out, delicate and wispy, the lace-edged leaves of one tree mingling with the shining gold arrowheads of the second. The air in the ellipse of negative space formed by the trunks shimmered faintly, as if heat from an unseen source distorted the light through it. And light came through it. Neither the unnatural darkness cast by Aidris Akalan nor the dreary drizzle of the day that had existed before touched that inner world. Sunlight glimmered there, illuminating jewellike flowers and catching the wings of butterflies and dragonflies. The lush trees, rolling meadows and pristine brook that sparkled just within view beckoned; this was Eden before the fall—perhaps, Jayjay thought, quite literally.

She moved forward but Matthiall stopped her with a hand on her shoulder and a shake of his head. "We can't go through until he invites us."

"But they're coming."

"It doesn't matter. This is Callion's domain, to my knowledge the last of the hidden worlds, and no one can enter it unless Callion brings him through."

Sophie stood close to Jay and Matthiall. The sounds of the hunters' voices grew nearer. "Can't you let your friend know it was an emergency?"

"It isn't that I *won't* go in," Matthiall told her in a patient whisper. "It's that I can't. The hidden world will resist our presence unless he opens it to us."

Jay hugged herself, listening to the calls that grew always closer. "How long will it take him to get here?"

"I don't know. He comes when he chooses."

"Does he at least know we're here?"

"I've done my best to tell him." Matthiall sagged against the crotch of the tree and closed his eyes.

Jay looked from the tree to the woods behind them, then back to the tree. She didn't see anyplace to hide if Callion didn't arrive in time. There would be little sense in running. All she and Sophie could do was wait.

"I smell them," something roared, far nearer than Jay had imagined the hunters could be.

"Quick! Through the gate," a rough voice said from inside the hidden world.

Matthiall acted without hesitation. In a fluid motion he grabbed Jay and picked her up and shoved her through the opening, grabbed Sophie and shoved her through, and flung himself in behind them. Jayjay heard baying from just behind her, and turned in time to see the faces of several warrags closing on the opening in the tree. Then, inexplicably, they stopped and stared, and their heads lifted and they began to howl.

"I closed the gate. Pity they saw into my realm before I did." A bolt of light shot out from the gate trees and enveloped the warrags; they screamed and crumbled into dust. "Now they won't tell their bitch what they saw."

Jay shivered; at the deadliness of the door and the coldness of the voice.

"Callion. I didn't think you were going to arrive in time," Matthiall said, and Jay turned away from the gate to see the man to whom he spoke.

Matthiall wasn't speaking to a man at all, but to an animal. The animal looked from him to Sophie, and from Sophie to her, and she tried not to stare. Callion's beady, anthracite eyes glittered; his broad, black, leathery nose twitched, and when he grinned at her, double rows of needlelike teeth gleamed. He stood about three feet high. His bare feet, claw-tipped and four-toed, were twice as long as hers, narrow and bony with a light coat of glossy honey-gold fur along them. Two black stripes ran from the knobby joint above his toes along the tops of his feet and disappeared into his pant legs. He'd belted the coarse blue homespun pants beneath his round belly with a length of what looked like hemp rope. He hadn't bothered with a shirt. Jayjay guessed that maybe with his fur, he didn't need one. His belly

was covered with short, creamy white fur that darkened to gold at the sides and back. The fur on his back
grew longer and coarser; four thick black stripes ran
from the nape of his neck down his spine. His coarse,
brushy hair was close-cropped and glossy black; it stood
up straight in all directions, making him look as if he'd
had a bad scare. He had no fur on his face, which was
a pale copper gold darker than the cream of his belly
but lighter than the fur of his back, and the lips that
curved over his short, tapering muzzle looked shock-
ingly human. But his broad, fur-covered shoulders and
short, muscular arms terminated in four-fingered hands
tipped with heavy digging claws that still trailed bits
of bark. He looked, she thought, like a very large, over-
dressed badger.

Callion returned his attention to Matthiall and said,
"Well, you certainly brought trouble to my doorstep this
time. She's sitting out there, you know, and unless I
overestimate her enormously, she's busy figuring out
a way to get through my front door."

"I'm sorry," Matthiall told him. "We had no other
choice."

"We had no other choice," the creature grumbled.
"No, I don't suppose you did. It's such a pity that I can't
kill all of them and be done with them." He turned
and bowed to Sophie and Jay. "Welcome," he said. "You
look like you've had a weary, miserable journey. I'll feed
you and offer you warm baths. I'd give you new clothes
if I had them, but since nothing I own is your size, I'll
have my nephew clean them for you while you bathe."

"Nephew?" Matthiall asked.

"A long-lost relative has come visiting." Callion tipped
his head far back to stare up at Matthiall. "Shall we
go in? Your friends seem quite tired."

Callion turned and pointed at a little wooden door
angled into the side of a small, artificial hillock covered with wildflowers. He looked back to Jay and

Sophie and bowed slightly. "My home. Not built for Alfkindir, not built for Machnan . . . built for me. Still, you'll manage well enough inside if you watch your heads."

He led them to the door and opened it for them, ushering them in before him. Jayjay had to duck to get through, and once inside she found she couldn't stand up straight in the corridor. The ceiling was about five feet high, which probably felt roomy to Callion.

When she looked at him and his home, she had a hard time picturing Callion as the rightful inhabitant of his Eden. He appeared to have constructed his house entirely by excavating tunnels and chambers into the hillside, then reinforcing his work with rough finished post-and-beam supports. He'd wasted no time on ornamentation and no time on fine finishing. The dovetail joints fit crudely, though they did look solid. In the entry hall, he'd fitted shelves between many of the posts, and filled the shelves with dried meats, dried herbs, jars and vials and bits and pieces of things Jayjay didn't recognize . . . and wasn't sure she cared to examine. Dim globes glowed along the corridors, a limited concession to visibility. The floors were dirt, the walls were dirt, and the ceilings were dirt.

"First door through," Callion said, pointing them down the hallway to the left. "I'll be with you as soon as I gather some food and drink. You'll want to eat before you wash. Once you're clean I'm sure you'll want to sleep for a while."

The room into which he'd directed them featured several homemade wooden benches built for someone with legs far shorter than Jay's. Its single window looked out onto a meadow; the view would have been prettier if the glass had been either clean or gone. A red rug of lumpish weave and dreadful design covered the floor, and several shelves with books and curios on them hid large portions of the walls. Callion appeared to have made use of a tree root that grew into the room; he'd cleaned it and was using it to dry another pair of homespun pants.

The three of them took seats, Sophie on one side of Jay and Matthiall on the other. They didn't talk much. They were alive, and they were probably safe for a while, but they were wet and cold and hungry and filthy and tired, and Jay didn't think they were very safe, or that even their marginal safety would last for long. She didn't want to talk. She wanted to recover. And then she wanted to go home.

Callion trotted through the door carrying a tray on which rested drinking glasses and little plates, a tall corked bottle and a corkscrew, some bread, a large bunch of dark purple grapes, a bowl of olives, a jar of Peter Pan peanut butter and a butter knife.

Jay and Sophie gasped in unison when they saw the peanut butter.

"Where did you get that?" Sophie asked, beating Jay to the question by microseconds.

Callion grinned. "I have my sources. I thought you might enjoy it. It is by far my favorite of all the foods the Machine World has invented."

"The Machine World?" Jay said.

"It describes your home well enough, doesn't it?"

Jay nodded.

So he knew the world they came from, and had some contact with it. Perhaps when he said he could help them, he'd been telling the truth. Maybe he could get them out of Glenraven and back to the Peanut Butter World.

He passed around the glasses and plates, struggled with the corkscrew but managed it at last, poured wine for each of them, then passed around the tray and waited while they loaded their plates with food.

"Eat, eat," he told them. "While you're eating, my nephew is heating the bathwater. When you're finished, tell me and I'll take you to your rooms. One for each of you . . . they're small rooms, and you're not small people, are you?" He chuckled, and poured more wine for the three of them.

Jay began to warm up. The wine was vivid emerald green, and it bit like a snake at the first sip, but after that first startling bite the warmth rolled down her throat and into her belly and flowed into her veins, and suddenly she was warm and nothing hurt. She ate as much food as she could hold, stuffing herself with juicy sun-sweet grapes and firm, fleshy, slightly salty olives, bread and peanut butter, cheese, and wine. More wine. Much more wine.

At last Callion was helping her to her feet and guiding her down the hall, and she could think, "Bath, bath," and "Bed, bed," and not much else at all. "Wine?" she asked Callion, and he laughed and said something that sounded very soft and blurry to her, and she was going to insist that he get her some more wine immediately when Callion guided her into a room and stood her in front of a mattress, and it rose up and hit her in the face.

I'm drunk, she thought, but that was silly. She'd only had three small glasses of wine. Nobody got drunk on just three little glasses of . . .

Fifty-four

"All three of them are soundly asleep." Hultif met his uncle outside of the third guest room. "How do you know none of them got too much of the drug, though?"

Callion glanced over at his nephew. "I don't know, and except for the one Matthiall called Jayjay, I don't care. The other two are essentially expendable. If Jayjay got too much, I can give her an antidote."

Hultif frowned and tried to see what his uncle was thinking from the expression on his face. He got nothing. "But according to the omens, all three of them are necessary if we wish to assure Aidris Akalan's overthrow."

"Oh, they are. And we'll use them. I've checked this from every possible angle," Callion assured him. Hultif noticed that his uncle was mixing herbs into a bag— preparing for some complex spell, no doubt. "I can't kill Matthiall outright; in some way I haven't yet deciphered, he's bound to Jayjay, and I can't be sure that she'll survive if he dies, at least not yet. Once I've bound her to me, his survival will cease to matter. But according to my predictions, if I throw him to the Machnan, my chances of successfully overthrowing the Akalan snake improve dramatically." He chuckled.

"Likewise, if I dump the other girl into Aidris Akalan's lap, she will apparently create enough of a diversion that I can take *my* Watchmistress candidate right into Cotha Maest under her nose and declare myself Watchmaster."

Hultif frowned. He offered a polite objection, carefully phrased; lesser relatives, after all, did not directly confront relatives as senior and powerful as Callion. "I don't remember the omens pointing in that direction, Uncle."

"How could you? They only began to point in that direction once these three landed on my doorstep."

"Of course." Hultif bowed slightly. "Will you be needing me immediately?"

"Not for a while." Callion was absorbed in his herb work. He didn't bother looking at Hultif, which was good for Hultif; he felt agitated and disturbed by his uncle's new plan, and feared his distress might show on his face.

"Then may I beg your indulgence for a short time. I have several things I must do to get ready for the things that are coming."

His uncle waved him off. "Go. Go. I'll call you when I need you."

Hultif hurried away. He wanted to consult the omens; he didn't wish to call his uncle a liar, but he had been under the impression that all three of these creatures who had landed on his uncle's doorstep had been essential, and he hadn't thought they'd been meant to serve as sacrifices.

Fifty-five

Aidris Akalan found the hidden door at last. By careful divination, she could trace its true form hidden within the flawless disguise the ancient master had cast over it. What she had found was one of the gate trees of the Aregen . . . the Aregen she had been certain she had destroyed, save for her servant Hultif. Apparently she had been deceived by more than Hultif's show of obedience, for this tree lived, and since it had admitted her enemies and shielded them from her, so did the Aregen monster who'd planted it.

She frowned. Matthiall and the two Machnan wizards were hiding in the Aregen's domain. She wanted to get them out, but she had marched her army under cover of false night and that had cost her dearly; when she reached the place where the trio had camped the night before, she'd stepped through the shields and triggered a trap set by one of them. That trap had been designed to drain her of magical energy, and though she'd gotten free of it, it too had cost. She did not have the energy left to root out this ancient enemy and destroy Matthiall and the Machnan wizards too.

Her band of hunters clustered around her; she'd pulled in the boundaries of her false night once she and her men caught up with the fugitives. She needed to save everything she had left.

Or perhaps she could make use of the Watchers, she thought.

They might be able to smash their way through the gate tree for her. Even if they couldn't, they could kill a few of the men she'd brought along with her and replenish her magical stores. At full strength, Aidris knew she was equal to the task of driving the Aregen out of his home and killing him; she would do that and kill the wizards and torture Matthiall. And then she would live forever.

Except her Watchers had abandoned her. They hadn't gone after Matthiall and the Machnan wizards. Instead, they had run. Had hidden. Why else had she reached the traitor and the two bitches before them?

But if she did not have the Watchers, she had nothing. No power. No immortality. She *had* to try to summon them.

She looked at her soldiers setting up their camps. Kin or Kin-hera, every one of them. Meat to the Watchers. And her.

She lifted her head and closed her eyes and sent her silent call racing through the forest, spreading out like ripples fleeing from a rock thrown into a pond. She rode the ripples, waiting for an answer. She tried to keep any feeling of need out of her summons. She wanted them to believe she called them from a position of power, as she had when she opened the Rift and drew them out of it a thousand years ago. She didn't want them to suspect she was weakened by her travails. She called, and got no response but silence.

She called again.

She waited, while the ripples spread out to fill Glenraven and began to bound back and overlap. The Watchers didn't answer. Aidris opened her eyes and frowned. She sent her message again.

The Watchers still didn't answer.

Fifty-six

Callion drew the circle around Matthiall's body and scattered some of the herbs across the unconscious Kin's chest. He murmured the words of an ancient holding spell; when he said the last of them, Matthiall's skin glowed softly. Then his breathing became imperceptible and his skin became pale, almost translucent, and parchment white.

"I don't dare kill you," Callion whispered, "but I can do something as good."

His spell would hold for a few hours, perhaps as much as a day. Once it wore off, Matthiall could become a problem. If Callion could not find a way to break the bond between him and Jayjay, without killing Jayjay, that problem wouldn't go away. Callion needed to find a place to put Matthiall.

He paced and thought. He wanted a place that would neutralize Matthiall's magic, some place that would hold him in . . . but a place that would protect him from outside enemies, too, because Callion knew he needed Jayjay, and if someone killed Matthiall and Jayjay died as a result, that would be the end of Callion's plans for a new Aregen empire.

A wizard's bell would be the perfect place, if he could find one that was sealed . . .

Callion began to laugh. From his lair, he spied on everyone in Glenraven. He recalled the uproar in Zearn that had resulted in the Sarijann wizard being walled into his tower. If Callion were to transport Matthiall into that bell—a difficult trick, but not an impossible one, since the bell hadn't been built with Aregen magic in mind—he could dispose of his own problem and create an interesting new one for the Machnan.

He settled onto his haunches and scratched a little divining triangle in the dirt. He held a hand over it and concentrated on pinpointing an empty space inside the Aptogurria in Zearn. The triangular line he'd drawn spun slowly until the leading point aimed itself at Callion's target; when it was done, the dirt inside of the scratched shape took on a leathery appearance and lifted up until it floated at eye level before Callion. The Aregen chuckled and drew a line through the air from the triangular badge to Matthiall's chest. The arrow crept along the invisible line he'd traced until it had settled itself on Matthiall.

"Go," Callion whispered.

Matthiall vanished.

Fifty-seven

Jayjay thrashed at the edge of a nightmare. In this dream someone held her head underwater; ripped her heart, still beating, from her chest; stole from her the one thing that could make her life complete.

The dream began only with feelings of dread and loss, but then it gathered form and substance. She found herself walking through a crowd. Walking . . . walking . . . through silence so thick and heavy and cruel it felt solid. It impeded her steps and weighed her down . . . walking past people who stared at her. They stood on both sides of a narrow path, and their cold, judgmental eyes followed her. Silent stares, cruel eyes. Walking, every step harder than the last.

She was walking down the aisle of a church. Getting married. Again.

"No one congratulates a woman who's getting married for the fourth time," a voice said. She recognized it as her own, but didn't know where it came from. "No one is happy for her. Even her friends will say, 'Well, I hope this one works out,' or 'I guess you know what you're doing.' They won't ever say 'That's wonderful,' or 'I'm so happy for you.' They aren't. And everyone else will roll their eyes or laugh or say something cutting. That's just the way it is."

A deep, rich, masculine voice said, "What difference does it make what other people say?"

She knew the voice, but lost as she was in the dream, she couldn't place a name to it. "It matters."

"Why?"

That was stupid. Because she had to live with the people who would turn their backs on her and laugh at her and remark on her stupidity or her poor choice of men or her trashiness. Anyone married more than once was tarred by a slight brush of trashiness, and more than twice . . . well, more than two marriages was the kiss of death.

"Don't you deserve love?"

"I've screwed up too many times."

"That isn't what I asked. Don't you deserve to be loved?"

"Everybody deserves to be loved."

"And I love you. I will love you and cherish you and spend the rest of my life with you. I can't promise I won't hurt you, but I won't intentionally hurt you. I won't leave you. I won't cheat on you. I will love you the way you deserve to be loved."

In her dream, Jay was nearing the pulpit. The crowd cleared, and she could see the man standing at the front of the church waiting for her. It was Matthiall.

She realized she had known that, but she didn't want to admit it to herself. She wanted to keep listening to his wonderful words. Jay looked at Matthiall and found that she desired him. She loved him. But Sophie would be horrified if Jay took up with a nonhuman. Her other friends would, too.

He'd saved her life. He loved her. She didn't know him very well, but she had known all three of her husbands before she married them—had known them for years. And those marriages had been nightmares.

Nightmares.

Nightmares.

She was *in* a nightmare. The church was full of her ex-husbands and her friends and the people she'd grown up with, with what was left of her family, with strangers who'd heard she was getting married again, and who wanted to come watch. People in the back of the church were sitting around on blankets, eating picnic lunches and pointing at her. Someone was selling hot dogs; she couldn't see the man but she could hear him shouting "Hot dogs! Hot dogs! Get'cher r-r-r-reeeddd-hot hot dogs!"

"I love you," she whispered to Matthiall.

She looked down at herself and realized she was standing there naked, and everyone she had ever known was pointing at her and laughing.

"I love you . . . but we could never work. I can't ever have anyone again; it simply doesn't work out for me."

And she turned and ran up the aisle, back the way she'd come, trying to get away from the probing eyes and mocking looks of the people who knew her and didn't think she measured up.

Fifty-eight

Yemus watched the simulacrums moving across his tabletop representation of Glenraven's Cavitarin Wood. His doppelganger made steady progress toward Aidris Akalan's troops, and the soldiers who followed it had not yet noticed that they pursued a wraith. Meanwhile, Jayjay and Sophie had disappeared from sight. This worried him, but he had faith that whatever they were doing would work toward the good of Glenraven. He'd given up on them once before, and look where that had gotten him. And for no reason. He wouldn't lose faith in them again.

A sudden chill in the room and a change in the air pressure caused him to look up; when he did, he saw the air near the walled-up door to the tower thickening and growing dark. It looked for a moment as if the air had sprouted a tunnel entrance. In another instant, Yemus realized that was exactly what he was looking at, for something fell out of the tunnel and landed on his floor with a thud; then the tunnel disappeared with a loud pop. He found himself looking at the unmoving body of a man. Yemus rose and walked over to him, wondering what magic could breach the Aptogurria's spell-shielded walls, and why anyone would employ that power to dump another man into his prison with him . . . and then he realized the man in the room with him wasn't a man at all. He was Alfkindir.

"Why—?"

He knelt and felt for a pulse; the Kin had one, but it was thready and fast. Yemus frowned and rolled the Kin over onto his back. The stranger had a feel of power surrounding him; Yemus guessed he was one of the Kin wizards, but that made the situation even stranger. Who would be strong enough to dispose of a Kin wizard . . . and to do it by breaking him into an unbreachable magical stronghold like the Aptogurria?

Aidris Akalan is involved, Yemus decided.

If Aidris was involved, that would make this man her enemy. If he was the Watchmistress's enemy, then Yemus could probably consider him a friend. If not a friend, at least a temporary ally.

Yemus went to his workbench and brought back an unraveler, a convenient little device his grandfather had developed when he was Zearn's chief wizard. Yemus lay the unraveler on the unconscious Kin's chest and activated it by feeding it a tiny amount of magical energy. The unraveler went to work, disassembling each spell on the man in reverse order.

First the unraveler tried to send him back where he'd come from, but it didn't have the power to do that. It followed the sequence required to do it, however, and Yemus got his first feel of his enemy's style. Then it began to disassemble a stasis spell. Again, that was done differently than Yemus would have done it. It was a spell that relied on brute force, not finesse—a spell done by someone with enormous power, someone who didn't have to conserve every trace of magical energy.

The spell fell away and the man began to wake up. Yemus discovered that in the meantime the unraveler had begun to disassemble another spell, and he quickly removed it and repaired the step it had begun to take apart; that spell appeared to be one the man had cast upon himself, and Yemus didn't think he'd appreciate having it disrupted.

The Kin opened his eyes and squinted up at the ceiling. He frowned, raised a hand to his forehead, and while he rubbed his temples, he moaned.

"How are you?" Yemus asked.

The Kin took notice of him for the first time. "Who are you . . . and what are you doing here?"

Yemus laughed. "I should be asking you the same thing. But from the looks of things, you've been through something bad; so . . . I'm Yemus Sarijann, First Wizard of Zearn. Only wizard now, of course . . . but . . ." He shrugged. "And I'm imprisoned in here, as you are."

"I know who you are, then." The Kin pushed himself toward a sitting position, but lost his balance and fell back. Yemus caught him before he could hit his head on the stone floor and helped him to sit.

"Thank you." The Kin looked around the room, then at Yemus. "I've heard of you," he said. "I'm Matthiall, son of Gerlin and Elloe, last of the Shae Kin." He nodded politely.

Yemus smiled. "Welcome to my humble abode."

"We are imprisoned?"

"Indeed. You find yourself in Zearn's Aptogurria, once my workplace and now my jail . . . and yours. Do you have any idea how you got here?"

Matthiall stood and walked slowly to the narrow slit window. He looked out; he didn't have to raise up on his toes to see the way Yemus did. With his back to Yemus, he said, "None . . . except that I went to an old friend for help, and when I woke up I was here instead of there."

Yemus thought of the odd magic, done in a style he had never seen. "What sort of old friend was this?"

"One of the last of the Aregen."

"The Masters? My God, I thought the Masters were extinct."

"Not entirely."

"I see." He pondered the wisdom of telling the Kin what he knew, then decided it couldn't hurt. "Your friend isn't much of a friend, I'd say. There was a spell on you, meant to keep you unconscious for a day or better. Powerful thing. And the magic that dumped you on my floor was no mean feat, either. The magic of both was new to me. It was power magic, spells that didn't need to lever a little magic to create a bigger effect."

"Callion sent me here, then." Matthiall turned and stared at Yemus. "I have to get out of here. He still has Jay and Sophie."

Ice froze in Yemus's blood. "Two outsiders? Women?"

Matthiall nodded. "You know them. From what I've been able to piece together, you were in some way responsible for bringing them here."

"And now they're in the hands of a Master?" Yemus shuddered. "Do you have any idea what he'll do?"

"I thought he would help me," Matthiall said. "Since I was so wrong about that, I don't expect anything else I can offer about the misborn little monster will have much value."

Yemus stood. "There's that." He walked to the table on which his simulacrums still went about their business. He looked down, and discovered that Sophie's simulacrum had reappeared. He pointed. "Sophie is right there. See her?" She stood still for just an instant; then she began running. Warrags chased her through the forest, and Kin raced to cut her off. They captured her. They dragged her to Aidris.

Yemus crouched over his board, whispering unintelligible prayers. Matthiall rested a hand on his shoulder and said nothing. The two men, Machnan and Kin, watched without daring to comment.

And Aidris pointed a finger at Sophie. An arc of brilliant red light shot from it, and the simulacrum of Sophie crumpled to the ground and lay still.

"No," Yemus whispered.

"No," Matthiall said.

But the unmoving form lay sprawled at the edge of Aidris Akalan's camp, and a faint black mist curled up around it and surrounded it.

Yemus dropped to his knees and stared. "No." His voice was pleading. "Please, no. Not dead."

He felt Matthiall's hand tighten, then release. "It's all over before it began. We've lost. My omens said we could not win without both of them."

"As did mine. Aidris wins, and we are destroyed."

Fifty-nine

She was already *dead*. Callion stared into his viewing bell and slammed a fist into the table, furious. Dead. His omens had assured him that if he threw her to Aidris, she would create enough confusion that Aidris and her flunkies would fail to notice his actions. They were supposed to take time to figure out what she was, and even longer to try to use her to get to him, before they finally killed her. He had intended to use that time to create a path from his domain to the throne room of Cotha Maest.

He closed his eyes and connected himself to the web that enclosed his domain. Now he wouldn't be able to get past Cotha Maest without alerting her to his actions. Aidris was still working on his gate, and she was getting closer. The Kin spell-magic was slower and weaker than the Aregen power-magic, just as the Machnan life-magic was weaker than the Kin magic; each creator race had made its creations less powerful than itself, thinking in this way to maintain control. Good theory, terrible execution, he thought. Because the "weaker" Aidris was about to come bursting through his door into his private domain, and all her greasy hordes were going to wash in after her, and by sheer numbers they would overwhelm him. Just as they had overwhelmed and destroyed so many of the Aregen.

He'd dropped Sophie at the edge of the Alfkindir camp. He'd felt a brief flash of power leaving his domain when he did, but that power wasn't part of Sophie; she had no more magic about her than her friend Jay. The power was connected to something else, something unrelated. And when he searched for the source of it near the place where he'd dropped Sophie, thinking that perhaps he'd sent one of his artifacts with her by accident, he discovered nothing but a book that she'd evidently had with her. There was no source of power—nothing that he could turn against Aidris Akalan.

He was furious. She shouldn't have been so fragile. Aidris shouldn't have been so efficient. Now he was going to have to change his plans, all because the two of them couldn't do anything right.

Sixty

free I am free I am free
lighter than air—as light as light—floating
*no one can make me go back there, back to the
darkness, back to the pain*
free I'm free I'm free
Mom?
*free I'm free I'm free and nothing can hurt me any-
more . . .*
Mom? You're here? Already?
Karen?
The lightness still filled her, but Sophie no longer
felt so giddy, so far from pain and suffering. The voice
she'd heard sounded precisely like Karen's, but Karen
was dead. Dead. And Sophie discovered that although
pain had grown distant and fuzzy, she was still capable
of feeling it. She felt it then.
Mom! It is you!
Sophie saw light shifting within the light, and suddenly she saw her daughter, not the way she had looked
as a child, but unmistakable nonetheless. She ran
toward Karen and embraced her; the two of them stood
wrapped in each other's arms for time that could have
been a moment or an infinity.

Oh, baby, how are you?

I'm fine, Mom. I've been waiting for you . . . but I didn't expect you yet.

Sophie laughed, swelling with bubbling effervescent joy. *Well, I'm here.*

Karen nodded, solemn and somehow not exuberant the way Sophie would have expected her to be. *I know. I just don't know why. I don't think you're supposed to be here yet.*

Sophie tried to imagine why she shouldn't be with Karen, and she couldn't. She tried to recall what she had been doing just before she found Karen, or where she had been, or how she had come to be where she was. All of that was a mystery.

I've been watching you, Mom. You were starting to do better. You were ready to live again.

Sophie looked at her daughter. *You were watching me?*

Always. I wanted you to be okay, and finally it looked like you were going to be.

Sophie thought, and then she nodded. Yes. She remembered that after all. Something had made her decide she wanted to live. She'd been struggling with her love for Mitch, but that struggle seemed so silly to her; all of a sudden she could see that she loved him more than she had the day she married him. She could feel her love for him, adult and solid and clear. She'd been confused about her friend Lorin . . . but why? Lorin was her friend. They'd known each other before, and would know each other again. But in this lifetime, they were going to be friends. Just friends.

How could things get so muddled?

And Karen had been watching over her, worrying about her, because she had let herself wander in the darkness, because she had refused to live her next day and her next; because she had, instead, hidden herself in the blanket of her pain and refused to go on. She'd known Karen wasn't gone, that death hadn't destroyed her daughter. Why hadn't she trusted what she knew?

Because I was afraid, she thought. *Afraid to live. But I changed all of that.*

How did I get here? she asked Karen.

Do you remember Glenraven? Do you remember Callion?

Suddenly Sophie did remember. *He poisoned me. He killed me.*

I know. But they still need you, Mom.

They . . . ?

You know who.

Sophie realized that when she thought about it, she knew the truth of that, too. A lot of people needed her. Mitch needed her. So did her friend Lorin. The child who was waiting for her to be ready so that he could be born needed her. People in Glenraven needed her. She had so much she had to do . . . so much living. So many things left undone.

But she was dead.

That seemed to be an insurmountable problem.

Sixty-one

Jayjay tried to rub her eyes, but her hands wouldn't move. She blinked instead, struggling to remember where she was and what was going on. Nothing made any sense.

Her arms were over her head. She tried to move them again, and finally realized that rope bound her wrists. The import of that sunk in and she shivered. Tied up was a bad sign. What had she done to get herself tied up? She tried to yell, and the sound came out muffled and unintelligible. Jay realized the awful taste in her mouth was a gag. She couldn't move her legs, either. Rope again.

And she felt like hell; weak and sick, nauseated, chilled, with her head throbbing and her sinuses blocked so that she almost couldn't breathe. She felt like she was getting a fever. Maybe she was coming down with the flu.

Maybe she was coming down with plague, considering where she was.

At last she got her eyes open in spite of the caked, gummy matter that held them shut.

Callion stood over her, smiling an unpleasant smile. "You're awake at last. The antidote worked. Good. I was beginning to fear that you would die, too, in spite of my best efforts, and I can't afford to lose you."

Too? Who had died? "Hwww vwwww?" she asked through the gag. It didn't sound too much like "who died" but Callion evidently got it.

"Aidris has already killed your friend Sophie." He shrugged, which involved an awkward movement of his badgerish shoulders. "It doesn't matter. I didn't need her anyway."

He turned his back on Jayjay and began doing something at a workbench covered with vials and canisters and an entire row of hard blue flames that shot steadily from the tips of coils of copper tubing. Another creature who looked very much like him stood off to one side, his gaze flicking from Callion to Jay and back.

Dead? Sophie was dead? Jay tried to get that thought clearly in her head, but her mind refused to accept it. Sophie was her best friend in the world, the person who had shared some of the biggest moments of her life. Sophie couldn't—simply could *not*—be dead.

Aidris. Aidris Akalan had killed her.

Callion turned back to Jay. "I do need *you*, however. According to every oracle I've been able to consult, you're to be the next Watchmistress of Glenraven. Since I have no wish to see my world fall to ruin in the hands of an outsider such as yourself, I'm going to have to bind the two of us together. I'll make you my *eyra*, the way Matthiall intended to. That will make me Watchmaster, and return control of Glenraven to the Aregen, which is where it belongs." Jay wished she could see his face. He clinked glass against glass, shook powdered something into a beaker, poured awful gloppy green stuff on top of it, then watched while the resulting mess changed from green to dark blue to black and began fizzing toward the beaker rim.

Sophie was dead?

Callion took a glass rod and stirred his concoction

vigorously; as he did, he spoke again. "Once you and I are established in Cotha Maest, I'm going to have to figure out what to do with you, of course. I can't kill you, any more than I can kill Matthiall now that he's bound himself to you. Once I unbind the two of you, he'll die. Who knows, maybe I'm mistaken and maybe he's dead already. It isn't important. He's dead or he'll die, and that's just one problem out of my way. But you . . . you're a disaster; you have no more magic in you than dead rock, and you're to be the next Watchmistress. I can see it. You'd erase the last of Glenraven's magic and turn our world into a carbon copy of your own stinking Machine World."

Jay tugged at the ropes that bound her wrists, trying not to make any noise. She needed to get away, to find Sophie and Aidris Akalan. Fury burned in her; Sophie didn't deserve to die. She had a life ahead of her. She was starting to find her way back from the dark place she'd been. Jay was going to make Aidris pay for what she'd done.

And she didn't dare sit still for Callion, either. He'd said he was going to break the bond between her and Matthiall, and that when he did, Matthiall would die. A part of her—the rational, Machine World part—insisted that was so much bullshit. The other part of her, though, the part that had immediately embraced Glenraven and called it home, said that it was nothing but truth. If Callion somehow broke the mystical bonds between them, Matthiall, whom she loved, would die.

No. That would not happen.

But Callion had bound her too well. As she fought, she felt the ropes tighten until she had to quit. They had completely cut off her circulation to her hands and feet.

"Maybe I can wall you up in the Aptogurria," Callion said. "Or maybe I should simply kill you. The Aregen, after all, are not bound by the Kinnish oaths taken during the binding of *eyran*." He added something else to the mess he was mixing, and it changed from black to water clear; bubbles rose in it and sparkled against the sides of the beaker and fizzed out the top.

Callion turned and grinned at her, his needle teeth gleaming. He held the beaker in one hand and lifted a metal rod from the line of flames with the other. Its tip glowed so hot it was almost white.

"Take the cloth from her mouth, Hultif," Callion said to the other Aregen who stood, watching. "She's going to drink this for me, and then she's going to bind herself to me willingly, or else I'm going to put her eye out with this." He waved the metal rod and his grin got bigger. He stared into Jay's eyes. "I want you to remember that for my purposes, you don't need eyes, you don't need ears, and you don't need a tongue. If you want to keep them, you'll drink this and not give me any trouble."

The other Aregen still stood off to one side, watching the two of them. Callion turned and glared at him. "Hultif, hurry up. We don't have much time before Aidris Akalan breaks down our door."

Hultif sighed and nodded. "Right." He came toward them and Callion returned his attention to her. He brought the poker close enough to her face that she could feel her cheek drying from its heat. When she winced away, he chuckled.

Jay caught movement from the corner of her eye, and saw the Aregen whom Callion had called Hultif bringing a club down on top of Callion's head. Callion cried out once, and as he did, searing pain flashed across Jay's cheek. He'd dropped the poker when Callion hit him, and it was burning a hole in her face. She screamed through the gag and thrashed, trying to move her head away from the horrible burning agony, trying to stop the pain.

Callion dropped out of sight, thudding to the floor.

"Hold still," Hultif said. He threw the poker across the room, then grasped her forehead firmly and turned her face toward him. "That left a nasty hole. I can see bone."

The pain was so fierce it was blinding. She tried to see him but red haze clouded her eyes and the agony stoppered her ears.

He said, "Hold still a moment; I can make the flesh grow back together." Hultif rested his claws on her burned flesh and for a moment the pain grew worse instead of better. Tears ran down her cheeks and she sobbed. But then the pain eased off; in another moment it was gone.

"That's left you with a scar, I'm afraid," the Aregen said. "I couldn't make the injury go away; I could only make it heal faster. The Aregen deal in power. The Machnan were the healers, but they have no magic left." He reached behind her and untied the gag and pulled it from her mouth.

"Thank you," she tried to say, but her mouth was so dry the words didn't come out.

Hultif worked at the ropes.

She sat up as her hands came free. As the blood rushed back into them, she rubbed them together, trying to ignore the pain. She said, "Is what he said about Sophie true?"

"Yes. Sophie is dead."

"What about Matthiall? Is he still alive?"

Hultif sighed. "You want the truth? Probably not. He's Kin—Old Line Kin at that—and Callion threw him into a Machnan tower while he was helpless. The Machnan in there probably killed him the second he materialized."

Jay gritted her teeth and nodded. Sophie dead. Matthiall gone. The wolves at the door, so to speak; Aidris and her monsters waited just outside the domain, and they weren't waiting passively, either. They were battering at the door and apparently having some success at it. Hope was gone, Glenraven was doomed, and she was going to die.

But, by God, she wasn't going to do it alone.

"Get me to Aidris."

He was untying her ankles. He glanced up at her and shook his head. "No point. We've already lost. The oracles were very clear on that; unless you and Sophie confronted Aidris together, you couldn't win."

"I don't give a damn whether I win or not," Jay said. "I know I can't win. I'm going to kill her for what she did to Sophie."

"She'll kill you. As soon as she sees you, she'll feel Glenraven's touch on you. She'll know you were destined to be the next Watchmistress, and because you're a rival, even though you're already beaten, she won't waste any time with you. She'll kill you as fast as she killed Sophie."

Jay could move her fingers again. She swung around and grabbed the little monster by both shoulders and shoved her face close to his. "Watchmistress? I'm not going to be anybody's Watchmistress. Don't you understand? This isn't about that anymore, if it ever was. I know I'm going to die. But she killed my friend, and she doesn't get that one free."

Hultif shook loose from her grip and blinked up at her. "Perhaps I can see what Glenraven wanted with you. But this is pointless, and I will not waste my time with pointless things. You have no magic, you have no talents, and you cannot hope to defeat the strongest Kintari Glenraven has ever seen. That is fact."

"Then why did you bother to help me? If you're just going to stand there and piss and moan about how helpless we are, why didn't you let your uncle or whatever he was force me to marry him? I suppose that's the correct analogy—marriage. At least he had a plan. At least he wasn't sitting here with his thumbs up his ass waiting for the end of the world."

Hultif barked; Jay realized that sound was his laugh. "No," he said, "my uncle never sat around with his . . . with his thumbs up his ass. So you want to do something?"

"I'm going to do something. You're going to show me how to get to Aidris, and I'm going to take her apart."

The little monster began to smile. "Well, if we're going to die making a great dramatic stand, I'll help you. She killed my entire family when I was an infant at the breast, and kept me as her slave for over a hundred years. I always intended to be the one who killed her."

"So let's go."

He nodded. "Indeed. Your belongings are in the corner there. If you have any weapons, I suggest you get them. You'll need them."

Jay had the sword Matthiall had given her, and the knife she'd been carrying around with her since she'd first arrived, the one she'd gotten from Lestovru. She strapped on the sword, then put on the dagger belt too, thinking that it was probably silly to do so; she had damned little experience with one blade, and none at all fighting with a sword and a *main gauche*.

"That's it?" Hultif raised the spots on his furry forehead where eyebrows would have been on a human. "Those are your weapons? Two sticks?"

"That's all I have."

"Well, maybe someday fools will write songs about how I diverted the evil Watchmistress with my magical talents of setting fires and summoning snow and creating a fine banquet out of trash while you attacked her with your two sticks. I'm sure they'll say we died bravely," he said. "Though I was hoping I wouldn't die at all." He sighed deeply. "Let's go."

Sixty-two

Sophie stopped communicating with Karen when she realized a silent crowd had gathered around her; they were people only in the way that shadows were people. They had shape and movement, but no depth or life. They fit the dark, empty nothingness of the place where she and Karen had met—fit the place and made it more forbidding and bleak than it had been. They were, she thought, appropriate denizens of the realm of the dead; they made no sound, but their presence seemed to weigh down the air she breathed and cast a cold, penetrating chill through her blood and bones, leaving her trembling even though they had not touched her.

She felt a distance spring up between her and Karen, a sudden frightening, painful void that yawned as large and hard and ugly as the death that had separated them the first time. "What's wrong?" she asked her daughter out loud.

Karen looked at her mother, eyes searching for something she didn't seem able to find. "You don't have much more time."

"Time? For what?"

"To decide."

Sophie felt lost. "Decide? What?"

"I can't tell you."

Not *I don't know*, but *I can't tell you.* "You know, don't you?"

"Yes." Karen nodded. "I know, but I'm not permitted to interfere any more than I have already."

Sophie looked at the shadow-drawn specters who waited and watched. "They're part of it."

"Yes."

"Can you tell me who they are?"

Karen held still, her head tipped to one side as if she were listening to a voice that only she could hear. Perhaps, Sophie thought, she was. After a moment, Karen nodded. "I can tell you. They are the souls of still-living Machnan, voluntarily held captive so that they can save their children from a terror that has oppressed their people for centuries."

"They have something to do with me," Sophie said. It wasn't a question, but Karen nodded when she said it.

"They do."

Sophie looked at them. She thought, I was chosen for Glenraven. Maybe because I had something to give to it, but I've gotten something in return. I've found the will to live again. I have something to go back to that I didn't have when I left. I have hope again. Karen isn't gone forever; death isn't the end of everything. I can have the courage to love again.

She considered destiny. Maybe it was real; but if it was, it wasn't the way some people painted it. Destiny didn't demand. It asked. It knocked. It offered, and if she wanted to, she knew she could turn her back on it. The souls of the Machnan were part of her destiny, but she understood that she was free to refuse them. They couldn't make her do whatever it was her destiny called for. She tested her theory.

"I could go with you, couldn't I? I could choose to die."

"Yes," Karen said.

"I could go back, too, without making any promises to anyone."

"Perhaps. That is certainly less likely."

"But I have a chance to do more. I have a chance to help these people. To help them help their children."

Karen nodded again, not saying anything.

The souls of the Machnan stirred, and in their almost-empty eyes, Sophie thought she could see faint flickerings of hope. Hope.

She thought she understood. She could give the Machnan their lives back the way Glenraven had given her life back to her. This was her destiny, and it was a destiny of love and compassion. She remembered the pain of loving Karen even before she was born and fearing for her future, of wanting the best for her and knowing that no matter how much she wanted the best, Karen would know pain and suffering. Sophie's destiny touched on the still-heavy anguish of losing the daughter she loved, and on the empathy she felt for these mothers and fathers who would barter their souls to save their children. She knew—*knew*—how that felt.

She could feel their love and their pain and she could do something to make a difference.

Karen rested her hands on Sophie's shoulders and leaned forward to stare into her mother's eyes. "It's time. You have to tell me . . . what are you going to do?"

Sophie felt her daughter's hands on her shoulders and remembered the way those same hands had felt when Karen was tiny; she remembered chubby baby fists clutching her finger, holding on so tightly. She remembered Karen's first smiles, her first steps, her first words. Many of the frightened souls who clustered around her knew those same feelings.

"I'm going to find a way back," she told her daughter. "I'll miss you, but I'll see you again someday. Now, though, I'm going to do what I can to help these people. I don't know what I can do, but whatever it is, I'll do it."

Sophie heard movement from the silent watchers; no longer silent, they were walking toward her from all sides, their shadowy forms nebulous, their faces full of hope.

Paper-dry voices whispered. "We don't know what you'll do, but we will try to take you back to do it."

"You can get me back to my body? You can make me live again?" Sophie asked, watching the shadow shapes drawing closer.

"We think we can," they said. They surrounded her, and as they did, Karen backed away. Sophie reached for her daughter, but Karen kept backing up. "If it hasn't been too long."

"Not yet," Sophie whispered.

"Now. There isn't any more time." She smiled, the smile that Sophie could never forget, had never stopped seeing. "But I'll still be here when you get back."

The souls of the Machnan began to flow into her, and she felt herself filling with a tingling, throbbing power; she felt the way she had felt when she touched the book, but the sensation was a thousand times stronger.

"We were the book," the souls whispered inside her head. "When you touched it, you felt us." They kept on melding with her, and she realized there had been more of them around her than she'd been able to see. Dozens became hundreds, hundreds became a thousand, that thousand multiplied, and the ranks of the bodiless souls thinned at last.

And the strangers' souls that melded inside of her soul whispered into her mind, "Now we try to go back."

Sixty-three

Aidris chanted. This was the old way to magic, the Kintari way. It was slower and weaker than the Aregen power magic she'd used to summon the Watchers, but it was her magic. She didn't have to consume the magic of others to do it. She didn't need anything but herself, and her concentration.

Her concentration had been hard to maintain.

What with the hiss of the endless pouring rain, the pitiful excuse for a Machnan wizard popping out of the gate at her, and enemy fighters approaching through the forest from the northeast, she'd lost her place in the spell twice, and both times she'd had to start from the beginning. She was out of practice; for almost a thousand years she'd done Aregen magic, achieving through sheer power what she now had to accomplish through finesse.

She'd lost some of her touch.

Her guards crouched just outside of the rain shield she'd spelled around herself with their ears cocked to the northeast, listening to the sounds they'd identified as approaching troops. Machnan, they'd said, moving forward on horseback. Then the distant shouts began; the first clashes of metal on metal, the first screams, the first howls of triumph. The elite warrag guard stood and quivered, hackles raised and bodies leaning forward, and their eagerness to charge into battle conveyed itself to Aidris even through the fine sweaty haze of her concentration. She kept the rhythm of the chant, though, and felt the subtle web of power build.

Then in the distance a warrag howled in anguish, and the four who guarded her reacted instinctively; they responded with howls of their own.

For the third time she stammered to a halt and felt the building energy shatter and scatter around her. She turned on her guards, fury locking her muscles into knots and twisting her hands into claws. "Go," she snarled. "Get away from me. Set your watch someplace where I cannot see your mindless faces or hear your animal voices. You stinking, sniveling, worthless wastes of flesh; go prove your mettle out there."

She pointed and the warrags tucked their tails along their bellies and slunk out of sight in four directions, to set up their watchposts. Worthless animals. The Kin had erred in creating them. They were too emotional and too attached to each other.

She wondered if she could undo them. As she dropped herself back into the half-tranced state of mind she had to maintain to weave the final component of the gate-opening spell, she thought that once she had concluded the business of this night, she would look into destroying or redesigning the warrags.

Sixty-four

"That helps a little," Jay said, watching the guards slink out of sight.

Jay and Hultif crouched just inside the opening in the gate tree. They could clearly see and hear the woman who stood on the other side, chanting and drawing diagrams in the air with her fingertips.

"Yes. But they're quick."

"I've fought one before," Jay said. "I know how fast they are."

Hultif turned and stared at her, surprise on his face. "Did you win?"

"We survived."

"That's as good as a win."

They watched Aidris begin her spell again. Behind her, lying crumpled on the ground against a tree, Jayjay could see Sophie's body. No obvious injury pointed to the cause of her death. Jay could see no blood, no scars, no wounds. But she could no longer pretend there was hope. Sophie was dead. And her killer still lived.

Sitting, watching Aidris, Jay had an idea. "You can make it snow, huh?"

Hultif jumped at the sound of her voice, and the fur on his body stood straight out. In other circumstances,

358

it would have been comical. He nodded, though, and smoothed his fur down. "Sometimes I can even summon a very good ice storm, though it does help if the weather is already miserable."

"Yeah," Jay said, watching the woman. "I'll bet that does help. So how long would it take you to get us some snow?"

"With it raining like this? Oh, I can change it to snow in merest minutes."

Jay nodded. The plan grew. "And you can start fires and make banquets. That's it?"

Hultif chuffed softly, and Jay read the sound as irritation. The peevish sound of his voice when he answered her told her she'd guessed right. "I'm very young, and mostly untrained. I can read the future too, though not when I am personally endangered. As I am now, for example." He cocked his head to one side and studied her. "You're very critical for someone who has no magic at all."

"I'm not critical of your magic. I was just wishing you could blast death rays from your fingertips or something like that."

"Sorry. No death rays. Had I been able to do that, yon bitch would have died at my hands long before now."

Jay nodded and considered for a moment his statement about looking into the future. "So you can't see the outcome of this?"

He glanced sidelong at her and said, "It doesn't take magic to see that. Fools could predict this outcome."

They were going to die. Right. Jay balled her hands into fists and glared at the hag on the other side of the opening.

"So if we're going to die anyway, why can't I just jump through the gate and run her through?"

"Before we can physically pass through the gate, we must open it. She will feel that; she cannot help but feel that, linked to the gate as she is. She will have the moment that it takes me to open it to prepare herself, and in that moment we will lose our surprise." He sighed. "And she is by far the better wizard of the two of us."

Jay nodded and thought for a moment. "But you can do your spells through the gate, can't you?"

"Yes."

"You could make it snow, or maybe set her on fire?"

"Yes."

"Okay. Can you start the fires quickly, or does it take you as long as it would to make it snow?"

"I can create the power spell so that it lacks nothing but the initiation word. Then I can hold it in readiness, and once cast, I can cast five or six more times before I have to stop and rebuild the spell."

"Fine. This is what I think we should do, then. You'll make it snow. If you can do ice, do ice. That ought to distract her. Then set a fire behind her—you can keep a fire burning in the rain?"

"Of course I can do that."

"Of course you can. Right. Endanger her with the fire, enough that she has to turn around to deal with it. While she's fighting that, you open the gate for me, and I jump through and kill her."

Hultif said, "You're asking me to do three things at once. Maintain snow, maintain a fire, and open the gate."

"You can't do that?"

"No one could do that."

"You can't make the snow keep itself going? That snow could provide us with a lot of cover. And it should be an obstacle to the rest of her people, especially if you can give us ice, too."

Hultif rocked back and forth on his haunches, muzzle tucked down to his chest. "Hmmmmm. Hmmmmm." He looked up at Aidris. "Snow first. Then the gate.

Then the fire. I will throw it at her as you go through. For short spells, if I have the temperature low enough, the snow will maintain itself."

"Fine. Then let's go, before she gets through the gate."

Hultif squinched his eyes shut and continued to rock and mumble and growl. Jay watched the torrents of rain that streamed down the tree trunk that made up the other side of the gate. They were water, and they stayed water, and she began to think that he'd been exaggerating his abilities. Then all of a sudden the hiss of the rain became the pounding of hail, mixed with freezing rain and a blizzard of snowflakes.

Aidris screamed in frustration and stared up at the sky. "What, by the demons of the Rift, is the meaning of this?"

Jay unsheathed her sword. "Yes."

The snow came down harder, and the ice and hail kept falling too. Banshee winds tore through the forest, blowing the flakes in spirals and swarms; green leaves and dead branches, ripped from the high canopy by the hailstones, created a secondary curtain of debris that further lessened visibility. The roar of wind and hail and icy rain drowned out Aidris's furious shouts, and the ever-thickening snow erased her, too.

"Now the gate," Jay said, and Hultif opened his eyes.

"Oh, my heavens," he murmured. "I wasn't expecting that." Then a smile stretched across his muzzle and all his needle teeth gleamed. "But of course. Every time she broke her concentration, her spell scattered, but the energy from it didn't go anywhere. It was just out there, building and building." He rubbed his paws together. "Oh, lovely. The serpent bit her own damned tail."

"Get the gate," Jay repeated.

Hultif nodded, and Jay saw the inside of the gate begin to glow with a warm golden light. She'd forgotten that. The golden glow would show up on the other side, too—maybe even through Hultif's blizzard. Probably even through his blizzard.

"She's going to know I'm coming through. Be quick with the fire or I'm dead before I can get to her."

"As fast as I can."

Jayjay had her sword in her right hand and her dagger in her left. She climbed into the crotch of the gate tree where the two main trees split and crouched there. She decided she would jump out, duck, roll to her left, and come up to the side of the Watchmistress. Maybe that would be enough to save her.

Maybe.

The snow and sleet and hail kept pounding against the invisible barrier between her and Aidris. Then, without warning, the storm slammed into her. Blinded, she jumped, rolled and turned, and blinking furiously, stood, turning to the place where she thought the Watchmistress would be.

She couldn't see anything.

Sixty-five

Hultif couldn't believe he'd managed such tremendous snows. He wondered if he could create as impressive a fire; wondered if the Watchmistress's stray magic would feed a conflagration as well as it fed a storm. With the gate snapped shut behind him and Aidris effectively locked out for still a while longer, he began casting a fire spell.

But before he could release it, he heard quick, stealthy footsteps behind him. He spun in time to see his uncle swing a massive hammer at his head.

He shrieked and leapt to one side. "Uncle! No! We can still beat the Watchmistress. Don't!"

He dodged as Callion, with blood running down his face, snarled and swung the hammer again. "You *interfered*, boy!"

"But the omens, Uncle. I checked the omens, and if you had followed through on your plan, we would have been doomed. You could not have won!"

Callion leapt and swung the hammer overhand; the massive metal head whistled past Hultif's ear and crashed into his shoulder as Callion slammed into him.

Hultif heard bones breaking as he toppled to the ground. He screamed and kicked out with both legs, flinging his uncle off of him. He rolled to his right side and with his good arm pushed himself to his feet. His left arm hung uselessly.

"I don't care about your omens! I could have won!" Callion swung the hammer again, but this time he lost his grip on the handle. It sailed past Hultif and smashed into the tree behind him so hard Hultif could feel the shock wave of its impact in the ground under his feet. He scrambled for the hammer as Callion lunged. He had the advantage of proximity; he came up with the tool and swung it. He hit Callion, but not solidly. He hadn't been in position to get a good backswing. The tree trunk blocked him. Nevertheless, he hit hard enough that Callion grunted and backed off.

"Glenraven chooses the Master of the Watch," Hultif said, stalking toward his uncle. "And Glenraven didn't choose you."

"Glenraven doesn't know what's good for her anymore. The realm is dying, and this idiotic choice is nothing but the sign of her spasming death throes."

"And your subversion of Glenraven's will is going to bring our world back to life, Uncle?"

He backed, his eyes shifting rapidly from side to side as he looked for another weapon. "The Aregen are the first Masters. We rule by right—and the time has come to reclaim our right."

"No. The time has come to let Glenraven breathe. Aidris tore open the Rift and bled her nearly dead, but Glenraven isn't dead yet. If that creature can let her heal, then I support her."

"You're a fool, and the child of fools. You're blinded by sentiment and tales of the glorious old days. I say we must create the glorious new days."

He tripped over a root and sprawled backward. Hultif hesitated for a second, looked back toward the gate tree where Jayjay had vanished into the storm, and turned to leap.

But Callion was no longer on the ground. He was no longer in sight.

Hultif spun, trying to find some sign of what had become of him, and felt a sharp tug as his uncle, who had somehow gotten behind him, grabbed the hammer away from him.

He charged immediately, ramming his head into his uncle's chest and clawing for his eyes with his good hand. The pain in his left shoulder, where the hammer had crushed bone, was a constant searing agony. He knew, however, that because he was fighting and moving, it wasn't as bad as it would become when he was still. He didn't give in to it.

In the back of his mind he wished the fire spell had been readied when his uncle attacked. He could have burned the old bastard. But there was no way to ready the spell while fighting; battles between wizards were only magical if the two stood off from each other with their shields already set, so that they could take the time to gather their power. Fighting close in, they did what others did. They bit and clawed and snapped and hit and stabbed.

Callion staggered backward with the hit, but caught his balance and lunged, swinging. Hultif scrambled back out of the way, in the position his uncle had been in instants before. He needed a weapon and he had nothing. For all his scorn of Jayjay's sword and knife, at that moment he wished he were so well armed.

"I . . . will . . . be . . . Master . . . of . . . the . . . Watch," Callion said, punctuating each word with a swing.

Hultif thought he saw one of his uncle's gardening hoes leaning against a tree near the garden clearing. All he had to do was jump the little stream and get it. Just a little stream, though its banks were steep and rock-lined.

He broke and ran, charging away from Callion; he

leapt and soared over the banks and slammed face-first into the ground on the other side, tripped by a slightly raised border of stones that he hadn't seen behind his uncle's greenery.

For an instant he was stunned, and he expected to feel the hammer smash down into the back of his skull before he could get to his feet again, but the blow didn't come.

Ignoring his injured arm, he flung himself forward and retrieved the hoe, then turned to face Callion, thinking that he had become the better armed of the two.

He was in time to see the light flicker out in the gate tree, and to see Callion vanish into the white cloak of snow.

Sixty-six

Yemus watched the simulacrums on the table. Matthiall crouched beside him, shaking his head. They'd been stunned when Jay burst out of the gate swinging a sword.

"Why has she not attacked Aidris, though?" Matthiall asked. "And why has Aidris not attacked her? They are, if your scale is right, so near they could almost touch."

"I can't tell what is going on," Yemus admitted. Something had happened that had thrown the whole battle into chaos. The Machnan, who had been winning, were now losing. Their horses had, for some reason, become useless. The animals slipped and staggered. People wandered past each other so close they could have whispered secrets in each others' ears, and yet they gave no sign that they suspected anyone near. The battles that had been engaged continued, but fighters fell and wiped their eyes and if they backed too far away from each other to catch their breath, suddenly acted as if the enemy with whom they had just been fighting had ceased to exist.

"Has someone cursed them with forgetfulness?" Yemus wondered.

"I cannot say. Someone has cursed them with something. They fight only if they fall right into each other. And why do they keep wiping their eyes?"

"It was raining," Yemus told him. "I did not create a simulacrum for the rain because it created a blur in the air that made the figures difficult to see."

"Then is it raining so hard they're blind?"

Yemus pursed his lips, then shrugged. "I can cast a simulacrum for the air to find out if they face a deluge." He tapped a finger on the table and murmured a few words. Suddenly the entire tabletop vanished in a dome of white.

"Snow?" Matthiall frowned. "Awfully early for that."

"It can't be natural."

"No. I shouldn't think so. But neither your people nor mine have the sheer power to control the weather." He growled. "So this comes either from Aidris, who gets her power from death, or from Callion, who has it naturally.

"Remove it. Better we can see what's happening, even if they can't."

Jay was feeling around in the blizzard, poking with her sword. She was headed in the wrong direction. Aidris had cast a light spell and appeared to be using it to try to find her way back to the gate tree, but she had gone right by it and was headed for the wrong tree.

"So Aidris didn't do it," Matthiall said.

"Evidently not."

Suddenly Yemus realized that the simulacrum of Sophie's body was no longer surrounded by black mist. He pointed it out to Matthiall.

"Perhaps something has gone amiss with your casting. Some of these other figures wear their death shrouds. Recast that one."

That seemed reasonable. Yemus blanked out the simulacrum of Sophie and cast another one. It didn't wear the black mist that signified death either. "What in the world . . . ?"

"She isn't moving."

"No."

"She hasn't moved since she fell there."

"No."

"Perhaps the blanket of snow is interfering with your casting."

The gate tree flared again, and this time an Aregen burst out of it.

"Oh, no," Yemus said. "Callion is there."

The Aregen stopped, rubbed his face vigorously, then tucked his head for a moment. Both men in the Aptogurria felt a trickle of power building in the simulacrum; that sensation indicated that he was preparing to cast a spell.

Callion stood a moment longer; then broke his stance and tipped his head skyward. Waiting.

Sixty-seven

she felt nothing and more nothing and the darkness
seemed that it would never end

and then smothering soaking poisonous cold so solid
so complete so real the cold became lead that encased
her limbs and shoved down on her chest and refused
her the air that was her birthright

frozen stiff arms and legs and the utter utter silence
of flesh without the rush of blood the surge of air the
pulsing pounding dance of the heart the million tiny
noises that were life she was dead

dead

hopelessly eternally dead but now with her living soul
encased in dead flesh dead and they had tried had tried
and fought and struggled but she had been too long
dead and now frozen she had no hope

and then sweet single thud like a drumstick on a lone
drum, one heartbeat

long silence, the drummer alone and without rhythm
and without response, the drummer had played his note
but the rest of the band hadn't come, he was alone on
the field alone and now he would give up

another beat

and a silence

and then, quicker, another
and another
and she felt the burning in her chest that was the
body begging for air and she breathed in breathed in
through a blanket of frozen something but the air still
came she filled her lungs with it and
held it
held it
drew in more and held it until it hurt and still she
breathed in and when the burning grew unbearable she
let her breath
out
with
a
rush that was ecstasy and triumph and promise
and she felt the fire start deep inside of her, and felt
it spread as warm blood began to stir again in her veins
And she twitched her fingers.
And they moved when she demanded that they
move.
She shrugged shoulders and bent knees and curled
herself forward into a sitting position.
Alive, she thought. My God. I'm alive.
She realized she was beyond just feeling. She could
think again.
My name is Sophie.
I'm in a lot of trouble.
I need to find a place to hide until I figure out what
is going on.

Sixty-eight

No battle plan survived the moment of engagement, Jayjay told herself. But the plan was supposed to at least get you to the battle before it fell apart.

She couldn't find Aidris anywhere, and she had the feeling that stumbling around through the blizzard, poking her sword into every dark shape she thought she saw, especially when those shapes turned out to be trees, was not sound tactics. But she didn't know what else to do. She hadn't counted on the ferocity of the blizzard, or the cold so bitter that her hand felt like it had frozen to the hilt of her sword. She hadn't counted on getting soaked through from the icy rain, or on her eyelashes sticking together. She had counted on Hultif's fires, and she could see none of those. Where summer had reigned only moments before, now winter locked in everything.

She couldn't get back through the gate, either, even assuming she could find the right tree. She was trapped, and she was freezing, and she was furious. Only an idiot would end up dying of exposure in the middle of summer because of her own moronic plan.

I should have just jumped out at her, Jay thought. She would have killed me but she would have died, too.

The snow began to thin, and a single warm tendril of air curled past her. For a moment she was grateful, but then she considered the larger implications of a break in the weather. First there had been no blast of fire, and now the snowstorm was dying. Something had happened to Hultif, hadn't it?

And that meant she was completely alone in dealing with Aidris Akalan. No magical backup. No diversions. No fire spells.

Aidris still didn't know she was in the woods. If the storm died and she hadn't found cover, she would lose the element of surprise, and the element of surprise was the only thing she had left. She fumbled around until she found a tree, and then she crouched beside it.

The blizzard continued to lose its power. She started being able to make out trunks between the increasingly large, wet flakes. The pounding of the tiny hailstones stopped and with them, the hissing that had been so overpowering she had ceased to hear it. With its absence, she heard fighting again.

Fewer flakes, and more rain, and the rain warmer against her skin. Maybe she wouldn't die of exposure after all. She heard Aidris before she saw her.

"The snow has hidden the damnable corpse! How am I to find the right tree again if I can't find the body?"

Two warrags were sniffing around on the white-blanketed ground fifty yards away, obviously looking for Sophie, while Aidris kicked at the snow around the base of each tree. Jay kept in a crouch, scooted around until a tree blocked the three of them from her sight, then ran forward, still crouched down. She didn't like the fact that Aidris was trying to use her best friend's body as a landmark. She wished she had her father's old Browning twelve-gauge over-and-under. Two slugs from that would solve all of Aidris's problems nice and fast, and a lot of other people's problems, too.

She didn't have the over-and-under. She had a sword, and a dagger, no backup, and no more cover from the weather. The snow turned into rain.

Line from a Dan Fogelberg song, she thought, annoyed with herself for the errant thought. How come I never met somebody at a checkout stand?

But she'd met somebody in a dungeon, and while that probably wouldn't have made for a chart-topping song, it would have made for a good life. She believed it would have.

It can't now, she thought. The game's all over now. She lined herself up behind cover and moved to the next tree, staying low and keeping quiet.

You're going to die for what you did, bitch, she thought. You hurt a hell of a lot of people, and you killed my best friend, and maybe I can't save the whole world, but I can light my one little candle before your friends take me out.

She smiled grimly. That's it. My contribution to life. My single real accomplishment. Not my books, not the novel I never got around to or never had the guts to try, not the kids I wanted but never had. The only thing I will ever have done that made a difference will have been this.

That sucks.

Sixty-nine

The warrags couldn't find the body, and Aidris couldn't find the body. The rain was washing away the snow and the Machnan wizard's corpse should have been exposed and visible.

It wasn't.

Aidris didn't think the warrags had dragged it off to eat it. She could still hear the sounds of fighting; they weren't stupid enough to stop for a snack in the middle of a battle.

She thought she knew what had happened. The gate had opened twice at the height of the snowstorm. She'd felt it, though she hadn't been able to see it. She expected an attack, but when one hadn't been forthcoming, she'd thought perhaps the people she and her army had trapped inside the Aregen domain had summoned the snowstorm for cover so that they could escape.

Now, though, she decided that for whatever reason, someone had come out, taken the corpse, and gone back in again.

She was going to have to find the gate tree the hard way.

"Guard me," she said, and three warrags took up their positions around her.

She didn't know how much time she had left. She could tell from the sound that the battle had intensified. Her army would only be able to help her after it had defeated the attackers. And perhaps some of the attackers would break through the lines to her guard and her. She needed to be through the gate before they could reach her. She needed to be able to drain whatever strength she could from the Aregen domain, and the soon-to-be dead people hiding in it.

She pulled her protective spells in tight and, holding her arms straight in front of her, chanted in a low, rhythmic monotone. As she chanted, she felt the shape of the area's magic grow around her. Her Kin and her Kin-hera, a bright bolt of something that felt Aregen and enormously powerful, the tree. Yes. She let the feel flow through her fingertips and she turned until the current was strongest. She followed it, moving slowly, chanting, taking her time; she was peripherally aware that her guard stalked at her sides and at her back, wary and waiting for trouble. She was peripherally aware of the fighting, of tension in the air, of something waiting to happen. But she kept chanting and kept moving until her fingers touched the right tree. She stopped chanting, released the spell, and all feelings of magic died.

And then, without expending any effort, she felt the surge of power again, but this time from off to one side. The signature of the magic, after all the centuries that she'd dealt with it, was unmistakable.

Her Watchers were returning.

They did not come with a wind, nor with the rustling of leaves. They did not howl or shriek or growl as they were wont to do most times. Instead they came in silence, their power unmistakable and inescapable. They swirled around her for a moment, silent, not touching her, a cloud of deadly fireflies that she was able to contain only because she had summoned them to blood and held them with blood.

She waited, not letting them find any fear in her.

They coalesced at last into the shape of her face. "We have decided," they said with a single voice that sounded much like hers.

"Decided."

"Yes. We did not know what we wanted, but now we have decided."

"I tell you what you can have," she said. "You don't tell me what you want."

"Have you forgotten your oath?"

Aidris couldn't be certain that she heard anger in the voice; it wasn't the voice of a real creature, after all, but only a construct. Still, she thought she felt anger.

"Have you forgotten that you were to bring me Matthiall and the hearts of his two wizards?"

"That has all changed."

"Has it?" Aidris recalled her intermittent anxiety that she had done something wrong in dealing with the Watchers, but she still could not recall what it might have been. The anxiety returned. If things had changed, she had done something careless, she thought. Something very small, and seemingly irrelevant. Something I said that I shouldn't have said, or something I shouldn't have said that I did.

She waited since there seemed to be nothing else to do.

"We have decided what we want."

"What do you want?"

"We want the blood of everything in this place. Now."

"That's ridiculous. If you hunt judiciously, you will hunt here forever. If you destroy everything at once, you will starve."

"No. We will go home. *You* will starve. But because this is what we want, you will give it to us, or we will devour you and still we will go home."

"What has given you the idea that I would let you do this?"

"This was your oath." For an instant the Watchers were silent. Then her own voice in her own tones said back to her, "Enough! I'll give you his blood. I said I would, didn't I? Have I ever broken a promise to you? I'll give you anything you want—I swear it. But don't bother me with that. Go now, and bring him to me quickly. And bring the hearts of the wizards he stole from me."

She caught and held her mistakes. Her first mistake had been to deal with the Watchers in an emotional state. Her second and third mistakes had come from the first, and they were unrecoverable. She had sworn to give the Watchers something without making the reward conditional on their successful completion of her task. And she had offered to give them something she couldn't afford to give.

So I could die now, or I can let them devour the world and die soon.

Let the world burn, she thought. *If I can't have Glenraven, no one will.*

"Take everything," she said. "I give you leave."

Seventy

Jay heard Aidris say, "Take everything," and then she saw something she couldn't believe. Sophie walked out from behind a tree, and said, "Take me first."

The firefly swarm enveloped her instantly, without warning. "No, Sophie," Jay shouted, but her shout wouldn't have mattered. Aidris had recognized Sophie, and she started to scream in that same instant.

And Sophie began to glow, but the spots of fire under her skin died out as quickly as they arose. The swarm that surrounded her began to hum with agitation, as if it were a swarm of bees disturbed by a boy with a stick. Aidris was standing there screaming and the three warrags, who had heard her condemn them to death, had fled, and Jay ran forward to attack.

The swarm lifted off of Sophie, who stood there unscathed. It thrashed and circled and raged, no longer one coherent entity but a thousand angry voices all shrieking at the same time. Aidris was frozen, staring from it to Sophie and back.

The buzzing and howling died down quickly and the firefly lights reformed into a face. "We cannot take her. She is multitudes, and the multitudes rebuild as we destroy. We cannot have everything in this world, so

you have broken bond with us." The face began to dis-integrate into its component parts, and as the face came apart, the voice became voices and the voices shrieked:
> you lied to us
> > lied you promised us
> everything
> > everything we wanted we needed
> needed you promised
> die we will kill you
> > drink your blood kill you
> kill

They swarmed around Aidris as they had around Sophie an instant before, and Jay just had time to think, Well, that solves a big part of my problem, when Callion appeared.

He didn't step out from behind a tree. He didn't come running. One minute he wasn't there and the next minute he was.

He intoned an alien command in a ringing voice; the shape and the sound of the words made Jayjay's skin crawl. They were powerful words rich with the taint of ancient evil. Without understanding them, her mind still formed pictures from them—pictures of a place beyond dark-ness, of a void and chaos and a brilliant, searching, inhuman mind that hungered for the fruits of evil the way an infant hungered for the breast. It sought out blood and pain and grief and fear; it created them, it devoured them, it moved on to new victims and new worlds.

The brilliant lights were only a part of that mind, but when Callion spoke, a darkness opened up within the forest—a darkness that was the Abyss.

At some far distant time and in some unknown place, Jay thought, a human saw what I am seeing and named that vision Hell.

Callion stopped speaking. The Abyss hung open and the quick, evil mind within looked out. The Watchers held still, no longer devouring Aidris.

Aidris, unmoving, stared at the rift in the fabric of the forest that opened into infinite darkness.

Sophie backed away, half a step at a time.

Jay, sword in hand, exposed to the sight of her enemies, held her breath and waited.

Callion said to her and to Aidris and to Sophie and perhaps to the thing that watched from the void, "I have been denied the realm I deserve. I have been denied the position of power that is my birthright. I have been rejected by this, my home. Hear me now. I have summoned the Rift, and I claim the services of that which waits. I would have let them scour Glenraven of life, but they could not. If they devoured Aidris Akalan, they would have returned to the Rift, and you and you"— he pointed from Sophie to Jay—"would have won. Instead, I claim by ancient spell and birthright the services of these, the Devourers and servants of the Rift for as long as I shall live. And I give to the Alfkindir Watchmistress Aidris Akalan youth and strength, that she may continue her reign, and with it continue Glenraven's suffering. You will never be Watchmistress of this realm." He glowered at Jay, and sniffed. "Meanwhile, I'll go where I'm appreciated. Writhe in Hell."

He vanished. The Watchers vanished.

And Aidris Akalan, visibly youthful, straight-backed and clear-eyed, smiled from Sophie to Jay, raised her hands, closed her eyes and began to chant.

White light streamed from her fingertips.

Jay charged forward clutching the sword and the dagger, and felt fire explode in her chest. She knew from the pain, the impossible pain, that she should have been dead when it hit and she couldn't understand why she wasn't. The pain got worse instead of better. She went to her knees, screaming, hanging on to the sword, still moving toward Aidris but not fast enough. Not fast enough. But she wasn't dead.

Sophie was at her side, pulling the dagger from her

left hand and running forward. How could she? Jay wondered. Aidris's blast struck her, too, but she kept going.

Jay forced herself to her feet, and Aidris screeched, "Die, you Machnan whores. Die! I am Watchmistress."

Sophie fought her way forward, through the blasts of magical fire, and inside of Jay something snapped. The pain suddenly halved itself, though no change was visible in Aidris. Jay ran again, and Aidris's eyes grew wide, and the fire that flew from her fingertips grew hotter and fiercer and still hotter. Jay and Sophie kept charging forward, making progress against the blasts that pounded them back. Closer and closer, close enough that Jay could see the sweat pouring from Aidris's forehead.

But Aidris found strength from somewhere. Her chanting grew louder yet, and the flames blasted Jayjay backward, step by grudging step.

The gate behind Aidris opened and Hultif appeared through it. He too cast a form of fire, but his fire caught at Aidris's clothing and began to burn it.

She shrieked. Her concentration wavered and her attack on Jay and Sophie weakened just enough that they could move forward again. Jay closed the gap first and rammed the sword into Aidris's belly, angling the blade upward and to her right, hoping that an Alfkindir heart was in the same place as a human heart.

Sophie, half a step behind her, slashed the dagger across Aidris's neck, and blood spurted over all three of them.

The fires from Aidris's spell got hotter and blasted higher again; Jay wondered if the Kin wizard were healing herself or if in her death throes she had poured the rest of her life into the magic.

The pain returned, worse than ever, and then, for a single instant it vanished almost completely.

The explosion inside of Jay's skull that followed that lessening of pain flung her to the ground and cast her into darkness and silence.

Seventy-one

Yemus crouched in the rubble of the Aptogurria, digging for Matthiall's body with his bare hands. Yemus was bleeding and his clothing was in shreds and he suspected a broken bone in his left shoulder, but he refused to take time for his own injuries. The Kin was trapped somewhere beneath the stones.

Torrin kept screaming, "What happened? What have you done?" until finally Yemus, not looking away from what he was doing, said, "Aidris is dead. She was about to win, but our two heroes kept at her and kept at her. Sophie—well, Sophie was dead, and I don't know how she came back to life. Jayjay was half bonded to the Kintari I'm trying to dig out. He took some of the blast that Aidris leveled at her, but he couldn't take enough. So I linked him to the Aptogurria, and it began absorbing Aidris's magic."

He found a hand and lifted away the rubble that freed the arm it was attached to. Yemus knelt, found a faint, thready pulse, and turned to his brother. "Help me," he snarled. "One of the saviors of Glenraven lies dying beneath your feet."

Torrin bent over and began clearing debris.

"I don't understand any of this. You were alone. And then you escaped. And now you are back."

"The only thing you need to understand right now," Yemus told him, "is that the backblast of magic from Aidris's death exploded the Aptogurria and sent its walls crashing down on us. We have to save him." He nodded at Matthiall, whose head, bleeding but uncrushed, he had just uncovered. "And then we have to lead the rest of your troops into the Cavitarin Wood against Aidris's forces. I don't know that the guards who are fighting there right now will last much longer without our aid. And they fight to save the life of our new Watchmistress."

Seventy-two

"Please breathe," the voice said again. "Please . . . please. Take a deep breath if you can."

Jay realized that voice had been talking for a long time, exhorting her to move, to breathe, to open her eyes. She tried to comply, but the pain was terrible.

"Come on, Jay. Open your eyes." That voice was Sophie's.

Jay remembered Sophie being dead; at least she thought she remembered that. And then she remembered the fight with Aidris. And pain. And her sword cut and Sophie's attack with the dagger. And blood.

Aidris . . .

"Aidris is dead?" she asked.

She opened her eyes in spite of the pain. She was lying on a canopied bed in a huge stone-walled room. The room looked a lot like the room in the Wethquerin Zearn, actually. She wondered if perhaps it was. Sophie stood beside her, very much alive though battered and bruised. She grinned when she saw Jay looking up at her, and bent down and hugged her.

"What happened?" Jay asked.

"We won."

"Yeah, I figured that. We're still alive . . . sort of."

She gave Sophie a weak grin meant to show that she was joking. "I mean what went wrong there at the end?"

Sophie said, "I'll let Yemus explain it. He wanted to talk with you when you were awake."

A young woman in what Jay recognized as Sarijann livery led Yemus into the room. He looked like he'd been the unpopular referee at an elephant football game, and she wondered if she were as battered and bruised. Sophie helped her sit up and propped cushions behind her.

Yemus pulled a chair up beside the bed and settled into it.

"How are you feeling?"

"I'll be better when I know what's going on."

He nodded. "Glenraven has chosen you as its Watchmistress."

Jay said, "Callion and Hultif said the same thing."

"Yes. Well, Glenraven cannot make you stay, but if you leave, I can tell you that our world is unlikely to have much hope of survival. After the centuries-long misrule of Aidris Akalan, Glenraven has her first breath of hope in the rule of the hero she chose."

"What about Sophie? We both came here."

"You were both chosen as heroes, but not as Masters of the Watch. You alone have some quality that our world believes it cannot survive without. It guided the spirits of the Machnan to you, and now it waits to hear how you will choose."

Yemus looked at her, sighed and added, "And I wait, too. We need you here, Jay. When I sold you the book, I didn't think you were the right one. But you beat Aidris Akalan. In spite of everything, you got through to her and you beat her. You and Sophie." He smiled at Sophie, then looked back to Jay. "And we're going to need you in the future. The Machnan have their magic back, and we think with the alliance you forged with the Aregen and some of the Kin you'll have a chance of leading Glenraven into an era of real prosperity. I don't think it's going to be easy, but I also think that you alone in the world can do it. And the other problems remain."

"Other problems?"

"The Rift is open and the Aregen wizard Callion got away."

Jay nodded. She remembered that.

She leaned back and closed her eyes. She thought of the world she'd left behind. She loved her writing, but that was her one real source of happiness. The rest of her life had been unfortunate at best, and disastrous at worst. And Glenraven still sang to her as it had the first moment she'd seen it. In some way she couldn't understand, it was the home she'd always dreamed of.

"Could I go back and visit Sophie and my family sometimes?"

Sophie looked sad, and Yemus shook his head slowly. "No. As Watchmistress, you would bind yourself body and soul to Glenraven. You cannot leave her any more than she can leave you. In the rites of the Master of the Watch, you become the ears that listen to the voice of this world. And when you speak, her voice and your voice become one."

"I would lose myself?"

Yemus snorted. "If Glenraven had that much control, Aidris Akalan would never have happened. No, your love for the world and her love for you will let you hear what she needs and will keep you from doing the things that would destroy her. You are her choice, Jay. Please don't reject her."

Rejection. Jay thought of another of her many mistakes, her rejection of Matthiall's love. She asked, "If I am Watchmistress, must I be alone?"

"No. You can take a bondmate or an *eyra*, raise children, have grandchildren."

She nodded. "And what will Sophie say when she goes home?"

"She will say that you died. She will take proof."

Jay looked at Sophie.

Sophie said, "I've known since I got here that this place was going to change our lives, Jay. It's changed mine for the better. I know what I want now. I know who I am again. And I know that I'm a survivor."

"You're my best friend."

"Even if we never see each other again, we'll always be friends."

"I know."

"Find the life you've been searching for, Jay. Take it and don't look back."

"Yes."

And she looked to Yemus. "Yes," she said. "I'll stay."

Seventy-three

The ceremony was simple. Jay stood in a small stone amphitheater and made her promises to Glenraven. She promised that she would love the world and listen to her needs. She promised that she would care for all the people of Glenraven and that she would seek fairness and truth in her dealings with them. She promised she would do her best always, and that she would be kind.

Her promises were not a written litany. They were from her heart, and they were given not just to the world of Glenraven but to its people, thousands of whom crowded the stone rows of the amphitheater, the hill above it, and the grassy knolls to either side.

Then Hultif, Yemus and Matthiall, the three wizards chosen by their people to represent the three-senior races, knelt before her and kissed her hand. Yemus drew blood from her finger and dropped it into a bowl of earth. Then he and the other two wizards took handfuls of the earth and scattered it to the four winds.

And the voice of Glenraven whispered in her heart. *Welcome at last, daughter and friend. Finally you can hear me in other than your dreams. Finally we can speak one to the other. I have waited for you for a very long time.*

Seventy-four

Sophie was the first to hug her when the ceremony was over. "Good luck," she said. "Be happy."

Jay frowned. She looked at Sophie, wanting to see something other than what she saw. "That sounds like good-bye."

"It is. It has to be. I wanted to see you become the new Watchmistress, and I guess I wanted to know that you were going to be okay, but I need to get back home. I don't belong here. It isn't my world."

Jay wanted to say that she was wrong, that it could be her world too, but she couldn't. She could feel inside of her that Sophie was right, and that Glenraven, grateful as she was to Sophie, knew that Sophie could never belong to her.

"Hug Mitch for me when you get back, will you? And don't tell Steven to drop dead, no matter how much you might want to."

Sophie laughed. "I'd kind of planned on doing that, actually."

"I figured you might. That's why I said something. I've found my life. I don't resent the fact that he has his. I'm just glad I'm not involved with it anymore."

She stopped and swallowed, fighting unexpected tears. "I wish you could stay a few more days."

"I know. But I could never stay long enough to make saying good-bye easier." Sophie nodded at a man who stood on the side of the hill holding three horses. "My guide is waiting."

They hugged, and Jay started to cry in earnest. Sophie did too.

"Best friends are forever," Sophie said.

Jay nodded and caught her breath and wiped her eyes. "Be happy," she said. "And don't forget me."

"Never."

Seventy-five

When the last of the people who wanted to embrace her and welcome her had gone home, Matthiall walked beside her toward her new home, a little house in Zearn.

"You could have taken a castle," he said. "Servants. You could have had anything you wanted."

"I got what I wanted."

"Everything?"

She looked at him. "No. Not everything. I made one mistake, and I need to repair that."

A worried frown creased his forehead. "What mistake did you make?"

She reached out her hand and took his. "I'm afraid," she told him. "I've spent a long time being afraid, and that fear doesn't go away quickly or easily. Please be patient with me. When you said you loved me, that old fear overwhelmed me, and I said I didn't love you."

She stopped and turned to face him, and looked up into his pale, beautiful eyes.

"And I do love you, Matthiall. I do."

Seventy-six

Sophie pedaled out of the tunnel and waved to her guide to stop. She stood staring down at the maybe-Roman road she and Jay had ridden in on, and she felt the cold air sting her cheeks. Winter was coming to the mountains—coming too soon. The cold air matched the chill she carried inside of her.

The guide carried a corpse with him. It was a perfect duplicate of Jayjay's body. Sophie would tell anyone who asked that Jay had fallen off the side of a mountain and broken her neck. The injuries to the body would confirm that story.

No one would go looking for Glenraven. The guide told her that after they left it, the ancient road would disappear. Not even Sophie would be able to find it again.

Sometimes there is no going back, she told herself. Jay will be happy. So will I. Only this part hurts, and the pain from this moment will grow duller with time.

I wouldn't change any of this.

She lifted her foot onto her pedal, ready to move on, and a lump in her pocket stopped her. She reached in and pulled out the book.

Fodor's Glenraven, it said for just an instant. Then

393

the letters blurred and ran and faded, and when she looked at it again, it said *Fodor's Spain.*

That was it. The last of Glenraven's magic was gone from her life.

She waved to the guide, and they started down the last lap of the road home.

Her own magic waited ahead.